JOHN BUNYAN.

THE

PILGRIM'S PROGRESS

FROM

This World to that which is to Come.

DELIVERED UNDER

THE SIMILITUDE OF A DREAM.

BY

JOHN BUNYAN.

WITH PORTRAIT AND MEMOIR OF THE AUTHOR,

BY

THE REV. T. SCOTT.

PHILADELPHIA:
CLAXTON, REMSEN & HAFFELFINGER,
Nos. 819 & 821 MARKET STREET.
1869.

PREFACE.

The high estimation in which 'The Pilgrim's Progress' has been held for above a century, sufficiently evinces its intrinsic value: and there is every reason to suppose, that it will be read with admiration and advantage for ages to come; probably till the consummation of all things.

The pious Christian, in proportion to 'his growth in grace and in the knowledge of the Lord Jesus,' derives more and more instruction from repeated perusals of this remarkable book; while his enlarged experience and extended observation enable him to unfold, with progressive evidence, the meaning of the agreeable similitudes employed by its ingenious author. And even the careless or uninstructed reader is fascinated to attention, by the simple and artless manner in which the interesting narrative is arranged. Nor should this be represented as a mere amusement, which answers no farther purpose: for it has been observed by men of great discernment,

and acquaintance with the human mind, that
young persons, having perused the Pilgrim
as a pleasing tale, have often retained a remembrance of its leading incidents, which,
after continuing perhaps in a dormant state
for several years, has at length germinated,
as it were, into the most important and seasonable instruction ; while the events of their
own lives placed it before their minds in a new
and affecting point of view. It may, therefore, be questioned, whether modern ages
have produced any work which has more
promoted the best interests of mankind.

These observations indeed more especially
apply to the first part of the Pilgrim's Progress ; that being complete in itself, and in
all respects superior to the second. Yet this,
also, contains many edifying and interesting
passages ; though in unity of design, in arrangement of incident, and in simplicity of
allegory, it is not comparable to the other.
Indeed, the author, in his first effort, had nearly exhausted his subject ; and nothing remained, for this second attempt, but a few
detached episodes (so to speak) to his original
plan : nor could any vigour of genius have
wrought them up to an equal degree of excellence. It must, however, be allowed, that
Mr. Bunyan here frequently sinks below himself, both in fertility of invention, force of
imagination, and aptness of illustration : nay,
he sometimes even stoops to a puerile play of
fancy, and a refined nicety in explaining
doctrines, which do not at all accord with the

rest of the work. But the same grand principles of evangelical and practical religion, which stamp an inestimable value on the first part, are in the second also exhibited with equal purity, though not with equal simplicity : and, on many occasions, the author rises superior to his disadvantages ; and introduces characters, or incidents, which arrest the attention, and interest the heart of every pious and intelligent reader.

It would not perhaps be difficult to shew, that the Pilgrim's Progress, as first published, is as really an original production of vigorous native genius, as any of those works, in prose or verse, which have excited the admiration of mankind, through successive ages, and in different nations. It does not indeed possess those ornaments which are often mistaken for intrinsic excellence : but the rudeness of its style (which at the same time is characteristic of the subject) concurs to prove it a most extraordinary book : for, had it not been written with very great ingenuity, a religious treatise, evidently inculcating doctrines always offensive, but now more unfashionable than formerly, would not, in so homely a garb, have so durably attracted the attention of a polished age and nation Yet it is undeniable, that Bunyan's Pilgrim continues to be read and admired by vast multitudes ; while publications on a similar plan, by persons of respectable learning and talents, are consigned to almost total neglect and oblivion !

1*

This is not, however that view of the work, which entitles it to its highest honour, or most endears it to the pious mind : for, comparing it with the other productions of the same author (which are indeed edifying to the humble believer, but not much suited to the taste of the ingenious,) we shall be led to conclude, that in penning this he was favoured with a peculiar measure of the Divine assistance : especially when we recollect, that, within the confines of a jail, he was able so to delineate the Christian's course, with its various difficulties, perils, conflicts, &c., that scarcely any thing seems to have escaped his notice. Indeed, the accurate observer of the church in his own days, and the learned student of ecclesiastical history, must be equally surprised to find, that hardly one remarkable character, good or bad, or mixed in any manner or proportion imaginable ; or that one fatal delusion, bye-path, or injurious mistake, can be singled out, which may not be paralleled in the Pilgrim's Progress : that is, as to the grand outlines ; for the minutiæ, about which bigoted and frivolous minds waste their zeal and force, are, with very few exceptions, wisely passed over. This circumstance is not only surprising, but it suggest an argument, not easily answered, in support of the truth of those religious sentiments, which are now often derided under the title of orthodoxy ; for every part of this singular book exclusively suits the different descriptions of such as profess those doctrines ; and relates the experiences, mistakes, falls, recoveries distresses, temptations, conflicts, supports, and consolations of serious persons of this class in our own times, as exactly as if it had been penned from the observation of them, and for their immediate benefit: while, like the sacred Scriptures, it remains a sealed book to all who are strangers to evangelical religion.

These remarks may very properly be concluded with the words of a justly admired poet of the present day, who in the following lines has fully sanctioned all that has been here advanced—

'Oh thou, whom, borne on Fancy's eager wing
Back to the season of life's happy spring,
I pleas'd remember, and while mem'ry yet
Holds fast her office here, can ne'er forget,
Ingenious dreamer, in whose well-told tale
Sweet fiction and sweet truth alike prevail,
Whose hum'rous vein, strong sense, and simple style,
May teach the gayest, make the gravest smile,
Witty, and well employ'd, and, like thy Lord,
Speaking in parables his slighted word—
I name thee not, lest so despised a name
Should move a sneer at thy deserved fame ;
Yet e'en in transitory life's late day
That mingles all my brown with sober gray,
Revere the man, whose Pilgrim marks the road
And guides the progress of the soul to God.
'Twere well with most, if books that could engage
Their childhood, pleased them at a riper age ;
The man approving what had charmed the boy,
Would die at last in comfort, peace, and joy,
And not with curses on his art who stole
The gem of truth from his unguarded soul.'

                              Cowper, Tirocinium, v. 129

In respect of the present edition of the Pilgrim's Progress it may be proper to ob-

serve, that it having become general to pub-
lish every approved work in such a style of
elegance, and with such decorations, as may
recommend it to a place in the collections of
the curious and affluent, and thus attract the
notice of those who would perhaps otherwise
have overlooked it ; something of this nature
was proposed by the proprietors of this edition, who deemed it requisite that it should
be accompanied with original explanatory
notes.   Several persons have indeed already
favoured the public with illustrations of this
kind : but as the proprietors did not deem
that consideration a sufficient reason for
omitting this part of their design ; so the editor, on mature deliberation, did not think
himself precluded by it from communicating
his sentiments on a favourite book, according
to a plan he had formed in his own mind
Every man, who thinks for himself, has his
own view of a subject, which commonly varies,
more or less, from the sentiments of others,
whom he nevertheless esteems and loves
with great cordiality : and the great Head of
the church has intrusted different talents to
his servants, to qualify them for usefulness
among distinct descriptions of persons.   It is
indeed incontrovertable, that some men will
receive the great truths of Christianity with
candour and docility, when exhibited in a
style and manner suited to their peculiar
taste, who disregard and reject them, when
conveyed in language which numbers, perhaps
justly, think far more interesting and affect-

ing. It need not, therefore, be apprehended, that the labours of different writers on the same subject should materially interfere with each other : rather we may indulge a hope, that, as far as they accord to this standard of divine truth, they will, in different circles, promote the common cause of vital godliness.

The editor's aim, in this attempt to elucidate the Pilgrim's Progress, is, to give a brief key to the grand outlines of the allegory, from which the attentive reader may obtain a general idea of the author's design as he proceeds ; to bestow more pains in fixing the precise meaning of those parts, which might most perplex the reader, and which seem to have most escaped the notice, or divided the sentiments of expositors ; to state and establish, compendiously but clearly, those doctrinal, practical, and experimental views of Christianity, which Mr. Bunyan meant to convey, guarding them carefully from those extremes and perversions which he never favoured, but which too frequently increase men's prejudices against them ; to delineate the more prominent features of his various characters, with a special reference to the present state of religious profession, and with cautions to the reader, to distinguish accurately what he approves from the defects even of true pilgrims ; and, in fine, to give as just a representation, as may be, of the author's sentiments concerning the right way to heaven ; and of the many false ways, and bye paths, which prove injurious to all who ven-

ture into them, and fatal to unnumbered multitudes. In executing this plan, no information that he can procure is neglected ; but he
does not invariably adhere to the sentiments
of any man : and while his dependance is
placed, as he hopes, on the promised teaching of the Holy Spirit, he does not think
himself authorized to spare any pains, in en
deavouring to render the publication acceptable and useful.

The text is, in most places, printed as it
stands in those old editions, which may be
supposed to contain the author's own terms ;
which latter editors have frequently modern-
ized. A few obsolete or unclassical words,
and unusual phrases, seem to become the
character of the Pilgrim ; and they are often
more emphatical than any which can be
substituted in their stead. A few exceptions,
however, are made to this rule ; as the author, if living, would certainly change some
expressions for others less offensive to modern
ears. Great pains have been taken to collate
different copies of the work, and to examine
every scriptural reference ; in order to render
this edition, in all respects, as correct as possible. The author's marginal references
seemed so essential a part of the work, that it
was deemed indispensably requisite to insert
them in their places. But as the other marginal notes do not appear to convey any material instruction distinct from that contained
in the text, and to be principally useful in
pointing out any passage, to which the read-

er might wish to refer, it was thought most advisable to omit them.

Mr. Bunyan prefixed to each part of the Pilgrim's Progress a copy of verses : but as his poetry does not much suit the taste of these days, it hath been deemed expedient to omit them. That prefixed to the first part is entitled, ' The Author's Apology for his Book ;' but it is now generally allowed, that the book, so far from needing an apology, indeed merits the highest commendation. In this he informs us, that he was unawares drawn into the allegory, when employed about another work ; that the farther he proceeded, the more rapidly did ideas flow into his mind ; that this induced him to form it into a separate book ; and that shewing it to his friends,

> ' Some said, John, print it ; others said, Not so ;
> Some said, It might do good ; others said, No.'

The public will not hesitate in determining which opinion was the result of the deeper penetration ; but will wonder, that a long apology for such a publication should have been deemed necessary. This was, however, the case ; and the author, having solidly, though rather verbosely, answered several objections, and adduced some obvious arguments in very unpoetical rhymes, concludes with these lines, which may serve as a favourable specimen of the whole :—

> ' Would'st thou divert thyself from melancholy ?
> Would'st thou be pleasant, yet be far from folly ?
> Would'st thou read riddles and their explanation ?

Or else be drowned in thy contemplation?
Dost thou love picking meat? Or would'st thou see
A man i' the clouds, and hear him speak to thee?
Would'st thou be in a dream, and yet not sleep?
Or would'st thou in a moment laugh and weep?
Or would'st thou lose thyself, and catch no harm?
And find thyself again without a charm?
Would'st read thyself, and read thou know'st not what,
And yet know whither thou art blest or not,
By reading the same lines? O then come hither,
And lay my book, thy heart and head together.'

The poem prefixed to the second part, in a kind of dialogue with his book, is less interesting; and serves to shew, that the pious author had a more favourable opinion of its comparative merit than posterity has formed; which is no singular case. It is, therefore, presumed, that the omission of it in this edition will not be thought to require any farther apology with the more judicious admirers of the work. Some verses are likewise found at the bottom of certain places that accompanied the old editions, which they, who omit the plates, or substitute others, know not where to insert. To shew all regard, however, to every thing that Mr. Bunyan wrote as a part of the work, such as are most material may be found in the notes on the incidents to which they refer

                                T. SCOTT.

THE LIFE OF JOHN BUNYAN

THE celebrated author of the Pilgrim's Progress was born, A. D. 1628, at Elstow, a small village near Bedford. His father earned his bread by the low occupation of a common tinker; but he bore a fair character, and took care that his son, whom he brought up to the same business, should be taught to read and write. We are told, indeed, that he quickly forgot all he had learned, through his extreme profligacy; yet it is probable, that he retained so much as enabled him to recover the rest, when his mind became better disposed, and that it was very useful to him in the subsequent part of his life.

The materials, from which an account of this valuable man must be compiled, are so scanty and confused, that nothing very satisfactory should be expected. He seems from his earliest youth to have been greatly addicted to impiety and profligacy; yet he was interrupted in his course by continual alarms and convictions, which were sometimes peculiarly overwhelming, but had no other effect at the time, than to extort from him the most absurd wishes that can be imagined. A copious narrative of these early conflicts and crimes is contained in a treatise published by himself, under the title of 'Grace abounding to the chief of Sinners'.

During this part of his life he was twice preserved from the most imminent danger of drowning : and being a soldier in the parlia ment's army at the siege of Leicester, A. D. 1645, he was drawn out to stand centinel : but one of his comrades, having by his own desire taken his place, was shot through the head on his post ; and thus Bunyan was reserved by the all disposing hand of God for better purposes. He seems, however, to have made progressive advances in wickedness, and to have become the ringleader of youth in every kind of profaneness and excess.

His career of vice received a considerable check, in consequence of his marriage with the daughter of a person, who had been very religious in his way, and remarkably bold in reproving vice, but who was then dead. His wife's discourse to him concerning her father's piety excited him to go regularly to church : and as she brought him, for her whole portion, The practice of Piety, and the Plain Man's Pathway to Heaven, he employed himself frequently in reading these books.

The events recorded of our author are so destitute of dates, or regard to the order in which they happened, that no clear arrangement can now be made of them : but it is probable, that this new attention to religion, though ineffectual to the reformation of his conduct, rendered him more susceptible of convictions ; and his vigorous imagination, at the time wholly unrestrained by knowledge or discretion, laid him open to a variety of impressions, sleeping and waking, which he verily supposed to arise from words spoken to him, or objects presented before his bodily senses ; and he never after was able to break the association of ideas thus formed in his mind. Accordingly he says, that one day, when he was engaged in diversion with his companions, ' A voice did suddenly dart from heaven into my soul, which said, Wilt thou leave thy sins and go to heaven, or have thy sins and go to hell ?' The consciousness of his wicked course of life, accompanied with the recollection of the truths he had read, suddenly meeting, as it were, in his mind, thus produced a violent alarm, and made such an impression on his imagination, that he seemed to have heard these words, and to have seen Christ frowning and menacing him. But we must not suppose, that there was any miracle wrought ; nor could there be any occasion for a new revelation to suggest or enforce so scriptural a warning. This may serve as a specimen of those impressions which constitute a large part of his religious experience ; but which need not be particularized in this place.

He was next tempted to conclude, that it was then too late to repent or seek salvation ; and, as he ignorantly listened to the suggestion, he indulged his corrupt inclinations without restraint, imagining that this was the only way in which he could possibly have the least expectation of pleasure.

While he was proceeding in this wretched course, a woman of very bad character reproved him with great severity for profane swearing ; declaring, in the strongest expressions, that he exceeded in it all men she had ever heard. This made him greatly ashamed, when he reflected that he was too vile even for such a bad woman to endure : so that from that time he began to break off that odious custom. His guilty and terrified mind was also prepared to admit the most alarming impressions during his sleep ; and he had such a dream about the day of judgment, and its awful circumstances and consequences, as powerfully influenced his conduct. There was indeed, nothing extraordinary in this, for such dreams are not uncommon to men under deep convictions ; yet the Lord was doubtless, by all these means, secretly influencing his heart, and warning him to flee from the wrath to come.

He was, however, reluctant to part with his irreligious associates and vain pleasures ; till the conversation of a poor man, who came in his way, induced him to read the Bible, especially the preceptive and historical parts of it ; and this put him upon an entire reformation of his conduct, insomuch that his neighbours were greatly astonished at the change which they had witnessed. In this manner he went on for about a year ; at some times satisfied with himself, and at others distressed with fears and consciousness of guilt. He seems ever after to have considered all the convictions and desires, which he at this time experienced, as wholly originating from natural principles; but in this perhaps some persons will venture to dissent from him A self-righteousness, accompanied with self-complacancy, and furnishing incentives to pride, is indeed a full proof of unregeneracy. But conscientiousness, connected with disquietudes, humiliation for sin, and a disposition to wait for divine teaching, is an effect and evidence of life, though the mind be yet darkened with ignorance, error and prejudice. And he that hath given life will give it more abundantly; for, ' the path of the just is as the shining light, that shineth more and more unto the perfect day.'

While Bunyan was in this state of mind he went, in the course of his trade as a tinker, to Bedford; where he overheard some women discoursing about regeneration; and though he could not understand their meaning he was greatly affected by observing the earnestness, cheerfulness, and humility of their behaviour; and was also convinced, that his views of religion were at that time very defective. Being thus led to frequent their company, he was brought as it were into a new world. Such an entire change took place in his sentiments, dispositions, and affections; and his mind was so deeply engaged in contemplating the great concerns of eternity, and the things pertaining to the kingdom of God, that he found it very difficult to employ his thoughts on any secular affairs.

But this extraordinary flow of affections, not being attended by a proportionable measure of doctrinal information, laid him open to various attempts of Satan and his emissaries. The Ranters, a set of the vilest antinomians that almost ever existed, first assailed him, by one of their party, who had formerly been Mr. Bunyan's companion in vice : but he overacted his part ; and, proceeding even to deny the being of a God, probably furnished the character of Atheist in the ' Pilgrim's Progress.' While Mr. Bunyan was engaged in reading the books of the Ranters, not being able to form his judgment about them, he was led to offer up the following prayer :—' O Lord, I am a fool, am not able to know the truth from error : Lord, leave me not to my own blindness, either to approve or condemn this doctrine. If it be of God, let me not despise it ; if it be of the devil, let me not embrace it. Lord, I lay my soul in this matter only at thy foot ; let me not be deceived, I humbly beseech thee.' This most suitable request the Lord graciously answered ; he soon saw through the delusions of the Ranters ; and probably referred to them, under the character of Self-will, in the second part of this work.

The epistles of St. Paul, which he now read with great attention, but without any guide or instructer, gave occasion to his being assulted by many sore temptations. He found the apostle continually speaking of faith ; and he could find no way by which he might under-

stand the meaning of that word, or discover
whether he was a believer or not ; so that,
mistaking the words of Christ (Matt. xvii. 20,)
he was tempted to seek a solution of his difficulty by trying to work a miracle ; he thought,
however, it would be right to pray before he
made the attempt, and this induced him to
desist, though his difficulties still remained
He was delivered from great perplexities about
the doctrine of election, by reflecting, that
none ' ever trusted in God and was confounded ;' and therefore it would be best for him to
trust in God, and leave election, as a ' secret
thing,' with the Lord, to whom it belonged
And the general invitations of the Gospel and
the assurance that ' yet there is room,' helped
him to repel the temptation to conclude, that
the day of grace was past.

This brief account of his temptations and escapes may teach others the best way of re
sisting similar suggestions ; and it shews us,
that numbers are durably harassed by such
perplexities, for want of doctrinal knowledge
and faithful instructors and counsellors. He
was, however, afterwards enabled, by means
of these inward trials, to caution others to
better effect, and more tenderly to sympathize
with the tempted.

After some time Mr. Bunyan became ac
quainted with Mr. Gifford, an Antipædobaptist minister at Bedford, whose conversation
was very useful to him : yet he was in some
respects more discouraged than ever, by fuller discoveries of those evils in his heart,

which he had not before noticed; and by doubts concerning the truth of the Scriptures, which his entire ignorance of the evidences by which they are authenticated rendered durably perplexing to him. He was, however, at length relieved by a sermon he heard on the love of Christ; though the grounds, on which he derived satisfaction and encouragement from it, are not very accurately stated. Soon after this he was admitted, by adult baptism, a member of Mr. Gifford's church, A. D. 1655, being then twenty-seven years of age; and after a little time was earnestly desired by the congregation to expound or preach, in a manner which is customary among the dissenters, as a preparation to the ministry. For a while he resisted their importunity, under a deep sense of his incompetency; but at length he was prevailed upon to speak in a small company, which he did greatly to their satisfaction and edification. Having been thus proved for a considerable time, he was at length called forth, and set apart by fasting and prayer to the ministerial office, which he executed with faithfulness and success during a long course of years; though frequently with the greatest trepidation and inward disquietude.

As he was baptized 1655, and imprisoned 1660, he could not have been long engaged in the work previous to that event; and it does not appear whether he obtained a stated employment as a minister, or whether he only preached occasionally, and continued to work

at his trade, as many dissenters very lauda-
bly do, when called to minister among poor
people, that they may not be ' burthensome
to them.' Previous, however, to the restoration of Charles II., when the churches were
principally filled by those, who have since
been distinguished as nonconformists, he was
expected to preach in a church near Cam-
bridge ; and a student of that university, not
remarkable for sobriety, observing a concourse
of people, was induced by curiosity to hear
' the tinker prate ;' but the discourse made
an unexpected impression on his mind ; he
embraced every future opportunity of hearing
Mr. Bunyan ; and at length became an eminent preacher in Cambridgeshire.

When the restoration took place, and, contrary to equity, engagements, and sound policy, the laws were framed and executed with
a severity, evidently intended to exclude every man, who scrupled the least tittle of the
doctrine, liturgy, discipline, or government of
the established church, Mr. Bunyan was one
of the first that suffered by them : for, being
courageous and unreserved, he went on in
his ministerial work without any disguise ; and
November 12, 1660, was apprehended by a
warrant from Justice Wingate at Harlington,
near Bedford, with sixty other persons, and
committed to the country jail. Security was
offered for his appearance at the sessions ;
but it was refused, as his sureties would not
consent that he should be restricted from
preaching any more. He was accordingly

confined till the quarter-sessions, when his
indictment stated, 'That John Bunyan, of
the town of Bedford, labourer, had devilishly
and perniciously abstained from coming to
church to hear divine service ; and was a
common upholder of several unlawful meet-
ings and conventicles, to the great disturbance
and distraction of the good subjects of this
kingdom, contrary to the laws of our sovereign
Lord the King.' The facts charged upon
him in this absurd indictment were never
proved, as no witnesses were produced. He
had confessed, in conversation with the magistrates, that he was a dissenter, and had
preached ; these words, being considered as
equivalent to conviction, were recorded
against him, and as he refused to conform he
was sentenced to perpetual banishment.
This sentence indeed was not executed ; but
he was confined in Bedford jail more than
twelve years, notwithstanding several attempts
were made to obtain his deliverance !

During this tedious imprisonment, or, at
least, part of it, he had no books, except a bible, and Fox's Martyrology : yet in this situation he penned the Pilgrim's Progress, and
many other treatises. He was only thirty-two
years of age, when he was imprisoned ; he
had spent his youth in the most disadvantageous manner imaginable ; had been no more
than five years a member of the church at
Bedford ; and less time a preacher of the
Gospel : yet in this admired allegory he appears to have been most intimately acquaint-

ed with all the variety of characters, which ministers, long employed in the sacred service, and eminent for judgment and sagacity, have observed among professors or opposers of evangelical truth !

No fewer than sixty dissenters, and two ministers, were confined with Mr. Bunyan in this jail ; and as some were discharged, others were committed during the time of his imprisonment : but this painful situation afforded him an opportunity of privately exercising his ministry to good effect. He learned in prison to make tagged thread laces, in the intervals of his other labours, and by this employment provided in the most unexceptionable manner for himself and his family. He seems to have been endued with extraordinary patience and courage, and to have experienced abundant consolations, while enduring these hardships : he was however sometimes distressed about his family, especially his eldest daughter, who was blind ; but in these trying seasons he received comfort from meditating on the promises of Scripture (Jer. xv. 11 ; xlix. 11.)

He was at some times favoured by the jailors, and permitted to see his family and friends, and, during the former part of his imprisonment, was even allowed to go out occasionally, and once to take a journey to London, probably to see whether some legal redress might not be obtained, according to some intimations given by Sir Matthew Hale, when petitions in his favour were laid before the judges. But this indulgence of the jailor exposing him to great danger, Mr. Bunyan was afterwards more closely confined. Hence I suppose, has arisen the opinion, which commonly prevails, that he was imprisoned at different times : but he seems never to have been set at liberty, and then recommitted ; though his hardships and restraints were greater at one time than at another.

In the last year of his imprisonment (A. D. 1671,) he was chosen pastor of the dissenting church at Bedford ; though it does not appear what opportunity he could have of exercising his pastoral office, except within the precincts of the jail. He was however liberated soon after, through the good offices of Dr. Barlow, bishop of Lincoln, after many fruitless attempts had been made for that purpose Thus terminated his tedious, severe, and even illegal, imprisonment, which had given him abundant opportunity for the exercise of patience and meekness ; and which seems to have been overruled, both for his own spiritual improvement, and the furtherance of the Gospel ; by leading him to study, and to form habits of close reflection, and accurate investigation of various subjects, in order to pen his several treatises : when probably he would neither have thought so deeply, nor written so well, had he been more at ease, and at liberty.

A short time after his enlargement, he built a meeting-house at Bedford, by the voluntary contributions of his friends ; and here he

statedly preached to large auditories, till his
death, without meeting with any remarkable
molestation. He used to come up to London
every year, where he preached among the
nonconformists with great acceptance ; and
it is said that Dr. Owen frequently attended
on these occasions, and expressed his approbation in very decided language. He also
made stated circuits into other parts of Eng-
land ; and animated his brethren to bear the
cross patiently, to obey God rather than man,
and to leave all consequences with him. He
was at the same time peculiarly attentive to
the temporal wants of those who suffered for
conscience-sake, and of the sick or afflicted ;
and he employed his influence very successfully, in reconciling differences among professors of the Gospel, and thus preventing disgraceful and burthensome litigations. He
was very exact in family religion, and the instruction of his children ; being principally
concerned for their spiritual interests, and
comparatively indifferent about their temporal prosperity. He therefore declined the liberal proposal of a wealthy citizen of London,
to take his son as an apprentice without any
premium, saying, 'God did not send me to advance my family, but to preach the Gospel :'
probably disliking the business, or situation,
as unfavourable to piety.

Nothing material is recorded concerning
him, between his enlargement in 1672, and
his death in 1688. It is said, that he clearly
saw through the designs of the court, in fa

vour of popery, when the indulgence was
granted to the dissenters, by James II., in
1687 : but that he advised his brethren to
avail themselves of the sunshine, by diligent
endeavours to spread the Gospel ; and to
prepare for an approaching storm by fasting
and prayer. The next year he took a journey
in very bad weather from London to Reading,
Berks, to make up a breach between a father
and his son, with whom he had some acquaintance ; and having happily effected his
last work and labour of love, he returned to
his lodgings on Snow-hill, apparently in good
health ; but very wet with the heavy rain that
was then falling ; and soon after he was seized with a fever, which in ten days terminated
his useful life. He bore his malady with
great patience and composure, and died in a
very comfortable and triumphant manner,
Aug. 31, 1688, aged sixty years ; after having exercised his ministry about thirty-two.
He lies buried in Bunhill-fields, where a
tomb-stone to his memory may still be seen.
He was twice married ; by his first wife he
left four children, one of which, a daughter
named Mary, who was blind, died before
him. He was married to his second wife A.
D. 1658, two years before his imprisonment,
by whom he seems not to have had any children : she survived him about four years.
Concerning the other branches of his family
we have not been able to gain any information.

Mr. Bunyan was tall and broad set, though not corpulent ; he had a ruddy complexion, with sparkling eyes, and hair inclined to red, but, in his old age, sprinkled with gray. His whole appearance was plain, and his dress always simple and unaffected. He published sixty tracts, which equalled the number of years he lived. The Pilgrim's Progress had passed through more than fifty editions in 1784.

His character seems to have been uniformly good, from the time when he was brought acquainted with the blessed Gospel of Christ ; and though his countenance was rather stern, and his manner rough, yet he was very mild, modest, and affable, in his behaviour. He was backward to speak much, except on particular occasions, and remarkably averse to boasting ; ready to submit to the judgment of others, and disposed to forgive injuries, to follow peace with all men, and to employ himself as a peace-maker : yet he was steady to his principles, and bold in reproving sin without respect of persons. Many slanders were spread concerning him during the course of his ministry, some of which he refuted ; they have however all died away, and no one now pretends to say any thing to his disadvantage, except as his firm attachment to his creed, and his practice as a Calvinist, a dissenter, and an Antipædobaptist, has been called bigotry ; and as the account given of his own experience has been misunderstood, or misrepresented.

He was undoubtedly endued with extraordinary natural talents ; his understanding discernment, memory, invention, and imagination, were remarkably sound and vigorous. so that he made very great proficiency in the knowledge of scriptural divinity, though brought up in ignorance ; but he never made much progress in human learning.   Even such persons, as did not favour his religious principles, have done ample justice to his mental powers.   The celebrated Dr. Johnson ranks the Pilgrim's Progress among a very few books indeed, of which the reader, when he comes to the conclusion, wishes they had been longer ; and allows it to rank high among the works of original genius.   (Piozzi's Anecdotes of Johnson, Boswell's life o. Johnson, vol. ii. p. 97, 2d edit.)   But it is above all things wonderful, that Bunyan's imagination, fertile and vigorous in a very great degree, and wholly untutored by the rules of learning, should in this instance have been so disciplined by sound judgment, and deep acquaintance with the Scripture, as to produce, in the form of an allegory, one of the fairest and most unexceptionable treatises on the system of Calvinism, that can be found in the English language.   In several of his other publications his imagination sometimes carried him beyond just bounds : but here he avoids all extremes, and seems not to deviate either to the right hand or to the left.   Perhaps, as he was himself liable to depression of spirit, and had passed through deep distresses, the view he gives of the pilgrim's temptation may be too gloomy ; but he has shown in the course of the work, that this arose principally from inadequate views of evangelical truth, and the want of Christian communion, with the benefits to be derived from the counsels of faithful minister   T. SCOTT.

3*

THE

PILGRIM'S PROGRESS.

PART I.

As I walked through the wilderness of this
world, I lighted on a certain place where was
a den,* and laid me down in that place to
sleep ; and as I slept I dreamed a dream. I
dreamed and behold, I saw † a man clothed

*·Mr. Bunyan was confined, at different times, about twelve
years in Bedford jail, for exercising his ministry contrary to
the statutes then in force. This was ' the den, in which he
slept and dreamed :' here he penned this instructive allegory,
and many other useful works, which evince that he was neither soured nor disheartened by persecution. The Christian,
who understands what usage he ought to expect in this evil
world, comparing our present measure of religious liberty
with the rigours of that age, will see abundant cause for gratitude ; but they, who are disposed to complain, can never be at
a loss for topics, while so much is amiss among all ranks and
orders of men, and in the conduct of every individual.

† ' I saw'—The allegory opens with a description of the
principal character to which it relates. The view, which the
author in his dream had of him, as ' clothed in rags,' implies
that all men are sinners, in their dispositions, affections and
conduct ; that their supposed virtues are radically defective,
and worthless in the sight of God ; that the pilgrim has discovered this in his own case, so that he perceives his own
righteousnesses to be insufficient for justification, even as sordid rags would be unsuitable raiment for those who stand be-

with rags, standing in a certain place, with
his face from his own house, a book in his
hand, and a great burthen upon his back (Isa.
lxiv. 6 ; Luke xiv. 33 ; Psal xxxviii. 4 ;
Hab. ii. 2.) I looked, and saw him open the
book and read therein ; and as he read he
wept and trembled ; and not being able longer to contain, he brake out with a lamentable cry, saying, ' What shall I do ?' (Acts,
ii. 37.)

fore kings. His ' face turned from his own house' represents
the sinner convinced that it is absolutely necessary to subordin
ate all other concerns to the care of his immortal soul, and to renounce every thing which interferes with that grand object :
this makes him lose his former relish for the pleasures of sin,
and even for the most lawful temporal satisfactions, while he
trembles at the thought of impending destruction (Heb. xi. 8.
24—27.) ' The book in his hand,' &c. instructs us, that
sinners discover their real state and character, by reading and
believing the Scriptures ; that their first attention is often directed to the denunciations of the wrath to come contained in
them, and that such persons cannot but continue to search
the word of God, though their grief and alarm be increased
by every perusal. The ' burthen upon his back' represents
that distressing sense of guilt, and fear of wrath, which deeply convinced sinners cannot shake off ; ' the remembrance of
their sins is grievous to them, the burthen of them is intolerable :' their consciences are oppressed with guilt, even on
account of those actions in which their neighbours perceive
no harm ; their hearts tremble at the prospect of dangers of
which others have no apprehension ; and they see an absolute
necessity of escaping from a situation in which others live
most securely : for true faith, from the very first, ' sees things
that are invisible.' In one way or other, therefore, they soon
manifest the earnestness of their minds, in inquiring ' what
they must do to be saved ?' The circumstances of these humiliating convictions exceedingly vary ; but the life of faith
and grace always begins with them : and they, who are wholly
strangers to this experience, are Christians only in name and
form :—

' He knows no hope, who never knew a fear.'
                                        Cowper.

In this plight* therefore he went home, and refrained himself as long as he could, that his wife and children should not perceive his dis-

* 'In this plight'.—The contempt or indignation, which worldly people express towards those who are distressed in conscience, commonly induces them to conceal their inquietude as long as they can, even from their relatives ; but this soon becomes impracticable. Natural affection also, connected with a view of the extreme danger to which a man sees the objects of his most tender attachments exposed, but of which they have no apprehensions, will extort such earnest representations, warnings, and entreaties, as are here expressed. The city of Destruction (as it is afterwards called) signifies this present evil world, as doomed to the flames ; or the condition of careless sinners, immersed in secular pursuits and pleasures, neglecting eternal things, and exposed to the unquenchable fire of hell, ' at the day of judgment and perdition of ungodly men.' They who are ignorant of the Scriptures, and unaccustomed to compare their own conduct with the Divine law, will be amazed at such discourse ; and, instead of duly regarding the warnings given them, will commonly ascribe them to enthusiasm or insanity ; and as prophets, apostles, and the Son of God himself, were looked upon in this light by their contemporaries, we may be sure that no prudence, excellence, or benevolence, can exempt the consistent believer from the trial. Near relations will generally be the first to form this opinion of his case ; and will devise various expedients to quiet his mind : diversions, company, feastings, absence from serious friends or books, will be prescribed : and by these means a false peace often succeeds a transient alarm. But when a genuine humiliating discovery of the evil and desert of sin has been made to the soul, such expedients will not alleviate, but increase, the anguish ; and will be followed by still greater earnestness about a man's own salvation, and that of others. This commonly strengthens prejudice, and induces obduracy : and contemptuous pity gives place to resentment, ill usage, derision, or neglect. The disconsolate believer will then be driven into retirement, and relieve his burthened mind by reading the Scriptures, and meditation on his doleful case, with compassionate prayers for his despisers : and thus he sows in tears that seed from which the harvest of his future joy will surely be produced.

tress ; but he could not be silent long, because
that his trouble increased : wherefore at length
he brake his mind to his wife and children,
and thus he began to talk to them : ' O my
dear wife,' said he ' and you the children of my
bowels, I your dear friend am in myself undone,
by reason of a burthen that lieth hard upon
me : moreover, I am certainly informed that
this our city will be burned with fire from
heaven ; in which fearful overthrow, both myself, with thee my wife, and you my sweet
babes, shall miserably come to ruin, except
(the which yet I see not) some way of escape
may be found, whereby we may be delivered.'
At this his relations were sore amazed ; not
for that they believed that what he had said to
them was true, but because they thought some
frenzy distemper had got into his head ; therefore, it drawing towards night, and they hop-
ing that sleep might settle his brains, with all
haste they got him to bed : but the night was
as troublesome to him as the day ; wherefore,
instead of sleeping, he spent it in sighs and
tears.   So when the morning was come they
would know how he did : he told them ' worse
and worse.'   He also set to talking to them
again, but they began to be hardened. They
also thought to drive away his distemper by
harsh and surly carriage to him ; sometimes
they would deride, sometimes they would
chide, and sometimes they would quite neglect him.   Wherefore he began to retire himself to his chamber, to pray for and pity them ;
and also to condole his own misery.   He

would also walk solitarily in the fields, sometimes reading and sometimes praying ; and
thus for some days he spent his time.

Now I saw* upon a time when he was walking in the fields, that he was (as he was wont)
reading in his book, and greatly distressed in
his mind ; and as he read, he burst out, as he
had done before, crying, ' What shall I do to
be saved ?' (Acts xvi. 30, 31.)

I saw also that he looked this way and that
way, as if he would run ; yet he stood still,
because (as I perceived) he could not tell
which way to go.   I looked then, and saw a
man named Evangelist coming to him, and he
asked, ' Wherefore dost thou cry ?'

He answered, Sir, I perceive by the book
in my hand that I am condemned to die, and
after that to come to judgment ; and I find
that I am not willing to do the first, nor able
to do the second (Heb. ix 27 ; Job xvi. 21, 22 ;
Ezek. xxii. 14.)

Then said Evangelist, Why not willing to
die, since this life is attended with so many
evils ?   The man answered, Because I fear
that this burthen that is upon my back will
sink me lower than the grave, and I shall fall

* ' Now I saw'—The Scriptures are indeed sufficient to
make us wise unto salvation, as well as to shew us our guilt
and danger ; yet the Lord commonly uses the ministry of his
servants to direct, into the way of peace, even those who
nave previously discovered their lost condition.   Though
convinced of the necessity of escaping from impending ruin,
they hesitate, not knowing what to do, till Providence brings
     acquainted with some faithful preacher of the Gospel,
     instructions afford an explicit answer to their secret
     after the way of salvation.

into Tophet (Isa. xxx 33.) And, Sir, if I be
not fit to go to prison, I am not fit to go to judg
ment, and from thence to execution ; and the
thoughts of these things make me cry.

Then said Evangelist,* If this be thy condition, why standest thou still ? He answered, Because I know not whither to go. Then
he gave him a parchment roll ; and there was
written within, ' Flee from the wrath to come'
(Matt. iii. 7)

The man therefore read it, and, looking
upon Evangelist very carefully, said, Whither must I flee ?† Then said Evangelist, point-

* ' Then said'—The able minister of Christ will deem it
necessary to enforce the warning, ' flee from the wrath to
come,' even upon those who are alarmed about their souls ;
because this is the proper way of exciting them to diligence
and decision, and of preserving them from procrastination.
They, therefore, who would persuade such persons, that their
fears are groundless, their guilt far less than they suppose,
and their danger imaginary, use the most effectual means of
soothing them into a fatal security. Nor can any discoveries
of henious guilt or helpless ruin in themselves produce despondency, provided the salvation of the Gospel be fully exhibited,
and proposed to them.

† ' Whither'—The awakened sinner may be incapable for a
time of perceiving the way of salvation by faith in Christ ;
for divine illumination is often very gradual. Thus, though
the pilgrim could not see the gate, when Evangelist pointed it out to him, he thought he could discern the shining
light. Upright inquirers attend to the general instructions
and encouragements of Scripture, and the declarations of the
pardoning mercy of God ; which by degrees lead them to the
knowledge of Christ, and to faith in him : for, as our author
says in a marginal note, ' Christ, and the way to him, cannot
be found without the word.' Thus instructed, the pilgrim
' began to run ;' for no persuasions or considerations can
induce the man, who is duly in earnest about salvation,
to neglect those things which he knows to be his present duty '
but it must be expected that carnal relations will oppose his

ing with his finger over a very wide field, Do
you see yonder wicket gate ? (Matt. vii. 13,
14.) The man said, No. Then said the other, Do you see yonder shining light ? (Psal
cxix. 105 ; 2 Pet. i. 14.) He said, I think I
do. Then said Evangelist, Keep that light
in your eye, and go up directly thereto, so
shalt thou see the gate ; at which when thou
knockest it shall be told thee what thou shalt
do. So I saw in my dream that the man be
gan to run. Now he had not run far from
his own door but his wife and children perceiving it began to cry after him to return
(Luke xiv. 26 ;) but the man put his fingers in
his ears, and ran on, crying ' Life ! life ! eternal life !' So he looked not behind him (Gen.
xix. 17 ; 2 Cor. iv. 18,) but fled towards the
middle of the plain.

The neighbours* also came out to see him

especially as it appears to them destructive of all their prospects of worldly advantage. The following lines are here
subjoined to a very rude engraving :—

    ' Christian no sooner leaves the world but meets
    Evangelist, who lovingly him greets
    With tidings of another ; and doth shew
    Him how to mount to that from this below.'

* ' The neighbours'—The attention of numbers is in general excited when one of their companions in sin and van'ty
engages in religion and forsakes the party. He soon becomes
the topic of conversation among them : their minds are vari-
ously affected ; some ridicule, others rail, threaten, attempt
force, or employ artifice, to withdraw him from his purpose ;
according to their different dispositions, situations, or relations to him. Most of them, however, soon desist, and leave
him to his choice. But two characters are not so easily
shaken off ; these our author has named Obstinate and Pliable, to denote their opposite propensities. The former,

run : and as he ran, some mocked, others
threatened, and some cried after him to re
turn ; and among those that did so there were
two that were resolved to fetch him back by
force. The name of one was Obstinate, and
the name of the other Pliable. Now by this
time the man was got a good distance from
them ; but however they were resolved to pursue him, which they did, and in a little time
they overtook him. Then said the man,
Neighbours, wherefore are you come ? They
said, To persuade you to go back with us ,
but he said, That can by no means be : you
dwell, said he, in the city of Destruction ; the
place also where I was born ; I see it to be
so ; and dying there, sooner or later, you will
sink lower than the grave, into a place that
burns with fire and brimstone : be content,
good neighbours, and go along with me.

through a resolute pride and stoutness of heart, persists in attempting to bring back the new convert to his worldly pursuits : the latter from a natural easiness of temper and sus-
ceptibility of impression, is pliant to persuasion, and readily
consents to make a profession of religion.

The subsequent dialogue admirably illustrates the characters of the speakers. Christian, for so he is henceforth called) is firm, decided, bold, and sanguine :—Obstinate is profane, scornful, self-sufficient, and disposed to contemn God's
word, when it interferes with his worldly interests .:—Pliable
is yielding, and easily induced to engage in things, of which
he understands neither the nature nor the consequences.
Christian's plain warnings and earnest entreaties ; Obstinate's contempt of believers, as ' crazy-headed coxcombs,'
and his exclamation when Pliable inclines to be a pilgrim,
' What, more fools still ?' are admirably characteristic ; and
shew that such things are peculiar to no age or place, but always accompany serious godliness, as the shadow does the
substance.

What, said Obstinate, and leave our friends and our comforts behind us ?

Yes, said Christian (for that was his name ;) because that all which you shall forsake is not worthy to be compared with a little of that that I am seeking to enjoy ; and if you will go along with me, and hold it, you shall fare as I myself ; for there where I go is enough and to spare (Luke xv. 17 :) come away, and prove my words.

Obst. What are the things you seek, since you leave all the world to find them ?

Chr. I seek an 'inheritance incorruptible, undefiled, and that fadeth not away ; and it is laid up in heaven' (1 Pet. i. 4—6 ; Heb. xi. 6, 16,) and safe there, to be bestowed at the time appointed on them that diligently seek it. Read it so, if you will, in my book.

Tush, said Obstinate, away with your book : will you go back with us or no ?

No, not I, said the other, because I have laid my hand to the plough (Luke ix. 62.)

Obst. Come then, neighbour Pliable, let us turn again and go home without him : there is a company of these crazy-headed coxcombs, that when they take a fancy by the end are wiser in their own eyes than seven men that can render a reason.

Then said Pliable, Don't revile ; if what the good Christian says is true, the things he looks after are better than ours ; my heart inclines to go with my neighbour.

Obst. What more fools still ? be ruled by me, and go back ; who knows whither such a brain-sick fellow will lead you ? Go back, go back, and be wise.

Chr. Nay, but do thou come with thy neighbour Pliable ; there are such thing to be had which I spake of, and many more glories besides : if you believe not me read here in this book ; and, for the truth of what is expressed therein, behold all is confirmed by the blood of him that made it (Heb. ix. 17—22.)

Well, neighbour Obstinate, saith Pliable, I begin to come to a point : I intend to go along with this good man, and to cast in my lot with him : but, my good companion, do you know the way to this desired place ?

Chr. I am directed by a man, whose name is Evangelist, to speed me to a little gate that is before us, where we shall receive instructions about the way.

Pli. Come then, good neighbour, let us be going. Then they went both together.

And I will go back to my place, said Obstinate ; I will be no companion of such misled fantastical fellows.

Now I saw* in my dream, that when Obstinate was gone back, Christian and Pliable

---

* ' Now I saw'—This conversation between Christian and Pliable marks the difference in their characters, as well as the measure of the new convert's attainments. The want of a due apprehension of eternal things is evidently the primary defect of all who oppose or neglect religion ; but more maturity of judgment and experience are requisite to discover, that many professors are equally strangers to a realizing view ' of the powers and terrors of what is yet unseen.' The men represented by Pliable disregard these subjects ; they inquire eagerly about the good things to be enjoyed, but not in any proportion about the way of salvation, the difficulties to

went talking over the plain ; and thus they began their discourse.

Chr. Come, neighbour Pliable, how do
you do ? I am glad you are persuaded to go
along with me ; had even Obstinate himself
but felt what I have felt of the powers and
terrors of what is yet unseen, he would not
thus lightly have given us the back.

Pli. Come, neighbour Christian, since
there are none but us two here, tell me now
farther, what the things are, and how to be
enjoyed, whither we are going.

Chr. I can better conceive of them with
my mind than speak of them with my tongue ;
but yet, since you are desirous to know, I
will read of them in my book.

Pli. And do you think that the words of
your book are certainly true ?

be encountered, or the danger of coming short : and new converts, being zealous, sanguine, and unsuspecting, are naturally led to enlarge on the descriptions of heavenly felicity given
in Scripture. As these are generally figurative or negative,
such unhumbled professors, annexing carnal ideas to them,
are greatly delighted ; and, not being retarded by any distressing remorse and terror, or feeling the opposition of corrupt nature, they are often more zealous, and seem to proceed faster in external duties than true converts. They take
it for granted that all the privileges of the Gospel belong to
them ; and, being very confident, zealous, and joyful, they
often censure those who are really fighting the good fight of
faith. There are also systems diligently propagated, which
marvellously encourage this delusion, excite a high flow of
false affections, especially of a mere selfish gratitude to a
supposed benefactor for imaginary benefits, which is considered as a very high attainment : till the event proves them to
be like the Israelites at the Red Sea, who ' believed the
Lord's words, and sang his praise ; but soon forgat his
works, and waited not for his counsel' (Psalm cvi. 12—24.)

4*

Chr. Yes, verily, for it was made by him that cannot lie (Tit. i. 2.)

Pli. Well said ; what things are they ?

Chr. There is an endless kingdom to be inhabited, and everlasting life to be given us, that we may inhabit that kingdom forever (Isa. xiv. 17 ; John x. 27—29.)

Pli. Well said ; and what else ?

Chr. There are crowns of glory to be given us ; and garments that will make us shine like the sun in the firmament of heaven (2 Tim. iv. 8 ; Rev. xxii. 5 ; Matt. xiii. 43.)

Pli. This is very pleasant ; and what else ?

Chr. There shall be no more crying nor sorrow ; for he that is owner of the place will wipe all tears from our eyes (Isa. xxv. 8 ; Rev. vii. 16, 17 ; xxi. 4.)

Pli. And what company shall we have there ?

Chr. There we shall be with seraphim and cherubim, creatures that will dazzle your eyes to look on them (Isa. vi. 2 ; 1 Thess. iv. 16, 17.) There also you shall meet with thousands and ten thousands that have gone before us to that place ; none of them are hurtful, but loving and holy ; every one walking in the sight of God, and standing in his presence with acceptance for ever. In a word, there we shall see the elders with their golden crowns (Rev. iv. 4 ;) there we shall see holy virgins with their golden harps (Rev. xiv. 1—5 ;) there we shall see men that by the world were cut in pieces, burnt in flames, eaten of beasts, drowned in the seas, for the

love that they bare to the Lord of the place ;
all well, and clothed with immortality as with
a garment (John xii. 25 ; 2 Cor. v. 2—4.)

Pli. The hearing of this is enough to ravish one's heart ; but are these things to be
enjoyed ? How shall we get to be sharers
thereof ?

Chr. The Lord the governor of the country hath recorded that in this book ; the substance of which is, if we be truly willing to
have it he will bestow it upon us freely (Isa
iv. 1—3 ; John vi. 37 ; vii. 37 ; Rev. xxi. 6 ;
xxii. 17.)

Pli. Well, my good companion, glad am I
to hear of these things ; come on, let us mend
our pace.

Chr. I cannot go so fast as I would, by
reason of this burthen that is on my back.

Now I saw in my dream, that just as they
had ended this talk, they drew nigh to a very
miry slough* that was in the midst of the

* ' Miry slough'—The slough of Despond represents those
discouraging fears which often harass new converts. It is
distinguished from the alarms which induced Christian to leave
the city, and ' flee from the wrath to come :' for the anxious
apprehensions of one who is diligently seeking salvation are
very different from those which excited him to inquire after
it.   The latter are reasonable and useful, and arise from faith
in God's word : but the former are groundless, they result
from remaining ignorance, inattention, and unbelief, and
greatly retard the pilgrim in his progress. They should also
be carefully distinguished from those doubts and discouragements, which assault the established Christian ; for these are
generally the consequence of negligence, or yielding to temptation ; whereas new converts fall into their despondings,
when most diligent according to the light they have received :
and, if some conscientious persons seem to meet with this
slough in every part of their pilgrimage, it arises from an

plain, and they, being heedless, did both fall
suddenly into the bog. The name of the

immature judgment, erroneous sentiments, or peculiar temptations. When the diligent student of the Scriptures obtains
such an acquaintance with the perfect holiness of God, the
spirituality of his law, the inexpressible evil of sin, and his
own obligations and transgressions, as greatly exceeds the
measure in which he discerns the free and full salvation of the
Gospel, his humiliation will verge nearer and nearer to despondency. This, however, is not essential to repentance, but
arises from misapprehension ; though few in proportion whol-
y escape it. The *mire* of the slough represents that idea
which desponding persons entertain of themselves and their
situation, as altogether vile and loathsome ; and their confessions and self-abasing complaints, which render them contemptible in the opinion of others. As every attempt to rescue themselves discovers to them more of the latent evil of
their hearts, they seem to grow worse and worse ; and, for
want of a clear understanding of the Gospel, they have no
firm ground to tread on, and know neither where they are,
or what they must do. But how could Pliable fall into this
slough, seeing he had no such views of God or his law, of
himself, or of sin, as this condition seems to pre-suppose ?
To this it may be answered, that men can hardly associate
with religious persons, and hear their discourse, confessions, and complaints, or become acquainted with any part
of Scripture, without making some alarming and mortifying
discoveries concerning themselves. These transient convictions taking place when they fancied they were about to become very good, and succeeding to great self-complacency,
constitute a grievous disappointment ; and they ascribe their
uneasiness to the new doctrine they have heard. But, though
Pliable fell into the slough, Christian ' by reason of his burthen' sank the deepest ; for the true believer's humiliation
for sin tends greatly to increase his fear of wrath. Superficial professors, expecting the promised happiness without
trouble or suffering, are often very angry at those who were
the means of inducing them to think of religion ; as if they
had deceived them : and, being destitute of true faith, their
only object is, at any rate to get rid of their uneasiness
This is a species of stony-ground hearers abounding in every
part of the church, who are offended and fall away, by means
of a little *inward* disquietude, before any *outward* tribulation arises because of the word.

slough was Despond. Here therefore they
wallowed for a time, being grievously bedaubed with dirt ; and Christian, because of the
burthen that was on his back, began to sink
in the mire.

Then said Phable, Ah ! neighbour Christian, where are you now ?

Truly, said Christian I do not know.

At that Pliable began to be offended, and
angrily said to his fellow, Is this the happiness
you have told me all this while of ? If we have
such ill speed at our first setting out, what
may we expect betwixt this and our journey's
end ? May I get out again with my life, you
shall possess the brave country alone for me.
And with that he gave a desperate struggle
or two, and got out of the mire on that side
of the slough which was next his own house ;
so away he went, and Christian saw him no
more.

Wherefore* Christian was left to tumble in

* 'Wherefore'—Christian dreaded the doom of his city
more than the slough. Many persons, under deep distress
of conscience, are afraid of relief, lest it should prove delu-
sive.   Deliverance from wrath and the blessings of salvation
appear to them so valuable, that all else is comparatively trivial : desponding fears may connect with their religious diligence ; but despair would be the consequence of a return to
their former course of sin : if they perish, therefore, it shall
be whilst earnestly struggling, under deep discouragement,
after that salvation, for which their souls even faint within
them.   Their own efforts, indeed, fail to extricate them :
but in due time the Lord will send them assistance   This is
described by the allegorical person named Help, who may
represent the instruments by which they receive encouragement : a service in which it is a privilege to be employed !—
Fear is also personified : in the midst of the new convert's
discourse on the joys of heaven, fears of wrath often cast him

the slough of Despond alone ; but still he endeavoured to struggle to that side of the slough that was farthest from his own house, and next to the wicket-gate : the which he did, but could not get out because of the burthen that was upon his back. But I beheld in my dream, that a man came to him, whose name was Help, and asked him, What he did there?

Sir, said Christian, I was bid to go this way by a man called Evangelist, who directed me also to yonder gate, that I might escape the wrath to come. And as I was going thither, I fell in here

Help. But why did you not look for the steps ?

Chr. Fear followed me so hard that I fled the next way, and fell in.

Help. Then said he, Give me thy hand ; so he gave him his hand, and he drew him out and set him upon sound ground, and bid him go on his way (Psal. xi. 2.)

Then I stepped* to him that plucked him out

into despondency, while he so thinks of the terrors of the Lord, as to overlook his precious promises.

* 'Then I stepped'—This account of the slough, which our author in his vision received from Help, coincides with the preceding explanation. Increasing knowledge produces deeper self-debasement : hence discouraging fears arise in men's minds lest they should at last perish ; and objections against themselves continually accumulate, till they fall into habitual despondency, unless they constantly attend to the encouragements of the Scripture, or, in the apostle's language, have their ' feet shod with the preparation of the Gospel of peace.' As this state of mind is distressing and enfeebling in itself, and often furnishes enemies with a plausible objection to religion, the servants of God have always attempted to preserve humble inquirers from it, by various scriptural in-

and said, Sir, wherefore, since over this p ace
is the way from the city of Destruction to yonder gate, is that this plat is not mended, that
poor travellers might go thither with some security? And he said unto me, This miry slough
is such a place as cannot be mended ; it is
the descent whither the scum and filth that
attends conviction for sin doth continually run,
and therefore it was called the slough of Despond : for still, as the sinner is awakened
about his lost condition, there arises in his soul
many fears and doubts and discouraging apprehensions, which all of them get together,
and settle in this place. And this is the reason of the badness of the ground.

It is not the pleasure of the king that this
place should remain so bad (Isa. xxxv. 3. 4)
his labourers also have, by the direction of
his majesty's surveyors, been for above this

structions and consolatory topics : yet their success is not adequate to their wishes ; for the Lord is pleased to permit
numbers to be thus discouraged, in order to detect the false
professor, and to render the upright more watchful and humble. Our author in a marginal note, explains the steps to
mean, ' the promises of forgiveness and acceptance to life by
faith in Christ ;' which includes the general invitations, and
the various encouragements given in Scripture to all who
seek the salvation of the Lord, and diligently use the appointed means. It was evidently his opinion, that the path from
destruction to life lies by this slough ; and that none are indeed in the narrow way, who have neither struggled through
it, nor gone over it by means of the steps. The ' chance of
weather' seems to denote those seasons when peculiar temptations, excepting sinful passions, confuse the minds of new
converts ; and so, losing sight of the promises, they sink into
despondency during humiliating experiences : but faith in
Christ, and in the mercy of God through him, sets the pilgrim's feet on good ground.

sixteen hundred years employed about this
patch of ground, if perhaps it might have been
mended : yea, and to my knowledge, said he,
here have been swallowed up at least twenty
thousand cart-loads ; yea, millions of wholesome instructions, that have at all seasons
been brought from all places of the king's dominions (and they that can tell say, they are
the best materials to make good the ground o.
the place,) if so be it might have been mended : but it is the slough of Despond still, and
so will be when they have done what they
can.

True there are, by the direction of the law-
giver, certain good and substantial steps placed even through the very midst of the slough ;
but at such times as this place doth much
spew out its filth, as it doth against change o.
weather, these steps are hardly seen ; or i.
they be, men through the dizziness of their
heads step beside ; and then they are bemir-
ed to purpose, notwithstanding the steps be
there : but the ground is good when they are
once got in at the gate. (1 Sam. xii. 22.)

Now I saw* in my dream, that by this time
Pliable was got home to his house. So his
neighbours came to visit him ; and some of
them called him wise man for coming back ;
and some called him fool for hazarding him-

* 'Now I saw'—They, who affect to despise real Chris-
Jians, often both express and feel great contempt for those
that cast off their profession ; such men are unable, for a
time, to resume their wonted confidence among their former
companions ; and this excites them to pay court to them by
reviling and deriding those whom they have forsaken.

self with Christian : others again did mock at his cowardliness, saying, 'Surely, since you began to venture, I would not have been so base to have given out for a few difficulties :' so Pliable sat sneaking among them. But at last he got more confidence, and then they all turned their tales, and began to deride poor Christian behind his back. And thus much concerning Pliable.

Now as Christian was walking solitarily by himself, he spied one afar off, crossing over the field to meet him, and their hap was to meet just as they were crossing the way of each other. The gentleman's name, that met him, was Mr. Worldly-Wiseman ;* he

* ' Worldly-Wiseman'—The wise men of this world carefully notice those who begin to turn their thoughts to religion, and attempt to counteract their conviction before the case becomes desperate : from their desponding fears they take occasion to insinuate that they are deluded or disordered in their minds ; that they make too much ado about religion ; and that a decent regard to it (which is all that is requisite) consists with the enjoyment of this life, and even conduces to secular advantage. Worldly-Wiseman, therefore, is a person of consequence, whose superiority gives him influence over poor pilgrims : he is a reputable and successful man ; prudent, sagacious, and acquainted with mankind ; moral and religious in his way, and qualified to give the very best counsel to those who wish to serve both God and Mammon : but he is decided in his judgment against all kinds and degrees of religion, which interfere with a man's worldly interest, disquiet his mind, or spoil his relish for outward enjoyments. He resides at Carnal-policy, a great town near the city of Destruction : for worldly prudence, modelling a man's religion, is as ruinous as open vice and impiety; though it be very prevalent among decent and virtuous people. Such men attend to the reports that are circulated about the conversion of their neighbours, and often watch their opportunity of entering into discourse with them.

dwelt in the town of Carnal-policy, a very great town, and also hard by from whence Christian came. This man then meeting with Christian, and having some inkling of him (for Christian's setting forth from the city of Destruction was much noised abroad, not only in the town where he dwelt, but also it began to be the town talk in some other places,) Mr. Worldly-Wiseman, therefore, having some guess of him by beholding his laborious going, by observing his sighs and groans, and the like, began thus to enter into some talk with Christian.

World. How now,* good fellow, whither away after this burthened manner ?

* ' How now'—There is great beauty in this dialogue, arising from the exact regard to character preserved throughout Indeed this forms one of our author's peculiar excellencies; as it is a very difficult attainment, and always manifests a superiority of genius. The self-satisfaction of Worldly-Wiseman, his contempt of Christian's capacity, sentiments, and pursuits; his affected sneering compassion, and his censure of Evangelist's advice; his representation of the dangers and hardship of the way, and of ' the desperate ventures' of religious people ' to obtain they know not what :' and his confident assumption, that Christian's concern arose from weakness of intellect, ' meddling with things too high' for him, hearkening to bad counsel (that is, reading the word of God, and attending to the preaching of the Gospel,) and from distraction, as the natural consequence, are most admirably characteristic. His arguments also are very specious, though wholly deduced from worldly considerations He does not say, that Evangelist had not pointed out the way of salvation, or that wicked men are not in danger of future misery; but he urges, that so much concern about sin and the eternal world takes men off from a proper regard to their secular interests, to the injury of their families; that it prevents their enjoying comfort in domestic life, or in other providential blessings; that it leads them into perilous and dis-

Chr. A burthened manner indeed, as ever, I think, poor creature had! And whereas you asked me, whither away? I tell you, Sir, I am going to yonder wicket-gate before me; for there, as I am informed, I shall be put in a way to be rid of my heavy burthen.

World. Hast thou a wife and children?

Chr. Yes: but I am so laden with this burthen that I cannot take that pleasure in them as formerly; methinks I am as if I had none (1 Cor. vii. 29.)

World. Wilt thou hearken to me if I give thee counsel?

Chr. If it be good I will; for I stand in need of good counsel.

World. I would advise thee, then, that thou

tressing situations, of which their first terrors and despondings are only an earnest; that a troubled conscience may be quieted in a more expeditious and easy manner; and that they may obtain credit, comfort, and manifold advantages, by following prudent counsel. On the other hand, Christian not only speaks according to his name, but consistently with the character of a young convert. He makes no secret of his disquietude and terrors, and declares, without reserve, the method in which he sought relief. He owns, that he had lost his relish for every earthly comfort, and he desires to receive good counsel: but while he is prepared to withstand all persuasions to return home, he is not upon his guard against the insiduous proposal of his carnal counsellor. He fears the wrath to come more than all the dreadful things which had been mentioned: but his earnestness to get present relief exposes him to the danger of seeking it in an unwarranted way. He has obtained from the Scriptures a conviction of his guilt and danger; but, not having also learned the instructions of life, he does not discern the fatal tendency of the plausible advice given him by so reputable a person. Every one, who has been in the way of making observations on these matters, must perceive how exactly this suits the case of numbers, when first brought to mind the one thing needful

with all speed get thyself rid of thy burthen for thou wilt never be settled in thy mind till then, nor canst thou enjoy the benefits of the blessings which God hath bestowed upon thee till then.

Chr. That is that which I seek for, even to be rid of this heavy burthen ; but get it off myself I cannot : nor is there any man in our country that can take it off my shoulders : therefore am I going this way, as I told you, that I may be rid of my burthen.

World. Who bid you go this way to be rid of your burthen ?

Chr. A man that appeared to me to be a very great and honourable person : his name, as I remember, is Evangelist

World. Beshrew him for his counsel ; there is not a more dangerous and troublesome way in the world than is that unto which he hath directed thee ; and that thou shalt find if thou wilt be ruled by his counsel. Thou hast met with something, as I perceive, already ; for I see the dirt of the slough of Despond is upon thee ; but that slough is the beginning of the sorrows that do attend those that go on in that way. Hear me, I am older than thou ; thou art like to meet with, on the way which thou goest, wearisomeness, painfulness, hunger, perils, nakedness, sword, lions, dragons, darkness, and, in a word, death, and what not ? These things are certainly true, having been confirmed by many testimonies. And why should a man so carelessly cast away himself by giving heed to a stranger ?

Chr. Why, Sir, this burthen upon my back is more terrible to me than are all these things which you have mentioned : nay, methinks I care not what I meet with in my way, if so be I can also meet with deliverance from my burthen.

World. How camest thou by the burthen at first.

Chr. By reading this book in my hand.

World. I thought so ; and it has happened unto thee as to other weak men, who, meddling with things too high for them, do suddenly fall into thy distractions ; which distractions do not only unman men (as thine I perceive have done thee,) but they run them upon desperate ventures to obtain they know not what.

Chr. I know what I would obtain; it is ease from my heavy burthen.

World. But why wilt thou seek for ease this way, seeing so many dangers attend it ? Especially since, hadst thou but patience to hear me, I could direct thee to the obtaining of what thou desirest, without the dangers that thou in this way wilt run thyself into Yea, and the remedy is at hand.   Besides, I will add, that, instead of these dangers, thou shalt meet with much safety, friendship, and content.

Chr. Sir, I pray open this secret to me.

World. Why in yonder village (the village is named Morality*) there dwells a gentleman

* ‘ Morality’—The village Morality, is the emblem of that large company, who in nations favoured with evelation ab-

5*

whose name is Legality, a very judicious man,
and a man of very good name, that has skill

atain from scandalous vices, and practise reputable duties,
without any true fear or love of God, or regard to his authority or glory. This, connected with a system of notions, and
a stint of external worship, is substituted in the place of Chris
tianity : but it is faulty in its principle, measure, and object :
results wholly from self-love ; is restricted to the outward ob
servance of some precepts selected from the Scriptures ; and
aims principally at the acquisition of reputation, distinction,
or temporal advantages, with no more than a subordinate respect even to the interests of eternity : it is destitute of humility,
delight, impartiality, and universality in obedience ; it leaves
the heart in the possession of some worldly idol, and never
advances a man to the rank of a spiritual worshipper, or renders him meet for the peculiar pleasures of heaven. Yet this
mutilated kind of religion draws multitudes off from attending either to the holy requirements of the law, or to the humbling doctrines of the Gospel. The most noted inhabitant
of this village does not derive his name, Legality, from making the law of God the rule of his conduct (for 'by the law is
the knowledge of sin,' which tends to increase the convinced
sinner's distress) , but from his teaching men to depend on a
defective obedience to a small part of the law, explained and
lowered, according to the method of the scribes and pharisees. Such teachers, however, are admired by the wise men
of this world, and are deemed very skilful in relieving troubled consciences, and recovering men from religious distractions.
His son Civility is the emblem of those, who persuade themselves and others, that a decent, benevolent, and obliging
behaviour, will secure men from all future punishment, and
ensure an inheritance in heaven, if indeed there be any such
place ! Such counsellors can ease the consciences of ignorant
persons, when superficially alarmed, almost as well as those
who superadd a form of godliness, a few doctrinal opinions,
and a regard to some precepts of the Gospel. Both are nigh
at hand in every place ; and the wise men of this world are ever
ready to direct convinced sinners to seek relief from them :
they allow, that it is better for those who have been immor-
al and profligate to reform their lives ; for this will meet with
the approbation of their relatives, and conduce to their advantage, while the strait gate and narrow way would prove their
ruin. Most pilgrims are assailed by such counsellors : and
many are not able to detect the fallacy of their reasonings till
their own folly corrects them.

to help men off with such burthens as thine is from their shoulders; yea, to my knowledge he hath done a great deal of good this way; ay, and besides, he hath skill to cure those that are somewhat crazed in their wits with their burthens. To him, as I said, thou mayest go and be helped presently. His house is not quite a mile from this place; and if he should not be at home himself, he hath a pretty young man to his son, whose name is Civility, that can do it (to speak on) as well as the old gentleman himself. There, I say, thou mayest be eased of thy burthen: and if thou art not minded to go back to thy former habitation, as indeed I would not wish thee, thou mayest send for thy wife and children to thee to this village; where there are houses now stand empty, one of which thou mayest have at reasonable rates: provision is there also cheap and good; and that which will make thy life more happy is, to be sure there thou shalt live by honest neighbours in credit and good fashion.

Now was Christian somewhat at a stand; but presently he concluded, If this be true, which this gentleman hath said, my wisest course is to take his advice; and with that he thus farther spake.

Chr. Sir, which is my way to this honest man's house?

World. Do you see yonder high hill?*

---

* 'High hill'—Christian must go past mount Sinai to the village Morality; not that such men, as depend on their own reformation and good works, pay a due regard to the holy

Chr. Yes, very well.

World. By that hill you must go, and the first house you come at is his.

So Christian turned out of his way to go to Mr. Legality's house for help. But behold, when he was got now hard by the hill, it seemed so high, and also that side of it that was next the way side did hang so much over, that Christian was afraid to venture farther, lest the hill should fall on his head; wherefore, there he stood still, and wotted not what to do. Also his burthen now seemed heavier to him than while he was in his way. There came also flashes of fire out of the hill, that made Christian afraid that he should be burned (Exod. xix. 16—18 ; Heb. xii. 21 ;) here, therefore, he sweat and did quake for fear. And now he began to be sorry that he had taken Mr. Worldly-Wiseman's counsel. And with that he saw Evangelist coming to meet him; at the sight also

law which was delivered from that mountain (for 'they are alive without the law'); but because they substitute their own scanty obedience in the place of Christ's righteousness and atonement. They, who are not duly humbled and enlightened, perceiving little danger, pass on quietly and securely: but the sinner, who is deeply convinced of his guilt, finds every attempt 'to establish his own righteousness' entirely abortive: the more narrowly he compares his conduct and character with the holy law, the greater is his alarm: and he trembles lest its curses should immediately fall upon him, with vengeance more tremendous than the most awful thunder. Then the counsels of worldly wisdom appear in their true light, and the sinner is prepared to welcome the Gospel of free salvation: but if the minister, whose instructions he had forsaken, meet him, his terror will unite with conscious shame; and he will even be tempted to shun his faithful friend, through fear of his merited reproofs.

of whom he began to blush for shame. So Evangelist drew nearer and nearer, and coming up to him, he looked upon him with a severe and dreadful countenance, and thus began to reason with Christian.

What dost thou here, Christian? said he. At which words Christian knew not what to answer: wherefore, at present, he stood speechless before him. Then said Evangelist farther, Art thou not the man that I found crying without the walls of the city of Destruction?

Chr. Yes, dear Sir, I am the man.

Evan. Did not I direct thee the way to the little wicket-gate?

Yes, dear Sir, said Christian.

Evan. How is it then that thou art so quickly turned aside? for thou art now out of the way.

Chr. I met with a gentleman, so soon as I had got over the slough of Despond, who persuaded me that I might, in the village before me, find a man that could take off my burthen.

Evan. What was he?

Chr. He looked like a gentleman, and talked much to me, and got me at last to yield; so I came hither; but when I beheld this hill, and how it hangs over the way, I suddenly made a stand, lest it should fall on my head.

Evan. What said that gentleman to you?

Chr. Why he asked me whither I was going; and I told him.

Evan. And what said he then ?

Chr. He asked me if I had a family ; and I told him. But, said I, I am so loaded with the burthen that is on my back, that I cannot take pleasure in them as formerly.

Evan. And what said he then ?

Chr. He bid me with speed get rid of my burthen ; and I told him it was ease that I sought. And, said I, I am therefore going to yonder gate to receive farther directions how I might get to the place of deliverance. So he said that he would shew me a better way, and short, not so attended with difficulties as the way, Sir, that you set me in, which way, said he, will direct you to a gentleman's house that has skill to take off these burthens : so I believed him, and turned out of that way into this, if haply I might be soon eased of my burthen. But when I came to this place, and beheld things as they are, I stopped for fear, as I said, of danger ; but now know not what to do.

Then, said Evangelist, stand still* a little, that I may shew thee the words of God. So

* ' Stand still'—Our author judged it right, in dealing with persons under great terror of conscience, to aim rather at preparing them for solid peace, than hastily to give them comfort. Men may be greatly dismayed, and in some degree truly humbled, yet not be truly sensible of the aggravation and degree of their guilt. In this case, farther instructions, as to the nature and heinousness of their offences, are needful to excite them to proper diligence and self-denial, and to prepare them for solid peace and comfort. Whereas a well-meant, compassionate, but injudicious, method, of proposing consolatory topics indiscriminately to all under trouble of conscience, lulls many into a fatal sleep ; and gives others a

he stood trembling.   Then said Evangelist,
'See that ye refuse not him that speaketh :
for if they escaped not who refused him that
spake on earth, much more shall not we escape if we turn away from him that speaketh
from heaven (Heb. xii. 25.)   He said moreover, ' Now the just shall live by faith ; but
if any man draw back, my soul shall have no
pleasure in him' (Heb. x. 38.)   He also did
thus apply them : Thou art the man that art
running into this misery ; thou hast begun to
reject the counsel of the Most High, and to
draw back thy foot from the way of peace,
even almost to the hazarding of thy perdition.

   Then Christian fell down at his feet as dead,
crying, ' Woe is me, for I am undone !' At

transient peace, which soon terminates in deep despondency :
like a wound, hastily skinned over by an ignorant practition-
er, instead of being soundly cured by the patient attention of
a skilful surgeon.   The communication of more knowledge
may, indeed, augment a man's terror and distress ; but it
will produce deeper humiliation, and thus effectually warn
him against carnal counsellors and legal dependences.   Whatever may be generally thought of ' turning aside' from the
Gospel, it is a direct refusal to hearken to Christ ; and they
who do so run into misery, and leave the way of peace, to the
hazard of their souls ; even though moral decency and formal piety be the result (Gal. v. 4.)   Such denunciations are
despised by the stout-hearted, but the contrite in spirit, when
conscious of this guilt, are cast by them into the deepest distress ; so that they would fall into despair did not the ministers
of Christ encourage them by evangelical topics.   The following
lines are here inserted, as before, in the old editions :—

> ' When Christians unto carnal men give ear,
> Out of their way they go, and pay for't dear :
> For Master Worldly-Wiseman can but shew
> A saint the way to bondage and to woe.'

the sight of which Evangelist caught him by the right hand, saying, 'All manner of sin and blasphemy shall be forgiven unto men :' 'be not faithless but believing.' Then did Christian again a little revive, and stood up trembling, as at first, before Evangelist.

Then Evangelist proceeded, saying, Give more earnest heed to the things that I shall tell thee of. I will now shew thee who it was that deluded thee, and who it was also to whom he sent thee. The man that met thee is one Worldly-Wiseman, and rightly is he so called ; partly because he savoureth only the doctrine of this world (1 John iv. 5), therefore he always goes to the town of Morality to church,* and partly because he loveth that doctrine best, for it saveth him best from the cross (Gal. vi. 12) ; and because he is of this carnal temper, therefore he seeketh to pervert my ways, though right. Now there are three things in this man's counsel that thou must utterly abhor : his turning thee out of the way ; his labouring to render the cross odious to thee ; and his setting thy feet in that way that leadeth unto the ministration of death.

First, thou must abhor his turning thee out of the way, yea, and thine own consenting

---

* 'To church'—Worldly-Wiseman goes to church at the town of Morality : for such men support their confidence and reputation for religion by attending on those preachers, who substitute a proud scanty morality in place of the Gospel. This coincides with their secular views, dispositions, and interests ; they avoid the cross, verily thinking they have found out the secret of reconciling the friendship of the world with the favour of God ; and then they set up for teachers of the same convenient system to their neighbours !

thereto ; because this is to reject the counsel of God for the sake of the counsel of a worldly-Wise man. The Lord says, ' Strive to enter in at the strait gate,' the gate to which I send thee, ' for strait is the gate that leadeth unto life, and few there be that find it' (Luke xiii. 24 ; Matt. vii. 13, 14.) From this little wicket-gate, and from the way thereto, hath this wicked man turned thee, to the bringing of thee almost to destruction. Hate, therefore, his turning thee out of the way, and abhor thyself for hearkening to him.

Secondly, thou must abhor his labouring to render the cross odious unto thee ; for thou art to ' prefer it before the treasures in Egypt' (Heb. xi. 25, 26.) Besides, the King of Glory hath told thee, that ' he that will save his life shall lose it :' and, ' he that comes after me, and hates not his father, and mother, and wife, and children, and brethren, and sisters, yea, and his own life also, cannot be my disciple' (Matt. x. 37—39 ; Mark viii. 34, 35 ; Luke xiv. 26, 27 ; John xii. 25.) I say, therefore, for a man to labour to persuade thee, that that shall be thy death, without which the truth hath said thou canst not have eternal life this doctrine thou must abhor

Thirdly, thou must hate his setting of thy feet in the way that leadeth to the ministration of death. And for this thou must consider to whom he sent thee, and also, how un able that person was to deliver thee from thy burthen.

He to whom* thou was sent for ease, being by name Legality, is 'the son of the bond-woman, which now is, and is in bondage with her children' (Gal. iv. 21---27 ;) and is, in a mystery, this mount Sinai, which thou has feared will fall on thy head. Now if she with her children are in bondage, how canst thou expect by them to be made free ? This Legality, therefore, is not able to set thee free from thy burthen. No man was as yet ever rid of his burthen by him ; no, nor ever is like to be. 'Ye cannot be justified by the works of the law ; for by deeds of the law no man living' can be rid of his burthen: therefore, Mr. Worldly-Wiseman is an alien, and Mr. Legality a cheat ; and for his son Civility, notwithstanding his simpering looks, he is

---

* 'He to whom'—When Christ had finished his work on earth, the Sinai covenant with Israel was abrogated. The Jews, therefore, by cleaving to the Mosaic law as a complex covenant of works, were left in bondage and under condemnation ; and all professed Christians, who thus depend on notions, sacraments, religious duties, and morality, to the neglect of Christ and the new covenant in his blood, are entangled in the same fatal error. Legality can only lead a man to a false peace ; it can never deliver a sinner from guilt, or quiet the conscience of one who is really humbled and enlightened. The Scriptures adduced by Evangelist are so pertinent and conclusive against the fashionable religion, which has at present almost superseded the Gospel, that they can never be fairly answered : nay, the more any man considers them as the testimony of God, the greater must be his alarm (even as if he heard the voice from mount Sinai out of the midst of the fire ;) unless he be conscious of having renounced every other confidence, to ' flee for refuge to lay hold on the hope set before us' in the Gospel. Such alarms prepare men to attend to the counsel of those who preach salvation by faith in Christ alone, provided there may yet be hope ; of which there is no reason to doubt.

but a hypocrite, and cannot help thee. Believe me, there is nothing in all this noise that thou hast heard of those sottish men, but a design to beguile thee of thy salvation, by turning thee from the way in which I had set thee. After this Evangelist called aloud to the heavens for confirmation of what he had said ; and with that, there came words and fire out of the mountain under which poor Christian stood, that made the hair of his flesh stand up The words were thus pronounced : 'As many as are of the works of the law are under the curse : for it is written, Cursed is every one that continueth not in all things which are written in the book of the law to do them' (Gal. iii. 10.)

Now Christian looked for nothing but death, and began to cry out lamentably, even cursing the time in which he met with Mr. Worldly-Wiseman ; still calling himself a thousand fools for hearkening to his counsel. He also was greatly ashamed to think that this gentleman's arguments, flowing only from the flesh, should have the prevalency with him as to cause him to forsake the right way. This done, he applied himself again to Evangelist, in words and sense as follows :—

Sir, what think you ? Is there hope ? May I now go back, and go up to the wicket-gate ? Shall I not be abandoned for this, and sent back from thence ashamed ? I am sorry I have harkened to this man's counsel ; but may my sin be forgiven ?

Then said Evangelist, to him, thy* sin is
very great, for by it thou hast committed two
evils ; thou hast forsaken the way that is
good, to tread in forbidden paths : yet will
the man at the gate receive thee, for he has
good will for men ; only, said he, take heed
that thou turn not aside again, ' lest thou perish from the way when his wrath is kindled
but a little' (Psal. ii. 12.) Then did Christian address himself to go back ; and Evangelist, after he had kissed him, gave him one smile,
and bid him God speed. So he went on with
haste, neither spake he to any man by the way ;
nor if any asked him would he vouchsafe
them any answer. He went like one that was
all the while treading on forbidden ground, and
could by no means think himself safe till again
he was got into the way which he left to follow Mr. Worldly-Wiseman's counsel. So in
process of time Christian got up to† the gate.

* ' Thy sin'—In attempting to encourage those who despond, we should by no means persuade them that their sins
are few or trivial, or even that they judge too hardly of their
own conduct ; nay, we should endeavour to convince them,
that their guilt is even far greater than they suppose ; though
not too great to be pardoned by the infinite mercy of God in
Christ Jesus : for this tends to take them off more speedily
from every vain attempt to justify themselves, and renders them
more unreserved in relying on Christ for acceptance. In the
midst of the most affectionate encouragements, the faithful
minister must also solemnly warn young converts not to turn
aside ; nor can the humble ever find confidence or comfort,
till they are conscious of having regained the way they had
forsaken.

† ' Got up to'—The gate, at which Christian desired admission, represents Christ himself, as received by the penitent
sinner in all his offices, and for all the purposes of salvation,
according to the measure of his explicit knowledge ; by which

Now over the gate there was written, ' Knock,
and it shall be opened unto you' (Matt. vii.
7, 8.)

he actually enters into a state of acceptance with God. The
Scriptures referred to were spoken by our Lord himself, previous to the full revelation of his character and redemption ;
and may be very properly explained of a man's finally and
decidedly renouncing his worldly and sinful pursuits, and engaging with diligence and self-denial in a life of devotedness
to God. ' The broad road leads to destruction ;' the gate
by which men enter into it is wide ; for we are all ' born in
sin and the children of wrath,' and ' turn every one to his
own way' of folly and transgression : but a strait gate opens
into ' the narrow way that leadeth unto life ;' and at this the
penitent finds admission with difficulty and conflict. As it is
strait (or, in the language of the allegory, a wicket, or a little
gate,) the convert cannot carry along with him any of his
sinful practices, ungodly companions, worldly idols, or carnal
confidences, when he strives to enter in at it ; nor can he effectually contend with those enemies that obstruct his passage,
unless he wrestle continually with God in prayer, for his gracious assistance. But, while we advert to these things, we
must not forget, that the sinner returns to God by faith in
Christ : genuine repentance comes from him and leads to
him ; and the true believer not only trusts in the Lord for
salvation, but also seeks his liberty and happiness in his service. To enter in this manner, by Christ the door, is so
contrary to man's pride and lusts, to the course of the world,
and to the temptations of the devil, that *striving* or *wrestling* is more necessary in this than it can be conceived to be
in any other kind of conversion. Various things commonly
precede this unreserved acceptance of Christ, in the experience of those who are born of God ; but they are not easily
distinguishable from many temporary convictions, impressions,
and starts of devotion, which evidently vanish and come to
nothing. Yet even this is judiciously distinguished by our author from that view of the cross by which Christian was delivered from his burthen, for reasons which will speedily be
stated. The following lines are here inserted, under an engraving :—

> ' He that would enter in, must first without
> Stand knocking at the gate, nor need he doubt,
> That is a knocker, but to enter in ;
> For God can love him, and forgive his sin.'

6*

He knocked therefore more than once or twice, saying—

> May I now enter here ? Will he within
> Open to sorry me, though I have been
> An undeserving rebel ? Then shall I
> Not fail to sing his lasting praise on high

At last there came a grave person to the gate, named Goodwill,* who asked who was there ? and whence he came ? and what he would have ?

Chr. Here is a poor burthened sinner. I come from the city of Destruction, but am going to mount Zion, that I may be delivered from the wrath to come. I would, therefore, Sir, since I am informed that by this gate is the way thither, know if you are willing to let me in.

* ' Goodwill'—Goodwill seems to be an allegorical person, the emblem of the compassionate love of God to sinners, in and through Jesus Christ (Luke ii. 14.) He ' came from heaven to do the will of him that sent him,' and ' he will in no wise cast out any that come to him,' either on account of their former sins, or their present mistakes, infirmities, evil propensities and habits, or peculiar temptations. ' He waits to be gracious,' till sinners apply by earnest persevering prayer for his salvation ; and even the preparation of heart which leads to this is not requisite to induce the Lord to receive them, but to make them willing to apply to him. Numbers give themselves no concern about their souls ; others, after convictions, turn back with Pliable, or finally cleave to the counsels of worldly wisdom : but all, who come to Christ with a real desire of his whole salvation, are cordially welcomed ; over them angels rejoice, and in them the Redeemer ' sees of the travail of his soul and is satisfied.' So that inquirers are greatly mistaken when they fear lest Christ should reject them ; since they need only dread being tempted to reject him, or being partial and hypocritical in their application o him.

I am willing with all my heart, said he. And with that he opened the gate.

So when* Christian was stepping in the other gave him a pull. Then said Christian, What means that? The other told him, 'A little distance from this gate there is erected a strong castle, of which Beelzebub is the captain; from thence both he and they that are with him shoot arrows at those that come up to this gate, if haply they may die before they can enter in.'

Then said Christian, I rejoice and tremble So when he was got in, the man of the gate asked him who directed him thither.

Chr. Evangelist bid me come hither and knock, as I did; and he said that you, Sir, would tell me what I must do.

Good. 'An open door is before thee, and no man can shut it.'

Chr. Now I begin to reap the benefits of my hazards.

* 'So when'—As sinners become more decided in applying to Christ, and assiduous in the means of grace, Satan, if permitted, will be more vehement in his endeavours to discourage them; that, if possible, he may induce them to desist, and so to come short of the prize. Indeed, the Lord will accomplish the good work which he hath begun by his special grace; but probably the powers of darkness cannot exactly distinguish between those impressions which are the effects of regeneration, and such as result from the excitement of natural passions. It is, however, certain, that they attempt to disturb those who earnestly cry for mercy, by various suggestions, to which they were wholly strangers, while satisfied with a form of godliness: and that the Christian's grand conflict, to the end of his course, consists in surmounting the hindrances and opposition that he experiences, in keeping near to the throne of grace, by fervent, importunate, and persevering prayer.

Good But how is it that you come alone ?

Chr. Because none of my neighbours saw their danger, as I saw mine.

Good. Did any of them know of your com-ing ?

Chr. Yes, my wife and children saw me at the first, and called after me to turn again ; also some of my neighbours stood crying and calling after me to return ; but I put my fingers in my ears, and so came on my way.

Good. But did none of them follow you to persuade you to go back ?

Chr. Yes, both Obstinate and Pliable : but when they saw that they could not prevail, Obstinate went railing back, but Pliable came with me a little way.

Good. But why did he not come through ?

Chr. We indeed came both together until we came at the slough of Despond, into the which we also suddenly fell. And then was my neighbour Pliable discouraged, and would not adventure farther. Wherefore, getting out again on that side next to his own house he told me I should possess the brave country alone for him : so he went his way, and I came mine ; he after Obstinate, and I to this gate.

Then said Goodwill, Alas, poor man ! is the celestial glory of so small esteem with him, that he counteth it not worth running the hazard of a few difficulties to obtain it ?

Truly, said Christian, I have said the truth of Pliable ; and if I should also say all the truth of myself, it will appear there is no bet-

terment* betwixt him and myself. It is true
he went back to his own house, but I also
turned aside to go into the way of death, being persuaded thereto by the carnal argument
of one Mr. Worldly-Wiseman.

Good. Oh, did he light upon you ? What,
he would have had you have sought for ease
at the hands of Mr. Legality ! they are both
of them very cheats. But did you take his
counsel ?

Chr. Yes, as far as I durst. I went to find
out Mr. Legality, until I thought that the
mountain that stands by his house would have
fallen upon my head ; wherefore there I was
forced to stop.

Good. That mountain has been the death
of many, and will be the death of many more.
It is well you escaped ; being by it not dashed in pieces.

Chr. Why, truly, I do not know what had
become of me there, had not Evangelist happily met me again as I was musing in the
midst of my dumps : but it was God's mercy
that he came to me again, for else I had
never come hither. But now I am come,

---

* ' Betterment'—Our author here puts a very emphatical
word into Christian's mouth (' there is no *betterment* betwixt him and myself ',) which later editors have changed
for *difference*. This is far from an improvement, though
the word be more classical : for grace had made an immense
difference between Christian and Pliable ; but the former
thought his conduct equally criminal, and therefore, in respect of their deservings, there was no *betterment* betwixt
them. There are many alterations of a similar nature, in
which the old copies have been generally followed ; but it
would preclude more useful matter were they constantly noted.

such an one as I am, more fit indeed for death by that mountain, than thus to stand talking with my Lord. But, oh! what a favour is this to me, that yet I am admitted entrance here.

Good. We make no objections against any, notwithstanding all that they have done before they come hither. 'They in no wise are cast out' (John vi. 37 ;) and therefore, good Christian, come a little way with me, and I will teach thee about the way thou must go. Look before thee; dost thou see this narrow* way? that is the way thou must go. It was cast up by the patriarchs, prophets,

* ' Narrow'—Christian, being admitted at the strait gate, is directed in the narrow way. In the broad road every man may choose a path suited to his inclinations, shift about to avoid difficulties, or accommodate himself to circumstances; and he will be sure of company agreeable to his taste. But Christians must follow one another in the narrow way, along the same track, surmounting difficulties, facing enemies, and bearing hardships, without any room to evade them : nor is any indulgence given to different tastes, habits, or propensities. It is, therefore, a straitened, or, as some render the word, an afflicted way ; being indeed an habitual course of repentance, faith, love, self-denial, patience, and mortification to sin and the world, according to the rule of the Holy Scriptures. Christ himself is the way, by which we come to the Father and walk with him; but true faith works by love, and ' sets us in the way of his steps' (Psalm lxxxv 13.) This path is also straight, as opposed to the crooked ways of wicked men (Psalm cxxv. 5 ;) for it consists in an uniform regard to piety, integrity, sincerity, and kindness at a distance from all the hypocrisies, frauds, and artifices by which ungodly men wind about, to avoid detection, keep up their credit, deceive others, or impose on themselves The question proposed by Christian implies, that believers are more afraid of missing the way, than encountering hard ships in it : and Goodwill's answer, that many ways *butted* down on it, or opened into it, in various directions, shews

Christ and his apostles, and it is as straight as
a rule can make it : this is the way thou must
go.

But, said Christian, are there no turnings
nor windings, by which a stranger may lose
his way ?

Good. Yes, there are many ways butt down
upon this, and they are crooked and wide :
but thus thou must distinguish the right from
the wrong, the right only being strait and nar
row (Matt. vii. 13, 14.)

Then I saw in my dream, that Christian
asked him* farther, if he could not help him
off with the burthen that was upon his back :
for as yet he had not got rid thereof, nor could
he by any means get it off without help.

that the careless and self-willed are extremely liable to be
deceived : but it follows, that all these ways are crooked and
wide ; they turn aside from the direct line of living faith and
holy obedience, and are more soothing, indulgent, and pleasing to corrupt nature than the path of life ; which lies straight
forward, and is everywhere contrary to the bias of the carnal
mind.

* ' Asked him'—A general reliance on the mercy of God
by faith in Christ, accompanied with consciousness of sincerity in applying for this salvation, gives some encouragement to the convinced sinner's hope ; and transient joys are
often vouchsafed in a large proportion to unestablished believers : but more distinct views of the glory of the Gospel
are necessary to abiding peace. The young convert's consolations resemble the breaking forth of the sun in a cloudy and
tempestuous day ; those of the experienced Christian, his
more constant light in settled weather, which is not long togeth
er interrupted, though it be sometimes dimmed by intervening
clouds. Believers should not, therefore, rest in such tran
sient glimpses, but press forward to more abiding peace and
joy : and, as Christ does not in general bestow this blessing
on the unestablished, the endeavours of ministers to do so must
be vain.

He told him, As to thy burthen, be content to bear it until thou comest to the place of deliverance ; for there it will fall from thy back of itself.

Then Christian began to gird up his loins, and to address himself to his journey. So the other told him, that by that he was gone some distance from the gate he would come at the house of* the Interpreter, at whose door he should knock, and he would shew him excellent things. Then Christian took his leave of his friend, and he again bid him God speed.

Then he went on till he came to the house of the Interpreter, where he knocked over and over : at last one came to the door, and asked who was there ?

Chr. Sir, here is a traveller, who was bid

* ' House of'—We continually meet with fresh proofs of our author's exact acquaintance with the Scriptures, his sound judgment, deep experience, and extensive observation. With great propriety he places the house of the Interpreter beyond the strait gate : for the knowledge of divine things, which precedes conversion to God by faith in Christ, is very scanty, compared with the diligent believer's subsequent attainments. A few leading truths deeply impressed on the heart, and producing efficacious fears, hopes, desires, and affections, characterize the state of a new-born babe : but reliance on the mercy of God through Jesus Christ prepares him to receive farther instruction : and, ' having tasted that the Lord is gracious, he desires the sincere milk of the word, that he may grow thereby.' The Interpreter is an emblem of the teaching of the Holy Spirit, according to the Scripture, by means of reading, hearing, praying, and meditating, accompanied by daily experience and observation. Believers depend on this continual teaching, and are not satisfied with human instruction, but look to the fountain of wisdom, that they may be delivered from prejudice, preserved from error, and enabled to profit by the ministry of the word.

by an acquaintance of the good man of this house to call here for my profit. I would therefore speak with the master of the house. So he called for the master of the house, who after a little time came to Christian, and asked him what he would have ?

Sir, said Christian, I am a man that am come from the city of Destruction, and am going to the mount Zion ; and I was told by the man that stands at the gate at the head of this way, that if I called here you would shew me excellent things, such as would be a help to me in my journey.

Then said the * Interpreter, Come in ; I will shew thee that which will be profitable to

---

* 'Then said'—The condescending love of the Holy Spirit, in readily granting the desires of those who apply for his teaching, notwithstanding their sins, prejudices, and slowness of heart to understand, can never sufficiently be admired (Psalm cxliii. 10). He employs men as his instruments, who, by explaining the Scriptures, may be said to ' light the candle :' but he alone efficaciously opens the mind to instruction. ' The secret of the Lord is with them that fear him' (Psalm xxv. 14). The Interpreter leads them apart to communicate to them heavenly wisdom, which is hidden from the most sagacious of worldly men. The first lesson here inculcated relates to the character of the true minister : for nothing can be more important to every one who inquires the way to heaven, than to be able to distinguish faithful pastors from hirelings, blind guides, and false teachers ; who are Satan's principal agents in deceiving mankind, and in preventing the stability, consistency, and fruitfulness of believers. This portrait and its key need no explanation : but all, who sustain, or mean to assume, the sacred office, should seriously examine it, clause by clause, with the Scriptures from which it is deduced ; inquiring impartially how far they resemble it, and praying earnestly for more exact conformity , and every one should be extremely careful not to intrust his soul to the guidance of those who are wholly unlike this emblematic rep-

thee. So he commanded his man to light a candle, and bid Christian follow him : so he had him into a private room, and bid his man open a door, the which when he had done, Christian saw the picture of a very grave person hang up against the wall ; and this was the fashion of it : it had eyes lifted up to eaven, the best of books in its hand, the law of truth was written upon its lips, the world was behind its back ; it stood as if it pleaded with men, and a crown of gold did hang over its head.

Then said Christian, What meaneth this ?

Interp. The man, whose picture this is, is one of a thousand ; he can beget children (1 Cor. iv. 15.) travail in birth with children (Gal. iv. 19.) and nurse them himself when they are born. And whereas thou seest him with his eyes lifted up to heaven, the best of books in his hand, and the law of truth written on his lips ; it is to shew thee, that his work is to know and unfold dark things to sinners ; even as also thou seest him stand as if he pleaded with men : and whereas thou seest the world as cast behind him, and that a crown

resentation. For surely a slothful, frivolous, dissipated, licentious, ambitious, profane, or contentious man, in the garb of a minister, cannot safely be trusted as a guide in the way to heaven! He, who never studies, or studies any thing in preference to the Bible, cannot be qualified to ' unfold dark things to sinners !' and he, who is abundantly more careful about his income, ease, or consequence, than about the souls of his flock, cannot be followed without the most evident danger and the most inexcusable folly ! For who would employ an ignorant, indolent, or fraudulent lawyer, or physician, merely because he happened to live in the same parish !

hangs over his head; that is to shew thee, that slighting and despising the things that are present, for the love that he hath to his Master's service, he is sure in the world that comes next to have glory for his reward. Now, said the Interpreter, I have shewed thee this picture first, because the man, whose picture this is, is the only man whom the Lord of the place whither thou art going hath authorized to be thy guide, in all difficult places thou mayest meet with in the way: wherefore, take good heed to what I have shewed thee, and bear well in thy mind what thou hast seen; lest in thy journey thou meet with some that pretend to lead thee right, but their way goes down to death.

Then he took* him by the hand, and led him into a very large parlour that was full of

* 'He took'—All true believers desire sanctification, of which the moral law is the standard: yet every attempt to produce conformity in heart and life to that standard, by regarding the precepts, apart from the truths and promises, of Scripture, excites and discovers the evils which before lay dormant in the heart; according to the significant emblem here adduced. Mere moral preaching, indeed, has no such effect: because, in the place of the divine law, it substitutes another rule, which is so vague, that self-flattery will enable almost any man, who is not scandalously vicious, to deem himself justified according to it: so that, instead of enmity being excited in the heart, he allows the rule by which he is approved; and loves his idea of God, because it accords so well with his own character. But, when the holy law is brought with energy to the conscience, its strictness, spirituality, and severity, awaken the latent enmity of the heart: the absolute self-denial it demands, even in the most plausible claims of self-love, its express prohibition of the darling sin, with the experienced impractibility of adequate obedience, and the awful sentence it denounces against every transgressor, concur in exciting opposition to it, and even to him who gave it

dust, because never swept; the which, after he had reviewed a little while, the Interpreter called for a man to sweep. Now when he began to sweep, the dust began so abundant-y to fly about, that Christian had almost there-with been choked. Then said the Interpreter to a damsel that stood by, Bring hither water and sprinkle the room; the which when she had done, it was swept and cleansed with pleasure.

Then said Christian, What means this?

The Interpreter answered, This parlour is the heart of a man, that was never sanctified by the sweet grace of the Gospel: the dust is his original sin and inward corruptions, that have defiled the whole man. He, that began to sweep at first, is the Law; but she, that brought that water and did sprinkle it, is the Gospel. Now whereas thou sawest, that so soon as the first began to sweep, the dust

Moreover, the consciousness of a hankering after things prohibited, and a conviction of the evil of such concupiscence, induce a man to conclude that he is viler than ever; and, indeed, clearer knowledge must aggravate the guilt of every sin. A little discouragement of this kind prevails with numbers to cease from all endeavours, at least for a season; supposing that at present it is impossible for them to serve God; but others, being more deeply humbled, and taken off from all self-confidence, are thus prepared to understand and welcome the free salvation of the Gospel. The law then appears disarmed of its curse, as the rule and standard of holiness; while righteousness and strength are sought by faith in Jesus Christ: the believer is encouraged by the truths and promises of the Gospel, excited by its motives, and inclined by the Holy Spirit, to desire advancing sanctification: while by the prevalence of hope and love his inward enmity is subdued, and he delights in 'cleansing himself from all filthiness of flesh and spirit, and perfecting holiness in the fear of God.'

did so fly about that the room by him could
not be cleansed, but that thou wast almost
choked therewith; this is to shew thee, that
the law instead of cleansing the heart, by its
working, from sin, doth revive, put strength
into, and increase it in the soul, even as it
doth discover and forbid it; for it doth not
give power to subdue it (Rom. v. 20; vii. 7
—11; 1 Cor. xv. 56.)

Again as thou sawest the damsel sprinkle
the room with water, upon which it was
cleansed with pleasure; this is to shew thee,
that when the Gospel comes in the sweet and
precious influences thereof to the heart, then,
I say, even as thou sawest the damsel lay the
dust by sprinkling the floor with water, so is
sin vanquished and subdued, and the soul
made clean through faith of it, and consequently fit for the King of glory to inhabit
(John xiv. 21—23; xv. 3; Acts xv. 9; Rom.
xvi. 25, 26; Eph. v. 26.)

I saw, moreover, in my dream, that the Interpreter took him by the hand, and had him in
a little room where sat two little children,* each

* 'Two children'—In this instructive emblem, Passion
represents the prevalence of the carnal affections over reason
and religion. Whatever be the object, this dominion of the
passions produces fretfulness and childish perverseness, when
a man cannot obtain the imagined good his heart is set upon,
which wholly relates to the present life. But this impatience
of delay or disappointment is succeeded by pride, insolence,
contempt of others, and inordinate momentary delight, if he
be indulged with the possession of his idol. Such men may
scorn believers as foolish and wretched: but they soon grow
dissatisfied with success, and speedily lavish away their good
things. On the other hand, Patience is the emblem of those
who quietly and meekly wait for future happiness, renounc-

one in his chair. The name of the eldest was Passion, and the name of the other Patience. Passion seemed to be much discontented, but Patience was very quiet. Then Christian asked, what is the reason of the discontent of Passion ? The Interpreter answered, The governor of them would have him stay for his best things till the beginning of the next year ; but he will have all now. But Patience is willing to wait.

Then I saw that one came to Passion and brought him a bag of treasure, and poured it down at his feet : the which he took up and rejoiced therein, and withall laughed Patience to scorn. But I beheld but a while, and he had lavished all away, and had nothing left him but rags.

Then said Christian to the Interpreter, Expound this matter more fully to me.

So he said, These two lads are figures : Passion of the men of this world, and Patience of the men of that which is to come. For as here thou seest Passion will have all now this

ing present things for the sake of it. True riches, honours, and pleasures are intended for them, but not here ; and as well educated little children, they simply wait for them till the appointed season, in the way of patience and obedience. Reason determines, that a greater and more permanent good hereafter is preferable to a less and fleeting enjoyment at present : faith realizes, as attainable, a felicity infinitely more valuable than all which this world can possibly propose to us ; so that in this respect the life of faith is the reign of reason over passion, while unbelief makes way for the triumph of passion over reason. Nor can any thing be more essential to practice religion than an abiding conviction, that it is the only true wisdom, uniformly and cheerfully to part with every temporal good, whenever it interferes with the grand concerns of eternity.

year, that is to say in this world ; so are the men of this world : they must have all their good things now, they cannot stay till next year, that is, until the next world, for their portion of good. That proverb, 'A bird in the hand is worth two in the bush,' is of more authority with them than are all the divine testimonies of the good world to come. But as thou sawest that he had quickly lavished all away, and had presently left him nothing but rags ; so will it be with all such men at the end of this world.

Then said Christian, Now I see that Patience has the best wisdom, and that upon many accounts : because he stays for the best things :—and also because he will have the glory of his, when the other has nothing but rags.

Interp. Nay, you may add another, to wit, the glory of the next world will never wear out ; but these are suddenly gone. Therefore Passion had not so much reason to laugh at Patience, because he had his good things first, as Patience will have to laugh at Passion because he had his best things last : for first must give place to last, because last must have its time to come ; but last gives place to nothing, for there is not another to succeed he, therefore, that hath his portion first must needs have a time to spend it ; but he that has his portion last must have it lastingly : therefore it is said of Dives, 'In thy lifetime thou receivedst thy good things, and likewise Lazarus evil things ; but now he is com-

forted and thou art tormented (Luke xvi.
19—31.)

Chr. Then I perceive it is not best to covet things that are now, but to wait for things
to come.

Interp. You say truth ; ' For the things
that are seen are temporal ; but the things
that are not seen are eternal' (2 Cor. iv. 18).
But, though this be so, yet, since things present and our fleshly appetite are such near
neighbours one to another ; and again, because things to come and carnal sense are
such strangers one to another ; therefore it
is that the first of these so suddenly fall into
amity, and that distance is so continually between the second.

Then I saw in my dream that the Inter-

" ' A fire'—The doctrine of the true believer's final perseverance is here stated in so guarded a manner as to preclude every abuse of it. The emblem implies, that the soul
is indeed quickened by special grace, and endued with holy
affections ; and this heavenly flame is not almost extinguish-
ed or covered with ashes for many years, and then revived a
little at the closing scene; but it ' burns higher and hotter,'
notwithstanding the opposition of depraved nature, and the
unremitted efforts of Satan to quench it ; for the Lord secretly feeds it with the oil of his grace. Unbelievers can
persevere in nothing but impiety or hypocrisy : when a professor remarkably loses the vigour of his affections, the reality of his conversion becomes doubtful, and he can take no
warranted encouragement from the doctrine in question ; but
when any one grows more spiritual, zealous, humble, and
exemplary, in the midst of harassing temptations, while he
gives the whole glory to the Lord, he may take comfort from
the assurance, that ' he shall be kept by his power, through
faith, unto salvation.' Yet the way, in which the tempted
are preserved, often so far exceeds their expectations, that
they are a wonder to themselves : every thing seems to concur in giving Satan advantage against them, and his efforts

preter took Christian by the hand, and led him into a place where was a fire* burning against a wall, and one standing by it, always casting much water upon it to quench it ; yet did the fire burn higher and hotter.

Then said Christian, What means this ?

The Interpreter answered, This fire is the work of grace that is wrought in the heart ; he that casts water upon it to extinguish and put it out, is the devil : but in that thou seest the fire notwithstanding burn higher and hotter, thou shalt also see the reason of that. So he had him about to the backside of the wall, where he saw a man with a vessel of oil in his hand, of which he did also continually cast, but secretly, into the fire.

Then said Christian, What means this ?

The Interpreter answered, This is Christ, who continually with the oil of his grace maintains the work already begun in the heart : by the means of which, notwithstanding what the devil can do, the souls of his people prove gracious still (2 Cor. xii. 9). And in that thou sawest that the man stood behind the wall to maintain the fire ; that is to teach thee, that it is hard for the tempted to see how this work of grace is maintained in the soul.

appear very successful ; yet they continue from year to year, 'cleaving with purpose of heart unto the Lord,' trusting in his mercy, and desirous of living to his glory. The instruction especially inculcated by this emblem is, an entire reliance on the secret but powerful influence of divine grace, to maintain and carry on the sanctifying work that has been begun in the soul.

I saw also that the Interpreter took him again by the hand, and led him into a pleasant* place, where was builded a stately palace, beautiful to behold ; at the sight of which Christian was greatly delighted : he saw also upon the top thereof, certain persons walking, who were clothed all in gold.

Then said Christian, May we go in thither ?

Then the Interpreter took him and led him up towards the door of the palace ; and behold at the door stood a great company of men, as desirous to go in, but durst not. There also sat a man at a little distance from the door, at a table-side, with a book and his inkhorn before him, to take the name of him that should enter therein : he saw also, that in the doorway stood many men in armour to keep it, being resolved to do to the men that

---

* 'Pleasant'—Many desire the joys and glories of heaven (according to their carnal ideas of them,) but few are willing to 'fight the good fight of faith :' yet, without this fixed purpose of heart, the result of Divine grace, profession will end in apostacy :—'the man began to build, but was not able to finish.' This is emphatically taught us by the next emblem. Salvation is altogether free and without price: but we must learn to value it so highly as to venture or suffer 'the loss of all things that we may win Christ ;' or we shall not be able to break through the combined opposition of the world, the flesh, and the devil. If we fear any mischief that our enemies can attempt against us, more than coming short of salvation, we shall certainly perish, notwithstanding our notions and convictions. We should, therefore, count our cost, and pray for courage and constancy, that we may give in our names as in earnest to win the prize : then, 'putting on the whole armour of God,' and relying on his grace, we must fight our way through with patience and resolution ; while many, 'being harnessed and carrying bows,' shamefully 'turn back in the day of battle.'

would enter what hurt and mischief they could.
Now was Christian somewhat in amaze : at
last, when every man started back for fear
of the armed men, Christian saw a man of a
very stout countenance come up to the man
that sat there to write, saying, ' Set down my
name, Sir :' the which when he had done, he
saw the man draw his sword, and put a helmet upon his head, and rush towards the door
upon the armed men, who laid upon him with
deadly force ; but the man was not at all discouraged, but fell to cutting and hacking most
fiercely.   So after he had received and given
many wounds to those that attempted to keep
him out, he cut his way through them all,
and pressed forward into the palace ; at which
there was a pleasant voice heard from those
that were within, even of those that walked
upon the top of the palace, saying,

> Come in, come in ;
> Eternal glory thou shalt win.

So he went in, and was clothed with such garments as they.   Then Christian smiled, and
said, I think verily I know the meaning of
this.   Now, said Christian, let me go* hence.

* ' Let me go'—The time, spent in acquiring knowledge,
and sound judgment, is not lost, though it may seem to retard a man's progress, or interfere with his more active services : and the next emblem is admirably suited to teach
the young convert watchfulness and caution.   Christian's
discourse with the man in the iron cage sufficiently explains
the author's meaning ; but it has been observed by several
persons, that the man's opinion of his own case, does not
prove that it was indeed desperate.   Doubtless these fears
prevail in some cases of deep despondency, when there is

Nay, stay, said the Interpreter, till I have shewed thee a little more, and after that thou shalt go on thy way. So he took him by the hand again, and led him into a very dark room, where there sat a man in an iron cage

Now the man, to look on, seemed very sad. He sat with his eyes looking down to the ground, his hands folded together, and he sighed as if he would break his heart. Then said Christian, what means this ? At which the Interpreter bid him talk with the man.

Then said Christian to the man, What art thou ? The man answered, I am what I was not once.

Chr. What wert thou once ?

The man said, I was once a fair and flourishing professor, both in mine own eyes, and also in the eyes of others : I once was, as I thought, fair for the celestial city, and had then even joy at the thoughts that I should get thither (Luke viii. 13).

Chr. Well, but what art thou now ?

Man. I am now a man of despair, and am

every reason to conclude them groundless ; and we should always propose the free grace of the Gospel to those that have sinned in the most aggravated manner, when they become sensible of their guilt and danger : yet it is an awful fact, that some are thus ' shut up under despair,' beyond relief ; and ' It is impossible to renew them to repentance.' No true penitent, therefore, can be in this case : and we are commanded ' in meekness to instruct those that oppose themselves, if peradventure God will give them repentance.' But, at the same time, we should leave the doom of apparent apostates to God ; and improve their example, as a warning to ourselves and others, not to venture one step in so dangerous a path. This our author has judiciously attempted, and we should be careful no to counteract his obvious intention

shut up in it, as in this iron cage : **I cannot get out ; O now I cannot !**

Chr. But how camest thou in this condition ?

Man. I left off to watch and be sober ; I laid the reins upon the neck of my lusts ; I sinned against the light of the word, and the goodness of God : I have grieved the Spirit, and he is gone ; I tempted the devil, and he is come to me ; I have provoked God to anger, and he has left me ; I have so hardened my heart that I cannot repent.

Then said Christian to the Interpreter, But is there no hope for such a man as this ? Ask him, said the Interpreter.

Then said Christian, Is there no hope, but you must be kept in the iron cage of despair ?

Man. No, not at all.

Chr. Why ? the Son of the Blessed is very pitiful.

Man. I have crucified him to myself afresh ; I have despised his person, I have despised his righteousness, I have counted his blood an unholy thing, I have done despite to the Spirit of grace (Luke xix. 14 ; Heb. vi. 4 —6 ; x. 28, 29) ; therefore I have shut myself out of all the promises, and there now remains to me nothing but threatenings, dreadful threatenings, fearful threatenings, of certain judgment and fiery indignation, which shall devour me as an adversary.

Chr. For what did you bring yourself into his condition ?

VOL. I.   8

Man. For the lusts, pleasures, and profits of this world, in the enjoyment of which I did then promise myself much delight ; but now every one of those things also bite me and gnaw me like a burning worm.

Chr. But canst thou not repent and turn ?

Man. God hath denied me repentance. His word gives me no encouragement to believe ; yea, himself hath shut me up in this iron cage ; nor can all the men in the world let me out. O eternity ! eternity ! how shall I grapple with the misery that I must meet with in eternity !

Then said the Interpreter to Christian, Let this man's misery be remembered by thee, and be an everlasting caution to thee.

Well, said Christian, this is fearful ! God help me to watch and be sober, and to pray that I may shun the cause of this man's misery. Sir, is it not time for me to go on my way now ?

Interp. Tarry till I shall shew thee one thing more, and then thou shalt go on thy way.

So he took Christian by the hand again, and led him into a chamber where there was one rising out of bed ; and as he put on his raiment he shook and trembled. Then said Christian, Why doth this man thus tremble ? The Interpreter then bid him tell to Christian the reason of his so doing. So he began and said, This night as I was in my sleep I dreamed, and behold, the heavens grew exceeding black ; also it thundered and lighten-

ed in most fearful wise, that it put me into an
agony : so I looked up in my dream, and saw
the clouds rack at an unusual rate ; upon
which I heard a great sound of a trumpet,
and saw also a man sit upon a cloud, attended
with the thousands of heaven : they were all
in flaming fire, also the heavens were on a
ourning flame.   I heard then a voice saying,
' Arise, ye dead, and come to judgment ;' and
with that the rocks rent, the graves opened,
and the dead that were therein came forth
(John v. 28, 29 ; 1 Cor. xv. 51—58 ; 2 Thess
i. 7—10 ; Jude 14, 15 ; Rev. xx. 11—15) ;
some of them were exceeding glad, and look
ed upwards ; and some sought to hide them
selves under the mountains (Ps. 1. 1—3. 22 ,
Isa. xxvi. 20, 21 ; Mic. vii. 16, 17) : then I
saw the man that sat upon the cloud open the
book, and bid the world draw near.   Ye.
there was, by reason of a fierce flame which
issued out and came before him, a convenient
distance betwixt him and them, as betwixt
the judge and the prisoners at the bar (Dan. vii.
9, 10 ; Mal. iii. 2, 3).   I heard it also proclaimed to them that attended on the man
that sat on the cloud, ' Gather together the
tares, the chaff, and stubble, and cast them
into the burning lake :' and with that the bottomless pit opened just whereabout I stood ;
out of the mouth of which there came, in an
abundant manner, smoke, and coals of fire,
with hideous noises.   It was also said to the
same persons, ' Gather my wheat into the
garner' (Mal. iv. 1 ; Matt. iii. 2 ; xiii. 30 ;·

Luke iii. 17). And with that I saw many catched up and carried away into the clouds (1 Thess. iv. 13—18), but I was left behind I also sought to hide myself, but I could not, for the man that sat upon the cloud still kept his eye upon me ; my sins also came in my mind, and my conscience did accuse me on every side (Rom. ii. 14, 15.) Upon this I awaked from my sleep.

Chr. But what was it that made you so afraid of this sight ?

Man. Why I thought that the day of judgment was come, and that I was not ready for it : but this frighted me most, that the angels gathered up several and left me behind ; also the pit of hell opened her mouth just where I stood. My conscience too afflicted me ; and, as I thought, the Judge had always his eye upon me, shewing indignation in his countenance

Then said the Interpreter to Christian, Hast thou considered all these things ?

Chr. Yes ; and they put me in hope* and fear.

* In hope'—Our safety consists in a due proportion of hope and fear : when devoid of hope, we resemble a ship without an anchor ; when unrestrained by fear, we are like the same vessel under full sail, without ballast (1 Pet. i. 13—17.) Indiscriminate censures of all fear as the result of unbelief, and unguarded commendations of strong confidence, without respect to the spirit and conduct of professors, not only leads to much self-deception, but also tends to make believers unstable, unwatchful, and even uncomfortable ; for the humble often cannot attain to that confidence, that is represented almost as essential to faith ; and true comfort is the effect of watchfulness, diligence, and circumspection. Upon the whole

Interp Well, keep all things so in thy mind, that they may be as a goad in thy sides, to prick thee forward in the way thou must go.—Then Christian began to gird up his loins, and to address himself to his journey. Then said the Interpreter, The Comforter be always with thee, good Christian, to guide thee in the way that leads to the city. So Christian went on his way, saying—

> Here I have seen things rare and profitable;
> Things pleasant, dreadful, things to make me stable
> In what I have begun to take in hand:
> Then let me think on them, and understand
> Wherefore they shew'd me were; and let me be
> Thankful, O good Interpreter, to thee.

Now I saw* in my dream, that the highway, up which Christian was to go, was fenced on

what lessons could possibly have been selected of greater importance, or more suited to establish the new convert, than these are, which our author has most ingeniously and agreeably inculcated, under the emblem of the Interpreter's curiosities? They are indeed the principal subjects which faithful ministers enforce, publicly and in private, on all who begin to profess the Gospel; and which every true disciple of Christ daily seeks to have more clearly discovered to his mind, and more deeply impressed upon his heart.

* 'Now I saw'—Divine illumination in many respects tends to quicken the believer's hopes and fears, and to increase his earnestness and diligence; but nothing can finally relieve him from his burthen, except the clear discovery of the nature and glory of redemption. With more general views of the subject, and an implicit reliance on God's mercy through Jesus Christ, the humbled sinner enters the way of life, which is walled by salvation: yet he is oppressed with an habitual sense of guilt, and often bowed down with fears, till 'the Comforter, who glorifies Christ, receives of his, and shews it to him' (John xvi. 14.) When in this divine light the soul contemplates the Redeemer's cross, and discerns more clearly his love to lost sinners in thus dying for them

8*

either side with a wall, and that wall was called Salvation (Isa. xxvi. 1). Up this way therefore did burthened Christian run, but not without great difficulty, because of the load on his back.

He ran thus till he came at a place somewhat ascending, and upon that place stood a cross, and a little below, in the bottom, a sepulchre. So I saw in my dream, that just as Christian came up with the cross, his burthen loosed from off his shoulders, and fell

the motive and efficacy of his intense sufferings; the glory of the Divine perfections harmoniously displayed in this surprising expedient for saving the lost; the honour of the Divine law and government, and the evil and desert of sin, most energetically proclaimed in this way of pardoning transgressors and reconciling enemies; and the perfect freeness and sufficiency of this salvation; then 'his conscience is purged from dead works to serve the living God,' by a simple reliance on the atoning blood of Emmanuel. This deliverance from the burthen of guilt is in some respects final, as to the well-instructed and consistent believer; his former sins are buried, no more to be his terror and distress. He will indeed be deeply humbled under a sense of his guilt, and sometimes he may question his acceptance; but his distress, before he understood the way of deliverance, was habitual, except in a few transient seasons of relief, and often oppressed him when most diligent and watchful; but now he is only burthened when he has been betrayed into sin, or when struggling with peculiar temptations; and he constantly finds relief by looking to the cross. Many indeed never attain to this habitual peace: this is the effect of remaining ignorance, error, or negligence, which scriptural instuctions are the proper means of obviating. But it was not probable that our author should, so to speak, draw the character of his hero from the lowest order of hopeful professors; it may rather call for our admiration, that, in an allegory (which is the peculiar effort of a vigorous imagination) he was preserved, by uncommon strength of mind and depth of judgment, from stating Christian's experience above the general attainments of consistent believers, under solid instructions.

from off his back, and began to tumble, and
so continued to do till it came to the mouth
of the sepulchre, where it fell in, and I saw
it no more.

Then was Christian glad and lightsome,
and said with a merry heart, ' He hath given
me rest by his sorrow, and life by his death.'
Then he stood a while to look and wonder ;
for it was very surprising to him, that the
sight of the cross should thus ease him of his
burthen. He looked,* therefore, and looked

* ' He looked'—Christian's tears, amidst his gladness, intimate that deliverance from guilt, by faith in the atoning
sacrifice of Christ, tends to increase humiliation, sorrow for
sin, and abhorrence of it ; though it mingles even those affections with a sweet and solid pleasure. By the ' three
shining ones,' the author might allude to the ministration of
angels as conducive to the comfort of the heirs of salvation ;
but he could not mean to ascribe Christian's confidence to
any impressions, or suggestions of texts to him by a voice,
or in a dream ; any more than he intended, by his views of
the cross, to sanction the account that persons of heated imagination have given, of their having seen one hang on a
cross, covered with blood, who told them their sins were
pardoned ; while it has been evident, that they never understood the spiritual glory, or the sanctifying tendency of the
doctrine of a crucified Saviour. Such things are the mere
delusions of enthusiasm, from which our author was remarkably free : but the nature of an allegory led him to this method of describing the happy change that takes place in the
pilgrim's experience, when he obtains peace and joy in believing. His uniform doctrine sufficiently shews that he considered spiritual apprehensions of the nature of the atonement as the only source of genuine peace and comfort. And,
as the ' mark in the forehead' plainly signifies the renewa.
of the soul to holiness, so that the mind of Christ may appear in the outward conduct, connected with an open profession of faith, while the ' roll with a seal upon it' denotes
such an assurance of acceptance, as appears most clear and
satisfactory, when the believer most attentively compares his
views experiences desires, and purposes, with the Holy

again, even till the springs that were in his head sent the water down his cheeks (Zech xii. 10). Now, as he stood looking and weeping, behold three shining ones came to him, and saluted him with ' Peace be to thee.' So the first said to him, 'Thy sins be forgiven thee' (Mark ii. 5) ; the second stripped him of his rags, and clothed him with change of raiment ; the third also set a mark on his forehead, and gave him a roll with a seal upon it (Zech. iii. 4 ; Eph. i 13), which he bid him look on as he ran, and that he should give it in at the celestial gate ; so they went their way. Then Christian gave three leaps for joy, and went on singing—

Scriptures ; so he could not possibly intend to ascribe such effects to any other agent than the Holy Spirit ; who by enabling a man to exercise all filial affections towards God in an enlarged degree, as ' the Spirit of adoption bears witness' with his conscience, that God is reconciled to him, having pardoned all his sins ; that he is justified by faith in the righteousness of Emmanuel ; and that he is a child of God, and an heir of heaven. These things are clear and intelligible to those who have experienced this happy change ; and the abiding effects of their joy in the Lord, upon their dispositions and conduct (like the impression of the seal after the wax is cooled) distinguish it from the confidence and comfort of hypocrites and enthusiasts. It must, however, continue to be ' the secret of the Lord, with them that fear him,' ' hidden manna,' and ' a white stone, having in it a new name written, which no man knoweth saving he that receiveth it' (Psalm xv. 14 ; Rev. ii. 17.) Here again we meet with an engraving, and the following lines :—

' Who's this ? The Pilgrim. How ! 'Tis very true
Old things are past away ; all's become new.
Strange ! he's another man, upon my word ;
They be fine feathers that make a fine bird

Thus far did I come laden with my sin,
Nor could aught ease the grief that I was in,
Till I came hither; what a place is this!
Must here be the beginning of my bliss?
Must here the burthen fall from off my back?
Must here the strings that bind it to me crack!
Blest cross! blest sepulchre! blest rather be
The man that there was put to shame for me:

I saw* then in my dream that he went on thus even until he came at the bottom, where he saw, a little out of the way, three men fast asleep, with fetters upon their heels. The name of the one was Simple, another Sloth, and the third Presumption.

Christian then seeing them lie in this case went to them, if peradventure he might awake

---

* 'I saw'—We were before informed, that other ways 'butted down upon' the strait way; and the connexion of the allegory required the introduction of various characters, besides that of the true believer. Many may outwardly walk in the ways of religion, and seem to be pilgrims, who are destitute of those 'things which accompany salvation.' The three allegorical persons next introduced are nearly related; they appear to be pilgrims, but are a little out of the way, asleep, and fettered. Many of this description are found, where the truth is preached, as well as elsewhere: they hear and learn to talk about the Gospel; have transient convictions, which are soon quieted; cleave to the world, and rest more securely in the bondage of sin and Satan, by means of their profession of religion. They reject or pervert all instruction, hate all trouble, yet are confident that every thing is and will be well with them, while teachers, after their own hearts, lull them with a syren's song, by confounding the form with the power of godliness; and if any one attempt, in the most affectionate manner to warn them of their danger, they answer (according to the tenor of the words here used,) 'Mind your own business; we see no danger; you shall not disturb our composure, or induce us to make so much ado about religion: see to yourselves, and leave us to ourselves.' Thus they sleep on till death and judgment awake them.

them; and cried, You are like them t at
sleep on the top of a mast (Prov. xxiii. 34),
for the dead sea is under you, a gulph that
hath no bottom: awake, therefore, and come
away; be willing also, and I will help you off
with your irons. He also told them, If he
that goeth about like a roaring lion comes by,
you will certainly become a prey to his teeth
(1 Pet. v. 8). With that they looked upon
him, and began to reply in this sort: Simple
said, 'I see no danger;' Sloth said, 'Yet a
little more sleep;' and Presumption said,
'Every vat must stand upon its own bottom.'
And so they laid down to sleep again, and
Christian went on his way.

Yet* was he troubled to think, that men in
that danger should so little esteem the kind-

---

* 'Yet'—The true Christian will always be troubled when
he thinks of the vain confidence of many professors: but he is
more surprised by it at first than afterwards; for he sets out
with the idea, that all apparently religious people sincerely
seek the salvation of God: but at length experience draws his
attention to those parts of Scriptures which mention tares
among the wheat, and foolish virgins among the wise. Formalist and Hypocrisy soon come in this way; these near relations represent such as by notions and external observances
deceive themselves, and those who more grossly attempt to
impose upon others. They are both actuated by vain glory,
and seek the applause of men in their religious profession and
most zealous performances; while the credit thus acquired
subserves also their temporal interest: but repentance, conversion, and the life of faith, would not only cost them too
much labour, but destroy the very principle by which they
are actuated. By a much 'shorter cut,' they become a part
of the visible church, are satisfied with a form of godliness,
and kept in countenance by great numbers among every description of professing Christians, and the example of multitudes in every age. Their confidence, however, will not
bear the light of Scripture; they therefore shrink from inves-

ness of him that so freely offered to help them, both by the awakening of them, counselling of them, and proffering to help them off with their irons. And as he was troubled thereabout, he spied two men come tumbling over the wall on the left hand of the narrow way ; and they made up apace to him. The name of the one was Formalist, and the name of the other Hypocrisy. So, as I said, they drew up unto him, who thus entered with them into discourse.

Chr. Gentlemen, whence come you, and whither go you ?

Form. & Hyp. We were born in the land of Vain-glory, and are going for praise to mount Zion.

Chr. Why came you not in at the gate which standeth at the beginning of the way ? Know you not that it is written, that ' He that cometh not in by the door, but climbeth up some other way, the same is a thief and a robber ?' (John x. 1).

They said, that to go to the gate of entrance was by all their countrymen counted too far about ; and that therefore their usual way was to make a short cut of it, and to climb over the wall, as they had done.

Chr. But will it not be counted a trespass against the Lord of the city whither we are bound, thus to violate his revealed will ?

They told him, that, as for that, he needed

tigation, and treat with derision and reproaches all who would convince them of their fatal mistake, or shew them the real nature of evangelical religion.

not trouble his head there about ; for what they did they had custom for , and could produce, if need were, testimony that would witness it for more than a thousand years.

But said Christian, will your practice stand a trial at law ?

They told him, that custom, it being of so long standing as above a thousand years, would doubtless now be admitted as a thing legal by an impartial judge ; and besides, say they, if we get into the way, what's matter which way we get in ? If we are in, we are in · thou art but in the way, who, as we perceive, came in at the gate ; and we are also in the way, that came tumbling over the wall : wherein now is thy condition better than ours ?

Chr. I walk by the rule of my master, you walk by the rude working of your fancies. You are counted thieves already by the Lord of the way, therefore I doubt you will not be found true men at the end of the way. You come in by yourselves without his direction, and shall go out by yourselves without his mercy.

To this they made but little answer ; only they bid him look to himself. Then I saw that they went on every man in his way, without much conference one with another ; save that these two men told Christian, that, as to laws and ordinances, they doubted not but they should as conscientiously do them as he ; therefore, said they, we see not wherein thou differest from us, but by the coat that is on thy back, which was, as we trow, given thee by some of the neighbours, to hide the shame of thy nakedness.

Chr. By laws and ordinances you will not be saved (Gal. ii. 16), since you came not in by the door. And as for this coat that is on my back, it was given me by the Lord of the place whither I go ; and that, as you say, to cover my nakedness with. And I take it as a token of kindness to me ; for I had nothing but rags before : and besides, thus I comfort myself as I go ; Surely, think I, when I come to the gate of the city, the Lord thereof will know me for good, since I have his coat on my back ; a coat that he gave me freely in the day that he stripped me of my rags. I have, moreover, a mark in my forehead, of which perhaps you have taken no notice, which one of my Lord's most intimate associates fixed there in the day that my burthen fell off my shoulders. I will tell to you, moreover, that I had then given me a roll sealed, to comfort me by reading as I go on the way ; I was also bid to give it in at the celestial gate, in token of my certain going in after it : all which things I doubt you want, and want them because you came not in at the gate.

To these things they gave him no answer ; only they looked upon each other and laughed Then I saw that they went on all, save that* Christian kept before, who had no more

* 'Save that'—Even such Christians as are most assured of their acceptance, and competent to perceive the awful dan-

talk but with himself, and that sometimes sighingly and sometimes comfortably : also he would be often reading in the roll that one of the shining ones gave him, by which he was refreshed.

I beheld then that they all went on till they came to the foot of the hill* Difficulty ; at the bottom of which was a spring. There were also in the same place two other ways, besides that which came straight from the gate ; one turned to the left hand and the other to the right, at the bottom of the hill ; but the narrow way lay right up the hill, and the name of the going up the side of the hill is called Difficulty. Christian went now to the spring, and drank thereof to refresh himself (Isa. xlix. 10), and began to go up the hill, saying—

> The hill, though high, I covet to ascend,
> The difficulty will not me offend ;
> For I perceive the way to life lies here :
> Come, pluck up, heart, let's neither faint nor fear.
> Better, though difficult, the right way to go,
> Than wrong, though easy, where the end is woe

sions of false professors, find cause for sighs amidst their com forts, when employed in serious retired self-reflection. Nothing can exclude the uneasiness which arises from indwelling sin, with its unavoidable effects, and from the crimes and miseries they witness around them

* ' Hill'—The hill Difficulty represents those circumstan ces which require peculiar self-denial and exertion, that commonly prove the believer's sincerity, after he has first obtained a good hope through grace.'—The opposition of the world, the renunciation of temporal interests, or the painful task of overcoming inveterate evil habits or constitutional propensi ties (which during his first anxious earnestness seemed perhaps to be destroyed, though in fact they were only susperd

The other two also came on the foot of the
hill; but when they saw that the hill was
steep and high, and that there were two other ways to go; and supposing also that these
two ways might meet again with that up which
Christian went, on the other side of the hill,
therefore they were resolved to go into those
ways. Now the name of one of those ways
was Danger, and the name of the other Destruction. So the one took the way which is called
Danger, which did lead him into a great wood;
and the other took directly up the way to
Destruction, which led him into a wide field,
full of dark mountains, where he stumbled and
fell, and rose no more.

ed) : these and such like trials prove a severe test; but there
is no hope, except in pressing forward; and the encouragements, received under the faithful ministry of the Gospel,
prepare the soul for every conflict and effort. There are,
however, bye-ways; and the difficulty may be avoided without a man's renouncing his profession : he may decline the
self-denying duty, or refuse the demanded sacrifice, and find
some plausible excuse to his own conscience, or among his
neighbours. But the true believer will be suspicious of these
easier ways, on the right hand or the left : his path lies
straight forward, and cannot be travelled without ascending
the hill ; which he desires to do, because his grand concern is
to be found right at last. On the contrary, they who chiefly
desire, at a cheap rate, to keep up their credit and confidence, will venture into perilous or ruinous paths, till they
either openly apostatize, or get entangled in some fatal delusion, and are heard of no more among the people of God
These lines are here inserted—

> ' Shall they who wrong begin yet rightly end ?
> Shall they at all have safety for their friend ?
> No, no ; in headstrong manner they set out,
> And headlong they will fall at last, no doubt.'

I looked* then after Christian to see him go
up the hill, where I perceived he fell from running to going, and from going to clambering
upon his hands and his knees, because of the
steepness of the place. Now about the mid-
way to the top of the hill was a pleasant arbour, made by the Lord of the hill for the refreshing of weary travellers ; thither, therefore, Christian got, where also he sat down to
rest him : then he pulled his roll out of his
bosom, and read therein to his comfort ; he
also now began afresh to take a review of the
coat or garment that was given him as he
stood by the cross. Thus pleasing himself
awhile, he at last fell into a slumber, and
thence into a fast sleep, which detained him
in that place until it was almost night ; and

---

* ' I looked'—The difficulties of believers often seem to increase as they proceed ; this damps their spirits, and they find
more painful exertion requisite in pressing forward, than they
expected, expecially when they were rejoicing in the Lord :
he however helps them, and provides for their refreshment,
that they may not faint. But, whether their trials be mod-
erated, or remarkable divine consolations be vouchsafed, it
is, alas ! very common for them to presume too much on
their perseverance hitherto, and on the privileges to which
they have been admitted : thus their ardour abates, their diligence and vigilance are relaxed, and they venture to allow
themselves some respite from exertion. Then drowsiness
steals upon them, darkness envelops their souls, the evidences
of their acceptance are obscured or lost, and the event would
be fatal, did not the Lord excite them to renewed earnestness
by salutary warnings and alarms. Nor are believers at any
time more exposed to this temptation, than when outward
ease hath succeeded to great hardships, patiently and con
scientiously endured ; for at such a crisis they are least dispos
ed to question their own sicerity ; and Satan is sure to employ
all his subtlety to lull them into such a security as is in fact
an abuse of the Lord's special goodness vouchsafed to them.

in his sleep his roll fell out of his hand. Now, as he was sleeping there came one to him and awaked him, saying, 'Go to the ant, thou sluggard; consider her ways, and be wise' (Prov. vi 7). And with that Christian suddenly started up, and sped him on his way, and went apace till he came to the top of the hill.

Now when he was got up to the top of the hill there came two men* running to meet him amain; the name of the one was Timorous,

* 'Two men'—Some persons are better prepared to struggle through difficulties, than to face dangers; alarming convictions will induce them to exercise a temporary self-denial, and to exert themselves with diligence; yet the very appearance of persecution will drive them back to their forsaken courses and companions. Through unbelief, distrust, and timidity they fear the rage of men more than the wrath of God; and never consider how easily the Lord can restrain or disarm the fiercest persecutors. Even true Christians are sometimes alarmed by the discourse of such persons; but, as they believe the word of God, they are 'moved by fear' to go forward at all hazards: such terrors, as induce mere professors to apostacy, excite upright souls to renewed self-examination by the Holy Scriptures, that they may 'rejoice in hope' amidst their perils and tribulations; and this often tends to discover to them those decays and losses, in respect of the vigour of holy affection, and the evidences of their acceptance, which had before escaped their notice. Christian's perplexity, fear, sorrow, remorse, redoubled earnestness, complaints, and self-reproachings, when he missed his roll, and went back to seek it, exactly suit the experience of humble and conscientious believers, when unwatchfulness has brought their state into uncertainty; but they do not at all accord to that of professors, who strive against all doubts indiscriminately, more than against any sin whatever, which is not connected with open scandal; who strive hard to keep up their confidence against evidence, amidst continued negligence and allowed sins; and exclaim against sighs, tears, and tenderness of conscience, as legality and unbelief. Bunyan would have excluded such professors from the company of his pilgrims, though they often pass muster in modern times.

and of the other Mistrust : to whom Christian said, Sirs, what is the matter you run the wrong way ? Timorous answered, that they were going to the city of Zion, and had got up that difficult place ; but, said he, the farther we go the more danger we meet with ; wherefore we turned, and are going back again.

Yes, said Mistrust, for just before us lies a couple of lions in the way (whether sleeping or waking we know not) ; and we could not think, if we came within reach, but they would presently pull us in pieces.

Then said Christian, You make me afraid ; but whither shall I flee to be safe ? If I go back to my own country, that is prepared for fire and brimstone, and I shall certainly perish there : If I can get to the celestial city, I am sure to be in safety there :—I must venture :—to go back is nothing but death ; to go forward is fear of death, and life everlasting beyond it : —I will yet go forward. So Mistrust and Timorous ran down the hill, and Christian went on his way. But thinking again of what he had heard from the men, he felt in his bosom for his roll, that he might read therein and be comforted ; but he felt and found it not. Then was Christian in great distress, and knew not what to do ; for he wanted that which used to relieve him, and that which should have been his pass into the celestial city. Here therefore he began to be much perplexed, and knew not what to do. At last he bethought himself, that he had slept in the arbour that is on the

side of the hill ; and falling down upon his
knees he asked God forgiveness for that foolish act, and then went back to look for his roll
But all the way he went back, who can sufficiently set forth the sorrow of Christian's
heart ? Sometimes he sighed, sometimes he
wept, and oftentimes he chid himself for being so foolish to fall asleep in that place, which
was erected only for a little refreshment for
his weariness. Thus, therefore, he went
back, carefully looking on this side and on
that, all the way as he went, if happily he
might find the roll that had been his comfort
so many times in his journey. He went thus
till he came again in sight of the arbour where
he sat and slept ; but that sight renewed his sorrow the more, by bringing again, even afresh,
his evil of sleeping unto his mind. Thus
therefore he now went on bewailing his sinful
sleep, saying, ' O wretched man that I am !'
that I should sleep in the day-time ! (1 Thess.
v. 7, 8 ; Rev. ii. 4, 5.) That I should sleep
in the midst of difficulty ! That I should so
indulge the flesh, as to use that rest for ease
to my flesh, which the Lord of the hill hath
erected only for the relief of the spirits of pilgrims ! How many steps have I took in vain !
Thus it happened to Israel, for their sin they
were sent back again by the way of the Red
Sea : and I am made to tread those steps with
sorrow, which I might have trod with delight,
had it not have been for this sinful sleep.
How far might I have been on my way by
this time ! I am made to tread those steps

thrice over, which I needed to have trod but once ; yea, now also I am like to be benighted, for the day is almost spent : O that I had not slept !

Now* by this time he was come to the arbour again, where for a while he sat down and wept ; but at last (as God would have it) looking sorrowfully down under the settle, there he spied his roll ; the which he with trembling and haste catched up and put in his bosom. But who can tell how joyful this man was when he had gotten his roll again ? For this roll was the assurance of his life, and acceptance at the desired haven. Therefore he laid it up in his bosom, gave God thanks for directing his eye to the place where it lay, and with joy and tears betook himself again to his journey. But O how nimbly now did he go up the rest of the hill !---Yet † before he got

* ' Now'—By means of extraordinary diligence, with renewed application to the blood of Christ, the believer will in time recover his warranted confidence, and God will ' restore to him the joy of his salvation :' but he must, as it were, pass repeatedly over the same ground with sorrow, which, had it not been for his negligence, he might have passed at once with comfort.

Instead of the words, ' as God would have it,' all the old copies read, ' as Christian would have it ;' which must mean, that the Lord fully granted his desires. But modern editors have substituted, ' as Providence would have it,' which is indeed clear sense, but not much in our author's manner, who perhaps would rather have ascribed Christian's success to special grace ; yet, as some mistake seems to have crept into the old editions, I have ventured my conjecture in the emendation of it, of which the reader may judge for himself.

† ' Yet'—Believers may recover their evidences of acceptance, and yet suffer many troubles as the effects of their past unwatchfulness. The Lord rebukes and chastens those whom

up, the sun went down upon Christian ; and
this made him again recall the vanity of his
sleeping to his remembrance ; and thus he
again began to condole with himself : 'O
thou sinful sleep ! how for thy sake am I like to
be benighted in my journey ! I must walk
without the sun, darkness must cover the path
of my feet, and I must hear the noise of doleful creatures, because of my sinful sleep !'
Now also he remembered the story that Mistrust and Timorous told him of, how they were
frighted with the sight of the lions. Then
said Christian to himself again, these beasts
range in the night for their prey ; and if they
should meet with me in the dark how should
I shift them ? how should I escape being by
them torn in pieces ? Thus he went on. But,
while he was bewailing his unhappy miscar-
riage, he lifted up his eyes, and behold there
was a very stately palace before him, the
name of which was Beautiful,* and it stood by
the highway side.

he loves : genuine comfort springs immediately from the vigorous exercise of holy affections in communion with God,
which may be suspended even when no doubts are entertained of final salvation ; and the true penitent is least disposed
to forgive himself, when most satisfied that the Lord hath forgive him

   * ' Beautiful'—Hitherto Christian had been a solitary pilgrim ; but we must next consider him as admitted to the communion of the faithful, and joining with them in the most solemn public ordinances. This is represented under the emblem of the house Beautiful, and the pilgrim's entertainment
in it. Mr. Bunyan was a protestant dissenter, an *Indepen-
dant* in respect of church government and discipline, and ar
Anti-pædo-baptist, or one who deemed adult professors of
repentance and faith the only proper subjects of baptism, and

So I saw in my dream, that he made haste and went forward, that if possible he might get lodging there. Now before he had gone far he entered into a very narrow passage, which was about a furlong off the Porter's lodge : and looking very narrowly before him as he went he spied two lions* in the way. Now,

immersion the only proper mode of administering that ordinance. He must, therefore, have intended to describe especially the admission of the new convert as a member of a dissenting church (which consists of the communicants only) upon a profession of faith, and with adult baptism by immersion : but as he held open communion with *Pædo-baptists*, the last circumstance is not necessarily included. Indeed he has expressed himself so candidly and cautiously, that his representations may suit the admission of new members into the society of professed Christians in any communion, where a serious regard to spiritual religion is in this respect maintained. It may, perhaps, be questioned how far, in the present state of things, this is practicable ; but we can scarcely deny it to be very desirable, that Christian societies should be formed according to the principles here exhibited : such would indeed be very beautiful, honourable to God, conducive to mutual edification, and examples to the world around them Different expedients also may be adopted for thus promoting the communion of the saints : but surely more might be done than is at present, perhaps any where, were all concerned to attempt it boldly, earnestly, and with united efforts.

* ' Lions'—A public profession of faith exposes a man to more opposition from relatives and neighbours than a private attention to religion ; and in our author's days, it was commonly the signal for persecution ; for which reason he places the lions in the road to the house Beautiful. Sense perceives the danger to which an open profession of religion may expose a man, and the imagination through the suggestions of Satan, xceedingly magnifies them ; faith alone can discern the secret restraints which the Lord lays on the minds of opposers ; and even believers are apt to be fearful and distrustful on such occasions. But the vigilant pastors of the flock obviate their fears, and by seasonable admonitions animate them to press forward, assured that nothing shall do them any real harm and that all shall eventually prove beneficia' to them We

thought he, I see the danger that Mistrust and Timorous were driven back by. (The lions were chained, but he saw not the chains.) Then he was afraid, and thought nothing but death was before him. But the porter at the lodge, whose name is Watchful, perceiving that Christian made a halt, as if he would go back, cried unto him, saying, ' Is thy strength so small ? (Mark iv. 40.) ' Fear not the lions, for they are chained, and are placed there for trial of faith where it is, and for discovery of those that have none : keep in the midst of the path, and no hurt shall come unto thee.'

Then I saw that he went on trembling for fear of the lions ; but taking good heed to the directions of the porter, he heard them roar, but they did him no harm. Then he clapped his hands, and went on till he came and stood before the gate where the porter was Then said Christian to the porter, Sir, what house is this ? And, May I lodge here to-night ? The porter answered, This house was built by the Lord of the hill, and he built it for the relief and security of pilgrims. This porter* also asked whence he was ? and whither he was going ?

---

meet with the following lines in the old copies, which though misplaced in most of them, may refer to the pilgrim's present situation.

' Difficulty is behind, fear is before,
Though he's got on the hill, the lions roar :
A Christian man is never long at ease ;
When one fright's gone, another doth him sieze.'

* ' This porter'—The porter's inquiries and Christian's answers exhibit our author's sentiments on the caution with which members should be admitted into the communion of

Chr I am come from the city of Destruction, and am going to mount Zion ; but, because the sun is now set, I desire, if I may, to lodge here to-night.

Por. What is your name ?

Chr. My name is now Christian, but my name at the first was Graceless : I came of the race of Japheth (Gen. ix. 27), whom God will persuade to dwell in the tents of Shem.

Por. But how doth it happen that you come so late ? The sun is set.

Chr. I had been here sooner, but that,

the faithful ; and it very properly shews, how ministers by private conversation, may form a judgment of a man's profession, whether it be intelligent and the result of experience, or notional and formal. Christian assigned his sinful sleeping as the cause of his arriving so late : when believers are oppressed with prevailing doubts of their acceptance, they are backward in joining themselves to God's people ; and this often tempts them to sinful delays, instead of exciting them to greater diligence. The subsequent discourse of Discretion with the pilgrim represents such precautions and inquiries into the character and views of a professor, as may be made use of by any body of Christians, in order to prevent the intrusion of improper persons. The answers, given to the several questions proposed, constitute the proper external qualifications for admission to the Lord's table, when there is nothing in a man's principles and conduct inconsistent with them : the Lord alone can judge how far they accord to the inward dispositions and affections of the heart. By the little discourse of others belonging to the family with Christian previous to his admission, the author probably meant, the members should be admitted into Christian societies with the approbation, at least, of the most prudent, pious, and candid part of those that constitute them ; and according to the dictates of those graces or endowments here personified. By giving him ' something to eat before supper,' he probably referred to those preparatory sermons and devotions, by which the administration of the Lord's supper was then frequently and with great propriety introduced.

wretched man that I am! I slept in the arbour that stands on the hill-side. Nay, I had notwithstanding that, been here much sooner, but that in my sleep I lost my evidence, and came without it to the brow of the hill; and then feeling for it and finding it not, I was forced, with sorrow of heart, to go back to the place where I slept my sleep; where I found it, and now I am come.

Por. Well, I will call out one of the virgins of this place, who will, if she like your talk, bring you in to the rest of the family, according to the rules of the house. So Watchful the porter: ang a bell, at the sound of which came out at the door of the house a grave and beautiful damsel, named Discretion, and asked why she was called?

The porter answered, This man is in a journey from the city of Destruction to mount Zion; but being weary and benighted, he asked me if he might lodge here to-night: so I told him I would call for thee, who, after discourse had with him, mayest do as seemeth thee good, even according to the law of the house.

Then she asked him whence he was? and whither he was going? and he told her She asked him also how he got in the way? and he told her. Then she asked him what he had seen and met with in the way? and he told her. And at last she asked his name. So he said, It is Christian: and I have so much the more a desire to lodge here to-night, because, by what I perceive, this place was

built by the Lord of the hill for the relief and
security of pilgrims. So she smiled, but the
water stood in her eyes ; and after a little
pause she said, I will call forth two or three
more of the family. So she ran to the door,
and called out Prudence, Piety, and Charity,
who after a little more discourse with him,
had him into the family ; and many of them
meeting him at the threshold of the house
said, 'Come in, thou blessed of the Lord,
this house was built by the Lord of the hill,
on purpose to entertain such pilgrims in.'
Then he bowed his head, and followed them
into the house. So when he was come in and
sat down, they gave him something to eat,
and consented together, that, until supper was
ready, some of them should have some particular discourse with Christian, for the best
improvement of time ; and they appointed
Piety, and Prudence, and Charity, to discourse with him ; and thus they began.

Pi. Come* good Christian, since we have
been so loving to you, to receive you into
our house this night, let us, if perhaps we may
better ourselves thereby, talk with you of all
things that have happened to you in your pilgrimage.

---

* ' Come'—The farther conversation of Piety and her
companions with Christian was subsequent to his admission,
and represents the advantage of the communion of the saints,
and the best method of conducting it. To lead believers to a
serious review of the way in which they have been led hitherto is every way profitable, as it tends to increase humiliation, gratitude, faith, and hope ; and must, therefore, proportionably conduce to the glory of God, and the edification
of their brethren.

Chr. With a very good will; and I am glad that you are so well disposed.

Pi. What moved you at first to betake yourself to a pilgrim's life?

Chr. I was driven out of my native country by a dreadful sound that was in mine ears; to wit, that unavoidable destruction did attend me if I abode in that place where I was.

Pi. But how did it happen that you came out of your country this way?

Chr It was as God would have it; for when I was under the fears of destruction, I did not know whither to go; but by chance there came a man, even to me as I was trembling and weeping, whose name is Evangelist, and he directed me to the wicket-gate, which else I should never have found, and so set me into the way that hath led me directly to this house.

Pi. But did you not come by the house of the Interpreter?

Chr. Yes, and did see such things there, the remembrance of which will stick by me as long as I live; especially three things; to wit, how Christ, in despite of Satan, maintains his work of grace in the heart; how the man had sinned himself quite out of hopes of God's mercy; and also the dream of him that thought in his sleep the day of judgment was come.

Pi. Why, did you hear him tell his dream?

Chr. Yes, and a dreadful one it was, I thought; it made my heart ache as he was telling of it; but yet I am glad I heard it.

Pi. Was this all you saw at the house of
the Interpreter ?

Chr. No ; he took me and had me where
he shewed me a stately palace, and how the
people were clad in gold that were in it ; and
how there came a venturous man, and cut his
way through the armed men that stood in the
door to keep him out ; and how he was bid
to come in and win eternal glory : methought
those things did ravish my heart. I would
have staid at that good man's house a twelve-
month, but that I knew I had farther to go.

Pi. And what saw you else in the way ?

Chr. Saw ! Why, I went but a little farther, and I saw One, as I thought in my
mind, hang bleeding upon a tree ; and the
very sight of him made my burthen fall off
my back (for I groaned under a very heavy
burthen, but then it fell down from off me)
It was a strange thing to me, for I never saw
such a thing before : yea, and while I stood
looking up (for then I could not forbear
looking) three shining ones came to me : one
of them testified that my sins were forgiven
me ; another stripped me of my rags, and
gave me this embroidered coat which you see ;
and the third set the mark which you see in
my forehead, and gave me this sealed roll
(and with that he plucked it out of his bosom).

Pi But you saw more than this, did you
not ?

Chr The things that I have told you were
the best, yet some other matters I saw ; as

namely, I saw three men, Simple, Sloth, and Presumption, lie asleep, a little out of the way as I came, with irons upon their heels ; but do you think I could awake them ! I also saw Formality and Hypocrisy come tumbling over the wall, to go, as they pretended, to Zion, but they were quickly lost ; even as I myself did tell them, but they would not believe. But, above all, I found it hard work to get up this hill, and as hard to come by the lions' mouths ; and truly, if it had not been for the good man, the porter, that stands at the gate, I do not know but that, after all, I might have gone back again ; but now, I thank God, I am here ; and I thank you for receiving of me.

Then Prudence* thought good to ask him a few questions, and desired his answer to .nem.

Pr. Do you not think sometimes of the country from whence you came ?

Chr. Yes, but with much shame and de-

* 'Prudence'—Men may learn by human teaching to profess any doctrine, and relate any experience ; nay, general convictions, transient affections, and distinct notions may impose upon the man himself, and he may mistake them for true conversion. The best method of avoiding this dangerous rock consists in daily self-examination, and constant prayer to be preserved from it ; and, as far as we are concerned, to form a judgment of others, in order to perform our several duties towards them, prudence is especially required, and will suggest such questions as follow in this place. The true Christian's inmost feelings will best explain the answers, which no exposition can elucidate to those who are unacquainted with the conflict to which they refer. The golden hours (fleeting and precious) are earnests of the everlasting holy felicity of heaven.

10*

testation : truly, if I had been mindful of that country from whence I came out, I might have had opportunity to have returned ; but now I desire a better country, that is, a heavenly one (Heb. xi. 16).

Pr. Do you not yet bear away with you some of the things that then you were conversant withal ?

Chr. Yes, but greatly against my will ; especially my inward and carnal cogitations, with which all my countrymen, as well as myself, were delighted : but now all those things are my grief ; and might I but choose mine own things, I would choose never to think of those things more ; but when I would be doing of that which is best, that which is worst is with me (Rom. vii).

Pr. Do you not find sometimes as if those things were vanquished, which at other times are your perplexity ?

Chr. Yes, but that is but seldom ; but they are to me golden hours in which such things happen to me.

Pr. Can you remember by what means you find your annoyances at times as if they were vanquished ?

Chr. Yes ; when I think what I saw at the cross, that will do it ; and when I look upon my embroidered coat, that will do it ; and when I look into the roll that I carry in my bosom, that will do it ; and when my thoughts wax warm about whither I am going, that will do it.

Pr. And what is it that makes you so desirous to go to mount Zion ?

Chr. Why, then I hope to see him alive that did hang dead on the cross; and there I hope to be rid of all those things that to this day are an annoyance to me; there they say there is no death (Isa. xxv. 8; Rev. xxi. 4); and there I shall dwell with such company as I like best. For, to tell you the truth, I love him because I was by him eased of my burthen; and I am weary of my inward sickness. I would fain be where I shall die no more, and with the company that shall continually cry, 'Holy holy, holy.'

Then said Charity* to Christian, Have you a family? are you a married man?

Chr. I have a wife and four small children.

Char. And why did you not bring them along with you?

Then Christian wept, and said, Oh, how willingly would I have done it! but they were all of them utterly averse to my going on pilgrimage.

Char. But you should have talked to them, and have endeavoured to have shewn them the danger of being left behind.

Chr. So I did; and told them also what

---

* ' Charity'—When a man knows the value of his own soul, he will become greatly solicitous for the souls of others. It is, therefore, a very suspicious circumstance, when a professor shews no earnestness in persuading those he loves best to seek salvation also; and it is absurd to excuse this negligence by arguments taken from God's secret purposes, when these have no influence on the conduct of the same persons in their temporal concerns. Charity's discourse with Christian shews what our author thought to be the duties of believers in this most important concern, and what he understood to be the real reasons why carnal men reject the Gospel.

God had shewed to me of the destruction of our city ; but I seemed to them as one that mocked, and they believed me not (Gen. xix. 14).

Char. And did you pray to God that he would bless your counsel to them ?

Chr. Yes, and that with much affection ; for you must think that my wife and poor children were very dear unto me.

Char. But did you tell them of your own sorrow, and fear of destruction ? for I suppose that destruction was visible enough to you.

Chr. Yes, over, and over, and over. They might also see my fears in my countenance, in my tears, and also in my trembling under the apprehension of the judgments that did hang over our heads ; but all was not sufficient to prevail with them to come with me.

Char. But what could they say for themselves why they came not ?

Chr. Why, my wife was afraid of losing this world ; and my children were given to the foolish delights of youth : so, what by one thing and what by another, they left me to wander in this manner alone.

Char. But did you not with your vain life damp all that you by words used by way of persuasion to bring them away with you ?

Chr. Indeed I cannot commend my life, for I am conscious to myself of many failings therein : I know also, that a man by his conversation, may soon overthrow what by argument or persuasion he doth labour to fasten

upon others for their good. Yet this I can
say, I was very weary of giving them occasion, by any unseemly action, to make them
averse to going on pilgrimage. Yea, for this
very thing they would tell me I was too precise ; and that I denied myself of things, for
their sakes, in which they saw no evil. Nay,
I think I may say, that if what they saw in
me did hinder them, it was my great tenderness in sinning against God, or of doing any
wrong to my neighbour.

Chr. Indeed Cain hated his brother, ' because his own works were evil, and his brother's righteous' (1 John iii. 12) ; and if thy
wife and children have been offended with
thee for this, they thereby shew themselves
to be implacable to good ; and thou hast delivered thy soul from their blood (Ezek. iii. 19).

Now I saw in my dream, that thus they
sat talking together until supper* was ready.
So when they had made ready, they sat down

---

* ' Supper'—The administration of the Lord's supper is
here emblematically described. In it the person, humiliation, sufferings, and death of Christ, with the motive and
event of them, are kept in perpetual remembrance. By seriously contemplating these interesting subjects, with the
emblems of his body wounded, and his blood sl ed, before
our eyes ; and by professing our cordial acceptance of his
purchased salvation, and surrender of ourselves to his service ; we find every holy affection revived and invigorated,
and our souls melted into deep repentance, inspired with
calm confidence, animated to thankful, zealous, self-denying
obedience, and softened into tender affection for our fellow Christians, with compassionate forgiving love of our
most inveterate enemies. The believer will readily apply
the allegorical representation of ' the Lord of the hill' (Isa.
xxv. 6, 7) to the love of Christ for lost sinners, which no
words can adequately describe, for it passeth knowledge '

to meat. Now the table was furnished with fat things, and with wine that was well refined ; and all their talk at the table was about the Lord of the hill ; as, namely, about what he had done, and wherefore he did what he did, and why he had builded that house ; and by what they said, I perceived that he had been a great warrior, and had fought with and slain him that had the power of death (Heb. ii. 14, 15) ; but not without great danger to himself ; which made me love him the more.

For, as they said, and as I believe, said Christian, he did it with the loss of much blood. But that which put glory of grace into all he did, was, that he did it out of pure love to his country. And besides, there were some of them of the household that said they had been and spoke with him since he did die on the cross ; and they have attested, that they had it from his own lips, that he is such a lover of poor pilgrims, that the like is not to be found from the east to the west.

They, moreover, gave an instance of what they affirmed, and that was, he had stripped himself of his glory that he might do this for the poor ; and that they heard him say and affirm, that he would not dwell in the mount of Zion alone. They said, moreover, that he had made many pilgrims princes, though by nature, they were beggars born, and their original had been the dunghill (1 Sam. ii. 8 ; Ps. cxiii. 7).

Thus they discoursed together till late at

night; and after they had committed them
selves to their Lord for protection, they be
took themselves to rest.   The pilgrim they
laid in a large upper chamber, whose window
opened towards the sun rising : the name of
the chamber was Peace,* where he slept till
break of day, and then he awoke and sang—

> Where am I now ! Is this the love and care
> Of Jesus, for the men that pilgrims are
> Thus to provide ! That I should be forgiven,
> And dwell already the next door to heaven !

So in the morning they all got up, and, af
ter some more discourse, they told him that he
should not depart till they had shewed him the
rarities of that place.   And first they had him
into the study,† where they shewed him re
cords of the greatest antiquity ; in which, as I
remember in my dream, they shewed him,
first, the pedigree of the Lord of the hill, that
he was the Son of the Ancient-of-days, and
came by that eternal generation : here also
were more fully recorded the acts that he had

---

* ' Peace'—That peace of conscience and serenity of mind,
which follows a humble upright profession of faith in Christ,
and communion with him and his people, is not the effect of
a mere outward observance ; but of that inward disposition,
of the heart which is thus cultivated, and of the Lord's bles
sing on his own appointments. This is here represented by
the chamber Peace : it raises the soul above the care and
bustle of this vain world, and springs from the healing beams
of the Sun of righteousness.

† ' Study'—Christian communion, properly conducted,
tends to enlarge the believer's acquaintance with the Holy
Scriptures : and this conduces to the increase of faith, hope,
love, patience, and fortitude ; to animate the soul in emula
ting the illustrious examples there exhibited, and to furnish
instruction for every good work.

done, and the names of many hundreds that he had taken into his service; and now he had placed them in such habitations that could neither by length of days, nor decays of nature, be dissolved.

Then they read to him some of the worthy acts that some of his servants had done; as how they had 'subdued kingdoms, wrought righteousness, obtained promises, stopped the mouths of lions, quenched the violence of fire, escaped the edge of the sword, out of weakness were made strong, waxed valiant in fight, and turned to flight the armies of the aliens' (Heb. xi. 33, 34).

Then they read again in another part of the records of the house, where it was shewed how willing the Lord was to receive into his favour any, even any, though they in time past had offered great affronts to his person and proceedings. Here also were several other histories of many other famous things, of all which Christian had a view, as of things both ancient and modern, together with prophecies and predictions of things that have their certain accomplishment, both to the dread and amazement of enemies, and the comfort and solace of pilgrims.

The next day they took him and had him into the armoury,* where they shewed him all

* 'Armoury'—The provision, which is made in Christ and his fulness, for maintaining and increasing, in the hearts of his people, those holy dispositions and affections, by the vigorous exercise of which victory is obtained over all their enemies, is here represented by the armoury (Eph. vi. 10—18; 1 Thes. v. 6). This suffices for all who seek to be supplied

manner of furniture which their Lord had provided for pilgrims, as sword, shield, helmet, breast-plate, all-prayer, and shoes that would not wear out. And there was here enough of this to harness out as many men, for the service of their Lord, as there be stars in the heaven for multitude.

They also shewed him some of the engines, with which some of his servants had done wonderful things. They showed him Moses's rod; the hammer and nail with which Jael slew Sisera; the pitchers, trumpets, and lamps too, with which Gideon put to flight the armies of Midian. Then they shewed him the ox's goad, wherewith Shamgar slew six hundred men. They shewed him also the jaw-bone with which Sampson did such mighty feats: they shewed him moreover the sling and stone with which David slew Goliah of Gath; and the sword also with which their Lord will kill the man of sin, in the day that he shall rise up to the prey. They shewed him besides many excellent things, with which Christian was much delighted. This done, they went to their rest again.

Then I saw in my dream, that on the morrow he got up to go forwards, but they desir-

from it, how many soever they be. We ought, therefore, 'to take to ourselves the whole armour of God,' and 'put it on,' by diligently using all the means of grace; and we may assist others by our exhortations, counsels, example, and prayers, in doing the same. The following allusions to the Scripture history, which have a peculiar propriety in an allegory, intimate, that the means of grace are made effectual by the power of God, which we should depend on in implicit obedience to his appointments.

ed him to stay till the next day also ; **and**
then, said they, we will, if the day be clear,
shew you the Delectable Mountains,* which
they said, would yet farther add to his comfort, because they were nearer the desired
haven than the place where at present he
was ; so he consented and staid. When the
morning was up, they had him to the top of
the house, and bid him look south : so he did
and behold, at a great distance (Isa. xxxiii. 16
17), he saw a most pleasant mountainous
country, beautified with woods, vineyards,
fruits of all sorts, flowers also, with springs and
fountains, very delectable to behold. Then
he asked the name of the country. They said,
it was Emmanuel's Land ; and it is as common, say they, as this hill is, to and for all the
pilgrims. And when thou comest there, from
thence thou mayest see to the gate of the Celestial City, as the shepheards that live there
will make appear.

Now he† bethought himself of setting forward, and they were willing he should. But

* ' Mountains'—The delectable mountains, as seen at a
distance, represent those distinct views of the privileges and
consolations attainable in this life, with which believers are
sometimes favoured, when attending on divine ordinances, or
diligently making a subsequent improvement of them. The
hopes thus inspired prepare them for meeting and pressing
forward through dangers and hadships ; this is the pre-emi-
nent advantage of Christian communion, and can only be enjoyed at some special seasons, when the Sun of righteousness
shines upon the soul.

† ' Now he'—The ordinances of public or social worship are
only the means of being religious, not the essence o' religion itself. Having renewed our strength by waiting the
Lord, we must go forward, by attending with increasing

first, said they, let us go again into the armoury. So they did ; and when he came there they harnessed him from head to foot with what was of proof, lest perhaps he should meet with assaults in the way. He being therefore thus accoutred, walked out with his friends to the gate, and there asked the porter, if he saw any pilgrims pass by ? Then the porter answered, Yes.

Chr. Pray did you know him ?

Port. I asked his name, and he told me it was Faithful.

O, said Christian, I know him ; he is my townsman, my near neighbour, he comes from the place where I was born : how far do you think he may be before ?

Port. He is got by this time below the hill.

Well, said Christian, good porter, the Lord be with thee, and add to all thy blessings much increase, for the kindness thou hast shewed to me.

Then he began to go forward : But Discretion, Piety, Charity, and Prudence, would accompany him down* to the foot of the hill.

diligence to the duties of our several stations, and preparing to resist temptations, which often assault us after special seasons of divine consolation. Ministers, therefore, and experienced believers should warn young converts to expect trials and conflicts, and recommend to them such companions as may be a comfort and help in their pilgrimage.

* 'Down'—The humiliation requisite for receiving Christ, obtaining peace and making a good confession of the faith, is general and indistinct, compared with that which subsequent trials and conflicts will produce ; and the Lord commonly dispenses comfort and humiliating experiences alternately, that the believer may neither be elated nor depressed above measure (1 Cor. xii 1—5) ; the valley of Humilia-

So they went on together, reiterating their former discourses, till they came to go down the hill. Then said Christian, As it was difficult coming up, so, so far as I can see, it is dangerous going down. Yes, said Prudence, so it is; for it is a hard matter for a man to go down into the valley of Humiliation, as thou art now, and to catch no slip by the way; therefore, said they, are we come out to accompany thee down the hill. So he began to go down, but very warily, yet he caught a slip or two.

Then I saw in my dream, that these good companions, when Christian was gone down to the bottom of the hill, gave him a loaf of bread, a bottle of wine, and a cluster of raisins; and then he went on his way.

But now, in this valley of Humiliation, poor Christian was hard put to it; for he had gone but a little way before he spied * a foul

tion therefore, is very judiciously placed beyond the house Beautiful. Some explain it to signify a Christian's outward circumstances, when reduced to poverty, or subjected to great temporal loss by professing the Gospel; and perhaps the author had this idea in his mind; yet it could only be viewed as the means of producing inward humiliation. In going down into the valley, the believer will greatly need the assistance of discretion, piety, charity, and prudence, and the recollection of the instructions and counsels of such Christians as are eminent for these endowments: for humiliating dispensations and experiences exite the latent evils of the heart, and often cause men to speak and act unadvisedly; so that, notwithstanding every precaution, the review will commonly discover many things, which demand the remorse and sorrow of deep repentance.

* 'Spied'—Under discouraging circumstances the believer will often be tempted to murmur, despond or seek relief from the world. Finding that his too sanguine expectations are

fiend coming over the field to meet him : his name is Apollyon. Then did Christian begin to be afraid, and to cast in his mind whether to go back or stand his ground. But he considered again that he had no armour for

not answered, that he grows worse rather than better in his own opinion of himself, that his comforts are transitory, and that much reproach, contempt, and loss, are incurred by his profession of religion, discontent will often rise up in his heart, and weakness of faith will expose him to sharp conflicts.—Mr. Bunyan, having experienced, in an uncommon degree, the most dreadful temptations, was probably led by that circumstance to speak on this subject in language not very intelligible to those who have been exempted from such painful exercises of mind. The nature of his work required, that they should be described under outward emblems ; but the inward suggestions of evil spirits are especially intended. These seem to have peculiar access to the imagination, and are able to paint before that illusive faculty the most alluring or terrifying representations, as if they were realities. Apollyon signifies the destroyer (Rev. ix. 11) ; and in carrying on the work of destruction, fallen angels endeavour by various devices to deter men from prayer, and to render them afraid of those things, without which the life of faith cannot be maintained ; in order that, after convictions, they may be led to give up religion, as the only method of recovering composure of mind. Many, 'having no root in themselves,' thus gradually fall away ; and others are greatly retarded : but the well instructed believer sees no safety, except in facing his enemy. If there appears to be danger, in persevering, ruin is inevitable if he desist (for Christian ' had no armour for his back') ; even fear, therefore, will in that case induce a man to stand his ground, and the more resolutely he resists temptation, the sooner will he regain his tranquillity : for when he suggestions of Satan excite us to pray more fervently, and to be more diligent in every service, that enemy will ' flee from us.' Perhaps some may remember a time when they were so harassed as almost to despair of relief ; who have since been so entirely delivered, that, were it not for the recollection of their own past experience, they would be ready to ascribe all such things to disease or enthusiasm, notwithstanding all that the Scripture contains on the subject.

11*

his back, and therefore thought that to turn the back to him might give him greater advantage, with ease to pierce him with his darts ; therefore he resolved to venture, and stand his ground : for thought he, had I no more in mine eye than the saving of my life, it would be the best way to stand.

So he* went on, and Apollyon met him

* ' So he'—The description of Apollyon implies, that the combat afterwards recorded particularly represented the terrors by which evil spirits attempt to drive professors out of their path. Other temptations, though perhaps more dangerous, are not so distressing : ' Satan can transform himself into an angel of light ;' and indeed he is a very Proteus, who can assume any form, as best suits his purpose. As all have been overcome by the temptations of the devil, and ' of whom a man is overcome, of the same is he brought into bondage ;' so by usurpation, he is become the god and prince of this world, and we have all been his slaves. But believers, having been redeemed by the blood of Christ, ' are made free from sin and become the servants of God :' and the abiding conviction, that all the subjects of sin and Satan must perish, concurs with their experience of its hard bondage, in fortifying them against every temptation to return to it. Sensible of their obligations to God as their Creator and Governor, they have deeply repented of their past rebellions ; and having obtained mercy, feel themselves bound by gratitude and the most solemn engagements to cleave to him and his service. Their difficulties and discouragements cannot induce them to believe that they ' have changed for the worse ;' nor will they be influenced by the numbers who apostatize, from love to the world and dread of the cross ; for they are ' rooted and grounded in love,' and not merely moved by fears and hopes. They are sure that the Lord is able to deliver them from their enemies ; and should the wicked be permitted to prosper in their malicious devices, they know enough of his plan, to rely on his wisdom, truth, and love in the midst of sufferings. Thus they have answers ready for every suggestion ; even such answers as Christian had been furnished with at the house of the Interpreter. If such temptations prove ineffectual, Satan will perhaps assault the believer, by representing to his mind, with every possible ag-

Now the monster was hideous to behold : he was clothed with scales like a fish (and they are his pride) ; he had wings like a dragon, feet like a bear, and out of his belly came fire and smoke, and his mouth was as the mouth of a lion. When he was come up to Christian, he beheld him with a disdainful countenance, and thus began to question with him.

Apol. Whence came you ? and whither are you bound ?

Chr. I am come from the city of Destruction, which is the place of all evil, and am going to the city of Zion.

Apol. By this I perceive thou art one of my subjects ; for all that country is mine, and I am the prince and god of it. How is it then that thou hast run away from thy king ? Were it not for that I hope thou mayest do me more service, I would strike thee now, at one blow, to the ground.

Chr. I was born indeed in your dominions, but your service was hard, and your wages such as a man could not live on, ' for the wag-

gravation, the several instances of his misconduct, since he professed the Gospel, in order to heighten his apprehensions of being found at last a hypocrite : when the soul is discouraged and gloomy, he will be as assiduous in representing every false step to be a horrid crime inconsistent with a state of grace, as he is at other times in persuading men, that the most flagrant violations of the Divine law are mere trifles In repelling such suggestions, the well-instructed believer will neither deny the charge, nor extenuate his guilt ; but he will flee for refuge to the free-grace of the Gospel, and take com fort from the consciousness that he now hates, and groans under the remains of those evils, which once he wholly lived in without remorse ; thence inferring, that ' his sins, though many, are forgiven.'

es of sin is death' (Rom. vi. 23) ; therefore, when I was come to years, I did, as other considerate persons do, look out if perhaps I might mend myself.

Apol. There is no prince that will thus lightly lose his subjects, neither will I as yet lose thee ; but since thou complainest of thy service and wages, be content to go back what our country will afford, I do here promise to give thee.

Chr. But I have let myself to another, even to the king of princes ; and how can I with fairness go back with thee ?

Apol. Thou hast done in this according to the proverb, ' Changed a bad for a worse ;' but it is ordinary for those that have professed themselves his servants, after awhile to give him the slip, and return again to me. Do thou so too, and all shall be well.

Chr. I have given him my faith, and sworn my allegiance to him : how then can I go back from this, and not be hanged as a traitor?

Apol. Thou didst the same to me, and yet I am willing to pass by all, if now thou wilt yet turn again and go back.

Chr. What I promised thee was in my nonage ; and besides, I count that the prince, under whose banner now I stand, is able to absolve me ; yea, and to pardon also what I did as to my compliance with thee : and, besides, O thou destroying Apollyon, to speak truth, I like his service, his wages, his servants, his government, his company, and country, better than thine ; and therefore, leave off to persuade me farther ; I am his servant, and I wi'l follow him.

Apol. Cons'der again, when thou art in cool blood, what thou art like to meet with in the way that thou goest.   Thou knowest that, for the most part, his servants come to an ill end, because they are transgressors against me and my ways.   How many of them have been put to shameful deaths ! And besides, thou countest his service better than mine, whereas he never came yet from the place where he is to deliver any that served him out of their hands ; but, as for me, how many times as all the world very well knows, have I delivered, either by power or fraud, those that have faithfully served me, from him and his, though taken by them : and so I will deliver thee.

Chr. His forbearing at present to deliver them is on purpose to try their love, whether they will cleave to him to the end ; and, as for the ill end thou sayest they come to, that is most glorious in their account : for, present deliverance, they do not much expect it ; for they stay for their glory, and then they shall have it, when their Prince comes in his and the glory of the angels.

Apol. Thou hast already been unfaithful in thy service to him ; and how dost thou think to receive wages of him ?

Chr. Wherein, O Apollyon, have I been unfaithful to him ?

Apol Thou didst faint at first setting out,

when thou wast almost choked in the gulf of Despond; thou didst attempt wrong ways to be rid of thy burthen, whereas thou shouldest have stayed till thy Prince had taken it off; thou didst sinfully sleep, and lose thy choice things; thou wast also almost persuaded to go back at the sight of the lions; and when thou talkest of thy journey, and of what thou hast heard and seen, thou art inwardly desirous of vain glory in all that thou sayest or doest.

Chr. All this is true, and much more which thou hast left out; but the Prince, whom I serve and honour, is merciful and ready to forgive. But besides, these infirmities possessed me in thy country; for there I sucked them in, and I have groaned under them, been sorry for them, and have obtained pardon of my Prince.

Then Apollyon broke out into a grievous rage,* saying, I am an enemy to this Prince;

* 'Rage'—Thus far Christian's contest with Apollyon is intelligible and instructive to every experienced believer: what follows is more difficult. But if we duly reflect upon the Lord's permission to Satan, in respect of Job, with the efforts and effects that followed; and if we compare it with the tempter's desire of sifting Peter and the other apostles as wheat—we shall not be greatly at a loss about our author's meaning. This enemy is sometimes gratified with such an arrangement of outward dispensations as most favours his assaults: so that the believer's path seems to be wholly obstructed. The Lord himself appears to have forsaken him, or even to fight against him; and his appointments are deemed contrary to his promises. This gives Satan an oportunity of suggesting hard thoughts of God and his ways, doubts about the truth of the Scriptures, and desponding fears of a fatal event to a self-denying course of religion. Many such 'fiery darts' may be repelled or quenched by the shield of

I hate his person, his laws, and people ; I am come out on purpose to withstand thee.

faith ; but there are seasons (as some of us well know) when they are poured in so incessantly, and receive such plausibility from facts, and when they so interrupt a man while praying, reading, or meditating, that he is tempted to intermit religious duties, to avoid their horrid concomitants. The evils of the heart, which seemed before to be subdued, are at these times so excited by means of the imagination, that they apparently prevail more than ever, rendering every service an abomination, as well as a burthen ; so that the harassed soul, alarmed, baffled, defiled, self-detested, and thinking that God and his servants unite in abhorring him, is ready to give up all hope, to doubt all his former principles, to seek refuge in some heretical or antinomian system, or to attempt the dissipation of his melancholy gloom, by joining again in the vanities of the world. Thus the enemy ' wounds him in his understanding, faith, and conversation' (according to the author's marginal interpretation of his meaning), yet he cannot find relief in this manner ; but is inwardly constrained, with renewed efforts, to return to the conflict. But when such temptations are long continued, resistance will gradually become more feeble ; the distressed believer will be ready to give up every thing ; and when the enemy plies him closely with infidel suggestions, to which his circumstances give a specious occasion, he may be thrown down, and ' his sword may fly out of his hand :' so that for a time he may be unable to give any credit to the truth of the Scriptures, by which alone he was before enabled to repel the tempter. This is a dreadful case : and could true faith thus finally and entirely fail, even real Christians must perish. Satan hath succeeded against many professors, with half these advantages ; and he may be supposed at least, to boast that he is sure of such as are thus cast down. But the advocate above ' prays' for his disciples, ' that their faith should not fail' (Luke xxii. 31, 32). So that, though Peter fell with Judas, he was not left to perish with him. The Christian, therefore, though ' almost pressed to death,' and ready ' to despair of life, will, by the special grace of God, be helped again to seize his sword, and to use it with more effect than ever. The Holy Spirit will bring to his mind, with the most convincing energy, the evidences of the divine inspiration of the Scripture, and enable him to rely on the promises : and thus, at length, the enemy will be put to flight, by testimonies of holy w

Chr. Apollyon, beware what you do, for I
am in the king's highway, the way of holiness ,
therefore take heed to yourself.

Then Apollyon straddled quite over the
whole breadth of the way, and said, I am void
of fear in this matter ; prepare thyself to
die ; for I swear by my infernal den, that

pertinently adduced, and more clearly understood than before. Experience will teach some readers to understand
these things, and they will know how to compassionate and
make allowances for the mistakes of the tempted : and others, who have been graciously exempted from, perhaps, the
deepest anguish known on earth (though commonly not of
long duration), should learn from the testimony of their brethren, to allow the reality of these distresses, and sympathize
with the sufferers ; and not (like Job's friends) to join with
Satan in aggravating their sorrows. We may allow, that
constitution, partial disease, and errors in judgment, expose
some men more than others to such assaults ; yet these are
only occasions, and evil spirits are assuredly the agents in
thus harassing serious persons. It is indeed of the greatest
importance to be well established in the faith : they, who in
ordinary cases are satisfied with general convictions and comfortable feelings, without being able to give a reason for their
hope, may be driven to the most tremendous extremities,
should God permit them to be thus assaulted : for they have
no fixed principles to which they may resort in such an
emergency ; and perhaps some degree of mistake always gives
Satan his principal advantage on these occasions. Yet men
of the most sober minds and sound judgment, when in a better state of bodily health than usual, and in all other respects
more rational, have experienced such distressing temptations of this kind, as they could scarcely have believed on the
report of others ; and when delivered, they cannot look
back on the past without the greatest consternation. Besides the verses, by which Christian gave thanks to his
great deliverer, we meet in the old copies with these lines :—

A more unequal match can hardly be,
Christian must fight an angel ; but you see,
The valiant man by handling sword and shield,
Doth make him, though a dragon, quit the field,'

thou shalt go no farther : here will I spill thy soul.

And with that he threw a flaming dart at his breast ; but Christian had a shield in his hand, with which he caught it, and so prevented the danger of that.

Then did Christian draw, for he saw it was time to bester him ; and Apollyon as fast made at him, throwing darts as thick as hail ; by the which notwithstanding all that Christian could do to avoid it, Apollyon wounded him in his head, his hand, and foot. This made Christian give a little back : Apollyon, therefore, followed his work amain, and Christiar again took courage, and resisted as manfully as he could. This sore combat lasted for above half a day, even till Christian was almost quite spent ; for you must know, that Christian, by reason of his wounds, must needs grow weaker and weaker.

Then Apollyon, spying his opportunity, began to gather up close to Christian, and, wrestling with him, gave him a dreadful fall ; and with that Christian's sword flew out of his hand. Then said Apollyon, I am sure of thee now ; and with that he had almost pressed him to death, so that Christian began to despair of life. But, as God would have it, while Apollyon was fetching his last blow, thereby to make a full end of this good man, Christian nimbly stretched out his hand for his sword, and caught it, saying, ' Rejoice not against me, O mine enemy ! when I fall, I shall arise' Mic. vii. 8) ; and with that gave him a deadly thrust, which made him give back, as one that had received his mortal wound. Christian perceiving that, made at him again, saying, 'Nay, in all these we are more than conquerors, through him that loved us' (Rom. viii. 37—39 ; Jam. iv. 7) ; and with that Apollyon spread forth his dragon's wings and sped him away, that Christian saw him no more.

In this combat no man can imagine, unless he had seen and heard, as I did, what yelling and hideous roaring Apollyon made all the time of the fight ; he spake like a dragon : and, on the other side, what sighs and groans burst from Christian's heart. I never saw him all the while give so much as one pleasant look, till he perceived he had wounded Apollyon with his two-edged sword ; then indeed he did smile and look upward ! But it was the dreadfullest fight that ever I saw.

So when the battle was over, Christian said, I will here give thanks to him that hath delivered me out of the mouth of the lion, to him that did help me against Apollyon. And so he did, saying,

> Great Beelzebub, the captain of this fiend,
> Design'd my ruin ; therefore to this end
> He sent him harness'd out ; and he with rage
> That hellish was did fiercely me engage :
> But blessed Michael helped me, and I
> By dint of sword did quickly make him fly :
> Therefore to him let me give lasting praise
> And thanks, and bless his holy name always.

Then there came to him a hand* with some

---

* ' A hand'—When the believer has obtained the victory over temptation, the Lord will graciously heal all the wounds

of the leaves of the tree of life, the which
Christian took and applied to the wounds that
he had received in the battle, and was healed
immediately. He also sat down in that place
to eat bread, and to drink of that bottle that
was given him a little before : so being refreshed, he addressed himself to his journey
with his sword drawn in his hand ; for he said,
I know not but some other enemy may be at
hand.   But he met with no other affront from
Apollyon quite through the valley.

Now at the end of this valley was another,
called the valley* of the Shadow of Death,

he received in the conflict ; pardoning his sins, rectifying his
mistakes, and renewing his strength and comfort, through the
mediation of Christ, and by the influences of the Holy Spirit : so that the most distressing experiences are often succeeded by the sweetest confidence and serenity of mind, and
the greatest alacrity in the ways of God. 'The leaves of the
tree of life' (Rev. xxii. 2), represent the present benefits of
the redemption of Christ : ' the hand' may be the emblem of
those whom the Lord employs, as instruments in restoring to
his discouraged servants ' the joy of his salvation.' The believer thus healed and refreshed, by meditation on the death
of Christ, and other religious exercises, rests not in one victory, but presses forward, prepared for new conflicts ; yet the
enemy, once decidedly put to flight, seldom repeats the same
assaults, at least for some time ; because he will generally
find the victor upon his guard on that side, though he may be
surprised in some other way.

* ' The valley'—The valley of the Shadow of Death seems
intended to represent a variation of inward distress, conflict,
and alarm, which arise from prevailing darkness and insensi-
bility of mind, rendering a man reluctant to religious duties,
and dull in the performance of them, which makes way for
manifold apprehensions and temptations. The words, quoted
from the prophet, describe the waste howling wilderness
through which Israel journeyed to Canaan ; which typified
the believer's pilgrimage through this world to heaven. From
this we may infer, that the author meant in general, that such

and Christian must needs go through it, because the way to the Celestial City lay through

dreary seasons may be expected, as very few believers wholly escape them : but we must not suppose, that he intended
to convey an idea, that all experience these trials in the same
order or degree as Christian did. While men rest in forms
and notions, they generally expect nothing in religious ordinances but to finish a task, and to enjoy the satisfaction of
having done their supposed duty; but the spiritual worshipper, at some times, finds his soul filled with clear light and
holy affection ; 'it is good for him to draw nigh to God;'
and 'his soul is satisfied as with marrow and fatness, while
he praises his God with joyful lips :' at other times, dulness
and heaviness oppress him; he feels little exercise of faith,
hope, desire, reverence, love, or gratitude ; he seems to address an unknown or absent God, and rather to mock than
to worship him; divine things appear obscure and almost
unreal ; and every returning season of devotion, or reiterated
effort to lift up his heart to God, ends in disappointment ; so
that religion becomes his burthen instead of his delight.
Evils before unnoticed are now perceived to mingle with his
services ; for his self-knowledge is advanced; his remedy
seems to increase his disease ; he suspects that all his former
joy was a delusion, and is ready to conclude, that 'God had
forgotten to be gracious, and hath shut up his loving-kindness
in displeasure.' These experiences, sufficiently painful in
themselves, are often rendered more distressing, by erroneous expectations of uninterrupted comfort, or by reading
books, or hearkening to instructions, which state things un-
scripturally ; representing comfort as the evidence of acceptance, assurance as the essence of faith, impressions or visions as the witness of the Spirit ; or perfection as attainable in this life, nay, actually attained by all the regenerate ;
as if this were the church triumphant, and not the church
militant. The state of the body also, as disordered by ner-
vous or hypochondriacal affections, gives energy to the distressing inferences which men often draw from their dark
frame of mind ; and indeed indisposition may often operate
as a direct cause of it ; though the influences of the Holy
Spirit will overcome this, and all other impediments to comfort, when 'he sheds abroad the love of God in the heart.'
Evil spirits never fail, when permitted, to take advantage of
a disordered state, whether of body or mind, to mislead, entangle, perplex, or defile the soul. Persons of a melancholic

the midst of it Now this valley is a very solitary place. The prophet Jeremiah thus describes it : 'A wilderness, a land of deserts and of pits ; a land of drought, and of the *shadow of death* ; a land that no man,' but a Christian, ' passeth through, and where no man dwelt' (Jer. ii. 6).

Now here Christian was worse put to than in his fight with Apollyon ; as by the sequel you shall see.

I saw then in my dream, that when Christian was got on the borders of the Shadow of Death, there met him two men,* children of

temperature, when not aware of the particular causes whence their gloom originates, are apt to ascribe it wholly to desertion, which exceedingly enhances their distress ; and, as our author had been greatly harassed in this way, he has given us a larger proportion of this shade than is generally met with by consistent believers, or than the Scriptures give us reason to expect : and probably he meant to state the outlines of his own experience in the pilgrimage of Christian.

* ' Two men'—These men were spies, not pilgrims : they related what they had observed at a distance, but had never experienced. They represent those who have been conversant with godly people ; and ' bring an evil report on the good land,' to prejudice the minds of numbers against the right ways of the Lord. Such men pretend to have made trial of religion, and found it to be a comfortless and dreary pursuit ; they give a caricatured discription of the sighs, groans, terrors, and distresses of pious persons, and of all the dreadful things to be seen and heard among them : they avail themselves of every unguarded or hyperbolical expression, which escapes a tempted believer ; of the enthusiastic representations which some people give of their experience ; and even of the figurative language, which is often employed in speaking of inward conflicts under images taken from external things. Thus they endeavour to excuse their own apostacy, and to expose to contempt the cause which they have deserted. Nothing they can say, however, concerning the disorder or confusion to which religion may sometimes

12*

them that brought up an evil report of the good land (Numb. xiii.), making haste to go back ; to whom Christian spake as follows :—

Whither are you going ?

They said, Back ! back ! and we would have you to do so too, if either life or peace is prized by you.

Why, what's the matter ? said Christian.

Matter ! said they, we were going that way as you are going, and went as far as we durst ; and indeed we were almost past coming back ; for had we gone a little farther we had not been here to bring the news to thee.

But what have you met with ? said Christian.

Men. Why we were almost in the valley of the Shadow of Death (Ps. xliv. 19), but that by good hap we looked before us, and saw the danger before we came to it.

But what have you seen ? said Christian.

Men. Seen ! why the valley itself, which is as dark as pitch ; we also saw there the hob-goblins, statyrs, and dragons of the pit ; we heard also in that valley a continual howling and yelling, as of people under unutterable misery, who there sat bound in affliction and irons ; and over that valley hang the dis-couraging clouds of confusion : death also doth always spread his wings over it (Job iii.

give occasion, can induce the believer to conclude that he has mistaken his way, or that it would be advisable for him to turn back, or deviate into any bye-path : though they will excite him so vigilance and circumspection. As those spies do so much mischief by their misrepresentations, we should be careful to give them as little occasion as we possibly can

5 ; x. 22). In a word, it is every whit dreadful, being utterly without order.

Then said Christian, I perceive not yet, by what you have said, but that this is my way to the desired haven.

Men. Be it thy way ; we will not choose it for ours.

So they parted ; and Christian went on his way, but still with his sword drawn in his hand, for fear lest he should be assaulted.

I saw then in my dream, so far as this valley reached there was on the right hand a very deep ditch ;* that ditch is it into which the blind

* 'Deep ditch'—The fatal presumption, into which men are soothed, through ignorance and various kinds of false doctrine, so that they conclude themselves safe without any warrant from Scripture, is intended by the 'deep ditch,' into which 'the blind lead the blind and perish with them.' This is often done by men who reciprocally criminate and despise each other. 'The dangerous quag,' on the other side of the narrow way represents the opposite extreme—despair of God's mercy ; and the mire of it agrees with that of the slough of Despond. In these opposite ways multitudes continually perish ; some concluding that there is no fear, others that there is no hope. But the danger to which a real believer is exposed, of verging towards one of these extremes in times of inward darkness and disconsolation, is especially implied. They, who have had much opportunity of conversing with professors of the Gospel, have met with many persons who once were zealous and comfortable, but their religious affections have declined ; their duties are comparatively scanty, formal, and joyless ; their walk unsteady, and their hearts dark, cold, and barren ; they call themselves backsliders and complain of desertion, yet they have no hearts to use proper means of revival but love to be soothed in their present condition ; and quiet themselves by presuming that they are true believers, and abusing the doctrine of final perseverance. Many of this cast are wholly deceived; others partially, and will be recovered by severe but salutary rebukes and chastenings. Even the consistent well-instructed Christian, when greatly

hath led the blind in all ages, and hath both there miserably perished. Again, behold, on the left hand there was a very dangerous quag, into which if even a good man falls he finds no bottom for his foot to stand on : into this quag king David once did fall, and had, no

discouraged, may be powerfully tempted to seek peace of mind, by arguing with himself on the safety of his state, or trying to be satisfied without his former spiritual affections and holy consolations : and Satan will find prompters to suggest to him, that this is the case of all experienced believers, and that fervency of love belongs only to young converts, who are strangers to their own hearts. This is the more plausible, because the increase of sound judgment and abiding spiritual affections abates that earnestness (often indiscreet and disproportioned), which sprang from mere selfish principles : and, when religious profession is cheap and common, many retain it, who have scarce any appearance of spirituality, and who infects others with their contagious converse and example. But while the conscientious believer, amidst his deepest discouragements, dreads and shuns this presumption, he is liable to sink into despondency ; and may be led to condemn all his past experience as unreal ; to rank himself among stony-ground hearers ; to conclude that it is useless for him to pray or seek any more ; and to lie down in enfeebling dejection. Again, perceiving this danger, he finds it very difficult, in the present dark state of his soul, to avoid it, without seeming to abuse the free grace of the gospel. This experience must create much distress, perplexity, and confusion ; and make way for many dark and terrifying temptations ; so that, though a man be not harassed with doubts about the truth of the Scriptures, he will be enable to make much use of them for his direction and comfort ; and earnest, instant prayer must be his only resource. Cases sometimes occur, in which, through a concurrence of circumstances, this alarming and perplexing experience continues and increases for some time : but the true Christian will be, as it were, constrained to press forward, and by faith will at length put his enemies to flight. Some have thought, that the general notions of apparitions may be alluded to, as giving the tempter an occasion of increasing the terror of such persons as are in that respect credulous and timorous.

doubt, therein been smothered, had not he that is able plucked him out (Ps. lxix. 14).

The pathway was here also exceeding narrow, and therefore good Christian was the more put to it ; for when he sought in the dark to shun the ditch on the one hand, he was ready to tip over into the mire on the other ; also when he sought to escape the mire, without great carefulness he would be ready to fall into the ditch. Thus he went on, and I heard him here sigh bitterly ; for besides the danger mentioned above, the pathway was here so dark, that oft-times when he lifted up his foot to go forward, he knew not where, nor upon what, he should set it next.

About the midst of the valley, I perceived the mouth of hell to be, and it stood also hard by the way-side ; now, though Christian, what shall I do ? and ever and anon the flame and smoke would come out in such abundance, with sparks and hideous noises (things that cared not for Christian's sword, as did Apollyon before), that he was forced to put up his sword, and betake himself to another weapon, called *all-prayer* ; so he cried, in my hearing ' O Lord, I beseech thee, deliver my soul (Ps. cxvi. 4. Ephes. vi. 18). Thus he went on a great while, yet still the flames would be reaching towards him ; also he heard doleful voices, and rushing to and fro, so that sometimes he thought he should be torn in pieces, or trodden down like mire in the streets. This frightful sight was seen, and these dreadful noises were heard by him for several miles together; and coming to a place where he thought he heard a company of fiends coming forward to meet him, he stopt, and began to muse what he had best to do: sometimes he had half a thought to go back; then again he thought he might be half way through the valley; he remembered also how he had already vanquished many a danger; and that the danger of going back might be much more than for to go forward. So he resolved to go on; yet the fiends seemed to come nearer and nearer: but when they were come even almost at him, he cried out with a most vehement voice, ' I will walk in the strength of the Lord God;' so they gave back and came no farther.

One thing* I would not let slip: I took notice, that now poor Christian was so confound-

* ' One thing'—The case here intended is not uncommon among conscientious persons under urgent temptations. Imaginations are suddenly excited in their minds, with which their previous thoughts had no connexion, even as if words were spoken to them: these often imply nard censures of God, his service or decrees, which they abhor as direct blasphemy; or harass them with other hateful ideas: yet, instead of considering, that such suggestions distress them, in exact proportion as they are opposite to the prevailing disposition of their hearts, and that their dread and hatred of them are evidences of love to God, they consider them as unpardonably criminal, inconsistent with a state of grace, and a mark of final reprobation. Whereas, had such things coincided with the state of their minds, they would have been defiling but not distressing; and instead of rejecting them at once with decided abhorrence, they would have given them entertainment, and employed their minds about them, as much as they dared: ' for the carnal mind is enmity against God,' and can only be deterred from blasphemy, on many occasions, by the dread of his vengeance. Our author had been so much baffled by this stratagem of the tempter, that it would have been extraordin

ed that he did not know his own voice ; and
thus I perceived it : just when he was coming
over against the mouth of the burning pit, one
of the wicked ones got behind him, and stepped up softly to him, and whisperingly suggested many grievous blasphemies to him,
which he verily thought had proceeded from
his own mind. This put Christian more to it
than any thing that he met with before, even
to think that he should now blaspheme him
that he loved so much before ; yet if he could
have helped it he would not have done it : but
he had not the discretion either to stop his
ears, or to know from whence the blasphemies
came.

When Christian had travelled in this disconsolate condition some considerable time,
he thought he heard the voice* of a man, as

ary had he omitted it : for the subsequent discovery he made
of his mistake, and of the way of resisting the devil in this
case, qualified him to give suitable cautions to others. The
intrusion of such thoughts should excite us to greater earnestness in prayer, pious meditations, or adoring praises ; for
this, above all other things, will in the event be found to close
the mind most effectually against them.—The following lines
come in here, as before—

   ' Poor man ! where art thou now ? thy day is night :
   Good man, be not cast down, thou yet art right.
   The way to heav'n lies by the gates of hell :
   Cheer up, hold out, with thee it shall go well.'

* ' The voice'—Nothing more effectually supports the
tempted than to learn, that others, whom they consider as
believers, have been or are in similar circumstances : for the
idea, that such a state of mind as they experience is inconsistent with true faith, gives the enemy his principal advantage
against them. Indeed this often proves the means of their
deliverance ; for in due season that light, affection, and

going before him, saying, 'though I walk through the valley of the shadow of ·death I will fear no ill, for thou art with me' (Ps. xxiii. 4).

Then he was glad, and that for these reasons : First, Because he gathered from thence, that some who feared God were in this valley as well as himself : Secondly, For that he perceived God was with them, though in that dark and dismal state ; and why not, thought he, with me ? though by reason of the impediment that attends this place I cannot perceive it (Job ix. 11). Thirdly, For that he hoped (could he overtake them) to have company by and by. So he went on, and called to him that was before ; but he knew not what to answer, for that he also thought himself to be alone. And by-and-bye the day broke : then said Christian, he hath 'turned the shadow of death into the morning' (Amos v. 8).

Now morning being come he looked back, not out of desire to return, but to see by the light of the day what hazards he had gone through in the dark : so he saw more perfectly the ditch that was on the one hand, and the quag that was on the other ; also how narrow the way was which led betwixt them both also now he saw the hobgoblins, and satyrs,

consolation, for which they have long mourned, thirsted, prayed, and waited, will be vouchsafed them ; and the review of the dangers they had escaped, now more clearly discerned than before, will enlarge their hearts with admiring gratitude to their great and gracious deliverer.

and dragons of the pit, but all afar off, for after break of the day they came not nigh;
yet they were discovered to him, according to that which is written, 'He discovereth deep things out of darkness, and bringeth out to light the shadow of death' (Job
xii. 22).

Now was Christian much affected with his
deliverance from all the dangers of his solitary way; which dangers, though he feared
them more before, yet he saw them more
clearly now, because the light of the day
made them conspicuous to him. And about
this time the sun was rising, and this was another mercy to Christian; for you must note,
that though the first part of the valley of the
Shadow of Death was dangerous, yet this
second part,* which he was yet to go, was,
if possible, far more dangerous: for, from
the place where he now stood even to the
end of the valley, the way was all along set

---

* 'Second part'—Various interpretations are given of this
second part of the valley, which only shew, that the author's
precise idea in it lies more remote from general apprehension
than in other passages: for they all coincide with some of
the difficulties or dangers that are clearly described under
other emblems. I would not indeed be too confident, but, I
apprehend, in general we are taught by it, that believers are
not most in danger when under the deepest distress; that
the snares and devices of the enemy are so many and various,
through the several stages of our pilgrimage, as to baffle all
description or enumeration; and that all the emblems of the
valley of humiliation, and of the shadow of death, could not
fully represent the thousandth part of them. Were it not,
therefore, that the Lord undertakes to guide his people, by
the light of his word and Spirit, they never could possibly escape them all.

full of snares, traps, gins, and nets, here, and so full of pits, pitfalls, deep holes, and shelvings down, there, that had it been dark, as it was when he came the first part of the way, had he had a thousand souls they had in reason been cast away : but as I said, just now the sun was rising. Then said he, ' his candle shineth on my head, and by his light I go through darkness (Job xxix. 3).

In this light therefore he came to the end of the valley. Now I saw in my dream, that at the end of this valley lay blood, bones, ashes, and mangled bodies of men, even of pilgrims that had gone this way formerly : and while I was musing what should be the reason, I spied a little before me a cave, where two giants, Pope* and Pagan, dwelt in old time ; by whose power and tyranny the men, whose bones, blood, ashes, &c., lay there, were cruelly put to death. But by this place Christian went without much danger, whereat I somewhat wondered : but I have learnt since, that Pagan has been dead many a day ; and, as for the other, though he be yet alive, he is by reason of age, and

* ' Pope'—The inhabitants of Britain are not thought to be in any immediate danger, either from Pope or Pagan Yet something very like the philosophical part of paganism seems to be rising from the dead, while popery grows more infirm than ever : and as, even by the confession of the late king of Prussia, who was a steady friend to the philosophical infidels, they ' are by no means favourable to general toleration,' it is not improbable but pagan persecution may also in due time revive. Our author, however, has described no other persecution than what Protestants in his time carried on against one another with very great alacrity.

also of the many shrewd brushes that he met
with in his younger days, grown so crazy and
stiff in his joints, that he now can do little
more than sit in his cave's mouth, grinning at
pilgrims as they go by, and biting his nails
because he cannot come at them.

So I saw that Christian went on his way;
yet, at the sight of the old man, that sat in
the mouth of the cave, he could not tell what
to think; especially because he spake to
him, though he could not go after him, saying, ' You will never mend till more of you
be burned.'   But he held his peace, and set
a good face on it, and so went by and catched no hurt.   Then sang Christian,

> O world of wonders! (I can say no less)
> That I should be preserv'd in that distress
> That I have met with here! O blessed be
> That hand that from it hath delivered me!
> Dangers in darkness, devils, hell, and sin,
> Did compass me while I this vale was in;
> Yea, snares, and pits, and traps, and nets did lie
> My path about, that worthless silly I
> Might have been catch'd, entangled, and cast down:
> But since I live let Jesus wear the crown.

Now as Christian went on his way he came
to a little ascent,* which was up-cast on purpose that pilgrims might see before them. Up

---

* ' Ascent'—This may represent those moments of
couragement, in which tempted believers rise superior t
their difficulties; and are animated to desire the company
of their brethren, whom dejection under humiliating experiences disposes them to shun. The conduct of Christian inti-
mates, that believers are sometimes ready to hinder one another, by making their own attainments and progress a
standard for their brethren; but the lively exercise of faith

there, therefore, Christian went ; and looking
forward he saw Faithful before him upon his
iourney. Then said Christian aloud, 'Ho
ho ! so ho ! stay, and I will be your companion.' At that Faithful looked behind him, to
whom Christian cried, ' Stay, stay, till I come
to you ;' but Faithful answered, ' No, I am
upon my life, and the avenger of blood is behind me.'

At this Christian was somewhat moved, and
putting to all his strength he quickly got up
with Faithful, and did also overrun him ; so
the last was first. Then did Christian vain-
gloriously smile, because he had gotten the
start of his brother : but not taking good
heed to his feet he suddenly stumbled and fell,
and could not rise again until Faithful came
up to help him.

Then I saw in my dream they went very
lovingly on together, and had sweet discourse
of all things that had happened to them in
their pilgrimage ; and thus Christian began :--

My honoured and well-beloved brother
Faithful,* I am glad that I have overtaken

renders men intent on pressing forward, and more apt to
fear the society of such as would influence them to loiter
than to stop for them. This tends to excite an useful emula-
tion ; but while it promotes diligence, it often gives occasion to those risings of vain glory and self-preference, which
are the forerunners of some humiliating fall : thus believers
often are left to feel their need of help from the very persons
whom they have foolishly undervalued. Such experiences,
however, give occasion to those mutual good offices, which
unite them more closely in the nearest ties of tender affection.

* ' Faithful'—This episode, so to speak, with others of the
same kind, gives our author a happy advantage of vary-

you ; and that God has so tempered our spirits that we can walk as companions in this so pleasant a path.

Faith. I had thought, dear friend, to have had your company quite from our town, but you did get the start of me ; wherefore I was forced to come thus much of the way alone

Chr. How long did you stay in the city of Destruction, before you set out after me on your pilgrimage ?

Faith. Till I could stay no longer ; for there was great talk presently after you were gone out, that our city would in a short time with fire from heaven be burned down to the ground.

Chr. What ! did your neighbours talk so ?

Faith. Yes, it was for a while in every body's mouth.

Chr. What ! and did no more of them but you come out to escape the danger ?

Faith. Though there was, as I said, a great

ing the characters and experiences of Christians, as found in real life ; and of thus avoiding the common fault of making one man a standard for others, in the circumstances of his religious progress. It often happens, that they who have been acquainted before their conversion, and hear little of each other for some time after, find at length that they were led to attend to religion about the same period, without having opportunity or courage to confer together about it. The decided separation of a sinner from his old companions, and his avowed dread of the wrath to come, frequently excites alarms and serious thoughts in the minds of others, which they are not able wholly to shake off. In many indeed this is a mere floating, transient notion, insufficient to overcome the propensities of the carnal mind ; but when it arises from a real belief of God's testimony it will at length produce a happy change.

13*

talk there-about, yet I do not think they did firmly believe it. For in the heat of the discourse, I heard some of them deridingly speak of you and your desperate journey, for so they called this your pilgrimage. But I did believe, and do still, that the end of our city will be with fire and brimstone from above ; and therefore I have made my escape.

Chr. Did you hear no talk of neighbour Pliable.*

Faith. Yes, Christian, I heard that he followed you till he come at the slough of Despond ; where, as some said, he fell in ; but he would not be known to have so done ; but I am sure he was soundly bedaubed with that kind of dirt.

Chr. And what said the neighbours to him ?

Faith. He has since his going back been had greatly in derision, and that among all sorts of people ; some do mock and despise him, and scarcely will any set him on work. He is now seven times worse than if he had never gone out of the city.

Chr. But why should they be so against him, since they also despised the way that he forsook ?

* ' Pliable'—Apostates are often ashamed to own they have had convictions : their careless companions assume a kind of superiority over them ; they do not think them hearty in the cause of ungodliness, and they despise their cowardice and versatility : on the other hand such persons feel that they want an apology, and have recourse to contemptible lies and slanders, with abject servility ; while they shun religious people, as afraid of their arguments, warnings, and expostulations.

Faith. O they say, 'Hang him; he is a turncoat! he was not true to his profession.' I think God has stirred up even his enemies to hiss at him, and make him a proverb, because he hath forsaken the way (Jer. xxix. 18, 19).

Chr. Had you no talk with him, before you came out?

Faith. I met him once in the streets, but he leered away on the other side, as one ashamed of what he had done; so I spake not to him.

Chr. Well, at my first setting out I had hopes of that man; but now I fear he will perish in the overthrow of the city: for 'it hath happened to him according to the true proverb, the dog is turned to his vomit again; and the sow that was washed, to her wallowing in her mire' (2 Pet. ii. 22).

Faith. They are my fears of him too: but who can hinder that which will be?

Well, neighbour Faithful, said Christian, let us leave him, and talk of things that more immediately concern ourselves. Tell me now what you have met with in the way as you came; for I know you have met with some things, or else it may be writ for a wonder.

Faith. I escaped* the slough that I perceived you fell into, and got up to the gate without that danger: only I met with one,

---

* 'Escaped'—Some men are preserved from desponding fears, and the suggestions of worldly wisdom, by receiving more distinct views of the general truths of the Gospel; and

whose name was Wanton, that had like to have done me a mischief.

Chr. It was well you escaped her net : Joseph was hard put to it by her, and he escaped her as you did ; but it had like to have cost him his life (Gen. xxxix. 11—13.) But what did she do to you ?

Faith. You cannot think, but that you know something, what a flattering tongue she had ; she lay at me hard to turn aside with her, promising me all manner of content.

Chr. Nay, she did not promise you the content of a good conscience.

Faith. You know that I mean all carnal and fleshly content.

Chr. Thank God you have escaped her : ' the abhorred of the Lord shall fall into her ditch (Prov. xxii. 14).

Faith. Nay, I know not whether I did wholly escape her or no.

Chr. Why, I trow you did not consent to her desires.

Faith. No, not to defile myself, for I remembered an old writing that I had seen, which

thus they proceed with less hesitation and interruption in applying to Christ for salvation : yet, perhaps, their temperature, turn of mind, habits of life, and peculiar situation, render them more accessible to temptations of another kind ; and they may be more in danger from the fascinations of fleshly lusts. Thus in different ways the Lord makes his people sensible of their depravity, weakness, and exposed situation ; while he so moderates the temptation, or interposes for their deliverance, that they are preserved, and taught to ascribe all the glory to his name.

said, 'her steps take hold on hell' (Prov. v. 5; Job, xxxi. 1). So I shut mine eyes because I would not be bewitched with her looks: then she railed on me, and I went my way.

Chr. Did you meet with no other assault as you came?

Faith. When I came to the foot of the hill called Difficulty,* I met with a very aged man, who asked me what I was, and whither bound? I told him that I was a pilgrim going to the Celestial City. Then said the old man, Thou lookest like an honest fellow; wilt thou be content to dwell with me, for the wages that I shall give thee? Then I asked him his name, and where he dwelt? He said his name was Adam the first, and that he dwelt in the town of Deceit (Ephes. iv. 22). I asked him then what was his work? and what the wages that he would give? He told

---

* 'Difficulty'—Those Christians, who by strong faith or assured hope, endure hardships more cheerfully than their brethren, are often exposed to greater danger from the allurements of outward objects, exciting the remaining propensities of corrupt nature. Deep humiliation and great anxiety about the event, in many instances, tend to repress the lusts of the heart, by supplying a continual succession of other thoughts and cares; while constant encouragement, readily attained, too often leaves a man to experience them more forcibly. Nay, the same persons, who under pressing solicitude seem to be entirely delivered from some peculiar corruptions, find them revive and become very troublesome, when they have obtained more confidence about their salvation. The old Adam, the corrupt nature, proves a constant snare to many believers, by its hankering after the pleasures, riches, honours, and pride of the world; nor can the victory be secured without great difficulty and trouble, and strong faith and fervent prayer

I farther asked what house he kept, and what other servants he had ? so he told me, that his house was maintained with all the dainties in the world ; and that his servants were those of his own begetting. Then I asked how many children he had ? He said, that he had but three daughters, 'the Lust of the Flesh, the Lust of the eyes, and the Pride of Life' (1 John ii. 16) ; and that I should marry them if I would. Then I asked how long time he would have me to live with him ? and he told me, as long as he lived himself.

Chr. Well, and what conclusion came the old man and you to at last ?

Faith. Why, at first I found myself somewhat inclinable to go with the man, for I thought he spake very fair ; but looking in his forehead as I talked with him, I saw there written, ' Put off the old man with his deeds '

Chr. And how then ?

Faith. Then it came burning hot into my mind, whatever he said, and however he flattered, when he got me home to his house, he would sell me for a slave. So I bid him forbear to talk, for I would not come near to the door of his house. Then he reviled me, and told me, that he would send such a one after me that should make my way bitter to my soul. So I turned to go away from him ; but just as I turned myself to go thence, I felt him take hold of my flesh, and he gave me such a deadly twitch back, that I thought he had pulled part of me after himself : this

made me cry, O wretched man ! (Rom. vii
24.)   So I went on my way up the hill.

Now, when I had got about half way up, I
looked behind me and saw one coming after
me, swift as the wind ; so he overtook me just
about the place where the settle stands.

Just there, said Christian, did I set down
to rest me ; but being overcome with sleep I
there lost this roll out of my bosom.

Faith   But, good brother, hear me out : so
soon as the man overtook me, he was but a
word and a blow, for down he knocked me,
and laid me for dead.   But when I was a little come to myself again, I asked him wherefore he served me so ? He said, because of
my secret inclining to Adam the first : and
with that he struck me another deadly blow
on the breast, and beat me down backward :
so I lay at his foot as dead as before.   When
I came to myself again I cried him mercy ;
but he said, I know not how to shew mercy ;
and with that knocked me down again.   He
had doubtless made an end of me, but that
one came by and bid him forbear.

Chr. Who was that that bid him forbear ?

Faith. I did not know him at first, but as
he went by I perceived the holes in his hands
and in his side : then I concluded that he was
our Lord.   So I went up the hill.

Chr. That man that overtook you was Moses.*   He spareth none, neither knoweth he

* ' Moses'—The doctrine of Moses did not essentially differ from that of Christ : but the giving of the law, that ministration of condemnation to all sinners, formed so promi-

how to shew mercy to those that transgress his law.

Faith. I know it very well ; it was not the first time that he has met with me. It was he that came to me when I dwelt securely at home, and that told me he would burn my house over my head if I staid there.

Chr. But did you not see the house that stood there on the top of the hill on the side of which Moses met you ?

Faith. Yes, and the lions too, before I came at it :—but, for the lions, I think they were asleep, for it was about noon ; and, because I had so much of the day before me, I passed* by the porter and came down the hill.

nent a part of his dispensation, in which the Gospel was exhibited under types and shadows, that ' the law' is said to have been ' given by Moses,' while ' grace and truth came by Jesus Christ;' especially, as the shadows were of no farther use when the substance was come. Even such hankerings after worldly objects, as are effectually opposed and repressed, being contrary to the spirituality of the precept, ' Thou shalt not covet, often greatly discourage the new convert ; who does not duly recollect, that the Gospel brings relief to those who feel themselves justly condemned by the law. Yet these terrors produce deeper humiliation, and greater simplicity of dependance on the mercy of God in Christ Jesus, as ' the end of the law for righteousness to every one that believeth.' Many for a time escape discouragement, because they are but superficially acquainted with their own hearts , yet it is proper they should be farther instructed by such experiences as are here described, in order to their greater stability, tenderness of conscience, and compassion for their brethren, in the subsequent part of their pilgrimage.

* ' Passed'—This circumstance seems to imply, that, in our author's judgment, even eminent believers sometimes decline entering into communion with their brethren according to his views of it ; and that very lively affections and strong consolations may probably have rendered them less attentive to these externals. Indeed he deemed this a disad-

Chr. He told me, indeed, that he saw you go by; but I wish you had called at the house, for they would have shewed you so many rarities, that you would scarce have forgot them to the day of your death. But pray tell me, did you meet nobody in the valley of Humility?

Faith. Yes, I met with* one Discontent, who would willingly have persuaded me to go back again with him: his reason was, for that the valley was altogether without honour He told me moreover, that there to go was the way to disoblige all my friends, as Pride, Arrogancy, Self-conceit, Worldly-glory, with

vantage and a mistake (which is perhaps also intimated by Faithful's not calling at the house of the Interpreter), but not a sufficient reason why other Christians should not cordially unite with them. This is a beautiful example of that candour, in respect of those things about which pious persons differ, that consists with decided firmness in the great essentials of faith and holiness.

* 'I met with'—While some believers are most tried with inward fears and conflicts, others are more tempted to repine at the outward degradation, reproach, ridicule, and loss to which religion exposes them. A man perhaps, at first, may flatter himself with the hope of avoiding the peculiarities and eccentricities, which have brought enmity or contempt on some professors of the Gospel; and of ensuring respect and affection, by caution, uprightness, and benevolence; but farther experience and knowledge constrain him to adopt and avow sentiments, and associate with persons, that the world despises; and, seeing himself invincibly impelled by his conscience, to a line of conduct which ensures the reproach of enthusiasm and folly, the loss of friends, and manifold mortifications, he is powerfully assaulted by discontent; and tempted to repine, that the way to heaven lies through such humiliation and worldly disappointments; till the considerations, adduced in Faithful's answer, enable him at length to overcome this assailant, and to ' seek the honour that cometh from God only.

others, who he knew, as he said would be very much offended if I made such a fool of myself as to wade through this valley.

Chr. Well, and how did you answer him?

Faith. I told him, that although all these that he named might claim kindred of me, and that rightly (for indeed they were my relations according to the flesh), yet since I became a pilgrim they have disowned me, and I also have rejected them, and therefore they are to me now no more than if they had never been of my lineage. I told him, moreover, that as to this valley he had quite misrepresented the thing; for 'before honour is humility, and a haughty spirit before a fall.' Therefore, said I, I had rather go through this valley to the honour that was so accounted by the wisest, than choose that which he esteemed most worthy our affections.

Chr. Met you with nothing else in that valley?

Faith. Yes, I met* with Shame; but of

---

* 'Yes, I met'—Persons of a peculiar turn of mind, when enabled to overcome temptations to discontent about worldly degradation, are exceedingly prone to be influenced by a false shame, and to profess religion in a timid and cautious manner; to be afraid of speaking all their mind in some places and companies, even when the most favourable opportunity occurs; to shun in part the society of those whom they most love and esteem, lest they should be involved in the contempt which is cast on them; to be reserved and inconstant in attending on the ordinances of God, entering a protest against vice and irreligion, bearing testimony to the truth, and in attempting to promote the Gospel: being apprehensive lest these things should deduct from their reputation for good sense, prudence, learning, or liberality of sentiment. Men, who are least exposed to those conflicts in

all the men that I met with in my pilgrimage,
he, I think, bears the wrong name. The other
would be said nay, after a little argumenta-
tion and somewhat else ; but that bold-faced
Shame would never have done.

Chr. Why, what did he say to you ?

Faith. What ! why he objected against religion itself ; he said, it was a pitiful, low,
sneaking business for a man to mind religion ; he said, that a tender conscience was
an unmanly thing ; and that for a man to

which Christian was engaged, are often most baffled by this
enemy ; nor can others make proper allowances for them in
this case, any more than they can for such as experience
those dark temptations, of which they have no conception.
Constitution, habits, connexions, extensive acquaintance
with mankind, and an excess of sensibility, united to that
pride which is common to man, continually suggest objections to every thing that the world despises, which they can
hardly answer to themselves, and excite such alarms as they
cannot get over ; while a delicate sense of propriety, and the
specious name of prudence, supply them with a kind of half
excuse for their timidity. The excessive trouble which this
criminal and unreasonable shame occasions some persons
contrary to their judgment, convictions, arguments, endeavours, and prayers, gave our author the idea, that ' this enemy bears a wrong name.' Many a suggestion made to the
mind in this respect from time to time is so natural, and has
so strong a party within (especially in those who are more
desirous of honour than of wealth or pleasure), that men
can scarcely help feeling for the moment as if there were
truth in it, though they know, upon reflection, that it is most
irrational. Nay, these feelings insensibly warp men's conduct ; though they are continually self-condemned on the retrospect. There are some who hardly ever get the better
of this false shame ; and it often brings their sincerity into
doubt, both with themselves and others : but flourishing
Christians at length in good measure rise superior to it, by
such considerations as are here adduced, and by earnest persevering prayer.

watch over his words and ways, so as to tie up himself from that hectoring liberty that the brave spirits of the times accustom themselves unto, would make him the ridicule of the times. He objected also, that but few mighty, rich, or wise, were ever of my opinion ; nor any of them neither, before they were persuaded to be fools, and to be of a voluntary fondness to venture the loss of all for nobody knows what (John vii. 48 ; 1 Cor. i. 26 ; iii. 18 ; Phil. iii. 7---9). He moreover objected the base and low estate and condition of those that were chiefly the pilgrims of the times in which they lived ; also their ignorance, and want of understanding in all natural science. Yea, he did hold me to it at that rate also about a great many more things than here I relate ; as, that it was a shame to sit whining and mourning under a sermon, and a shame to come sighing and groaning home ; that it was a shame to ask my neighbour forgiveness for petty faults, or to make restitution where I have taken from any. He said also, that religion made a man grow strange to the great, because of a few vices, which are called by finer names ; and made him own and respect the base, because of the same religious fraternity : and is not this, said he, a shame ?

Chr. And what did you say to him ?

Faith. Say ! I could not tell what to say at first. Yea, he put me so to it that my blood came up in my face : even this Shame fetched it up, and had almost beat me quite off.

But at last I began to consider, that 'that which is highly esteemed among men is had in abomination with God' (Luke xvi. 15). And I thought again, this Shame tells me what men are, but it tells me nothing what God or the word of God is. And I thought moreover that at the day of doom we shall not be doomed to death or fire, according to the hectoring spirits of the world, but according to the wisdom and law of the Highest. Therefore, thought I, what God says is best indeed, is best, though all the men in the world are against it: seeing then that God prefers his religion; seeing God prefers a tender conscience; seeing they that make themselves fools for the kingdom of heaven are wisest; and that the poor man that loveth Christ is richer than the greatest man in the world that hates him——Shame, depart, thou art an enemy to my salvation; shall I entertain thee against my sovereign Lord? how then shall I look him in the face at his coming? Should I now be ashamed of his ways and servants, how can I expect the blessing? (Mark viii. 38.) But indeed this Shame was a bold villain; I could scarce shake him out of my company; yea, he would be haunting of me, and continually whispering me in the ear, with some one or other of the infirmities that attend religion: but at last I told him, it was but in vain to attempt farther in this business; for those things that he disdained in those did I see most glory: and so at last I got past this importunate one. And when I had shaken him off then I began to sing:

14*

The trials that those men do meet withal,
That are obedient to the heavenly call,
Are manifold, and suited to the flesh,
And come, and come, and come again afresh ;
That now, or some times else, we by them may
Be taken, overcome, and cast away.
O let the pilgrims, let the pilgrims, then,
Be vigilant, and quit themselves like men.

Chr. I am glad, my brother, that thou didst withstand this villain so bravely ; for of all, as thou sayest, I think he has the wrong name : for he is so bold as to follow us in the streets, and to attempt to put us to shame before all men ; that is, to make us ashamed of that which is good. But if he was not himself audacious, he would never attempt to do as he does : but let us still resist him, for, notwithstanding all his bravadoes, he promoteth the fool, and none else. ' The wise shall inherit glory,' said Solomon ; ' but shame shall be the promotion of fools' (Prov. iii. 35).

Faith. I think we must cry to him, for help against Shame, that would have us be valiant for truth upon the earth.

Chr. You say true : but did you meet nobody else in that valley ?

Faith. No, not I,* for I had sunshine all the

* ' No, not I'—Christian in great measure escaped the peculiar temptations that assaulted Faithful ; yet he sympathized with him : nor did the latter deem the gloomy experiences of his brother visionary or imaginative, though he had been exempted from such trials. One man, from a complication of causes, is exposed to temptations of which another is ignorant ; in this case he needs much sympathy, which he seldom meets with ; while they, who are severe on him, are liable to be harassed and baffled in another way, which, for want of coincidence in habit, temperature, and situation, he

rest of the way through that, and also through the valley of the Shadow of Death.

Chr. It was well for you ; I am sure it fared far otherwise with me : I had for a long season, as soon as almost I entered into that valley, a dreadful combat with that foul fiend Apollyon ; yet, I thought verily he would have killed me, especially when he got me down and chrushed me under him as if he would have chrushed me to pieces ; for as he threw me my sword flew out of my hand ; nay, he told me he was sure of me ; but I cried to God, and he heard me, and delivered me out of all my troubles. Then I entered into the valley of the Shadow of Death, and had no light for almost half the way through it. I thought I should have been killed there over and over ; but at last day brake, and the sun rose, and I went through that which was behind with far more ease and quiet.

Moreover I saw in my dream, that as they went on, Faithful, as he chanced to look on one side, saw a man, whose name* is Talka-

is equally prone to disregard. Thus believers are often led reciprocally to censure, suspect, despise, or dislike each other, on those very grounds which should render them useful and encouraging counsellors and companions.

* ' Whose name'—The character next introduced, under a most expressive name, is an admirable portrait, drawn by a masterly hand from some striking original, but exactly resembling numbers in every age and place, where the truths of the Gospel are generally known. Talkative is not thus called merely on account of his loquacity, but from the peculiarity of his religious profession, which gave scope to his natural propensity, by furnishing him with a copious subject, and enabling him to display his talents, or seek credit in the church, without the trouble and expense of experimental and practical

tive, walking at a distance beside them; for in this place there was room enough for them all to walk. He was a tall man, and something more comely at a distance then at hand. To this man Faithful addressed himself in this manner:

Friend, whither away? are you going to the heavenly country?

Talk. I am going to the same place.

Faith. That is well; then I hope we may have your good company?

Talk. With a very good will will I be your companion.

Faith. Come on then, and let us go together, and let us spend our time in discoursing of things that are profitable.

Talk. To talk of things that are good to me is very acceptable, with you or with any other; and I am glad that I have met with those that incline to so good a work; for, to speak the truth, there are but few that care thus to spend their time as they are in their travels; but choose much rather to be speak

godliness. Such vain talkers especially appear when religious profession is safe, cheap, and reputable; numbers keeping one another in countenance, preventing the odium of singularity, and even giving a prospect of secular advantage by connexion with religious societies. They may, therefore, be expected in our age and nation, particularly in populous places, where the preaching or profession of any doctrine excites little attention or surprise, but ensures regard and favour from a numerous body who hold the same opinions. Such men appear above others, pushing themselves into notice, and be coming more conspicuous than humble believers; but their profession, specious at a distance, will not endure a near and strict investigation.

ing of things to no profit : and this hath been a trouble to me.

Faith. That is indeed a thing to be lamented : for what thing so worthy of the use of the tongue and mouth of men on earth, as are the things of the God of heaven ?

Talk. I like you wonderful well, for your sayings are full of conviction : and, I will add, what things is so pleasant, and what so profitable, as to talk of the things of God ?

What things so pleasant ? that is, if a man hath any delight in things that are wonderful . for instance, if a man doth delight to talk of the history or the mystery of things ; or if a man doth love to talk of miracles, wonders, or signs—where shall he find things recorded so delightful, and so sweetly penned, as in the Holy Scripture ?

Faith. That's true : but to be profited by such things in our talk should be our chief design.

Talk. That is it that I said : for to talk of such things is most profitable ; for by so doing a man may get knowledge of many things ; as, of the vanity of earthly things, and the benefit of things above. Thus in general : but more particularly, by this a man may learn the necessity of the new birth ; the insufficiency of our works ; the need of Christ's righteousness, &c. Besides, by this a man may learn what it is to repent, to believe, to pray, to suffer, or the like : by this also a man may learn what are the great promises and consolations of the Gospel, to his own comfort.

Farther, by this a man may learn to refute false opinions, to vindicate the truth, and also to instruct the ignorant.

Faith. All this is true, and glad am I to hear these things from you.

Talk. Alas ! the want of this is the cause that so few understand the need of faith, and the necessity of a work of grace in their soul, in order to eternal life ; but ignorantly live in the works of the law, by the which a man can by no means obtain the kingdom of heaven.

Faith. But, by* your leave, heavenly knowl-

* 'But by'—Zealous and lively Christians, who are not well established in judgment and experience, are often greatly taken with the discourse of persons who speak with great fluency and speciousness on various subjects, with a semblance of truth and piety ; yet they sometimes feel, as it were, a defect in their harangues, which makes them hesitate, though they are easily satisfied with plausible explanations. Talkative's discourse is copied with surprising exactness from that of numbers, who learn doctrinally to discuss experimental subjects, of which they never felt the energy and efficacy in their own souls. Men of this stamp can take up any point in religion with great ease, and speak on it in a pompous ostentatious manner ; but the humble believer forgets himself, while from his inmost heart he expatiates on topics which he longs to recommend to those whom he addresses. Humility and charity, however, dispose the possessors to make the best of others, and to distrust themselves : so that, unless these graces be connected with proportionable depth of judgment, and acuteness of discernment, they render them open to deception, and liable to be deceived by vain-glorious talkers. It would be conceited and uncandid, they think, to suspect a man, who says so many good things, with great confidence and zeal ; their dissatisfacton with the conversation or sermon they suppose was their own fault ; if they disagreed with the speaker, probably they were in an error ; if a doubt arose in their minds about his spirit or motives, it might be imputed to their own pride and envy. Thus men

edge of these is the gift of God ; no man attaineth to them by human industry, or only by the talk of them.

Talk. All that I know very well ; for a man can receive nothing except it be given him from heaven ; all is of grace, not of works : I could give you a hundred scriptures for the confirmation of this.

Well then, said Faithful, what is that one thing that we shall at this time found our discourse upon ?

Talk. What you will : I will talk of things heavenly or things earthly ; things moral or things evangelical ; things sacred or things profane ; things past or things to come ; things foreign or things at home ; things more essential or things circumstantial ; provided that all be done to our profit.

Now did Faithful begin to wonder ; and stepping to Christian (for he walked all this while by himself) he said to him, but softly, What a brave companion have we got ! surely this man will make a very excellent pilgrim.

At this* Christian modestly smiled and said, This man with whom you are so taken, will be-

---

are seduced to sanction what they ought to protest against, and to admire those whom they should avoid ; and that even by means of their most amiable dispositions. What follows is peculiarly calculated to rectify such mistakes, and to expose the consequences of this ill judged candour.

* ' At this'—Those believers, who have made the most extensive and accurate observations on the state of religious profession in their own age and place, and are most acquainted with the internal history of the church in other lands or former periods, may be deemed inferior in charity to their

guile with this tongue of his twenty of them
that knew him not.

Faith. ·Do you know him then ?

Chr. Know him ! yes, better than he knows
himself !

Faith. Pray what is he ?

Chr. His name is Talkative ; he dwelleth
in our town ; I wonder that you should be a
stranger to him, only I consider that our town
is large.

Faith. Whose son is he ? and whereabouts
doth he dwell ?

Chr. He is the son of one Saywell, he
dwelt in Prating-row ; and is known, of all
that are acquainted with him, by the name
of Talkative in Prating-row ; and notwith
standing his fine tongue he is but a sorry fel
low.

Faith. Well, he seems to be a very pretty
man.

Chr. That is, to them that have not a

---

brethren ; because they surpass them in penetration, and clearly
perceive the mischiefs which arise from countenancing loose
professors. They would vie with them in ' doing good to all
men,' ' bearing with the infirmities of the weak,' ' restoring
such as are overtaken in a fault,' or in making allowances
for the tempted ; but they dare not sanction such professors
as talk about religion and disgrace it, as mislead the simple,
stumble the hopeful, prejudice the observing, and give enemies a plausible objection to the truth. Here charity con-
strains us to run the risk of being deemed uncharitable, by
unmasking a hypocrite, and undeceiving the deluded. We
must not indeed speak needlessly against any one, nor testify
more than we know to be true even against a suspected professor ; but we should shew, that vain talkers belong to the
world, though numbers class them among religious people, to
the great discredit of the cause.

thorough acquaintance with him ; for he is best abroad ; near home he is ugly enough . your saying, that he is a pretty man, brings to my mind what I have observed in the work of the painter, whose pictures shew best at a distance, but very near, more unpleasing.

Faith. I am ready to think you do but jest, because you smiled.

Chr. God forbid that I should jest (though I smiled) in this matter, or that I should accuse any falsely. I will give you a farther discovery of him . this man is for any company, and for any talk ; as he talketh now with you, so will he talk when he is on the ale bench ; and the more drink he hath in his crown the more of these things he hath in his mouth : religion hath no place in his heart, or house, or conversation ; and all he hath lieth in his tongue, and his religion is to make a noise therewith.

Faith. Say you so ! then I am in this man greatly deceived.

Chr. Deceived ! you may be sure of it : remember the proverb, ' They say, and do not ;' but ' the kingdom of God is not in word, but in power' (Matt. xxiii. 3 ; 1 Cor. iv. 20). He talketh of prayer, of repentance, of faith, and of the new-birth ; but he knows but only to talk of them. I have been in his family, and have observed him both at home and abroad ; and I know what I say of him is the truth. His house is as empty of religion as the white of an egg is of savour. There is there

neither prayer, nor sign of repentance for sin ;
yea, the brute, in his kind, serves God far
better than he. He is the very stain, reproach, and shame, of religion to all that know
him (Rom. ii. 23, 24) ; it can harldly have a
good word in all that end of the town where
he dwells, through him. Thus say the common people that know him, ' A saint abroad,
and a devil at home.' His poor family finds
it so ; he is such a churl, such a railer at, and
so unreasonable with, his servants, that they
neither know how to do for, or to speak to
him. Men that have any dealings with him
say it is better to deal with a Turk than with
him, for fairer dealings they shall have at his
hands. This Talkative, if it be possible, will
go beyond them, defraud, begile, and over-
reach them. Besides, he brings up his sons
to follow his steps ; and if he finds in any of
them a ' foolish timorousness' (for so he calls
the first appearance of a tender conscience)
he calls them fools and blockheads, and by no
means will employ them in much, or speak to
their commendations before others. For my
part, I am of opinion, that he has by his wicked life caused many to stumble and fall ; and
will be, if God prevents not, the ruin of many
more.

Faith. Well, my brother, I am bound to believe you ; not only because you say you
know him, but also because like a Christian
you make your reports of men. For I cannot think that you speak those things of ill will,
but because it is even so as you say.

Chr. Had I known him no more than you, I might perhaps have thought of him as at the first you did : yea, had he received this report at their hands only that are enemies to religion, I should have thought it had been a slander (a lot that often falls from bad men's mouth upon good men's names and professions) : but all these things yea, and a great many more as bad, of my own knowledge, I can prove him guilty of. Besides, good men are ashamed of him ; they can neither call him brother nor friend ; the very naming of him among them makes them blush if they know him.

Faith. Well, I see that* saying and doing

---

* ' I see that'—Talkative seems to have been introduced on purpose that the author might have a fair opportunity of stating his sentiments concerning the practical nature of religion, to which numbers in his day were too inattentive. This admired allegory has fully established the important distinction, between a dead and a living faith, on which the whole matter depends. We may boldly state every doctrine of grace, with all possible strength and clearness, and every objection must ultimately fall to the ground, all abuses be excluded, provided this distinction be fully and constantly insisted on : for they arise without exception from substituting some false notion of faith in the place of that living, active, and efficacious principle, which the Scriptures so constantly represent as the grand peculiarity of vital godliness. The language used in this passage is precisely the same as is now branded with the opprobrious epithet of *legal*, by numbers who would be thought to admire the Pilgrim ; as any impartial person must perceive, upon an attentive perusal of it : and, indeed, some expressions are used which they, who are accustomed to stand their trial before such as ' make a man an offender for a word,' have learned to avoid. ' The practice part' is more accurately defined to be the unfailing effect of that inward life which is the soul of religion, than the soul itself. True faith justifies indeed, as it forms the sinner's re-

are two things, and hereafter I shall better observe this distinction.

Chr. They are two things indeed, and are as diverse as are the soul and the body; for, as the body without the soul is but a dead carcase, so saying, if it be alone, is but a dead carcase also. The soul of religion is the practice part: 'pure religion and undefiled, before God and the Father, is this: to visit the fatherless and widows in their affliction, and to keep himself unspotted from the world' (James i. 22—27). This Talkative is not aware of; he thinks that hearing and saying will make a good Christian; and thus he deceiveth his own soul. Hearing is but as the sowing of the seed; talking is not sufficient to prove that fruit is indeed in the heart and life; and let us assure ourselves, that, at the day of doom, men shall be judged according to their fruit (Matt. xiii. 23); it will not be said then, 'Did you believe?' but, 'Were you doers, or talkers only?' and accordingly shall they be judged. The end of the world is compared to our harvest; and you know men at harvest regard nothing but fruit. Not that any thing can be accepted that is not of faith; but I speak this to shew you how insignificant the profession of Talkative will be at that day.

Faith. This brings to my mind that of Moses, by which he described the beast that

---

lation to, and union with, Christ; but it always 'works by love,' and influences to obedience: hence the inquiry at the day of judgment will be rather about the inseparable fruits of faith, then its essential properties and nature.

is clean (Lev. xi. ; Deut. xiv.) : he is such an one that parteth the hoof, and cheweth the cud ; not that parteth the hoof only, or that cheweth the cud only. The hare cheweth the cud, but yet is unclean, because he parteth not the hoof. And this truly resembleth Talkative , he cheweth the cud, he seeketh knowledge : he cheweth upon the word ; but he divideth not the hoof, he parteth not with the way of sinners ; but, as the hare, he retaineth the foot of a dog or bear, and therefore he is unclean.

Chr. You have spoken, for aught I know, the true Gospel sense of those texts. And I will add another thing : Paul calleth some men, yea, and those great talkers too, ' sounding brass and tinkling cymbals ;' that is, as he expounds them in another place, ' things without life giving sound' (1 Cor. xiii. 1—3 ; xiv. 7.) ' Things without life ;' that is, without the true faith and grace of the Gospel ; and consequently things that shall never be placed in the kingdom of heaven among those that are the children of life, though their sound, by their talk, be as it were the tongue or voice of an angel.

Faith. Well,* I was not so fond of his com-

* ' Well'—When we speak to loose professors, we should always keep two things in view ; either to get rid of such ensnaring and dishonourable companions, or to use proper means to convince them of their fatal mistake. There is indeed more hope of the most ignorant and careless sinners than of them : yet ' with God all things are possible,' and we should not despair of any, especially as the very same method is suited to both the ends proposed ; which the subsequent discourse most clearly evinces. Very plain and particular declarations of those things, by which true believers are distin-

pany at first, but am sick of it now. What shall we do to be rid of him?

Chr. Take my advice and do as I bid you, and you shall find that he will soon be sick of your company too, except God shall touch his heart and turn it.

Faith. What would you have me to do?

Chr. Why, go to him, and enter into some serious discourse about the power of religion; and ask him plainly, when he has approved of it (for that he will), whether this thing be set up in his heart, house, or conversation?

Then Faithful stepped forward again, and said to Talkative, Come, what cheer! how is it now?

Talk. Thank you, well; I thought we should have had a great deal of talk by this time.

guished from the most specious hypocrites (whether in conversation or preaching), are best calculated to undeceive and alarm false professors; and form the most commodious fan, by which the irreclaimable may be winnowed from the society of godly persons. This is of great importance; for they are Achans in the camp of Israel, spots and blemishes to every company that countenances them. Doctrinal or even practical discussions, if confined to general terms, will not startle them; they will mimic the language of experience, declaim against the wickedness of the world and the blindness of pharisees, and strenuously oppose the opinions held by some rival sect or party; they will endure the most awful declarations of the wrath of God against the wicked, supposing themselves to be unconcerned in them; nay, they will admit that they are backsliders, or inconsistent believers. But when the conversation or sermon compels them to complain, ' in so saying thou condemnest us also,' they will bear no longer, but seek refuge under more comfortable preachers, or in more candid company; and represent their faithful monitors as censorious, peevish, and melancholy men.

Faith. Well, if you will, we will fall to it now; and since you left it with me to state the question, let it be this : How doth the saving grace of God discover itself when it is in the heart of man ?

Talk. I perceive, then, that our talk must be about the power of things : well, it is a very good question, and I shall be willing to answer you; and take my answer in brief thus : first, where the grace of God is in the heart it causeth there a great outcry against sin. Secondly—

Faith. Nay, hold, let us consider of one at once : I think you should rather say, It shews itself by inclining the soul to abhor its sin.

Talk. Why, what difference is there between crying out against, and abhorring of, sin.

Faith. Oh ! a great deal. A man may cry out against sin of policy, but he cannot abhor it but by virtue of a godly antipathy against it : I have heard many cry out against sin in the pulpit, who yet can abide it well enough in the heart, house, and conversation. Joseph's mistress cried with a loud voice, as if she had been very holy; but she would willingly, notwithstanding that, have committed uncleanness with him (Gen. xxxix. 11—15). Some cry out against sin, even as the mother cries out against her child in her lap, when she calls it slut and naughty girl, and then falls to hugging and kissing it.

Talk. You lie at the catch, I perceive.

Faith. No, not I, I am only for setting things right. But what is the second thing where by you will prove a discovery of a work of grace in the heart ?

Talk. Great knowledge of Gospel mysteries

Faith. This sign should have been first : but, first or last, it is also false ; for knowledge, great knowledge, may be obtained in the mysteries of the Gospel, and yet no work of grace in the soul (1 Cor. xiii). Yea, if a man have all knowledge he may yet be nothing, and so consequently be no child of God. When Christ said, ' Do ye know all these things ?' and the disciples had answered, Yes ; he added, ' Blessed are ye, if ye do them.' He doth not lay the blessing in the knowing of them, but in the doing of them. For there is a knowledge that is not attended with doing : ' he that knoweth his master's will, and doeth it not.' A man may know like an angel, and yet be no Christian ; therefore your sign of it is not true. Indeed, to know is a thing that pleaseth talkers and boasters ; but to do is that which pleaseth God. Not that the heart can be good without knowledge ; for without that the heart is nought. There is* therefore knowledge

* ' There is'—Spiritual knowledge, obtained by an implicit belief of God's sure testimony under the teaching of the Holy Spirit, producing a hearty love of revealed truth, is always humbling, sanctifying, and transforming : but speculative knowledge is a mere notion of divine things, as distant from a man's own concern in them, or any due apprehension of their excellency and importance, which puffs up the heart with proud self-preference, feeds carnal and malignant passions, and leaves the possessor under the power of sin and Satan.

and knowledge ; knowledge that resteth in the bare speculation of things, and knowledge that is accompanied with the grace of faith and love, which puts a man upon doing even the will of God from the heart : the first of these will serve the talker ; but without the other the true Christian is not content · ' Give me understanding and I shall keep thy law ; yea, I shall observe it with my whole heart' (Ps. cxix. 34).

Talk. You lie at the catch again ; this is not for edification.

Faith. Well, if you please, propound another sign how this work of grace discovereth itself where it is.

Talk. Not I, for I see we shall not agree.

Faith. Well, if you will not, will you give me leave to do it ?

Talk. You may use your liberty.

Faith. A work of grace in the soul discovereth itself, either to him that hath it, or to standers by.

To him that hath it, thus : it gives him conviction of sin, especially of the defilement of his nature, and the sin of* unbelief, for

* ' The sin of '—Divine teaching convinces a man that he is justly condemned for his transgressions of the law, and cannot be saved unless he obtains an interest in the merits of Christ by faith ; and that unbelief, or neglect of this great salvation, springs from pride, aversion to the character, authority, and law of God, and love to sin and the world ; that it implies the guilt of treating the truth of God as a lie, despising his wisdom and mercy, demanding happiness as a debt from his justice, and defying his ' wrath revealed from heaven against all ungodliness and unrighteousness of men.' This conviction makes way for his discovering the suitable

the sake of which he is sure to be damned, if he findeth not mercy at God's hand by faith in Jesus Christ (Mark xvi. 16; John xvi. 8, 9; Rom. vii. 24). This sight and sense of things worketh in him sorrow and shame for sin; he findeth, moreover, revealed in him the Saviour of the world, and the absolute necessity of closing with him for life; at the which he findeth hungerings and thirstings after him; to which hungerings, &c., the promise is made (Ps. xxxviii. 18; Jer. xxxi. 19; Matt. v. 6; Acts iv. 12; Gal. i. 15, 16; Rev. xxi. 6). Now according to the strength or weakness of his faith in his Saviour, so is his joy and peace, so is his love to holiness, so are his desires to know him more, and also to serve him in this world. But though, I say, it discovereth itself thus unto him, yet it is but seldom that he is able to conclude

ness to his case of a free salvation by faith: he perceives the glory of the Divine perfections harmoniously displayed in the person and redemption of Christ; and his heart is inwardly drawn to close with the invitations of the Gospel, and to desire above all things the fulfilment of its exceedingly great and precious promises to his soul. The expression ' revealed in him,' is taken from St. Paul's account of his conversion (Gal. i. 16); but as that was extraordinary, without the intervention of means or instruments, perhaps it is not accurately applied to the ordinary experience of believers. Our author, however, evidently meant no more, than the illumination of the Holy Spirit enabling a man to understand, believe, admire, and love the truths of the Bible respecting Christ; and not any new revelation, declaring his interest in the Saviour, by a whisper, vision, or any such thing. These enthusiastic expectations and experiences have deceived many and stumbled more; and have done greater harm to the cause of evangelical religion than can be conceived or expressed.

that this is a work of grace ; because his corruptions now, and his abused reason, make his mind to misjudge in this matter : therefore in him that hath this work there is required a very sound judgment before he can with steadiness conclude that this is a work of grace.

To others, it is thus discovered : 1. By an experimental confession of his faith in Christ. 2. By a life answerable to that confession, to wit, a life of holiness ; heart-holiness, family-holiness (if he hath a family), and by conversation-holiness in the world ; which in the general teacheth him inwardly to abhor his sin, and himself for that, in secret ; to suppress it in his family, and to promote holiness in the world ; not by talk only, as a hypocrite or talkative person may do, but by a practical subjection in faith and love to the power of the word (Ps. l. 23 ; Ezek. xx 43 ; Matt. v. 8 ; John xiv. 15 ; Rom. x. 9, 10 ; Phil. iii. 17—20). And now, sir, as to this brief description of the work of grace, and also the discovery of it, if you have aught to object, object ; if not, then give me leave to propound to you a second question.

Talk. Nay, my part is not now to object but to hear : let me therefore have your second question.

Faith. It is* this : Do you experience this first part of the description of it ? and doth

---

* ' It is'—It is not enough to state practical and experimental subjects in the plainest and most distinguishing manner : we ought also to apply them to men's consciences, by

your life and conversation testify the same ?
or standeth your religion in word or tongue
and not in deed and truth ? Pray, if you incline to answer me in this, say no more than
you know the God above will say Amen to ;
and also nothing but what your conscience
can justify you in : ' for not he that commendeth himself is approved, but whom the Lord
commendeth.' Besides, to say I am thus and
thus, when my conversation and all my neigh
bours tell me I lie, is great wickedness.

Then Talkative at first began to blush ,
but, recovering himself, thus he replied : You
come now to experience, to conscience, and
God ; and to appeal to him for justification
of what is spoken : This kind of discourse I
did not expect ; nor am I disposed to give
an answer to such questions ; because I count
not myself bound thereto, unless you take
upon you to be a catechizer ; and though you
should so do, yet I may refuse to make you

the most solemn and particular interrogations. In preaching, indeed, care must be taken not to turn the thoughts of a
congregation to an individual ; yet we should aim to lead
every one to reflect on his own case, and excite his conscience
to perform the office of a faithful monitor. But in private,
when we have ground to suspect that men deceive themselves,
such plain dealing is the best evidence of disinterested love.
It is at present, alas ! much disused, and deemed inconsistent
with politeness ; so that, in many cases, such an attempt
would be considered as a direct outrage and insult : and perhaps, in some circles, the language of these plain pilgrims
might be exchanged for that which would be less offensive,
without deducting from its energy : yet zeal for the honour of
the Gospel, and love to the souls of men, are, no doubt,
grievously sacrificed to urbanity, in this age of courteous insincerity.

my judge. But I pray will you tell me why you ask me such questions?

Faith. Because I saw you forward to talk, and because I knew not that you had aught else but notion. Besides, to tell you all the truth, I have heard of you, that you are a man whose religion lies in talk, and that your conversation gives this your mouth-profession the lie. They say you are a spot among Christians; and that religion fareth the worse for your ungodly conversation; that some already have stumbled at your wicked ways, and that more are in danger of being destroyed thereby; your religion and an ale-house, and covetousness, and uncleanness, and swearing, and lying, and vain company-keeping, &c., will stand together. The proverb is true of you which is said of a whore, to wit, that 'she is a shame to all women;' so you are a shame to all professors.

Talk. Since you are ready to take up reports, and to judge so rashly as you do, I cannot but conclude you are some peevish or melancholic man, not fit to be discoursed with; —and so, adieu.

Then came up Christian and said to his brother, I told you how it would happen; your words and his lusts could not agree. He had rather leave your company than reform his life; but he is gone, as I said: let him go, the loss is no man's but his own: he has saved us the trouble of going from him; for he continuing (as I suppose he will do,) as he is, he would have been but a blot in your company : besides, the apostle says, ' from such* withdraw thyself.'

Faith. But I am glad we had this little discourse with him ; it may happen that he will think of it again : however I have dealt plainly with him, and so am clear of his blood if he perisheth.

Chr. You do well to talk so plainly to him as you did ; there is but little of this faithful dealing with men now-a-days, and that makes religion to stink so in the nostrils of many as it doth : for they are these talkative fools, whose religion is only in words, and are debauched and vain in their conversation, that, being so much admitted into the fellowship of the godly, do puzzle the world, blemish Christianity, and grieve the sincere. I wish that all men would deal with such as

* 'From such'—This apostolical rule is of the greatest importance. While conscientious Christians, from a mistaken candour, tolerate scandalous professors and associate with them, they seem to allow that they belong to the same family ; and the world will charge their immoralities on the doctrines of the Gospel, saying of those who profess them, ' they are all alike, if we could find them out.' But did all, who ' adorn the doctrine of God our Saviour,' withdraw from such men, their crimes would rest with themselves and the world would be compelled to see the difference between hypocrites and real Christians. This is also the most effectual method of exciting self-deceivers, or inconsistent professors to self-examination, and of thus bringing them to be ashamed and humbled in true repentance : at the same time, it tends to deprive such men of that influence which they often employ to mislead and pervert hopeful inquirers and unestablished believers. The best discipline would have but a partial effect in preventing these evils, if not followed up by this conduct of individuals ; and where the former cannot be obtained, the latter would produce happier consequences than believers in general can suppose.

vou have done ; then should they be either
made more comformable to religion, or the
company of saints would be too hot for them.
Then did Faithful say—

> How Talkative at first lifts up his plumes !
> How bravely doth he speak ! How he presumes
> To drive down all before him ! But so soon
> As Faithful talks of heart-work, like the moon
> That's past the full, into the wane he goes ;
> And so will all but he that heart-work knows.

Thus they went on talking of what they
had seen by the way, and so made that way
easy, which would otherwise no doubt have
been tedious to them : for now they went
through a wilderness.

Now when they had got almost quite out
of this wilderness, Faithful chanced to cast
his eye back, and spied one coming after
them, and he knew him. Oh ! said Faithful
to his brother, Who comes yonder ? Then
Christian looked, and said, it is my* good
friend Evangelist. Ay, and my good friend

* 'It is my'—The author, intending next to represent his
pilgrims as exposed to severe persecution, and to exhibit
in one view what Christians should expect, and may be exposed to, from the enmity of the world, very judiciously introduces that interesting scene by Evangelist's meeting them,
with suitable cautions, exhortations, and encouragements.
The minister, by whose faithful labours a man is first directed into the way of salvation, commonly retains great influence, and is considered with special affection, even when
various circumstances have placed him at a distance under
some other pastor. The conversation, therefore, of such a
beloved friend tends to recall to the minds of believers their
former fears, trials, and deliverances, which animate them
to encounter farther difficulties, and opens the way for seasonable counsels and admonitions.

too, said Faithful, for it was he that set me the way to the gate. Now as Evangelist came up unto them, he thus saluted them :

Peace be with you, dearly beloved ; and peace be to your helpers.

Chr. Welcome, welcome, my good Evangelist ; the sight of thy countenance brings to my remembrance thy ancient kindness and unwearied labours for my eternal good.

And a thousand times welcome, said good Faithful, thy company, O sweet Evangelist, how desirable is it to us poor pilgrims !

Then said Evangelist, How hath it fared with you my friends, since the time of our last parting ? what have you met with, and how have you behaved yourselves ?

Then Christian and Faithful told him of all things that had happened to them in the way ; and how, and with what difficulty, they had arrived to that place.

Right glad am I, said Evangelist, not that you have met with trials, but that you have been victors, and for that you have, notwithstanding many weaknesses, continued in the way to this very day. I say, right glad am I of this thing, and that for my own sake and yours. I have sowed and you have reaped ; and the day is coming when both he that sowed and they that reaped shall rejoice together ;' that is, if you hold out ; 'for in due time ye shall reap, if you faint not' (John iv. 36 ; Gal. vi. 9). The crown is before you and it is an incorruptible one ; so run that you may obtain it. Some there be that set

out for this crown, and after they have gone
far for it another comes in and takes it from
them ; 'hold fast therefore that you have
let no man take your crown' (1 Cor. ix. 24—
27 ; Rev. iii 11): you are not yet out of the
gunshot of the devil ; 'you have not resisted
unto blood, striving against sin :' let the kingdom be always before you, and believe stead-
fastly concerning things that are invisible ;
let nothing that is on this side the other world
get within you ; and, above all, look well to
your own hearts and to the lusts thereof, for
they are 'deceitful above all things, and desperately wicked :' set your faces like a flint ;
you have all power in heaven and earth on
your side.

Then Christian thanked him for his exhortation ; but told him withal, that they would
have him speak farther to them for their help
the rest of the way ; and the rather for that
they well knew that he was a prophet,* and
could tell them of things that might happen

* 'Prophet'—The able and faithful minister can foretel
many things, from his knowledge of the Scriptures, and enlarged experience and observation, of which his people are
not aware   He knows beforehand, that ' through much
tribulation they must enter into the king om of God ;' and
the circumstances of the times aid him in discerning what
trials and difficulties more especially await them.   A retired
life shelters a believer from the enmity of the world ; and
timid men are often tempted on this account to abide in the
wilderness, to choose obscurity and solitude, for the sake of
quiet and safety, to the neglect of those active services for
which they are qualified.   But when Christians are called
forth to a more public situation, they will need peculiar cautions and instructions : for inexperience renders men inattentive to the words of Scripture ; and they often do not at

16*

unto them, and how they might resist and overcome them. To which request Faithful also consented. So Evangelist began as followeth :

My sons, you have heard in the words of the truth of the Gospel, that ' you must through many tribulations enter into the kingdom of heaven :' and again, that ' in every city, bonds and afflictions abide on you ;' and therefore you cannot expect that you should go long on your pilgrimage without them, in some sort or other. You have found something of the truth of these testimonies upon you already, and more will immediately follow : for now, as you see, you are almost out of this wilderness, and therefore you will soon come into a town that you will by-and-bye see before you ; and in that town you will be hardly beset with enemies, who will strain hard but they will kill you ; and be you sure, that one or both of you must seal the testimony, which you hold, with blood : but ' be you faithful unto death, and the King will give you a crown of life.' He that shall die there, although his death will be unnatural, and his pains perhaps great, he will yet have the better of his fellow ; not only because he will be arrived at the Celestial City soonest, but because he will escape many iseries that the other will meet with in the est of his journey. But when you are come o the town, and shall find fulfilled what I have here related, then remember your friend,

all expect, or prepare for, the trials which are inseparable from those scenes, on which they are perhaps even impatient o enter.

and quit yourselves like men ; and ' commit the keeping of souls to your God in well-doing, as unto a faithful Creator.'

Then I saw in my dream, that, when they were got out of the wilderness, they presently saw a town before them ; the name* of

* ' The name'—Our author evidently designed to exhibit in his allegory the grand outlines of the difficulties, temptations, and sufferings, to which believers are exposed in this evil world; which, in a work of this nature, must be related as if they came upon them one after another in regular succession ; though in actual experience several may meet together, many may molest the same person again and again, and some harass him in every stage of his journey. We should, therefore, singly consider the instruction conveyed by every allegorical incident, without measuring our experience, or calculating our progress, by comparing them with circumstances, which might be reversed or altered with almost endless variety. In general, Vanity fair represents the wretched state of things, in those populous places especially, where true religion is neglected and persecuted ; and indeed of the whole world, ' as lying in wickedness,' and as distinguished from the church of redeemed sinners. This contiues the same (in respect of the general principles, conduct, and pursuits of mankind) through all ages and nations ; but Christians are called to mix more with it at some times than at others ; and Satan, its god and prince, is permitted to excite fierce persecution in some places and on some occasions, while at other times he is restrained. Many, therefore, seem to spend all their days in the midst of Vanity fair, and of continual insults or injuries ; while others are only sometimes thus exposed, and pass most of their lives unmolested ; and a few are favoured with so obscure a situation, and such peaceable times, that they are very little acquainted with these trials. Mr. Bunyan, living in the country, had frequent opportunities of witnessing those fairs, which are held first in one town and then in another; and of observing the pernicious effects of such a concourse of people drawn together by interest, or for the purposes of dissipation and debauchery, on the principles, morals, health, and circumstances of young persons especially He must also, doubtless, have found them to be a very dangerous snare to serious or hopeful persons: so that his delineation of this case, under allusions taken from such a

that town is Vanity ; and at that town there is a
fair kept, called Vanity fair : it is kept all the

scene, will be more interesting and affecting to those who
have been spectators of these things, than to such as have
moved in higher circles, or dwelt chiefly in populous cities.
Worldly men covet, pursue, grasp at, and contend for, the
things of time and sense, with such eagerness and violence,
that their conduct aptly resembles the bustle, selfishness, artifice, dissipation, riot, and tumult of a large crowded fair.
The profits, pleasures, honours, possessions, and distinctions
of the world, are as transient and frivolous as the events of
the fair-day ; with which the children are delighted, but
which every man of sense contemns. Solomon, after a com
plete experiment, pronounced the whole to be ' vanity of vanities ;' the veriest vanity imaginable, a complex vanity, an
accumulation of ciphers, a lottery consisting entirely of
blanks ; every earthly object being unsuitable to the wants
of the rational soul, unsubstantial, unstisfactory, irksome,
disappointing, and perishing. Yet this traffic of vanities is
kept up all the year ; because the carnal mind always hankers
after one or other of these worldly trifles, and longs ' for
change of follies, and relays of joy ;' while objects suited to
its feverish thirst are always at hand to allure it, deriving
their efficacy from continually pressing, as it were, on the senses. When our first parents were fatally prevailed on to
join Satan's apostacy, they ' forsook the Fountain of living
waters, to hew out for themselves broken cisterns ;' and the
idolatry, of seeking happiness from the creature instead of the
Creator, has been universal among all their posterity. Since
the promise of a Saviour opened to fallen men a door of hope,
the tempter has continually tried to allure them by outward
objects, or induce them by the dread of pain and suffering, to
' neglect so great salvation.' Thus the prince of the devils
sets up this fair ; and by teaching men to abuse the good
creatures of God to vile purposes, or to expect from them
such satisfaction as they were never meant to afford, he hath
used them as baits to the ambition, avarice, levity, and sensu-
ality of the carnal mind. No crime has ever been committed on earth, or conceived in the heart of man, which did not
arise from this universal apostacy and idolatry ; from the excess, to which the insufficiency of the object to answer the
proposed end gives rise ; and from the vile passions, which
the jarring interest or inclinations of numberless competitors
for honour, power, wealth, and pleasure, cannot fail to excite

year long : it beareth the name of Vanity fair, because the town where it is kept is 'lighter than vanity,' and also because all that is there sold, or that cometh thither, is vanity. As is the saying of the wise, 'All that cometh is vanity (Eccles. i. 2—14 ; ii. 11—17 ; xi. 8 ; Isa xi. 17).

This fair is no new-erected business, but a thing of ancient standing : I will shew you the original of it.

Almost five thousand years agone there were pilgrims walking to the Celestial City, as those two honest persons are ; and Beelzebub, Apollyon, and Legion, with their companions, perceiving, by the path that the pilgrims made, that their way to the city lay through this town of Vanity, they contrived here to set up a fair ; a fair, wherein should be sold all sorts of vanity ; and that it should last all the year long ; therefore at this fair are all such merchandize sold, as houses, lands, trades, places, honours, preferments, ti-

As the streams of impiety and vice, which flow from this source, are varied, according to men's constitutions, educations, habits, and situations; so different worldly pursuits predominate in divers nations, or stages of civilization. Hence the manifold variations in the human character, which equal the diversity of their complexions, shape, or capacities, though they be all of one nature. To this an allusion is made by ' the rows' in this fair. The merchandize of Rome, which suited a rude and ignorant age, has now given place to the more plausible wares of sceptical philosophers, which are more agreeable to the pride of learning and human reasoning. Even things lawful in themselves, when sought or possessed in a manner which is not consistent with ' seeking first the kingdom of God, and his righteousness,' become allurements of Satan, to draw sinners into his fatal snare.

tles, countries, kingdoms, lusts, pleasures ; and delights of all sorts, as whores, bawds, wives, husbands, children, masters, servants, lives, blood, bodies, souls, silver, gold, pearls, precious stones, and what not ?

And moreover, at this fair there is at all times to be seen juggling, cheats, games, plays, fools, apes, knaves, and rogues, and that of every kind.

Here are to be seen too, and that for nothing, thefts, murders, adulterers, false swearers, and that of a bloodred colour.

And as in other fairs of less moment there are several rows and streets under their proper names, where such wares are vended, so here likewise you have the proper places, rows, streets (*viz.* countries and kingdoms), where the wares of this fair are soonest to be found. Here is the Britain row, the French row, the Italian row, the Spanish row, the German row, where several sorts of vanities are to be sold. But as in other fairs some one commodity is as the chief of all the fair, so the ware of Rome and her merchandize is greatly promoted in the fair ; only our English nation, with some others, have taken a dislike thereat.

Now, as I said, the way* to the Celestial City lies just through the town where this lus-

* ' The way'—Christianity does not allow men to ' bury their talent in the earth,' or to put ' their light under a bushel :' they should not ' go out of the world,' or retire into cloisters and deserts, and, therefore, they must all go through this fair. Thus our Lord and Saviour endured all the temptations and sufferings of this evil world ; without being at al

ty fair is kept ; and he that will go to the city,
and yet not go through this town,' must needs
go out of the world.' The Prince of princes
himself, when here, went through this town
to his own country, and that upon a fair-day
too : yea, and as I think, it was Beelzebub,
the chief lord of this fair, that invited him to
buy of his vanities ; yea, would have made
him lord of the fair, would he but have done
him reverence as he went through the town ;
yea, because he was such a person of honour,
Beelzebub had him from street to street, and
shewed him all the kingdoms of the world in
a little time, that he might, if possible, allure
that Blessed One to cheapen and buy some
of his vanities ; but he had no mind to the
merchandize, and therefore left the town
without laying out so much as one farthing
upon these vanites (Matt. iv. 8, 9 ; Luke
iv. 5—7.) This fair, therefore, is an ancient thing, of long standing, and a very great
fair.

Now these pilgrims, as I said, must needs

impeded or entangled by them, or stepping in the least aside
to avoid them. The age in which he lived peculiarly abound-
ed in all possible allurements ; and he was exposed to such
enmity, contempt, and sufferings, as could never be exceeded or equalled. But ' he went about doing good ;' and his
whole conduct, as well as his indignant repulse of the tempter's insolent offer, hath shewn emphatically his judgment of
all earthly things, and exhibited to us ' an example, that we
should follow his steps.' Here are inserted the following
lines—

Behold Vanity Fair ! The pilgrims there
Are chained, and stoned beside :
Even so it was our Lord past here,
And on mount Calvary died.

go through this fair. Well, so they did ; but behold, even as they entered into the fair, all the*people in the fair were moved, and the

* ' All the'—The presence of real Christians in those places, where a large concourse of worldly men is collected, must produce a disturbance and effervescence. The smaller the number is of those whose actions, words, or silence protest against the prevalency of vice and irreligion, the fiercer the opposition that will be excited. A pious clergyman, on board a vessel, where he was a single exception to the general ungodliness that prevailed, once gave great offence by silently withdrawing, when oaths or unseemly discourse made his situation uneasy, and was called to account for so assuming a singularity ! Believers, appearing in character among worldly people, and not disguising their sentiments, will meet this opposition ; which more accommodating professors will escape. The believer's avowed dependance on the righteousness and atonement of Christ for acceptance, gives vast offence to those who rely on their own good works for justification : his conformity to the example, and obedience to the commandments of the Redeemer, render him a precise, unfashionable, uncouth character, in the judgment of those, who ' walk according to the course of this world ;' and they will deem him insane or outlandish for his oddities and peculiarities His discourse, seasoned with piety, humility, seriousness, sincerity, meekness and spirituality, so differs from the ' filthy conversation of the wicked,' and the polite dissimulation of the courtly, that they can have no intercourse with him, or he with them ; and if he speaks of the love of Christ, and the satisfaction of communion with him while they ' blaspheme the worthy name by which he is called,' they must be as barbarians to each other. But above all, the believer's contempt of worldly things, when they interfere with the will and glory of God, forms such a testimony against all the pursuits and conduct of carnal men, as must excite their greatest astonishment and indignation ; while he shuns with dread and abhorrence, as incompatible with salvation, those very things to which they wholly addict themselves without the least remorse ! When the scoffs of those, who ' think it strange that they will not run with them to the same excess of riot,' extort from them a more explicit declaration of their religious principles, it may be expected, that the reproaches and insults of their despisers will be increased ; and then all the mischief and confusion which follow will be laid to their charge!

town itself, as it were, in a hubbub about them ; and that for several reasons : for,

'There were no such disputes about religion before they came' to ' turn the world upside down ;' ' they exceedingly trouble the city,' town, or village, by their pious discourse and censorious example. Thus Satan takes occasion to excite men to persecute the church when he fears lest the servants of God should successfully disseminate their principles : persecuting princes and magistrates, his ' most trusty friend,' are deputed by him to molest and punish their peaceable subjects, for consientiously refusing conformity to the world, or for dissenting from doctrines and modes of worship, which they deem unscriptural. Thus the most valuable members of the community are banished, imprisoned, or murdered ; multitudes are tempted to hypocrisy ; encouragement is given to time-servers to seek secular advantages by acting contrary to their conscience ; the principles of sincerity and integrity are generally weakened or destroyed by multiplied prevarications and false professions ; and numerous instruments of cruelty and oppression are involved in this complication of atrocious crimes. Our author doubtless drew many of his portraits in this historical picture from originals then sufficiently known ; and if any think that he has heightened his colourings, it may furnish them with a subject for gratitude, and a reason for content and peaceable submission to our rulers. In Fox's Martyrs we meet with authenticated facts, that fully equal this allegorical representation ; nay, ' The Acts of the Apostles' give us the very same view of the subject. The contempt, injustice, and cruelty, with which persecutors treat the harmless disciples of Christ, makes way for the exhibition of that amiable conduct and spirit which accord to the precepts of Scripture, and the example of persecuted prophets and apostles ; this often produces the most happy effects on those who are less prejudiced, which still more exasperates determined opposers ; but, however, frequently occasions a short respite for the persecuted, while worldly people quarrel about them among themselves. And even if greater severity be at length determined on, in order to deter others from joining them, perseverance in prudence, meekness, and patience, amidst all the rage of their enemies, will bear testimony for them in the consciences of numbers ; their religion will appear beautiful, in proportion as their persecutors expose their own odious deformity ; God will be with them to comfort and deliver them ; he will be honoured by their

First, The pilgrims were clothed with such kind of raiment as was diverse from the raiment of any that traded in that fair. The people, therefore, of the fair made a great gazing upon them : some said they were fools (1 Cor. iv. 9, 10) ; some, they were bedlams ; and some, they were outlandish men.

Secondly, And as they wondered at their apparel, so they did likewise at their speech ; for few could understand what they said : they naturally spoke the language of Canaan ; but they that kept the fair were men of this world : so that from one end of the fair to the other they seemed barbarians each to the other.

Thirdly, But that which did not a little amuse the merchandizers was, that these pilgrims set very light by all their wares ; they cared not so much as to look upon them ; and if they called upon them to buy, they would put their fingers in their ears, and cry, 'Turn away mine eyes from beholding vanity' (Ps. cxix. 37) ; and look upwards, signifying that their trade and traffic was in heaven.

profession and behaviour, and many will derive the most important advantage from their patient sufferings, and cheerful fortitude in adhering to the truths of the Gospel. But when believers are put off their guard by ill usage ; when their zeal is rash, fierce, contentious, boasting, or disproportionate ; when they are provoked to render ' railing for railing,' or to act contrary to the plain precepts of Scripture ; then they bring guilt on their consciences, stumble their brethren, harden the hearts and open the mouths of opposers, dishonour God and the Gospel, and gratify the great enemy of souls ; who malignantly rejoices in their misconduct but is tortured when they endure sufferings in a proper manner.

One chanced, mocking, beholding the carriages of the men, to say unto men, 'What will ye buy?' but they, looking gravely upon him, said, 'We buy the truth' (Prov. xxiii. 23). At that there was an occasion taken to despise the men the more; some mocking, some taunting, some speaking reproachfully, and some calling upon others to smite them. At last things came to a hubbub and great stir in the fair, insomuch that all order was confounded. Now was word presently brought to the great one of the fair, who quickly came down, and deputed some of his most trusty friends to take those men into examination, about whom the fair was almost overturned. So the men were brought to examination; and they that sat upon them asked them whence they came, whither they went, and what they did there in such an unusual garb? The men told them, that they were pilgrims and strangers in the world; and that they were going to their own country, which was the heavenly Jerusalem (Heb. xi. 13—16); and that they had given no occasion to the men of the town, nor yet to the merchandizers, thus to abuse them, and to let them in their journey; except it was for that, when one asked them what they would buy, they said they would buy the truth. But they that were appointed to examine them, did not believe them to be any other than bedlams and mad, or else such as came to put all things into a confusion in the fair. Therefore they took them and beat them, and besmeared them with dirt, and then put them into the cage, that they might be made a spectacle to all the men of the fair. Therefore they lay for some time, and were made the object of any man's sport, or malice, or revenge; the great one of the fair laughing still at all that befel them. But the men being patient, and 'not rendering railing for railing, but contrariwise blessing,' and giving good words for bad and kindness for injuries done, some men in the fair, that were more observing and less prejudiced than the rest, began to check and blame the baser sort for their continual abuses done by them to the men; they therefore in angry manner let fly at them again, counting them as bad as the men in the cage, and telling them, that they seemed confederates, and should be made partakers of their misfortune. The other replied, that, for aught they could see, the men were quiet and sober, and intended nobody any harm; and that there were many that traded in their fair that were more worthy to be put into the cage, yea, and pillory too, than were the men that they had abused. Thus after divers words had passed on both sides (the men behaving themselves all the while very wisely and soberly before them), they fell to some blows among themselves, and did harm one to another. Then were these two poor men brought before their examiners again, and there charged as being guilty of the late hubbub that had been in the fair. So they beat them pitifully, and hanged irons upon them, and led them in chains up and down the fair, for an example and terror to others, lest any should speak in their behalf, or join themselves unto them. But Christian and Faithful behaved themselves yet more wisely, and received the ignominy and shame that was cast upon them with so much meekness and patience, that it won to their side (though but few in comparison of the rest) several of the men in the fair. This put the other party yet into a greater rage, insomuch that they concluded the death of these two men Wherefore they threatened, that the cage nor irons should serve their turn, but that they should die for the abuse they had done, and for deluding the men of the fair.

Then were they remanded to the cage again, until farther order should be taken with them. So they put them in and made their feet fast in the stocks.

Here, therefore, they called again to mind what they had heard from their faithful friend Evangelist, and were the more confirmed in their ways and sufferings by what he told them would happen to them. They also now comforted each other, that whose lot it was to suffer, even he should have the best on it; therefore each man secretly wished that he might have that preferment: but committing themselves to the all-wise dispose of Him that ruleth all things, with much content they abode in the condition in which they were, until they should be otherwise disposed of.

Then a convenient time being appointed, they brought them forth to their trial, in or

17*

der to their condemnation. When* the time
was come they were brought before their enemies, and arraigned. The judge's name
was Lord Hategood : their indictment was
one and the same in substance, though somewhat varying in form ; the contents whereof was this :

That they were enemies to, and disturbers
of, their trade ; that they had made commo-
tions and divisions in the town, and had won
a party to their own most dangerous opinions, in contempt of the law of their prince.
Then Faithful began to answer that he had
only set himself against that which had set itself against him that is higher than the highest. And, said he, as for disturbance, I make
none, being myself a man of peace ; the par-

---

* 'When'—The description of the process, instituted
against the pilgrims, is given in language taken from the
legal forms used in our courts of justice, which in Mr. Bunyan's
days were shamefully perverted to subserve the most iniqui-
tous oppressions. The allegorical narrative is framed in
such a manner, as emphatically exposes the secret reasons,
which influence men thus to persecute their inoffensive neighbours ; and the very names employed declare the several
corrupt principles of the heart, from whence this atrocious
conduct results. Enmity against God, and his holy character, law, worship, truth and servants, is the principal source
of persecution ; the judge in Faithful's trial. The interfer-
ence of spiritual religion with men's covetous, ambitious,
and sensual pursuits ; and the interruption it gives to their
false peace and unanimity in ungodliness or hypocrisy, which
it tends to expose and undermine, form the grounds of the indictment ; that is, when the persecuted can truly answer,
that they ' only set themselves against that which sets itself
against God ;' and when they do not suffer ' as evil-doers
busy-bodies in other men's matters,' ambitious competitors
for secular advantages, or contentious disputants about political questions.

ties that were won to us were won by beholding our truth and innocence ; and they are
only turned from the worse to better. And
as to the king you talk of, since he is Beelzebub, the enemy of our Lord, I defy him
and all his angels.

Then proclamation was made, that they
that had aught to say for their lord against
the prisoner at the bar, should forthwith appear and give in their evidence. So there
came in three witnesses,* to wit, Envy, Su-

---

* ' Witnesses'—These names of the witnesses declare the
characters of the most active instruments of persecution.
Even Pilate could perceive, that the Jewish scribes and
priests were actuated by envy, in delivering up Jesus to him.
His instructions discredited theirs, and diminished their reputation and influence ; he was more followed than they ;
and in proportion as he was deemed a teacher sent from
God, they were regarded as blind guides. Thus formal instructors and learned men, who are strangers to the power
of godliness, have always affected to despise the professors
and preachers of the Gospel as ignorant enthusiasts ; they
envy the reputation acquired by them, and are angry at the
success of their doctrines. If they have not the authority to
silence the minister, they will browbeat such of his hearers
as are within the reach of their influence ; especially if they
have affronted them, by forsaking their ministering instructions. If they cannot prevail upon ' the powers that be' to
interfere, they will employ reproaches, menaces, or even oppression, to obstruct the progress of evangelical ministers ;
should any obsolete law remain unrepealed, of which they
can take advantage, they will be the first to enforce it ; and
if the rulers engage in persecution, they will take the lead, as
prosecutors and witnesses. As this was remarkably the
case in our author's days, and as the history of the Old and
New Testament, and every authentic record of persecutions,
give the same view of it, we cannot be greatly at a loss to
know what was especially meant by this emblem. In other
respects there is seldom much in the circumstances of pious
persons, to excite the envy of their ungodly neighbours ; as
they despise their spiritual privileges and comforts.

perstition and Pickthank. They were then asked if they knew the prisoner at the bar ; and what they had to say for their lord the king against him ?

Then stood forth Envy, and said to this effect : My lord, I have known this man a long time, and will attest upon my oath before this honourable bench, that he is——

Judge. Hold, give him his oath.

So they sware him. Then he said, My lord, this man, notwithstanding his plausible name, is one of the vilest men in our country ; he neither regardeth prince nor people, law nor custom ; but doeth all that he can to possess all men with certain of his disloyal *

---

* ' Disloyal'—It has always been the practice of envious accusers to represent those who refuse religious conformity as disloyal and disaffected to the civil government of their country ; because they judge it right to obey God rather than man, how grievous then is it, that any who profess the Gospel should give plausibility to such calumnies ! how desirable for them, after the example, and in obedience to the precepts of Christ and his apostles, ' by well-doing to put to silence the ignorance of foolish men ;' ' to avoid all appearance of evil ;' ' to render to Cæsar the things that are Cæsar's ; and to constrain even enemies to bear testimony to their peaceable deportment ! this would exhibit their patient sufferings for conscience-sake as amiable and respectable in the eyes of all not immediately engaged in persecution ; and would give a sanction to their most bold and decided testimony against every kind of vice, irreligion, and false religion. But when they revile the persons of rulers, or make religion the pretext for intermeddling out of their place in political matters, and of attempting to disturb the peace of the community, they exceedingly strengthen men's prejudices against the doctrines of the Gospel, and the whole body of those who profess them, and thus give occasion, and furnish an excuse, for that very persecution, of which they complain, in other respects, with the greatest justice.

notions, which he in the general calls ' principles of faith and holiness.' And, in particular, I heard him once myself affirm, that Christianity and the customs of our town of Vanity were diametrically opposite, and could not be reconciled. By which saying, my lord, he doth at once not only condemn all our laudable doings, but us in the doing of them.

Then did the judge say unto him, Hast thou any more to say?

Envy. My Lord, I could say much more, only I would not be tedious to the court. Yet if need be when the other gentlemen have given in their evidence, rather than any thing shall be wanting that will dispatch him, I will enlarge my testimony against him. So he was bid to stand by.

Then they called * Superstition, and bid him look upon the prisoner; they also ask-

* ' They called'—Superstition represents another class of underling persecutors (for the principals are often masked infidels). Traditions, human inventions, forms, and externals, appear to them decent, venerable, and sacred ; and are mistaken, with pertinacious ignorance, for the substance of religion. As mere circumstances of worship, some of these may very well answer the purpose ; provided they be not imposed, magnified above their value, or substituted in the place of things essentially good : others are bad in their origin, use, tendency : yet the truths, ordinances, and commandments of God are made void, that men may keep them. What is pompous or burthensome appears to such men meritorious ; and the excitement of mere natural passions (as at a tragedy) is deemed a most needful help to true devotion. They are, therefore, eminently qualified to be witnesses against the faithful servants of God ; for they ' think they are thus doing him service, while they are opposing a company of profane despisers of their idolized forms ; a set of fanatics, heretics, and pestilent schismatics. The religious

ed him what he could say for their lord the king against him ? Then they sware him ; so he began :

My lord, I have no great acquaintance with this man nor do I desire to have farther knowledge of him ; however, this I know that he is a very pestilent fellow, from some discourse that the other day I had with him in this town ; for then, talking with him, I heard him say, that our religion was nought, and such by which a man could by no means please God. Which saying of his, my lord, your lordship very well knows what necessarily thence will follow, to wit, that we still do worship in vain, are yet in our sins, and finally shall be damned : and this is that which I have to say.

Then was * Pickthank sworn, and did say what he knew in the behalf of their lord the king against the prisoner at the bar.

zeal contracts and hardens their hearts, and the supposed goodness of the cause sanctifies their bitter rage, enmity, and calumny. The manifest odiousness of these proceedings should excite all who love the truth to keep at the utmost distance from such obstinate confidence and violence ; to discountenance them to the utmost, in the zealots of their own party ; and to leave the enemies of the Gospel, if possible, to monopolize this disgrace. For, hitherto, almost every party has been betrayed into it, when advanced to power, and given its opponents the most plausible arguments against it.

* 'Then was'—Pickthank represents a set of tools that persecutors continually use : men of no religious principle, who assume the appearance of zeal for any party, as may best promote their interests ; who inwardly despise both the superstitious and the spiritual worshipper ; and see nothing in the conduct or circumstances of the latter to excite their rage or envy. But if their superiors be disposed to

My lord, and you gentlemen all, this fellow I have known a long time, and have heard him speak things that ought not to be spoke ; for he hath railed on our noble prince Beelzebub, and hath spoken contemptuously of his honourable friends, whose names are the Lord Oldman, the Lord Carnaldelight, the Lord Luxurious, the Lord Desire-of-vain-glory, my old Lord Lechery, Sir Having Greedy, with all the rest of our nobility ; and he hath said moreover, that, if all men were of his mind, if possible, there is not one of these noblemen should have any longer a being in this town. Besides, he hath not been afraid to rail on you, my lord, who are now appointed to be his judge, calling you an ungodly villain, with many other such-like villifying terms, with which he hath bespattered most of the gentry of our town

When this Pickthank had told his tale, the judge directed his speech to the prisoner at the bar, saying, Thou renegade, heretic,

persecute, they will afford their assistance ; for preferment runs in this channel. So that they bear testimony against believers from avarice or ambition, and flatter the most execrable characters, in order to get forward in the world ; this being the grand object to which they readily sacrifice every thing else. The names of the persons, concerning whom Faithful spoke, shews that his crime consisted in protesting, by word and deed, against vices which the great too often think themselves privileged to commit without censure, and not in reviling the persons or misrepresenting the actions of superiors. The former may with great propriety be done at all times ; and on some occasions the testimony against sin cannot be too closely applied to the consciences of the guilty, without respect of persons · but the latter is always unjust and unscriptural.

and traitor, hast thou heard what these honest gentlemen have witnessed against thee ?

Faith. May I speak a few words in my own defence ?

Judge. Sirrah, sirrah, thou deservest to live no longer, but to be slain immediately upon the place ; yet, that all men may see our gentleness towards thee, let us hear what thou, vile renegade, hast to say.

Faith. I say* then, in answer to what Mr. Envy hath spoken, I never said aught but this, that what rule, or laws, or custom, or

---

* ' I say'—Faithful's defence is introduced by these lines, as in the foregoing instances—

' Now, Faithful, play the man, speak for thy God ;
Fear not the wicked's malice, nor their rod :
Speak boldly, man, the truth is on thy side ;
Die for it, and to life in triumph ride.'

Christians, in such circumstances, should be more concerned for the honour of God than for their own credit or safety : they should take occasion to bear a decided testimony to the truths, commandments, and institutions of Scripture; leaving it to their accusers, judges, or hearers, to determine what sentiments and practices are thus proved to be anti-christian, or what number of ' teachers in Israel' are exposed as blind guides. That faith (by which alone we approach to God, and acceptably worship him) has no other object than divine revelation ; nothing done without the express warrant of Scripture can be profitable to eternal life, whatever may be said for its expediency ; but every thing foisted into religion contrary to that sacred rule must be an abomination. Human faith may please men ; but without a divine faith it is impossible to please God, either in general or in any particular action. And as we seldom can speak against the vile lusts of men, without being judged by implication to rail against such as are notoriously addicted to them, we cannot be the followers of him ' whom the world hated, because he testified of it that its works were evil,' unless we be willing to risk all consequences in copying his example.

people, were flat against the word of God,
are diametrically opposite to Christianity. If
I have said amiss in this, convince me of my
error, and I am ready here before you to
make my recantation.

As to the second, to wit, Mr. Superstition.
and his charge against me, I said only this,
that in the worship of God there is required
a divine faith ; but there can be no divine
faith without a divine revelation of the will of
God. Therefore, whatever is thrust into the
worship of God that is not agreeable to divine revelation, cannot be done but by a human faith, which faith will not be profitable
to eternal life.

As to what Mr. Pickthank hath said, I say
(avoiding terms, as that I am said to rail, and
the like), that the prince of this town, with
all the rabblement, his attendants, by this
gentleman named, are more fit for being in
hell than in this town and country ; and so
the Lord have mercy upon me.

Then the judge* called to the jury (who all
this while stood by to hear and observe),

* ' The judge'—A more just and keen satirical description
of such legal iniquities can scarcely be imagined, than that
contained in this passage. The statutes and precedents adduced (with an humourous and well-imitated reference to the
style and manner in which charges are commonly given to
juries) shew what patterns persecuting legislators and magistrates choose to copy, and whose kingdom they labour to uphold. Nor can any impartial man deny, that the inference is
fair which our author meant the reader to deduce ; namely,
that nominal Protestants, enacting laws requiring conformity
to their own creeds and forms, and inflicting punishments on
such as peaceably dissent from them, are actually involved in

Gentlemen of the jury, you see this man, about whom so great an uproar hath been made in this town; you have also heard what these worthy gentlemen have witnessed against him; also you have heard his reply and confession; it lieth now in your breasts to hang him, or save his life; but yet I think meet to instruct you in our law.

the guilt of these heathen persecutors, and of their anti-christian successors; even if their doctrine and worship be allowed to be scriptural and spiritual. Such methods only serve to promote hypocrisy, and to expose the conscientious to the malice, envy, or avarice of the unprincipled. The names of the jurymen, and their general and particular verdicts, the cruel execution of Faithful, and the happy event of his sufferings, need no comment. It was not indeed the practice of the times, to which this representation belongs, to inflict death on those who were persecuted for conscience-sake; yet very great rigours were used; the system then adopted, if carried to its consequences, must have ended in the extermination of all nonconformists from the land; it was natural to expect still greater cruelty from persons, who were found capable of the severities already experienced; and without all doubt many actually lost their lives, in one way or other, by the persecutions to which they were exposed. All those who feel a disposition to employ the power of the magistrate against such as differ from them in religious matters, should attentively consider the contemptible and odious picture here delineated, with the most entire justice, of the whole race of persecutors, and of their characters, principles, motives, and conduct; that they may learn to hate and dread such an anti-christian practice, and shun the most remote approaches to it. On the other hand, they who are exposed to persecution, or in danger of it, should study the character and conduct of Faithful, that they may learn to suffer in a Christian spirit, and to adorn the Gospel in the fiery trial. The following lines are here introduced, as before—

'Brave Faithful! bravely done in word and deed!
Judge, witnesses, and jury have, instead
Of overcoming thee but shew their rage;
When they are dead, thou'lt live from age to age.'

There was an act made in the days of Pharaoh the Great, servant to our prince, that, lest those of a contrary religion should multiply and grow too strong for him, their males should be thrown into the river (Exod. i). There was an act also made in the days of Nebuchadnezzar the Great, another of his servants, that whoever would not fall down and worship his golden image, should be thrown into the fiery furnace (Dan. iii.). There was also an act made in the days of Darius, that whoso for some time called upon any god but him should be cast into the lion's den (Dan. vi). Now the substance of these laws this rebel has broken, not only in thought (which is not to be borne) but also in word and deed; which must therefore needs be intolerable.

For that of Pharaoh—his law was made upon suspicion, to prevent mischief, no crime yet being apparent; but here is a crime apparent. For the second and third—you see he disputeth against our religion; and for the treason he hath confessed, he deserveth to die the death.

Then went the jury out, whose names were Mr. Blindman, Mr. Nogood, Mr. Malice, Mr. Lovelust, Mr. Liveloose, Mr. Heady, Mr. Highmind, Mr. Enmity, Mr. Liar, Mr. Cruelty, Mr. Hatelight, and Mr. Implacable; who every one gave in his private verdict against him among themselves, and afterwards unanimously concluded to bring him in guilty before the judge. And first among themselves, Mr. Blindman, the foreman, said, 'I see clearly that this man is a heretic.' Then said Mr. Nogood, 'Away with such a fellow from the earth.' 'Ay,' said Mr. Malice, 'for I hate the very looks of him.' Then said Mr. Lovelust, 'I could never endure him.' 'Nor I,' said Mr. Liveloose, 'for he would always be condemning my way.' 'Hang him, hang him,' said Mr. Heady. 'A sorry scrub,' said Mr. Highmind. 'My heart riseth against him,' said Mr. Enmity. 'He is a rogue,' said Mr. Liar. 'Hanging is too good for him,' said Mr. Cruelty. 'Let us dispatch him out of the way,' said Mr. Hatelight. Then said Mr. Implacable, 'Might I have all the world given me, I could not be reconciled to him; therefore let us forthwith bring him in guilty of death.' And so they did; therefore he was presently condemned to be had from the place where he was to the place from whence he came, and there to be put to the most cruel death that could be invented.

They therefore brought him out to do with him according to their law; and first they scourged him, then they buffeted him, then they lanced his flesh with knives; after that they stoned him with stones, then pricked him with their swords; and last of all they burned him to ashes at the stake. Thus came Faithful to his end.

Now I saw that there stood behind the multitude a chariot and a couple of horses waiting for Faithful, who, so soon as his adversa nes had dispatched him, was taken up into it, and straightway was carried up through the clouds, with sound of trumpet, the nearest way to the Celestial gate. But as for* Christian, he had some respite, and was remanded back to prison; so he there remained for a space: but he that overrules all things, having the power of their rage in his own hand, so wrought it about that Christian for that time escaped them, and went his way.

And as he went he sang, saying,

> Well, Faithful, thou hast faithfully profest
> Unto thy Lord, of whom thou shalt be blest,
> When faithless ones, with all their vain delight,
> Are crying out under their hellish plight:
> Sing, Faithful, sing, and let thy name survive,
> For though they kill'd thee thou art yet alive.

Now I saw in my dream that Christian went not forth alone; for there was† one

* ' As for'—When the believer has done his work, the wrath of man may be permitted to expedite his removal to his heavenly inheritance, beyond which all the malice and power of earth and hell are utterly unavailing against him. Thus the apostles were preserved during Saul's persecution, and Peter was rescued from the hands of Herod. The Lord has various methods of protecting and liberating his servants; sometimes he intimidates their persecutors; the paroxysm of their fury abates; or they are disheartened by ill success in their efforts to extirpate the hated sect; the principals and instruments are left to quarrel among themselves; the cruelties they exercise so disgust the people, that they dare not proceed; political interests engage even ungodly princes to promote toleration, and chain up the demon persecution; or the Lord raises up one of his own servants to authority, that he may be a protector of his church, and disappoint the devices of his enemies.

† ' There was'—' The blood of the martyrs is the seed of the church;' for sufferings properly endured form the

whose name was Hopeful (being so made by
the beholding of Christian and Faithful in
their words and behaviour in their sufferings
at the fair) who joined himself unto him ; and
entering into a brotherly covenânt, told him
that he would be his companion. Thus one
died to bear testimony to the truth, and another
rises out of his ashes to be a companion with
Christian in his pilgrimage. This Hopeful
also told Christian, that there were many
more of the men in the fair that would take
their time and follow after.

So I saw, that quickly after they were got
out of the fair they overtook one that was going before them, whose name* was By-ends ;

convincing and useful kind of preaching. The name of
Christian's new companion denotes the opinion, which established believers form at first of such as begin to profess
the Gospel in an intelligent manner. The nature of an allegory rendered it impracticable to introduce the new convert,
as beginning his pilgrimage from the same place, or going
through the same scenes, as Christian had done ; neither
could Faithful, for the same reason, be represented as passing the river afterwards mentioned. But the brotherly covenant, in which Hopeful joined himself with his companion,
must be supposed to imply the substance of all that had been
spoken of, as necessary to his final acceptance.

* ' Whose name'—The character of By-ends, and the
group that attended him, forms a clear detection and merited
condemnation of a large company of false professors, which
is not at all inferior in importance to the preceding severe
satire on open persecutors. When ' rest is given to the
church,' hypocrites often multiply more than real Christians.
The name of this pretender to religion, and those of his
town and connexions, do not merely describe his original character and situation (as Christian was at first
called Graceless of the city of Destruction), but they denote
the nature of his religious profession. Believers look back
on their former principles and behaviour with shame and ab-

so they said to him, What countryman, Sir?
and how far go you this way? He told them

horrence; but hypocrites, when reproved for evident sins,
excuse them, because Christ came to save the lost, and shews
mercy to the chief of sinners. Christian would readily have
granted, that 'no good lived' at his native city; he had
therefore renounced it, with all his old connexions; but By-
ends hoped better of Fair-speech, and gloried in his honourable relations there. Yet he was ashamed of his name: for
men are unwilling to allow that they seek worldly advantages
by their religion, and nothing more. The names, afterwards
selected, are most emphatically descriptive of that whole
species, who, with multiplied variations, suppose 'that gain
is godliness;' as will manifestly appear to any reader, who
attentively considers them. The polite simulation and dissimulation, which some most courtly writers have inculcated,
as the summit of good breeding, the perfection of a finished
education, and the grand requisite for obtaining worldly distinctions, if introduced into religion, and adopted by professors or preachers of the Gospel, in connexion with fashionable accomplishments and an agreeable address, constitute the
most versatile, refined, and insinuating species of hypocrisy
that can be imagined; and a man of talents, of any occupation or profession, may render it very subservient to his interest, by ensuring the patronage or custom of those to
whom he attaches himself, without giving much umbrage to the
world, which may despise such a character, but will not deem
him worthy of hatred. He may assume any of the names
here provided for the purpose, as may best suit his line in
life; and may shape his course, in subserviency to his grand
concern, with considerable latitude, provided he has prudence
enough to keep clear of scandalous vices; he will not be
long in learning the beneficial art of using two tongues with
one mouth, or of looking one way and rowing another; and
perhaps he may improve his fortune by an honourable alliance
with some branch of the ancient family of the Feignings.
The grand difference betwixt this whole tribe, and the body
of true Christians, consists merely in these two things—the
latter seek salvation by their religion; the former profess it,
in order to obtain, in the most advantageous manner, friends,
patrons, customers, or applause: those follow the Lord habitually, whatever tribulations arise because of the word;
but these conceal or deny their profession, when, instead of
gaining by it, they are exposed to reproach or persecution

that he came from the town of Fair-speech
and he was going to the Celestial City, but
told them not his name.

From Fair-speech! said Christian: is
there any good that lives there? (Prov. xxvi
25.)

Yes, said By-ends, I hope.

Pray, Sir, what may I call you? said
Christian.

By. I am a stranger to you and you to me;
if you be going this way, I shall be glad of
your company; if not, I must be content.

This town of Fair-speech, said Christian,
I have heard of, and, as I remember, they say
it is a wealthy place.

By. Yes, I will assure you that it is; and I
have very many rich kindred there.

Chr. Pray who are your kindred there, if a
man may be so bold?

By. Almost the whole town; and, in particular, my Lord Turn-about, my Lord Time-
server, my Lord Fair-speech, from whose
ancestors the town first took its name; also
Mr. Smooth-man, Mr. Facing-both-ways,
Mr. Any-thing; and the parson of our parish, Mr. Two-tongues, was my mother's own
brother by father's side; and, to tell you the
truth, I am become a gentleman of good
quality, yet my great grandfather was but a
waterman, looking one way and rowing another, and I got most of my estate by the
same occupation.

Chr. Are you a married man?

By. Yes, and my wife is a very virtuous

woman, the daughter of a virtuous woman ; she was my lady Feigning's daughter, there- fore she came of a very honourable family, and is arrived to such a pitch of breeding, that she knows how to carry it to all, even to prince and peasant. It is true we somewhat differ in religion from those of the stricte' sort, yet but in two small points : First, we never strive against wind and tide ; Secondly, we are always most zealous when religion goes in his silver slippers ; we love much to walk with him in the street, if the sun shines, and the people applaud him.

Then Christian stepped a little aside to his fellow Hopeful, saying, It runs in my mind that this is one By-ends of Fair-speech ; and if it be he, we have as very a knave in our company as dwelleth in all these parts. Then said Hopeful, Ask him ; methinks he should not be ashamed of his name. So Christian came up with him again, and said, Sir, you* talk as if you knew something more than all the world doth ; and, if I take not my mark amiss, I deem I have half a guess of you : is not your name Mr. By-ends, of Fair-speech ?

* ' Sir you'—The downright people of the world know how to serve Mammon by neglecting and despising God and religion ; the disciples of Christ can serve God by renouncing the world and its friendship : but time-servers talk as if they had found out the secret of uniting these two discordant inter ests, and thus of knowing something more than all the world This is the most prominent feature in this group of portraits which in other respects exhibits to the spectator various dis- similarities, and contains the faces of persons belonging to every division of professed Christians in the world.

By. This is not* my name, but indeed it is a nickname that is given me by some that cannot abide me, and I must be content to bear it as a reproach, as other good men have borne theirs before me.

Chr. But did you never give occasion to men to call you by this name?

By. Never, never! the worst that ever I did to give them an occasion to give me this name was, that I had always the luck to jump in my judgment with the present way of the times, whatever it was; and my chance was to get thereby. But if things are thus cast upon me, let me count them a blessing; but let not the malicious load me therefore with reproach.

Chr. I thought indeed that you were the man that I heard of; and, to tell you what I think, I fear this name belongs to you more properly than you are willing we should think it doth.

---

* 'This is not'—When hypocrites are charged with their double-dealing and obvious crimes, they commonly set it down to the account of persecution, and class themselves with that blessed company, of whom 'all manner of evil is spoken falsely, for the name of Christ;' as if there were no difference between suffering as a Christian, and being exposed as a scandal to the name of Christianity! Thus they endeavour to quiet their minds, and keep up their credit; deeming themselves at the same time very prudent and fortunate, in shifting about so as to avoid the cross, and secure their temporal interests. The apostle says concerning these men, 'from such turn away;' and the decided manner in which Christian warns By-ends, and renounces his company, though perhaps too plain to be either approved or imitated in this courtly, candid age, is certainly warranted and required by the holy Scriptures.

By Well, if you will thus imagine, I cannot help it ; you will find me a fair company-
keeper if you will still admit me your associate.

Chr. If you will go with us you must go
against wind and tide ; the which, I perceive
is against your opinion ; you must also own
religion in his rags as well as when in his silver slippers, and stand by him too when
bound in irons as well as when he walketh the
streets with applause.

By. You must not impose, nor lord it over
my faith ; leave me to my liberty, and let me
go with you.

Chr. Not a step farther, unless you will do
in what I propound as we.

Then said By-ends, I shall never desert my
old principles, since they are harmless and
profitable. If I may not go with you I must
do as I did before you overtook me, even go
by myself, until some overtake me that will
be glad of my company.

Now I saw in my dream that Christian and
Hopeful forsook him, and kept their distance
before him ; but one of them looking back
saw three men following Mr. By-ends, and
behold, as they came up with him, he made
them a very low congee ; and they also gave
him a compliment. The men's name were,
Mr. Hold-the-world, Mr. Money-love, and
Mr. Save-all ; men that Mr. By-ends had
formerly been acquainted with ; for in their
minority they were school-fellows, and were
taught by one Mr. Gripeman, a schoolmaster

ın Love-gain, which is a market town in the county of Coveting, in the north. This schoolmaster taught them the art of getting, either by violence, cozenage, flattery, lying, or by putting on a guise of religion; and these four gentlemen had attained much of the art of their master, so that they could each of them have kept such a school themselves.

Well, when they had, as I said, thus saluted each other, Mr. Money-love said to Mr. By-ends, Who are they upon the road before us? for Christian and Hopeful were yet within their view.

By. They are a couple of far countrymen, that after their mode are going on pilgrimage.

Money. Alas! why did they not stay, that we might have had their good company? for they, and we,* and you, Sir, I hope, are all going on pilgrimage.

* ' They and we'—It might have been supposed, that the persons here introduced were settled inhabitants of the town of Vanity, or the city of Destruction; but indeed they profess themselves pilgrims, and are desirous, during the present sunshine, to associate with such; provided they will allow them, without censure, to hold the world, love money, and save all, whatever become of faith and holiness, or of honesty, piety, truth, and charity! Covetousness, whether it consists in rapaciously trying to get money (to hoard, or to lavish, to purchase consequence, power, or pleasure, or to support magnificence and the pride of life); or parsimony in the ordinary proportion of expenditure; or tenacity, when duty requires a man to part with it, is a vice not so easily defined as many others. At the same time it enables a man, in various ways, to reward those who can be induced to connive at it, and to render it dangerous to oppose him; so that it is not wonderful, that it generally finds more quarter, even among re-

By. We are so indeed ; but the men before us are so rigid, and love so much their own notions, and do also so lightly esteem the opinions of others, that let a man be ever so godly, yet if he jumps not with them in all things they thrust him quite out of their company.

Save. That's bad ; but we read of some that are righteous over much,* and such men's

ligious persons, than other vices, which are not marked with so black a brand in the holy Scriptures. Too many professors even ' bless the covetous, whom God abhorreth,' and speak to them as if they were doubtless true Christians ; because of their steadiness in the profession of a doctrinal system, and a mode of worship, attended by morality, where money is not concerned and scandal might be incurred, and a narrow disproportionate contribution from their abundance, to support the interest of society or a party. Thus the ' vile person is called liberal, and the churl is said to be bountiful;' and the idolatry of worshipping money has seldom been execrated equally with that of those, ' whose god is their belly ;' unless when it has been so enormous as to become a kind of insanity. The most frugal support of religious worship, with the most disinterested pastors and managers, is attended with an expense, that the poor of the flock are utterly unable to defray. By this opening, Hold-the-world and Money-love frequently obtain admission among pilgrims, and acquire undue influence in their concerns. And when the effect of remaining selfishness in the hearts of true believers, insinuating itself under the specious plea of prudence and necessity, and the ill consequences of unsound professors associating with them, are considered ; with the censure that must fall upon a few obscure individuals who attempt to stem such a torrent ; it will appear evident. that the rich, and they who are growing rich, have more need of self-examination and jealousy over their own hearts than any other persons ; because they will be less plainly warned and reproved, in public and private, than any of their inferiors.

* ' Over much'—This expression of Solomon was probably intended to caution us against excessive zeal for some detached parts of religion to the neglect of others, or against

rigidness prevails with them to judge and condemn all but themselves; but I pray what
and how many were the things wherein you
differed!

By. Why they, after their headstrong manner, conclude, that it is their duty to rush on
their journey all weathers; and I am for
waiting for wind and tide. They are for hazarding all for God at a clap, and I am for taking all advantages to secure my life and estate. They are for holding their notions,
though all other men be against them; but
I am for religion in what, and so far as the
times and my safety will bear it. They are
for religion when in rags and contempt; but
I am for him when he walks in his golden slippers, in the sunshine, and with applause.

Hold. Ay, and hold you* there still, good
Mr. By-ends; for my part, I can count him
but a fool, that having the liberty to keep

superstitious austerities and enthusiastical delusions, or any
extremes, which always lead men off from vital godliness;
but it is the constant plea of those, who neglect the most essential duties of their place and station, to avoid the cross,
and preserve their worldly interests; and thus ' they wrest
the Scriptures to their own destruction.'

* ' And hold you'—This dialogue is not all more absurd
and selfish than the discourse of many who attend on the
preaching of the Gospel, and expect to be thought believers.
They connect ' the wisdom of the serpent' with his craft and
malice, not with the harmlessness of the dove; if worldly
lucre be the honey, they imitate the bee, and only attend to
religion when they can gain by it: they cut and shape their
creed and conduct to suit the times, and to please those among
whom they live; they determine to keep what they have at
any rate, and to get more, if it can be done without open
scandal; never seriously recollecting that they are mere stew-
ards of providential advantages, of which a strict account

what he has shall be so unwise as to lose it. Let us be wise as serpents; it is best to make hay when the sun shines : you see how the bee lieth still in winter, and bestirs her only when she can have profit with pleasure. God sends sometimes rain and sometimes sunshine; if they be such fools to go through the first, yet let us be content to take fair weather along with us. For my part, I like that religion best that will stand with the security of God's good blessings unto us ; for who can imagine, that is ruled by his reason, since God has bestowed upon us the good things of this life, but that he would have us keep them for his sake ? Abraham and Solomon grew rich in religion. And Job says that a good man ' shall lay up gold as dust.' But he must not be such as the men before us, if they be as you have described them.

Save. I think that we are all agreed in this matter, and therefore there needs no more words about it.

Money. No, there needs no more words about this matter indeed ; for he that believes neither scripture nor reason (and you see we have both on our side) neither knows his own liberty, nor seeks his own safety.

By. My brethren, we are, you see, going all on pilgrimage, and for our better diver-

must at last be given ; and instead of willingly renouncing or expending them, for the Lord's sake, when his providence or commandment requires it, they determine to hoard them up for themselves and families, or to spend them in worldly indulgences ; and then quote and pervert Scripture to varnish over this base idolatry.

sion from things that are bad, give me leave to propound unto you this question :

Suppose a man, a minister, or a tradesman, &c., should have an advantage lie before him, to get the good blessings of this life, yet so as that he can by no means come by them, except, in appearance at least, he becomes extraordinary zealous in some points of religion that he meddled not with before—may he not use the means to attain his end, and yet be a right honest man ?

Money. I see the bottom of your question ; and, with these gentlemen's good leave I will endeavour to shape you an answer. And first, to speak to your question, as it concerns a minister himself. Suppose* a minister, a worthy man, possessed of but a very small benefice, and has in his eyes a greater, more fat and plump by far ; he has also now an opportunity of getting of it, yet so as by being more studious, by preaching more fre-

* 'Suppose'—There is a fund of satirical humour in the supposed case here stated with such gravity ; and if the author, in his accurate observations on mankind, selected his example from among the mercenaries that are the scandal of the established church, her most faithful friends will not greatly resent this conduct of a dissenter. The worthy clergyman seeks first (not 'the kingdom of God and his righteousness,' or the glory of God in the salvation of souls, but) a rich benefice, to attain this primary object means must be used ; and hypocritical pretensions to diligence, zeal, piety, with some change of doctrine merely to please men, seem most likely to succeed : and so this most base, prevaricating, selfish and ungodly plan is adopted ! In how many thousands of instances has this been an awful reality ! How often has it been pleaded for, as prudent and laudable by men, not only pretending to common honesty and sincerity, but calling themselves the disciples of Jesus Christ !

quently and zealously, and because the temper
of the people requires it, by altering of
some of his principles : for my part, I see no
reason but a man may do this, provided he
has a call, ay, and more a great deal besides
and yet be an honest man.   For why ?

1. His desire of a greater benefice is lawful ; this cannot be contradicted, since it is
set before* him by providence ; so then he
may get it if he can, making no questions for
conscience-sake.

2. Besides his desire after that benefice
makes him more studious, a more zealous
preacher, &c. ; and so makes him a better
man, yea, makes him better improve his parts ;
which is according to the mind of God.

3. Now, as for the complying with the

* ' Set before'—God permits Satan to bait his hook with
some worldly advantage, in order to induce men to renounce
their profession, expose their hypocrisy, or disgrace the Gospel ; and they, poor deluded mortals ! call it ' an opening of
providence.' The Lord indeed puts the object in their ways,
if they will break his commandments in order to seize upon
it : but he does it to prove them, and to shew whether they
most love him or their worldly interests ; but the devil thus
tempts them, that he may take them captive at his will.'
The arguments here adduced, by an admirable imitation
of the pleas used among unsound professors, are only valid
on the supposition that religion is a mere external appearance, and has nothing to do with the state of the heart and
affections ; and in short, that hypocrisy and piety are words
precisely of the same meaning. Upon the whole, the answer
of Christian, though somewhat rough, is so apposite and conclusive, that it is sufficient to fortify every honest and attentive mind against all the arguments which the whole tribe
of timeserving professors ever did or ever can adduce, in support of their ingenious schemes and assiduous efforts to reconcile religion with covetousness and the love of the world, or
to render it subservient to their secular interests.

19*

temper of his people, by deserting to serve them, some of his principles, this argueth that he is of a self-denying temper, of a sweet and winning deportment ; and so more fit for the ministerial functions.

4. I conclude, then, that a minister that changes a small for a great should not, for so doing, be judged as covetous ; but rather, since he is improved in his parts and industry thereby, be counted as one that pursues his call, and the opportunity put into his hand to do good.

And now to the second part of the question, which concerns the tradesman you mentioned : suppose such an one to have but a poor employ in the world ; but by becoming religious he may mend his market, perhaps get a rich wife, or more and far better customers to his shop. For my part, I see no reason but this may be lawfully done For why ?

1. To become religious is a virtue, by what means soever a men becomes so.

2. Nor is it unlawful to get a rich wife, or more custom to my shop.

3. Besides, the man that gets these by becoming religious, gets that which is good, of them that are good, by becoming good himself ; so then here is a good wife, and good customers, and good gain, and all these by becoming religious, which is good : therefore, to become religious to get all these is a good and profitable design.

This answer, thus made by this Mr. Money-love to Mr. By-end's question, was highly ap

plauded by them all ; wherefore they concluded upon the whole, that it was most
wholesome and advantageous. And because,
as they thought, no man was able to contra-
dict it, and because Christian and Hopeful
were yet within call, they jointly agreed to assault them with this question as soon as they
overtook them ; and the rather because they
had opposed Mr. By-ends before. So they
called after them, and they stopped and stood
still till they came up to them : but they concluded, as they went, that not Mr. By-ends,
but old Mr. Hold-the-world, should propound
the question to them ; because as they supposed, their answers to him would be without
the remainder of that heat that was kindled
between Mr. By-ends and them at their parting a little before.

So they came up to each other, and, after
a short salutation, Mr. Hold-the-world propounded the question to Christian and his fellow, and bid them to answer it if they could.

Then said Christian, Even a babe in religion may answer ten thousand such questions.
For if it be unlawful to follow Christ for
loaves, as it is, John vi., how much more is it
abominable to make of him and religion a
stalking horse to get and enjoy the world ?
Nor do we find any other than heathens, hypocrites, devils, and witches, that are of this
opinion.

Heathens : for when Hamor and Shechem
had a mind to the daughter and cattle of Jacob, and saw that there were no ways for

them to come at them, but by becoming circumcised, they say to their companions, ' If every male of us be circumcised, as they are circumcised, shall not their cattle, and their substance, and every beast of theirs, be ours ?' Their daughters and their cattle were that which they sought to obtain, and their religion the stalking-horse they made use of to come at them. Read the whole story, Genesis xxxiv. 20—24.

The hypocritical Pharisees were also of this religion : long prayers were their pretence, but to get widows' houses was their intent, and greater damnation was from God their judgment (Luke xx. 46, 47).

Judas the devil was also of this religion : he was religious for the bag, that he might be possessed of what was therein ; but he was lost, a cast-away, and the very son of perdition.

Simon the witch was of this religion too ; for he would have had the Holy Ghost, that he might have got money therewith ; and his sentence from Peter's mouth was accordingly (Acts viii. 13—23).

Neither will it out of my mind, but that that man, that takes up religion for the world, will throw away religion for the world ; for so surely as Judas designed the world in becoming religious, so surely did he also sell religion and his master for the same. To answer the question therefore affirmatively, as I perceive you have done, and to accept of, as authentic, such answer, is both heathenish, hyp

ocritical, and devillish ; and your reward will
De according to your works. Then they
stood staring one upon another, but had not
wherewith to answer Christian. Hopeful also approved of the soundness of Christian's
answer ; so there was a great silence among
them. Mr. By-ends and his company also
staggered and kept behind, that Christian and
Hopeful might out-go them. Then said
Christian to his fellow, If these men cannot
stand before the sentence of men, what will
they do with the sentence of God, and, if they
are mute when dealt with by vessels of clay,
what will they do when they shall be rebuked
by the flames of a devouring fire ?

Then Christian and Hopeful outwent them
again, and went till they came to a delicate*
plain, called Ease, where they went with
much content ; but that plain was but narrow,
so they were quickly got over it. Now at the
farther side of that plain was a little hill, called
Lucre, and in that hill a silver mine, which some
of them that had formerly gone that way, because of the rarity of it, had turned aside to
see ; but going too near the brim of the pit,

* ' Delicate'—When the church enjoys great outward
peace (which has hitherto been generally but a transient season) professors are peculiarly exposed to the temptation of
seeking worldly riches and distinctions, which at other times
seem too remote to have much attractive influence ; and
many of them are more disconcerted and disposed to murmur,
when excluded from a share of these idolized prizes, than
Christians in general appear to have been under the most
cruel persecutions. The hill Lucre with the silver mine is a
little out of the pilgrim's path, even in times of the greatest
outward rest and security.

the ground, being deceitful under them, broke, and they were slain : some also had been maimed there, and could not to their dying day be their own men again.

Then I saw in my dream, that a little off the road, over against the silver mine, stood*

* ' Stood'—We know not in what way the love of this present world influenced Demas to forsake St. Paul ; yet our author is fully warranted in thus using his name, and afterwards joining it with those of Gehazi, Judas, and others, who perished by the same idolatry. The love of money is not always connected with the desire of covetously hoarding it : it often arises from a vain affectation of gentility, which is emphatically implied by the epithet bestowed on Demas (*gentlemanlike*). The connections that professors form in a day of ease and prosperity, and the example of the world around them (without excepting some of those who would be thought to love the Gospel), seduce them insensibly into a style of living that they cannot afford, in order to avoid the imputation of being sordid and singular. An increasing family ensures additional expense ; and children genteelly educated naturally expect to be provided for accordingly. Thus debts are contracted, and gradually accumulate ; it is neither so easy or so reputable to retrench, as it was to launch out ; and numerous tempters induce men thus circumstanced to turn aside to the hill Lucre ; that is, to leave the direct path of probity and piety, that they may obtain supplies to their urgent and clamorous necessities. Young persons, when they first set out in life, often lay the foundation for innumerable evils, by vainly emulating the expensive style of those in the same line of business, or the same rank in the community ; who are enabled to support such expenses, either by extensive dealings, or by means that ought not to be used. Besides the bankruptcies which continually originate from this mistaken conduct, it is often found, that fair profits are inadequate to uphold that appearance which was at first needlessly assumed ; and so necessity is pleaded for engaging in those branches of trade, or seizing on those emoluments, which the conduct of worldly people screen from total scandal, but which are evidently contrary to the word of God, and the plain rule of exact truth and rectitude, and which render their consciences very uneasy. But who can bear the mortification of owning himself poorer than he was thought to

Demas (gentlemanlike) to call passengers to come and see ; who said to Christian and his

be ? Who dare risk the consequences of being suspected to be insolvent ? Professors in these circumstances are as likely to embrace Demas's invitation, as either By-ends, Money-love, or Save-all ; and if they be ' not drowned in destruction and perdition,' will ' fall into temptation and a snare, and pierce themselves through with many sorrows.' Men should therefore consider, that it is as unjust to contract debts for superfluous indulgences, or to obtain credit by false appearances of affluence, as it is to defraud by any other imposition ; and that this dishonesty makes way for innumerable temptations to more disgraceful species of the same crime ; not to speak of its absolute inconsistency with piety and charity But none are so much exposed to this snare as ministers and their families, when, having no private fortune, they are situated among the affluent and genteel : by yielding to this temptation, they are often incapacitated from paying their debts with punctuality ; they are tempted to degrade their office by stooping to unsuitable methods of extricating themselves out of difficulties, from which strict frugality would have preserved them, and by laying themselves under obligations to such men as are capable of abusing this purchased superiority ; and, above all, they are generally induced to place their children in situations and connexions, the most unfavourable to the interests of their souls, in order to procure them a genteel provision. If we form a judgment upon this subject from the Holy Scriptures, we shall not think of finding the true ministers of God among the higher classes in the community, in matters of internal appearance or indulgence. That information on a variety of subjects, which many of them have the opportunity of acquiring, may render them acceptable company to the affluent, especially to such as love them for their works' sake ; and even the exercise of Christian tempers will improve the urbanity acquired by a liberal education, where faithfulness is not concerned. But if a minister thinks, that the attention of the great or noble requires him to copy their expensive style of living, he greviously mistakes the matter ; for this will forfeit the opinion before entertained of his good sense and regard to propriety ; and his official declarations concerning the vanity of earthly things, and the Christian's indifference about them, will be suspected of insincerity, while it is observed, that he conforms to the world, as far or even farther than his circum-

fellow, Ho ! turn aside hither, and I will shew you a thing.

Chr. What thing so deserving as to turn us out of the way to see it ?

stances will admit : and thus respect will often be changed into disgust ; for the affluent do not choose to be too closely copied in those things which they deem their exclusive privileges, es pecially by one who (they must think) secretly depends on them to defray the expense of such an intrusive competition. The consistent minister of Christ will certainly desire to avoid every thing mean and sordid, to retrench in every other way rather than exhibit the appearance of penury : but, provided he and his family can maintain a decent simplicity, and the credit of punctuality in his payments, he will not think of aspiring any higher. If, in order to do this, he be compelled to exercise considerable self-denial, he will think little of it, while he looks more to Jesus and his apostles, than to the few of a superior rank who profess the Gospel : and could he afford something genteel and fashionable, he would deem it more desirable to devote a larger portion to pious and charitable uses, than to squander it in such a vain affectation. Perhaps Satan never carried a more important point, within the visible church, than when the opinion was adopted, that the clergy were gentlemen by profession, and he led them to infer from it, that they and their families ought to live in a genteel and fashionable style. As the body of the clergy have been mostly but slenderly provided for, when they were thus taught to imitate the appearance of the affluent, the most effectual step was taken to reduce them to an abject state of dependance ; to convert them into parasites and flatterers ; to render them very indulgent to the vices of the rich and great ; or even to tempt them to become the instruments of accomplishing their ambitious or licentious designs : and no small part of the selfishness and artifices of the clergy, which are now made a pretext for abolishing the order, and even for renouncing Christianity, have in fact originated from this fatal mist ike In proportion as the same principle is adopted by ministers of any description, similar effects will follow ; and a degree of dependance, inconsistent with unembarrassed faithfulness, must be the consequence : nor can we in all cases, and without respect of persons, ' declare the whole counsel of God,' unless we be willing, if required, to be, and appear as, the poor followers of him ' who had not where to lay his head.'

Demas. Here is a silver mine, and some digging in it for treasure ; if you will come with a little pains you may richly provide for yourselves.

Then said Hopeful, Let us* go see.

Not I, said Christian, I have heard of this place before now, and how many there have been slain ; and besides, that treasure is a snare to those that seek it, for it hindereth them in their pilgrimage.

Then Christian called to Demas, saying, Is not the place dangerous ? hath it not hindered many in their pilgrimage ?

Demas. Not very dangerous, except to those that are careless. But withal he blushed as he spake.

Then said Christian to Hopeful, let us not stir a step, but keep on our way.

Hope. I will warrant you, when By-ends comes up, if he hath the same invitations as we, he will turn in thither to see.

Chr. No doubt thereof, for his principles lead him that way, and a hundred to one but he dies there.

Then Demas called again, saying, But will you not come over and see ?

Then Christian roundly answered, saying, Demas, thou art an enemy to the right ways of the Lord of this way, and hast been already con

---

* ' Let us'—Inexperienced believers are very liable to be seduced by the example and persuasions of hypocrites ; and to deviate from the direct path, in order to obtain worldly advantages, by means that many deem fair and honourable In this case the counsel and warnings of an experienced companion are of the greatest moment.

demned for thine own turning aside, by one of his majesty's judges (2 Tim. iv. 10) ; and why seekest thou to bring us into the like condemnation ? besides, if we at all turn aside our Lord the king will certainly hear thereof, and will there put us to shame, where we should stand with boldness before him.

Demas cried again, that he also was one of their fraternity ; and that if they would tarry a little he also himself would walk with them.

Then said Christian, What is thy name ? Is it not the same by which I have called thee ?

Demas. Yea, my name is Demas ; I am the son of Abraham.

Chr. I know you : Gehazi was your great grandfather, and Judas your father, and you have trod in their steps : it is but a devilish prank that thou usest : thy father was hanged for a traitor, and thou deservest no better reward (2 Kings v. 20---27 ; Matt. xxvi. 14, 15 ; xxvii. 3----5). Assure thyself, that when we come to the king we will do him word of this thy behaviour. Thus they went their way.

By this time By-ends and his companions were come again within sight, and they, at the first beck, went over to Demas. Now, whether they fell into the pit by looking over the brink thereof, or whether they went down to dig, or whether they were smothered in the bottom by damps that commonly arise, of these things I am not certain ; but this I observed,

that they never were seen again in the way
Then sang Christian :—

> By-ends and silver Demas did agree;
> One calls, the other runs, that he may be
> A sharer in his lucre ; so these do
> Take up in this world, and no farther go.

Now I saw, that, just on the other side of
this plain, the pilgrims came to a place where
stood an old monument hard by the highway
side, and at the sight of which they were both
concerned, because of the strangeness of the
form thereof, for it seemed to them as if it had
been a woman transformed into the shape of a
pillar. Here, therefore, they stood looking
and looking upon it, but could not for a time
tell what they should make thereof : at last
Hopeful spied written upon the head thereof,
a writing in an unusual hand ; but he, being
no scholar, called to Christian (for he was
learned) to see if he could pick out the
meaning : so he came, and after a little laying of the letters together, he found the same
to be this, 'Remember Lot's wife.' So he
read it to his fellow; after which they both concluded, that that was the pillar of salt into which
Lot's wife was turned, for looking back with
a covetous heart when she was going from Sodom for safety (Gen. xix. 26). Which sudden
and amazing sight gave them occasion of this
discourse.

Chr. Ah, my brother ! this is a seasonable
sight: it came opportunely to us after the in
vitation which Demas gave us to come over
to view the hill Lucre; and had we gone over,

as he desired us, and as thou wast, inclined to do, my brother, we had, for aught I know, been made like this woman, a spectacle for those that shall come after to behold.

Hope. I am sorry that I was so foolish, and am made to wonder that I am not now as Lot's wife ; for wherein was the difference betwixt her sin and mine ? she only looked back, and I had a desire to go see : let grace be adored, and let me be ashamed that ever such a thing should be in mine heart.

Chr. Let us take notice of what we see here for our help for time to come : this woman escaped one judgment, for she fell not by the destruction of Sodom ; yet she was destroyed by another, as we see she is turned into a pillar of salt.

Hope. True, and she may be to us both caution and example ; caution, that we should shun her sin ; or a sign of what judgment will overtake such as shall not be prevented by such caution : so Corah, Dathan, and Abiram, with the two hundred and fifty men that perished in their sin, did also become a sign or example to beware (Numb. xxvi. 9, 10). But above* all, I muse at one thing, to wit, how

---

* ' But above'—It is indeed most wonderful, that men, who profess to believe the Bible, can so confidently attempt to reconcile the love of the world with the service of God ; when the instructions, warnings, and examples in Scripture, which shew the fatal consequences of such endeavours, are so numerous, express, and affecting ! If Lot's wife, who merely hankered after the possessions she had left behind in Sodom, and looked back with a design of returning, was made a monument of the Lord's vengeance, and a warning to all future ages, what will be the doom of those profes-

Demas and his fellows can stand so confidently yonder to look for that treasure, which this woman, but for looking behind her after (for we read not that she stept one foot out of the way), was turned into a pillar of salt ; especially since the judgment which overtook her did make her an axample within sight of where they are ; for they cannot choose but see her, did they but lift up their eyes.

Chr. It is a thing to be wondered at, and it argueth that their hearts are grown desperate in that case ; and I cannot tell whom to compare them to so fitly, as to them that pick pockets in the presence of the judge, or that will cut purses under the gallows.   It is said of the men of Sodom, that 'they were sinners exceedingly,' because they were sinners 'before the Lord,' that is, in his eyesight, and notwithstanding the kindnesses that he had shewed them ; for the land of Sodom was now like the garden of Eden heretofore (Gen. xiii. 10—13).   This therefore provoked him the more to jealousy, and made their plague as hot as the fire of the Lord out of heaven could make it.   And it is most rationally to be concluded, that such, even such as these are, they that shall sin in the sight, yea, and that too in despite of such examples that are set continually before them to caution

sors of the Gospel who habitually prefer worldly gain, or the vain pomp and indulgence that may be purchased with it, to the honour of Christ, and obedience to his most reasonable commandments ? The true cause of this infatuation is here assigned.

them to the contrary, must be partakers of the severest judgments.

Hope. Doubtless thou hast said the truth ; but what a mercy is it, that neither thou, but especially I, am not made myself this example ! This ministereth occasion to us to thank God, to fear before him, and always to 'remember Lot's wife.'

I saw then that they went on their way to a pleasant river, which David the king called 'the river of God,' but John, 'the river of the water of life' (Ps. lxv. 9 ; Ezek. xlvii ; Rev. xxii. 1). Now their way lay just upon the bank of the river : here therefore Christian and his companion walked with great delight ; they drank also the water of the river, which was pleasant,* and enlivening to their weary

---

* ' Pleasant —When Abraham had given place to his nephew Lot, and receded from his interest for the credit of his religion, he was immediately favoured with a most encouraging vision (Gen. xiii). Thus the pilgrims, having been enabled to resist the temptation to turn aside for lucre, were indulged with more abundant spiritual consolations (Mark x. 23—30). The Holy Spirit, the inexhaustible source of life, light, holiness, and joy, is represented by ' the river of God, even that river of the water of life, clear as a crystal, proceeding out of the throne of God, and of the Lamb' (Rev. xxii. 1). All believers partake of his sacred influences, which prepare the soul for heavenly felicity, and are earnest and pledges of it : but there are seasons when he communicates his holy comforts in larger measure ; when the Christian sees such glory in the salvation of Christ, so clearly ascertains his interest in it, and realizes his obligations and privileges with such lively exercises of adoring love, gratitude, and joy, that he is raised above his darkness and difficulties ; enjoys sweet communion with God ; forgets, for the moment, the pain of former conflicts, and the prospect of future trials ; finds his in bred corruptions reduced to a state of subjection, and his maladies healed by lively exercises of faith in the Son of God ;

spirits. Besides, on the banks of this river, on either side, were green trees for all manner of fruit ; and the leaves they ate to prevent surfeits, and other diseases that are incident to those that heat their blood by travels. On either side of the river was also a meadow, curiously beautified with lilies ; and it was green all the year long. In this meadow they lay down and slept : for here they might lie down safely (Ps. xxiii ; Isa. xiv. 30). When they awoke they gathered again of the fruits of the trees, and drank again of the water of the river, and then lay down again to sleep. Thus they did several days and nights. Then they sang :

> Behold ye how those crystal streams do glide
> To comfort pilgrims by the highway side.
> The meadows green, besides the fragrant smell,
> Yield dainties for them : and he that can tell
> What pleasant fruit, yea leaves, these trees do yield,
> Will soon sell all that he may buy this field.

So when they were disposed to go on (for they were not as yet at their journey's end), they ate, and drank, and departed.

and anticipates with unspeakable delight the glory that shall be revealed. Then communion with humble believers (the lilies that adorn the banks of the river) is very pleasant; and the soul's rest in God and his service is safe as well as happy; being widely different from every species of carnal security. Had this river meant the blessings of pardon, justification, and adoption, it would not have been thus occasionally introduced ; for these belong to believers at all times, without any interruption or variation ; but the more abundant consolations of the Spirit are not vouchsafed in the same manner, and on them the actual enjoyment of our privileges in a great measure depends.

Now I beheld in my dream, that they had
not jourreyed far but the river and the way
for a time parted ; at which they were not a
little sorry, yet they durst not go out of the
way.   Now the way* from the river was
rough, and their feet tender by reason of their
travels : so the souls of the   pilgrims were
much   discouraged   because   of   the   way

* ' Now the way'—Believers, even when in the path of duty, walking by faith, and supported by the sanctifying influences of the Spirit, may be abridged of those holy consolations
which they have experienced ; and if this trial be accompanied with temporal losses, poverty, sickness, the unkindness
of friends, or ill usage from the world, they may be greatly
discouraged ; and Satan may have a special advantage in
tempting them to discontent, distrust, envy, or coveting.
Thus, being more disposed to ' wish for a better way,' than
to pray earnestly for an increase of faith and patience, they
will be tempted to look out for some method of declining the
cross, or shifting the difficulty which wearies them : nor will
it be long before some expedient for a temporary relief will
be suggested.   The path of duty being rough, a bye-path is
discovered, which seems to lead the same way ; but, if they
will thus turn aside (though they need not break through a
hedge) they must go over a stile.   The commandments of
God mark out the path of holiness and safety ; but a deviation from the exact strictness of them may sometimes be plau-
sibly made, and circumstances seem to invite to it.   Men
imagine some providential interposition, giving ease to the
weary ; and they think that the precept may be interpreted
with some latitude ; that prudence should be exercised ; and
that scrupulousness about little things is a mark of legality.
Thus, by leaning to their own understanding and trusting in
their own hearts, instead of asking counsel of the Lord, they
hearken to the tempter.   Nor is it uncommon for Christians of
deeper experience, and more established reputation to mislead their juniors, by turning aside from the direct line of
obedience.   For the Lord leaves them to themselves to repress their self-confidence, and keep them entirely dependent
on him ; and thus teaches young converts to follow no man
farther than he follows Christ.

(Numo. xxi. 4). Wherefore still as they went on they wished for a better way. Now a little before them, there was on the left hand of the road a meadow, and a stile to go over into it ; and that meadow is called By-path-meadow. Then said Christian to his fellow, If this meadow lieth along by our way-side let us go over into it. Then he went to the stile to see, and behold a path lay along by the way on the other side of the fence. 'Tis according to my wish, said Christian, here is the easiest going ; come, good Hopeful, and let us go over.

Hope. But how if this path should lead us out of the way ?

That's not like, said the other. Look,* doth it not go along by the way-side ? So Hopeful, being persuaded by his fellow, went

---

* 'Look'—It would not be politic in Satan to tempt believers at first to flagrant crimes, at which their hearts would revolt ; but he draws them aside, under specious pretences, into such plausible deviations as seem to be of no bad repute or material consequence : but every wrong step makes way for farther temptations, and tends to render other sins apparently necessary ; and if it be a deliberate violation of the least precept in the smallest instance, from carnal motives, it involves such self-will, unbelief, ingratitude, and worldly idolatry, as will most certainly expose the believer to sharp rebukes and painful corrections. The example also of professors, of whom perhaps at the first interview too favourable an opinion has been formed, helps to bolster up the vain-confidence of him who has departed from the path of obedience : for these men express the strongest assurance, and venture to violate the precepts of Christ, under pretence of honouring his free grace, and knowing their liberty and privilege ! But darkness must soon envelop those who follow such guides, and the most extreme distress and danger are directly in the way they take.

after him over the stile. When they were gone over, and were got into the path, they found it very easy for their feet ; and withal, they, looking before them, spied a man walking as they did, and his name was vain confidence : so they called after him, and asked him whither that way led ? He said, to the celestial gate. Look, said Christian, did not I tell you so ? by this you may see we are right : so they followed, and he went before them. But behold the night came on, and it grew very dark ; so that they that went behind lost the sight of him that went before.

He therefore that went before (Vain-confidence by name), not seeing the way before him, fell* into a deep pit (Isa. ix. 16), which was on purpose there made by the prince of those grounds, to catch vain-glorious fools withal, and was dashed in pieces with his fall.

Now Christian and his fellow heard him fall : so they called to know the matter ; but there was none to answer, only they heard a groaning. Then said Hopeful, Where are we now ? Then was his fellow silent, as mistrusting that he had led him out of the way ; and now† it began to rain, and thunder, and

* 'Fell'—This circumstance perhaps represents the salutary effects which are sometimes produced in the hearts of offending believers, by the awful death of some vain-glorious professor, to whom they have given too much attention. The Lord, however, will deliver his servants from the temporary prevalence of vain-confidence, while presumptuous hypocrites perish in the pit of darkness and despair.

† 'And now'—The holy law condemns every transgression : when the Christian, therefore, hath fallen into any wilful sin, he is often led to fear that his faith is dead, that

lighten, in a most dreadful manner ; and the water rose amain.

Then Hopeful groaned in himself, saying, Oh that I had kept on my way !

Chr. Who could have thought that this path should have led us out of the way ?

Hope. I was afraid on't at the very first, and therefore gave you that gentle caution. I would have spoken plainer, but you are older than I.

Chr. Good brother, be not offended ; I am sorry I have brought thee out of the way, and that I have put thee into such imminent danger : pray, my brother, forgive me ; I did not do it of an evil intent.

Hope. Be comforted, my brother, for I forgive thee ; and believe, too, that this shall be for good.

Chr. I am glad I have with me a merciful brother ; but we must not stand thus ; let us try to go back again.

Hope. But, good brother, let me go before

Chr. No, if you please, let me go first,

he is still under the law, and that his person is condemned by it as well as his conduct ; and thus he is brought back again, as it were, to the tempest, thunder, and lightning of mount Sinai. The following dialogue is very natural and instructive, and exhibits that spirit of mutual tenderness, forbearance, and sympathy, which becomes Christians in such perplexing circumstances. They, who have misled others into sin, should not only ask forgiveness of God, but of them also ; and they, who have been drawn aside by the example and persuasion of their brethren, should be careful not to upbraid or discourage them, when they become sensible of their fault.

that if there be any danger I may be first
therein ; because by my means we are both
gone out of the way.

No, said Hopeful, you shall not go first ;
for your mind being troubled may lead you
out of the way again. Then, for their encouragement, they heard the voice of one
saying, ' Let thine heart* be towards the
highway ; even the way that thou wentest :

* ' Let thine'—When such as have turned aside are called
upon in Scripture to return to God and his ways, the exhortation implies a promise of acceptance to all who comply with
it, and may be considered as immediately addressed to every
one with whose character and situation it corresponds. It
might be thought indeed, that an experienced believer, when
convinced of any sin, would find little difficulty in returning
to his duty, and recovering his peace. But experience inculcates a very different instruction : a deliberate transgression, however trivial it might seem at the moment, appears
upon the retrospect to be an act of most ungrateful and aggravated rebellion ; so that it brings such darkness upon the
soul, and guilt on the conscience, as frequently causes a man
to suspect that his experiences have been a delusion. And,
when he would attempt to set out anew, it occurs to him,
that if all his past endeavours and expectations, for many
years, have been frustrated, he can entertain little hope of
better success hereafter ; as he knows not how to use other
means, or greater earnestness, than he hath already employed to no purpose. Nor will Satan ever fail, in these circumstances, to pour in such suggestions as may overwhelm the
soul with an apprehension that the case is hopeless, and God
inexorable. The believer will not, indeed, be prevailed
upon by these discouragements wholly to neglect all attempts
to recover his ground ; but he will often resemble a man who
is groping in the dark and cannot find his way, or who is
passing through a deep and rapid stream, and struggling
hard to keep his head above water. Thus the desire of present relief from intolerable distress will occupy his thoughts,
and expose him to the danger of quieting his conscience in
an unauthorized manner, by some erroneous opinion or conclusion.

turn aside' (Jer. xxxi. 21). But by this time
the waters were greatly risen, by reason of
which the way of going back was very dangerous. (Then I thought, that it is easier
going out of the way when we were in, than
going in when we are out). Yet they ad-
ventured to go back ; but it was so dark, and
the flood was so high, that in their going
back they had like to have been drowned nine
or ten times.

Neither could they, with all the skill they
had, get again to the stile that night. Wherefore at last, lighting under a little shelter,*

* ' Shelter'—When David had fallen in the depths of sin
and distress, he cried most earnestly to the Lord (Ps. cxxx) ;
and Jonah did the same in the fish's belly. Extraordinary cases require singular diligence ; even as greater exertion is
necessary to get out of a pit than to walk upon level ground.
When believers, therefore, have brought themselves, by transgression, into great terror and anguish of conscience, it is
foolish to expect that God will ' restore to them the joy of
his salvation,' till they have made the most unreserved confession of their guilt, humbly deprecated his deserved wrath
in persevering prayer, and used peculiar diligence in every
thing that accompanies repentance and faith in Christ,
and tends to greater watchfulness, circumspection, and self-
denial. But they often seek relief in a more compendious
way ; and, as they do not wholly omit their customary religious exercises, or vindicate and repeat their transgressions,
they endeavour to quiet themselves by general notions of
God's mercy through Jesus Christ, and the security of the
new covenant ; and the storm in their consciences subsiding,
they ' find a little shelter,' and ' wait for a more convenient
opportunity' of recovering their former life and vigour in religion. Indeed, the very circumstances which should excite
us to peculiar earnestness, tend, through the depravity of
our nature, to blind and stupify the heart : Peter and the other
disciples ' slept for sorrow,' when they were more especially
required ' to watch and pray, that they might not enter into
temptation.' Such repeated sins and mistakes bring below

they sat down there till the daybreak ; but being weary they fell asleep.   Now there was,

ers into deep distress.   Growing more and more heartless in
religion, and insensible in a most perilous situation, they are
led habitually to infer that they are hypocrites ; that the encouragements of Scripture belong not to them ; that prayer
itself will be of no use to them ; and, when they are at length
brought to reflection, they are taken prisoners by Despair,
and shut up in Doubting-castle.   This case should be carefully
distinguished from Christian's terrors in the city of Destruction, which induced him to ' flee from the wrath to come ;'
from the slough of Despond, into which he fell when diligently seeking salvation ; from the burthen he carried to the
cross ; from his conflict with Apollyon, and his troubles
in the valley of the Shadow of death ;   and even from the
terrors that seized him and Hopeful in By-path-meadow,
which would have speedily terminated if they had not slept
on forbidden ground, and stopped short of the refuge the Lord
hath provided.   Despair, like a tremendous giant, will at
last seize on the souls of all unbelievers ; and when Christians conclude, from some aggravated and pertinacious misconduct, that they belong to that company, even their acquaintance with the Scripture will expose them to be taken
captive by him in this world.   They do not indeed fall and
perish with Vain-confidence ; but for a season they find it
impossible to rise superior to prevailing gloomy doubts bor-
dering on despair, or to obtain the least comfortable hope of
deliverance, or encouragement to use the proper means of
seeking it.   Whenever we deliberately quit the plain path
of duty, to avoid hardship and self-denial, we trespass on
giant Despair's ground ; and are never out of his reach till
renewed exercises of deep repentance, and faith in Christ,
producing unreserved obedience, especially in that instance
where before we refused it, have set our feet in the highway
we had forsaken.   This we cannot attain to without the
special grace of God, which he may not see good immediately to communicate : in the mean time every effort must be
accompanied with discouragement and distress ; but if we
yield to another temptation, and, instead of persevering, amidst
our anxious fears, to cry to him for help, and wait his time
of shewing mercy, endeavour to bolster up some false confidence, and take shelter in a refuge of lies, the event will be
such as is here described.   It will be in vain, after such
perverseness, to pretend that we have inadvertently mis

not far from the place where they lay, a castle, called Doubting Castle, the owner whereof was giant Despair; and it was in his grounds they were now sleeping. Wherefore he getting up in the morning early, and walking up and down in his fields, caught Christian and Hopeful asleep in his grounds. Then with a grim and surly voice he bid them awake, and asked them whence they were, and what they did in his grounds? They told him they were pilgrims, and that they had lost their way. Then said the giant, You have this night trespassed on me by trampling in, and lying on, my ground, and therefore you must go along with me. So they were forced to go, because he was stronger than they. They also had but little to say, for they knew themselves in a fault The giant, therefore, drove them before him, and put them into his castle in a very dark dungeon, nasty, and stinking to the spirits of these two men. Here then* they lay, from

taken our way; ' our own hearts will condemn us;' how then can ' we have confidence in God, who is greater than our hearts and knoweth all things?' The grim giant will prove too strong for us, and shut us up in his noisome dungeon, and the recollection of our former hopes and comforts will only serve to aggravate our woe. These lines are here inserted—

> ' The pilgrims now, to gratify the flesh,
> Will seek its ease; but, oh! how they afresh
> Do thereby plunge themselves new griefs into!
> Who seek to please the flesh themselves undo.'

* ' Here then'—Perhaps this exact time was mentioned under the idea, that it was as long as life can generally be

Wednesday morning till Saturday night, without one bit of bread, or drop of drink, or light, or any to ask how they did : they were, therefore, here in evil case, and were far from friends and acquaintance (Ps. lxxxviii. 8). Now in this place Christian had double sorrow, because it was through his unadvised counsel that they were brought into this distress.

Now giant* Despair had a wife, and her name was Diffidence ; so when he was gone

supported in the situation here described. The believer may be brought by wilful sin to such a condition, that, to his own apprehension, destruction is inevitable. If a man may sink so low as to have no light or comfort from God's word and Spirit, nothing to sustain his dying faith and hope, no help or pity from his brethren, but severe sensures or more painful suspicions ; the horrors of an accusing conscience, the dread of God as an enemy, connected with sharp and multiplied corrections in his outward circumstances ; as the price of the ease or indulgence obtained by some wilful transgression ; who, that believes it, will take encouragement to sin from the doctrine of final perseverance ? Would a man, for a trivial gain, leap down a precipice, even if he could be sure that he should escape with his life ? No, the dread of the anguish of broken bones, and of being made a cripple to the end of his days, would effectually secure him from such a madness.

* ' Now giant'—Despair seldom fully seizes any man in this world ; and the strongest hold it can get of a true believer amounts only to a prevailing distrust of God's promises, with respect to his own case ; for this is accompanied with some small degree of latent hope, discoverable in its effects, though unperceived amidst the distressing feelings of the heart. Perhaps this was intended in the allegory by the circumstance of Despair's doing nothing to the pilgrims save at the instance of his wife Diffidence. Desponding fears, when they so prevail as to keep men from prayer, make way for temptations to suicide, as the only relief to their miseries ; but when true faith is in the heart, however it may seem to be wholly out of exercise, the temptation will be evidently overcome, provided actual insanity do not intervene ; and this is a

to bed he told his wife what he had done ; to wit, that he had taken a couple of prisoners, and cast them into his dungeon for trespassing on his grounds. Then he asked her also what he had best do farther to them. So she asked what they were, whence they came, and whither they were bound ; and he told her. Then she counselled him, that when he arose in the morning he should beat them without mercy. So when he arose, he getteth a grievous crab-tree cudgel, and goes down into the dungeon to them, and there first falls to rating of them as if they were dogs, although they gave him never a word of distaste ; then he falls upon them, and beat them fearfully, in such sort that they were not able to help themselves, or turn them upon the floor. This done he withdraws, and leaves them there to condole their misery, and to mourn under their distress ; so all that day they spent their time in nothing but sighs and bitter lamentations. The next night she talked with her husband about them farther, and understanding that they were yet alive, did advise him to counsel them to make away themselves ; so when morning was come, he goes to them in a surly manner as before, and perceiving them to be very sore with the stripes that he had given them the day before,

uncommon case among religious people, whatever slanders their enemies may circulate, in order to prejudice men's minds against the truth. The giant's 'fits in sunshiny weather,' seem to denote those transient glimpses of hope, which preserve believers from such dire extremities in their most discouraged seasons.

21*

he told them, that, since they were never
like to come out of that place, their only way
would be forthwith to make an end of themselves, either with knife, halter, or poison,
for why, said he, should you choose life, seeing it is attended with so much bitterness ?
But they desired him to let them go ; with
that he looked ugly upon them, and rushing
to them, had doubtless made an end of them
himself, but that he fell into one of his fits
(for he sometimes in sunshiny weather fell into fits), and lost for a time the use of his
hand. Wherefore he withdrew, and left
them, as before, to consider what to do.
Then did the prisoners consult between themselves whether it was best to take his counsel
or no ; and thus they began to discourse :—

Brother,* said Christian, what shall we do ?
The life that we now live is miserable : for

* ' Brother'—They, who have long walked with stable
peace in the ways of God, are often known to be more dejected, when sin hath filled their consciences with remorse,
than younger professors are ; especially if they have caused
others to offend, or brought any reproach on the Gospel.
Their conduct, as inconsistent with their former character
and profession, seems a decided proof of self-deception in
times past ; they deem it hopeless to begin all over again ; Satan endeavours to the utmost to dishearten new converts by
their example ; and the Lord permits them to be overwhelmed
for a time with discouragement, for a warning to others ; to
vindicate the honour of his truth, which they have disgraced ;
to counterpoise such attainments or services, as might otherwise ' exalt them above measure ;' and to shew that none
has any strength independent of him, and that he can make
use of the feeble to assist the strong, when he sees good.
Hopeful's arguments against self-murder are conclusive :
doubtless men in general venture on that awful crime, either
disbelieving or forgetting the Scripture doctrine of a future

my part, I know not whether it is best to live thus, or die out of hand ; 'my soul chooseth strangling rather than life' (Job vii. 15), and the grave is more easy for me than this dungeon. Shall we be ruled by the giant ?

Hope. Indeed our present condition is dreadful, and death would be far more welcome to me than thus for ever to abide ; but yet let us consider, the Lord of the country to which we are going hath said, 'Thou shalt do no murder ;' no, not to another man's person ; much more then are we forbidden to take his counsel to kill ourselves. Besides, he that kills another can but commit murder upon his body ; but, for one to kill himself, is to kill body and soul at once. And moreover, my brother, thou talkest of ease in the grave, but hast thou forgotten the hell whither for certain the murderers go ? for, 'no murderer hath eternal life,' &c. And let us consider again, that all the law is not in the hand of giant Despair : others, so far as I can understand, have been taken by him as well as we, and yet have escaped out of his hands. Who knows, but that God, that made the world,

and eternal state of retribution ; and it were sincerely to be wished, that all serious persons would avoid speaking of such as have put an end to their existence ; which certainly tends to mislead the mind of the tempted into very erroneous apprehensions of this most important subject. The subsequent discourse aptly represents the fluctuation of men's minds under great despondency ; their struggles against despair, with purposes at some future opportunity to seek deliverance ; their present irresolution ; and the way in which feeble hopes, and strong fears of future wrath, keep them from yielding to the suggestions of the enemy.

may cause that giant Despair may die ; or
that, at some time or other, he may forget to
lock us in ; or that he may in a short time
have another of his fits before us, and may
lose the use of his limbs ? and if ever that
should come to pass again, for my part, I
am resolved to pluck up the heart of a man,
and to try my utmost to get from under his
hand. I was a fool that I did not try to do it
before ; but however, my brother, let us be
patient, and endure awhile ; the time may
come that may give us a happy release ; but
let us not be our own murderers. With these
words Hopeful at present did moderate the
mind of his brother ; so that they continued
together, in the dark, that day, in their sad
and doleful condition.

Well, towards evening the giant goes down
into the dungeon again, to see if his prisoners
had taken his counsel : but when he came
there he found them alive ; and, truly, alive
was all ; for now, what for want of bread and
water, and by reason of the wounds they received when he beat them, they could do little but breathe. But, I say, he found them
alive ; at which he fell into a grievous rage,
and told them, that, seeing they had disobey-
ed his counsel, it should be worse with them
than if they had never been born.

At this they trembled greatly, and I think
that Christian fell into a swoon ; but, coming
a little to himself again, they renewed their
discourse about the giant's counsel, and
whether yet they had best take it or no. Now

Christian again seemed to be for doing it, but Hopeful made his second reply as followeth :—

My brother* said he, rememberest thou not how valiant thou hast been heretofore ? Apollyon could not crush thee, nor could all that thou didst hear or see, or feel, in the valley of the Shadow of Death ; what hardship, terror, and amazement, hast thou already gone through, and art thou now nothing but fears ? Thou seest that I am in the dungeon with thee, a far weaker man by nature than thou art ; also, the giant has wounded me as well as thee, and hath also cut off the bread and water from my mouth, and with that I mourn without the light.   But let us exercise a little more patience ; remember how thou playedst the man at Vanity fair, and was neither afraid of the chain or cage, nor yet of bloody death ; wherefore let us, at least to avoid the shame that becomes not a Christian to be found in, bear up with patience as well as we can.

Now night being come again and the giant and his wife being in bed, she asked him concerning the prisoners, and if they had taken his counsel : to which he replied, They are sturdy rogues, they choose rather to bear all

* 'My brother'—Serious recollection of past conflicts, dangers, and deliverances, is peculiarly useful to encourage confidence in the power and mercy of God, and patient waiting for him in the most difficult and perilous situations; and conference with our brethren, even if they, too, are under similar trials, is a very important means of resisting the devil, when he would tempt us to renounce our hope, and have recourse to desperate measures.

hardship than to make away themselves.
Then said she, Take them into the castle-
yard to-morrow, and shew them* the bones
and skulls of those that thou hast already dispatched, and make them believe, ere a week
comes to an end tnou also will tear them in
pieces, as you hast done their fellows before them.

So when the morning was come, the giant
goes to them again, and takes them into the
castle-yard, and shews them as his wife had
bidden him : these, said he, were pilgrims,
as you are, once, and they trespassed in my
grounds, as you have done ; and when I
thought fit I tore them in pieces, and so within ten days I will do you : get you down into your den again : and with that he beat
them all the way thither. They lay therefore all day on Suturday in a lamentable case,
as before.   Now when night was come, and

---

* ' Shew them'—The Scripture exhibits some examples
of apostates who have died in despair (as king Saul and Judas Iscariot), and several intimations are given of those to
whom nothing remains but a certain fearful looking for of judgment and fiery indignation. A few instances also have been
noticed, in different ages, of notorious apostates, who have
died in blasphemous rage and despair : these accord to the
man in the iron cage at the house of the Interpreter, and
are awful warnings to all professors, ' while they think they
stand, to take heed lest they fall.'   But the hypocrite generally overlooks the solemn caution ; and the humble Christian, having a tender conscience and an acquaintance with
the deceitfulness of his own heart, is very apt to consider his
wilful transgression as the unpardonable sin, and to verge
towards despair, from an apprehension that the doom of
former apostates will at length be his own.   This seems intended by the giant shewing the pilgrims the bones of those
he had slain, in order to induce them to self-murder.

when Mrs. Diffidence and her husband the giant, were got to bed, they began to renew their discourse of their prisoners ; and withal, the old giant wondered that he could neither by his blows nor counsel bring them to an end.   And with that his wife replied, I fear said she, that they live in hopes that some will come to relieve them, or that they have picklocks about them, by the means of which they hope to escape.   And sayest thou, so my dear ? said the giant ; I will therefore search them in the morning.

Well, on* Saturday about midnight they

---

* 'Well, on'—Perhaps the author selected Saturday at midnight for the precise time when the prisoners began to pray, in order to intimate, that the return of the Lord's day and that preparation which serious persons are reminded to make for it, as well as its sacred services, are often the happy means of recovering those that have fallen into sin and despondency. Nothing will be effectual for the recovering of such persons, till they ' begin to pray' with fervency, importunity, and perseverance. Ordinary diligence will here be unavailing : they have sought ease to the flesh, when they ought to have ' watched unto prayer ; and they must now watch and pray when others sleep ; at least they must struggle against their own reluctancy, and persist in repeated application to the mercy-seat, till they obtain a gracious answer. But such is our nature and situation, that in proportion as we have special need for earnestness in such devout exercises, our hearts are averse to them. The obedient child anticipates the pleasure of meeting his affectionate parent ; but when conscious of having offended, through a mixture of shame, fear, and pride, he hides himself, and keeps at a distance from him. Thus unbelief, guilt, and a proud aversion to unreserved self-abasement, wrought upon by Satan's temptations, keep even   believer, when he is fallen into any aggravated sin, from coming to his only friend, and availing himself of his sole remedy : ' he keeps silence though his bones wax old with his roaring all the day long' (Psalm xxxii, 3—5) But when this unbelieving stoutness of spirit is broken down,

began to pray, and continued in prayer till almost break of day

Now a little before it was day, good Christian as one half amazed, brake out into this passionate speech : What a fool, quoth he, am I, thus to lay in a stinking dungeon, when I may as well walk at liberty ? I have a key* in my

and the offender begins to cry fervently to God for mercy, with humiliating confessions, renewed application to the blood of Christ, and perseverance amidst delays and discouragements, it will not be very long ere he obtain complete deliverance from the gloomy dungeon of despair.

* 'A key'—The promise of eternal life to every one, without exception, who believeth in Christ, is here especially intended ; but without excluding any other of the exceeding great and precious promises of the Gospel. The believer, when enabled to recollect such as peculiarly suit his case, and feeling that he cordially desires the promised blessings, and truly expects them by reliance on the testimony and faithfulness of God, in his appointed way, has the key in his bosom, ' which will open any lock in Doubting Castle ;' and while he pleads them by the prayer of faith, depending on the merits and atonement of Emmanuel, ' coming to God through him,' he gradually resumes his confidence, and begins to wonder at his past despondency. Yet some remains of unbelief, a recollection of his aggravated guilt, and a fear lest he should presume, will render it difficult for him wholly to dismiss his discouraging doubts. But let it especially be noted, that the faith, which delivered the pilgrims from giant Despair's castle, induced them to return into the highway of obedience without delay, or making any more complaints of its roughness ; as also to walk in it with more circumspection than before ; and to devise every method of cautioning others against passing over the stile into By-path meadow. Whereas a dead faith and vain confidence will keep out all doubts and fears, even on forbidden ground, and under the walls of Despair's castle ; till at length the poor, deluded wretch will be unexpectedly and irresistibly seized upon, and made his prey. And if Christians will follow Vain confidence, and endeavour to keep up their hopes when neglecting their known duty, let them remember, that (whatever some men may pretend) they will surely be thus

bosom, called Promise, that will I am persuaded, open any lock in Doubting Castle. Then
said Hopeful, That's good news, good brother, pluck it out of thy bosom and try.

Then Christian pulled it out of his bosom,
and began to try at the dungeon door ; whose
bolt as he turned the key gave back, and the
door flew open with ease, and Christian and
Hopeful both came out. Then he went to
the outward door that leads into the castle-
yard, and with this key opened that door also. After he went to the iron gate, for that
must be opened too, but that lock went very
hard ; yet the key did open it. Then they
thrust open the gate to make their escape
with speed ; but the gate as it opened made
such a cracking that it waked giant Despair,
who hastily rising to pursue his prisoners felt
his limbs to fail, for his fits took him again,
so that he could by no means go after them.
Then they went on, and came to the king's
highway, and so were safe, because they
were out of his jurisdictions.

Now, when they were gone over the stile,
they began to contrive with themselves what
they should do at that stile, to prevent those
that shall come after from falling into the
hand of giant Despair. So they consented
to erect there a pillar, and to engrave upon
the side thereof this sentence, ' Over this

brought acquainted with Diffidence, immured in Doubting
Castle, and terribly bruised and frighted by giant Despair ;
nor will they be delivered till they have learned, by painful
experience, that the assurance of hope is inseparably connected with the self-denying obedience of faith and love.

stile is the way to Doubting Castle, which is kept by giant Despair, who despiseth the king of the celestial country, and seeks to destroy the holy pilgrims.' Many therefore that followed after read what was written, and escaped the danger. This done, they sang as follows :

Out of the way we went, and then we found
What 'twas to tread upon forbidden ground ;
And let them that come after have a care,
Lest they, for trespassing, his prisoners are
Whose castle's Doubting, and whose name's Despair.

They went then till they* came to the Delectable Mountains, which mountains belong

---

* 'Till they'—When offending believers are brought to deep repentance, renewed exercises of lively faith, and willing obedience in those self-denying duties which they had declined, the Lord ' restores to them the joy of his salvation,' and their former comforts become more abundant and permanent. The Delectable Mountains seem intended to represent those calm seasons of peace and comfort, which consistent Christians often experience in their old age. They have survived, in a considerable degree, the vehemence of their youthful passions, and have honourably performed their parts in the active scenes of life ; they are established, by long experience, in the simplicity of dependance and obedience ; the Lord graciously exempts them from peculiar trials and temptations ; their acquaintance with the ministers and people of God is enlarged, and they possess the respect, confidence, and affection of many esteemed friends ; they have much leisure for communion with God, and the immediate exercises of religion ; and they often converse with their brethren on the loving kindness and truth of the Lord, till ' their hearts burn within them.' Thus ' leaning on their staffs,' depending on the promises and perfections of God in assured faith and hope, they anticipate their future happiness ' with joy unspeakable and full of glory.' These things are represented under a variety of external images, according to the nature of an allegory. The shepherds and their flocks denote the more extensive acquaintance of many aged Christians with the ministers and churches of Christ,

to the lord of that hill of which we have spoken before : so they went up to the mountains, to behold the gardens and orchards, the vineyards and fountains of waters ; where also they drank and washed themselves, and did freely eat of the vineyards. Now there was on the tops of these mountains shepherds feeding their flocks, and they stood by the highway side. The pilgrims therefore went to them, and leaning upon their staves (as is common with weary pilgrims when they stand to talk with any by the way), they asked, ' Whose Delectable mountains are these ? and whose be the sheep that feed upon them ?'

Shep. The mountains are Emmanuel's land and they are within sight of his city ; and the sheep also are his, and he laid down his life for them.

Chr. Is this the way to the Celestial city ?

Shep. You are just in the way ?

Chr. How far is it thither ?

Shep. Too far* for any but those that shall get thither indeed.

the chief Shepherd, ' who laid down his life for the sheep.' This is ' Emmanuel's land ;' for, being detached from worldly engagements and connexions, they now spend their time almost wholly among the subjects of the Prince of Peace, and as in his more especial presence. The following lines are added here, as before—

> ' Mountains delectable they now ascend,
> Where shepherds be, which to them do commend
> Alluring things, and things that cautions are ;
> Pilgrims are steady kept by faith and fear.

* ' Too far'—The certainty of the final perseverance of true believers is continually exemplified in their actual per-

Chr. Is the way safe or dangerous?

Shep. Safe for those for whom it is to be safe; 'but transgressors shall fall therein' (Hos. xiv. 9).

Chr. Is there in this place any relief for pilgrims that are weary and faint in the way?

Shep. The Lord of these mountains hath given us a charge 'not to be forgetful to entertain strangers' (Heb. xiii. 1, 2); therefore the good of the place is before you. I also saw in my dream, that, when the shepherds perceived that they were wayfaring men, they also put questions to them, (to which they made answer, as in other places), as, whence came you? and, how got you into the way? and by what means have you so persevered therein? for but few of them that begin to come hither do show their faces on this mountain. But when the shepherds heard their answers, being pleased therewith, they looked very lovingly upon them, and said, Welcome to the Delectable Mountains.

The shepherds, I say, whose names* were

severing, notwithstanding all imaginable inward and outward impediments. Many hold the doctrine who are not interested in the privilege, and whose conduct eventually proves, that they 'had no root in themselves' (1. John ii. 19); but the true believer acquires new strength by his very trials and mistakes, and possesses increasing evidence that the new covenant is made with him; for, 'having obtained help of God,' he still 'continues in Christ's word,' and 'abides in him; and while temptations, persecutions, heresies, and afflictions, which stumble transgressors and detect hypocrites, tend to quicken, humble, sanctify, and establish him, he may assuredly conclude, that 'he shall be kept by the power of God, through faith, unto salvation.'

* 'Names'—These names imply much useful instruction,

Knowledge, Experience, Watchful and Sincere, took them by the hand, and had them to their tents, and made them partake of that which was ready at present. They said, moreover, we would that you should stay here awhile, to be acquainted with us, and yet more to solace yourselves with the good of these Delectable Mountains. They then told them, that they were content to stay : so they went to their rest that night, because it was very late.

Then I saw in my dream, that in the morning the Shepherds called up Christian and Hopeful to walk with them upon the mountains : so they went forth with them, and walked awhile, having a pleasant prospect on every side. Then said the shepherds one to another, shall we show these pilgrims some

both to ministers and Christians, by shewing them what endowments are most essential to the pastoral office. The attention given to preachers should not be proportioned to the degree of their confidence, vehemence, accomplishments, graceful delivery, eloquence, or politeness ; but to that of their knowledge of the Scriptures, and of every subject that relates to the glory of God and the salvation of souls ; their experience of the power of divine truth in their own hearts, of the faithfulness of God to his promises, of the believer's conflicts, difficulties, and dangers, and of the manifold devices of Satan to mislead, deceive, pervert, defile, or harass the souls of men ; their watchfulness over the people, as their constant business and unremitted care, to caution them against every snare, and to recover them out of every error, in to which they may be betrayed ; and their sincerity, as manifested by a disinterested unambitious, unassuming, patient, and affectionate conduct ; by proving that they deem themselves bound to practise their own instructions, and by a uniform attempt to convince the people, that they 'seek not theirs, but them.'

22*

wonders? So, when they had concluded to do it, they had them first to the top of a hill,*

'A hill'—Human nature always verges to extremes. In former times the least deviation from an established system of doctrine was reprobated as damnable heresy; and some persons, even at this day, tacitly laying claim to infallibility, deem every variation from their standard an error, and every error inconsistent with true piety. But the absurdity and bad effects of this bigotry having been discovered and exposed, it has become far more common to consider indifference about theological truth as essential to candour and liberality of sentiment; and to villify, as narrow-minded bigots, all who 'contend earnestly for the faith once delivered to the saints,' however averse they may be to persecution, or disposed to benevolence towards such as differ from them. The great end for which prophets and apostles were inspired, martyrs shed their blood, and the Son of God himself came into the world and died on the cross, is pronounced a matter of no moment: revelation is virtually rejected (for we may know, without the Bible, that men ought to be sober, honest, sincere, and benevolent); and those principles from which all genuine holiness must arise, are contemned as enthusiasm and foolishness! Some errors may indeed consist with true faith, (for who will say that he is in nothing mistaken?) yet no error is absolutely harmless; all must, in one way or other, originate from a wrong state of mind, or a faulty conduct, and proportionably counteract the design of revelation; and some are absolutely inconsistent with repentance, humility, faith, hope, love, spiritual worship, and holy obedience, and consequently incompatible with a state of acceptance and salvation. They are represented by 'the hill Error,' and a scriptural specimen is adduced. Professors fall into such delusions by indulging self-conceit, vain-glory, and curiosity; by 'leaning to their own understandings,' and intruding into the things they have not seen, vainly puffed up by their fleshly mind, and by speculating on subjects, which are too deep for them—for the fruit of 'the tree of knowledge,' in respect of religious opinions not expressly revealed, is still forbidden; and men vainly thinking it 'good for food, and a tree to be desired to make men wise,' and desiring 'to be as gods,' understanding and accounting for every thing, fall into destructive heresies, do immense mischief, and become awful examples for the warning of their contemporaries and successors.

called Error, which was very steep on the fartherest side, and bid them look down to the bottom. So Christian and Hopeful looked down, and saw at the bottom several men dashed all to pieces by a fall that they had from the top. Then said Christian, What meaneth this? The shepherds answered, Have you not heard of them that were made to err, by hearkening to Hymeneus and Philetus (2 Tim. ii. 17, 18), as concerning the faith of the resurrection of the body? They answered, Yea Then said the shepherds, those that you see lie dashed in pieces at the bottom of this mountain are they; and they have continued to this day unburied, as you see, for example to others to take heed how they clamber too high, or how they come too near the brink of this mountain.

Then I saw they had them to the top of another mountain, and the name of that is Caution, and bid them look afar off: which when they did they perceived, as they thought, several men walking up and down among the tombs that were there; and they perceived that the men were blind, because they stumbled sometimes upon the tombs, and because they could not get out from among them. Then said Christian, What means this?

The shepherds then answered, Did you not see a little below these mountains a stile*

* ' A stile'.—Many professors, turning aside from the line of conscientious obedience to escape difficulties, experience great distress of mind; which not being able to endure, they desperately endeavour to disbelieve or pervert all they have learned concerning religion: thus they are blinded by Satan

that leads into a meadow on the left hand of this way? They answered, Yes. Then said the shepherds, From that stile there goes a path that leads directly to Doubting Castle, which is kept by giant Despair, and these men (pointing to them among the tombs) came once on pilgrimage, as you do now, even till they came to that stile. And because the right way was rough in that place, they chose to go out of it into that meadow, and there were taken by giant Despair, and cast into Doubting Castle; where, after they had awhile been kept in the dungeon, he at last did put out their eyes, and led them among those tombs, where he has left them to wander to this very day, that the saying of the wise man might be fulfilled, 'He that wandereth out of the way of understanding shall remain in the congregation of the dead' (Prov. xxi. 16). Then Christian and Hopeful looked upon one another, with tears gushing out, but yet said nothing to the shepherds.

through their despondings, and are given over to strong delusions, as the just punishment of their wickedness (2 Thess. i. 11—13). Notwithstanding their profession, and the hopes long formed of them, they return to the company of those who are dead in sin, and buried in worldly pursuits; differing from them merely in a few speculative notions, and being far more hopeless than they. This is not only the case with many, at the first beginning of a religious profession, as of Pliable at the Slough of Despond, but with some at every stage of the journey. Such examples may very properly demand our tears of godly sorrow and fervent gratitude, when we reflect on our own misconduct and the loving-kindness of the Lord, who hath made us to differ, by first implanting, and then preserving faith in our hearts.

Then I saw in my dream that the shepherds had them to another place in a bottom, where was a door in the side of a hill, and they opened the door and bid them look in. They looked in therefore, and saw that within it was very dark and smoky; they also thought that they heard there a rumbling noise, as of fire, and a cry of some tormented; and that they smelt the scent of brimstone. Then said Christian, What means this? The shepherds told them, This is* a by-way to hell, a way that hypocrites go in at; namely, such as sell their birthright, with Esau; such as sell their master, with Judas; such as blaspheme the Gospel, with Alexander; and that lie and dissemble, with Ananias, and Sapphira his wife.

Then said Hopeful to the shepherds, I perceive that these had on them, even every one, a shew of pilgrimage, as we have now, had they not?

Shep. Yea, and held it a long time too.

---

* 'This is'—No man can see the heart of another, or certainly know him to be a true believer: it is, therefore, proper to warn the most approved persons, ' while they think, they stand, to take heed lest they fall.' Such cautions, with the diligence, watchfulness, self-examination, and prayer which they excite, are the means of perseverance and establishment to the upright. An event may be certain in itself, and yet inseparable from the method in which it is to be accomplished (Acts xxvii. 22—31); and it may appear very uncertain to the persons concerned, especially if they yield to remissness (1 Pet. iv. 18): so that prayer to the Almighty God for strength with continual watchfulness and attention to every part of practical religion, is absolutely necessary to ' the full assurance of hope unto the end' (Heb. vi 10—12.)

Hope. How far might they go on in pilgrimage in their days, since they notwithstanding were thus miserably cast away ?

Shep. Some farther, and some not so far as these mountains.

Then said the pilgrims one to another. We had need to cry to the strong for strength.

Shep. Ay, and you will have need to use it when you have it, too.

By this time the pilgrims had a desire to go forwards, and the shepherds a desire they should ; so they walked together towards the end of the mountains. Then said the shepherds one to another, Let us here shew the pilgrims the gates of the Celestial city, if they have skill to look through our prospect ive glass. The pilgrims then lovingly accepted the motion : so they had them to the top of a high hill, called Clear, and gave them the glass to look.

Then they essayed to look, but the remembrance of that last* thing that the shepherds had shewed them made their hands shake ; by means of which impediment they could not look steadily through the glass, yet

---

* 'That last'—Such is the infirmity of our nature, even when in a measure renovated, that it is almost impossible for us vigorously to exercise one holy affection, without failing in some other. When we confide in God with assured faith and hope, we commonly are defective in reverence, humility, and caution : on the other hand, a jealous of ourselves, and a salutary fear of coming short or drawing back generally weaken our confidence in God, and interfere with a joyful anticipation of our future inheritance. But, notwithstanding this deduction through our remaining unbelief, such experiences are very advantageous : ' Be not highminded, but, fear ; ed is he that feareth always.'

thought they saw something like the gate, and also some of the glory of the place. Then they went away and sang this song :—

> Thus by the shepherds secrets are reveal'd,
> Which from all other men are kept conceal'd :
> Come to the shepherds then, if you would see
> Things deep, things hid, and that mysterious be.

When they were about to depart, one of the shepherds gave them a note of the way. Another of them bid them beware of the flatterer. The third bid them take heed that they slept not upon the enchanted ground. And the fourth bid them good speed. So I awoke from my dream.

And I slept and dreamed again, and saw the same two pilgrims going down the mountains along the highway towards the city. Now a little* below these mountains on the

* 'Now a little'—Multitudes of ignorant persons entirely disregard God and religion ; others have a show of piety, which is grave, reserved, auster, distant, and connected with contemptuous enmity to evangelical truth : but there are some persons of a sprightly disposition, who are more conceited and vain-glorious than haughty and arrogant ; think well of themselves, and presume on the good opinion of their acquaintance ; are open and communicative, though they expose their ignorance continually ; fancy themselves very religious, and expect to be thought so by others ; are willing to associate with evangelical professors, as if they all meant the same thing ; and do not express contempt or enmity, unless urged to it in self-defence. This description of men seems to be represented by the character next introduced, about which the author has repeatedly bestowed much pains. Christian had soon done with Obstinate and Worldly-wiseman ; for such men, being outrageous against the Gospel, shun all intercourse with established professors, and little can be done to warn or undeceive them : but brisk, conceited, shallow persons, who are ambitious of being thought religious, are

left hand lieth the country of Conceit, from which country there comes into the way in which the pilgrims walked a little crooked lane. Here, therefore, they met with a very brisk lad that came out of that country, and his name was Ignorance. So Christian asked him from what parts he came, and whither he was going?

Ignor. Sir, I was born in the country that lieth off there a little on the left hand, and am going to the Celestial city.

Chr. But how do you think to get in at the gate? for you may find some difficulties there.

As other good people do, said he.

Chr. But what have you to shew at that gate, that may cause that gate to be opened to you?

---

shaken off with great difficulty; they are continually found among the hearers of the Gospel; often intrude themselves at the most sacred ordinances, when they have it in their power; and sometimes are favourably thought of, till further acquaintance proves their entire ignorance. Pride, in one form or another, is the universal fault of human nature; but the frivolous vain-glory of empty talkers differs exceedingly from the arrogance and formal self-importance of scribes and pharisees, and arise from a different constitution and education, and other habits and associations: this is the town of Conceit, where Ignorance resided. A lively disposition, a weak capacity, a confused judgment; the want of information about religion and almost every other subject; a proportionable blindness to those manifold deficiencies, and a pert, forward self-sufficiency, are the prominent features in this portrait; and if a full purse, secular influence, the ability of conferring favours, and power to excite fears, be added, the whole receives its highest finishing. With these observations on this peculiar character, and a few hints as we proceed, the plain language of the author on this subject will be perfectly intelligible to the attentive reader.

Ignor. I know my Lord's will, and have been a good liver ; I pay every man his own ; I pray, fast, pay tithes, and give alms, and have left my country for whither I am going

Chr. But thou camest not in at the wicket-gate that is at the head of this way ; thou camest in hither through that same crooked lane, and therefore I fear, however thou mayest think of thyself, when the reckoning-day shall come, thou wilt have laid to thy charge that thou art a thief and a robber, instead of getting admittance into the city.

Ignor. Gentlemen ye be utter strangers to me, I know you not ; be content to follow the religion of your country, and I will follow the religion of mine. I hope all will be well. And, as for the gate that you talk of, all the world knows that that is a great way off of our country. I cannot think that any men in all our parts do so much as know the way to it ; nor need they matter whether they do or no ; since we have, as you see, a fine pleasant green lane that comes down from our country the next way into the way.

When Christian saw that the man was wise in his own conceit, he said to Hopeful, whisperingly, ' There is more hope of a fool than him' (Prov. xxvi. 12) ; and said moreover, ' When he that is a fool walketh by the way, his wisdom faileth him, and he saith to every one that he is a fool' (Eccles. x. 3). What, shall* we talk farther with him, or outgo him

* ' What, shall'—It is best not to converse much at once with persons of this character ; but after a few warnings to

at present, and so leave him to think of what he hath heard already, and then stop again for him afterwards, and see if by degrees we can do any good by him ? Then said Hopeful,

> Let Ignorance a little while now muse
> On what is said, and let him not refuse
> Good counsel to embrace, lest he remain
> Still ignorant of what 's the chiefest gain
> God saith, those that no understanding have,
> Altho' he made them, them he will not save.

He farther added, It is not good, I think, to say to him all at once ; let us pass him by, if you will, and talk to him anon, even as he is ' able to bear it.'

So they both went on, and Ignorance he came after. Now when they had passed him a little way, they entered into a very dark lane,* where they met a man whom seven

leave them to their reflections : for their self-conceit is often cherished by altercations, in which they deem themselves very expert, however disgusting their discourse may be to others.

* ' Dark lane'—This seems to mean a season of prevalent impiety, and of great affliction to the people of God. Here the impartial author takes occasion to contrast the character of Ignorance with that of Turn away. Loose evangelical professors look down with supercilious disdain on those who do not understand the doctrines of grace ; and think themselves more enlightened, and better acquainted with the liberty of the Gospel, than more practical Christians : but in dark times such wanton professors often turn out damnable apostates, and the detection of their hypocrisy makes them ashamed to shew their faces among those believers, over whom they before affected a kind of superiority. When convictions subside, and Christ has not set up his kingdom in the heart, the unclean spirit resumes his former habitation, and takes to himself seven other spirits more wicked than

devils had bound with seven strong cords, and were carrying him back to the door that they saw on the side of the hill (Matt. xii. 45; Prov. v. 22). Now good Christian began to tremble, and so did Hopeful his companion; yet as the devils led away the man, Christian looked to see if he knew him; and he thought it might be one Turn-away that dwelt in the town of Apostacy. But he did not perfectly see his face, for he did hang his head like a thief that is found. But being gone past, Hopeful looked after him, and spied on his back a paper with this inscription, 'Wanton professor and damnable apostate.' Then* said Christian to his fellow,

himself, who bind the poor wretch faster than ever in the cords of sin and delusion: so that his last state in more hopeless than the first. Such apostacies make the hearts of the upright to tremble; but a recollection of the nature of Turnaway's profession and confidence explains the matter, and they recover their hope, and learn to take heed to themselves.

* 'Then'—The ensuing episode concerning Little-faith was evidently intended to prevent weak Christians being dismayed by the awful thing spoken of loose professors. In times of persecution, many professors openly return into the broad way to destruction: Thus Satan murders the souls of men, by threatening to kill their bodies; this is Dead-man's lane, leading back to Broad-way-gate. Believers, indeed, are preserved from thus drawing back to perdition: but the weak in faith, being faint-hearted, and mistrusting the promises and faithfulness of God, and betrayed into sinful compliances or negligences, they lie down to sleep when they have special need to watch and be sober; they conceal, or perhaps deny, their profession, are timid and inactive in duty, or in other respects act contrary to their consciences, and thus contract guilt. So that Faint-heart threatens and assaults them; Mistrust plunders them; and Guilt beats them down, and makes them almost despair of life. As the robbery was com-

Now I call to remembrance that which was told me, of a thing that happened to a good man hereabout. The name of the man was Little-faith, but a good man, and he dwelt in the town of Sincere. The thing was this : at the entering in at this passage, there comes down from Broad-way-gate a lane called Dead-man's lane ; so called, because of the murders that are commonly done there ; and this Little-faith going on pilgrimage, as we do now, chanced to sit down there and slept : now there happened at that time to come down the lane from Broad-way-gate three sturdy rogues, and their names were Faint-heart, Mistrust, and Guilt, three brothers; and they spying Little-faith where he was, came galloping up with speed. Now the good man was just awakened from his sleep, and was getting up to go on his journey. So they came up all to him, and with threatening language bid him stand. At this Little-faith looked as white as a clout, and had neither power to fight or flee. Then said Faint-heart, 'Deliver thy purse ; but he making no haste to do it (for he was loth to lose his money), Mistrust ran up to him, and thrusting his hand into his pocket pulled out thence a bag of silver. Then he cried out 'Thieves ! thieves !' With that Guilt, with a

mitted in the dark lane before mentioned, this seems to have been the author's precise meaning; but any unbelieving fears, that induce men to neglect the means of grace, or to adopt sinful expedients of securing themselves, which on the review must bring guilt and terror upon their consciences, may also be intended.

great club that was in his hand, struck Little-
faith on the head, and with that blow felled him
flat to the ground ; where he lay bleeding as
one that would bleed to death. All this
while the thieves stood by. But at last,*
they hearing that some were upon the road,
and fearing lest it should be one Great-grace,
that dwells in the city of Good-confidence, they
betook themselves to their heels, and left this
good man to shift for himself ; who getting
up, made shift to scramble on his way.—
This was the story.

Hope. But did they take from him all that
ever he had ?

Chr. No ; the place where his jewels†
were they never ransacked ; so those he kept

---

* ' At last'—As these robbers represent the inward effects
of unbelief, and disobedience, and not any outward enemies,
Great-grace seems to be the emblem of those believers, or
ministers, who, having honourably stood their ground, endeavour to restore the fallen, in the spirit of meekness, by suitable encouragements. The remembrance of such persons, and
their compassionate exhortations or honourble examples, help
to drive away entire despondency, and to inspire the trembling penitent with some hope of finding mercy and grace in
this time of urgent need. This may be allegorically represented by the flight of the robbers, when they heard that
Great-grace was on the road.

† ' Jewels'—The believer's union with Christ, and the
sanctification of the Spirit, sealing his acceptance and rendering him meet for heaven, are his invaluable and unaliena-
ble Jewels. But he may by sin loose his comforts, and not
be able to perceive the evidences of his own safety ; and even
if he be again enabled to hope that it will be well with him
in the event, he may be so harassed by the recollection of the
loss he has sustained, the effects of his misconduct on others,
and the obstructions he hath thrown in the way of his own
comfort and usefulness, that his future life may be rendered
a constant scene of disquietude and painful reflections. Thus

23*

still. But, as I was told, the good man was much afflicted for his loss; for the thieves got most of his spending money. That which they got not, as I said, were jewels; also he had a little odd money left, but scarce enough to bring him to his journey's end (1 Pet. iv. 18); nay, if I was not misinform ed, he was forced to beg as he went, to keep himself alive (for his jewels he might not sell). But beg and do what he could, 'he went,' as we say, 'with many a hungry belly,' the most part of the rest of the way.

Hope. But is it not a wonder they got not from him his certificate, by which he was to receive his admittance at the celestial gate?

Chr. It is a wonder: but they got not that; though they missed it not through any good cunning of his; for he being dismayed with their coming upon him, had neither power nor skill to hide any thing; so it was more by good providence than by his endeavour that they missed of that good thing (2 Tim i 14; 2 Pet. ii. 9).

Hope. But it must needs be a comfort to him that they got not his jewels from him.

Chr. It might have been great comfort to him, had he used it as he should; but they that told me the story said, that he made but little use of it all the rest of the way; and

the doctrine of the believer's final perseverance is both maintained and guarded from abuse: and it is not owing to a man's own care, but to the Lord's free mercy, powerful interposition, and new-covenant engagements, that unbelief and guilt do not rob him of his title to heaven, as well as of his comfort and confidence.

that, because of the dismay that he had in
the taking away his money. Indeed he forgot it a great part of the rest of his journey ;
and besides, when at any time it came into
his mind, and he began to be comforted
therewith, then would fresh thoughts of his
loss come again upon him, and those thoughts
would swallow up all.

Hope. Alas, poor man ! this could not but
be a great grief unto him !

Chr. Grief ! ay, a grief indeed. Would it
not have been so to any of us, had we been
used as he, to be robbed and wounded too,
and that in a strange place, as he was ? It is
a wonder he did not die with grief, poor
heart : I was told, that he scattered almost
all the rest of the way with nothing but
doleful and bitter complaints ; telling also to
all that overtook him, or that he overtook in
the way as he went, where he was robbed,
and how ; who they were that did it, and
what he lost ; how he was wounded, and that
he hardly escaped with life.

Hope. But it is a wonder* that his necessity did not put him upon selling or pawning
some of his jewels, that he might have
wherewith to relieve himself in his journey.

Chr. Thou talkest like one upon whose
head is the shell to this very day : for what

* 'Wonder'—Many professors, meeting with discouragements, give up their religion for the sake of this present world ;
but, if any thence argue, that true believers will copy their
example, they shew that they are not well established in
judgment, nor deeply acquainted with the nature of the divine life, or the objects of its supreme desires and peculiar
fears.

should he pawn them ? or to whom should he sell them ? In all that country where he was robbed his jewels were not accounted of; nor did he want that relief which could from thence be administered to him. Besides, had his jewels been missing at the gate of the Celestial city, he had (and that he knew well enough) been excluded from an inheritance there, and that would have been worse to him than the appearance and villany of ten thousand thieves.

Hope. Why art thou so tart, my brother ? Esau sold his birthright, and that for a mess of pottage (Heb. xii. 16) ; and that birthright was his greatest jewel : and, if he, why might not Little-faith do so too ?

Chr. Esau did sell his birthright indeed, and so do many besides, and by so doing exclude themselves from the chief blessing ; as also that caitiff did : but you must put a difference betwixt Esau and Little-faith, and also betwixt their estates. Esau's birthright was typical, but Little-faith's jewels were not so. Esau's belly was his god, but Little-faith's belly was not so. Esau's want lay in his fleshly appetite, Little-faith's did not so. Besides, Esau could see no farther than to the fulfilling of his lust : 'For I am at the point to die,' said he, ' and what good will this birthright do me ?' (Gen. xxv 29—34). But Little-faith, though it was his lot to have but a little faith, was by his little faith kept from such extravagances, and made to see and prize his jewels more than to sell them as Esau did his birthright. You read not any where that Esau had faith, no, not so much as a little ; therefore no marvel, if where the flesh only bears sway (as it will in that man where no faith is, to resist), if he sells his birthright, and his soul and all, and that to the devil of hell ; for it is with such as it is with the ass, 'who in her occasion cann_ be turned away' (Jer. ii. 24) ; when their minds are set upon their lusts, they will have them, whatever they cost. But Little-faith was of another temper, his mind was on things divine ; his livelihood was upon things that were spiritual and above ; therefore, to what end should he that is of such a temper sell his jewels (had there been any one that would have bought them) to fill his mind with empty things ? Will a man give a penny to fill his belly with hay ? or can you persuade the turtle-dove to live upon carrion like the crow ? Though faithless ones can, for carnal lusts, pawn, or mortgage, or sell, what they have, and themselves outright to boot, yet they that have faith, saving faith, though but little of it, cannot do so. Here, therefore, my brother, is thy mistake.

Hope. I acknowledge it ; but yet your severe reflection had almost made me angry.

Chr. Why ! I did but compare thee to some of the birds that are of the brisker sort, who will run to and fro in untrodden paths with the shell upon their heads : but pass by that, and consider the matter under de-bate, and all shall be well betwixt thee and me

Hope. But, Christian, these three fellows, I am persuaded in my heart, are but a company of cowards :* would they have run else, think you, as they did, at the noise of one that was coming on the road ? Why did not Little-faith pluck up a greater heart ? He might, methinks, have stood one brush with them, and have yielded, when there had been no remedy.

Chr. That they are cowards, many have said, but few have found it so in the time of trial. As for a great heart, Little-faith had

* ' Cowards'—The young convert views temptations, conflicts, and persecutions, in a very different light than experienced believers do. Warm with zeal, and full of confidence, which he imagines to be wholly genuine, and knowing comparatively little of his own heart, or the nature of the Christian conflict, the young convert resembles a new recruit, who is apt to boast what great things he will do ; but the old disciple, though much stronger in faith, and possessing habitually more vigour of holy affection, knows himself too well to boast, and speaks with modesty of the past, and diffidence of the future : like the veteran soldier of approved valour, who has often been in actual service. They who have boasted before-hand what they would do and suffer rather than deny the faith, have generally either proved apostates, or been taught their weakness by painful experience. And when a real believer has thus fallen, the recollection of past boastings will add to his remorse and terror, and Satan will attempt to drive them to despair : so that, indeed, ' no man can tell what in such a combat attends us, but he that has been in the battle himself.' Even they, who were most remarkable for strength of faith, have often been overcome in the hour of temptation ; and, when guilt got within them, they found it no easy matter to recover their hope and comfort : how then can the weak in faith be expected to overcome in such circumstances ? The accommodation of the passages from Job to this conflict seems merely intended to imply, that the assaults of Satan, on these occasions, are more terrible than any thing in the visible creation can be ; and that every possible advantage will be needful in order to withstand in the evil day.

none; and I perceive by thee, my brother, hadst thou been the man concerned, thou art but for a brush, and then to yield. And verily, since this is the height of thy stomach, now they are at a distance from us, should they appear to thee, as they did to him, they might put thee to second thoughts.

But consider again, they are but journeymen thieves; they serve under the king of the bottomless pit; who if need be, will come to their aid himself, and his voice is as the roaring of a lion (1 Pet. v. 8). I myself have been engaged as this Little-faith was, and I found it a terrible thing. These three villains set upon me, and I beginning like a Christian to resist, they gave out a call, and in came their master: I would, as the saying is, have given my life for a penny; but that, as God would have it, I was clothed with armour of proof. Ay, and yet, though I was so harnessed, I found it hard work to quit myself like a man, no man can tell what in that combat attends us, but he that hath been in the battle himself.

Hope Well, but they ran, you see, when they did but suppose that one Great-grace was in the way.

Chr True, they have often fled, both they and their master, when Great-grace hath appeared; and no marvel, for he is the King's champion: but, I trow, you will put some difference between Little-faith and the King's champion. All the King's subjects are not his champions; nor can they, when tried, do such feats of war as he. Is it meet to think that a little child should handle Goliah as David did? or that there should be the strength of an ox in a wren? Some are strong, some are weak; some have great faith, some have little; this man was one of the weak, and therefore he went to the wall.

Hope. I would it had been Great-grace for his sake.

Chr. If it had been he, he might have had his hands full: for I must tell you, that though Great-grace is excellent good at his weapon, and has, and can, so long as he keeps them at sword's point, do well enough with them, yet if they get within him, even Faint-heart, Mistrust, or the other, it will go hard but that they will throw up his heels; and when a man is down, you know, what can he do?

Whoso looks well upon Great-grace's face, shall see those scars and cuts there that shall easily give demonstration of what I say. Yea, once I heard that he should say (and that when he was in the combat), 'We despaired even of life.' How did these sturdy rogues and their fellows make David groan, mourn, and roar? Yea, Heman and Hezekiah too, though champions in their days, were forced to bestir them when by these assaulted; and yet, notwithstanding, they had their coats soundly brushed by them Peter, upon a time, would go try what he could do; but, though some do say of him that he is the prince of the apostles, they handled him so that they made him at last afraid of a sorry girl.

Besides, their king is at their whistle ; he is never out of hearing ; and if at any time they be put to the worst, he, if possible, comes in to help them : and of him it is said, ' the sword of him that layeth at him cannot hold ; the spear the dart, nor the harbargeon ; he esteemeth iron as straw, and brass as rotten wood ; the arrow cannot make him flee, sling-stones are turned, with him, into stubble ; darts are counted as stubble ; he laugheth at the shaking of a spear' (Job xli. 26— 24). What can a man do in this case ? It is true, if a man could at every turn have Job's horse, and had skill and courage to ride him, he might do notable things, for his neck is clothed with thunder, he will not be afraid as a grasshopper ; the glory of his nostrils is terrible ; he paweth in the valley, and rejoiceth in his strength ; he goeth on to meet the armed men ; he mocketh at fear, and is not affrighted, neither turneth he back from the sword : the quiver rattleth against him, the glittering spear and the shield ; he swalloweth the ground with fierceness and rage, neither believeth he that it is the sound of the trumpet. He saith among the trumpets Ha, ha ; and he smelleth the battle afar off, the thunder of the captain and the shoutings, (Job xxxix. 19—25).

But for such footmen as thee and I are, let us never desire to meet with an enemy, nor vaunt as if we could do better, when we hear of others that they have been foiled ; nor be tickled at the thought of our own manhood, for such commonly come by the worst when

tried. Peter of whom I made mention before, he would swagger, ay, he would ; he
would, as his vain mind prompted him to say,
do better, and stand more for his master than
all men : but who so foiled and run down by
those villains as he ?

When, therefore, we hear that such rob-
beries are done on the King's highway, two
things become us to do : first, to go out harnessed, and to be sure to take a shield with
us ; for it was for want of that that he
that laid so lustily at Leviathan could not
make him yield ; for, indeed, if that be
wanted he fears us not at all. Therefore he
that had skill hath said, ' Above all, take the
shield of faith, wherewith ye shall be able to
quench all the fiery darts of the wicked'
(Eph. vi. 16).

It is good also that we desire of the King
a convoy,* that he will go with us himself.
This made David rejoice when in the valley
of the Shadow of Death ; and Moses was
rather for dying where he stood than to go
one step without his God (Exod. xxxiii. 15).
O my brother, if he will but go along with us,
what need we be afraid of ten thousand that
shall set themselves against us ? but without
him the proud helpers fall under the slain
(Psal. iii. 5—8 ; xxvii. 1—3 ; Isa. x. 4).

* ' Convoy'—Instead of saying, ' though all men deny
thee, yet will not I,' it behoves us to use all means of grace
diligently, and to be instant in prayer, that the Lord himself
may protect us by his power, and animate us by his presence
and then only shall we be enabled to overcome both the fear
of man, and the temptations of the devil.

I, for my part, have been in the fray before now; and though, through the goodness of him that is best, I am, as you see, alive, yet I cannot boast of my manhood. Glad shall I be if I meet with no more such brunts; though I fear we are not got beyond all danger. However, since the lion and the bear have not as yet devoured me, I hope God will deliver us from the next uncircumcised Philistines. Then sung Christian—

> Poor Little-faith! has been among the thieves?
> Wast robb'd? remember this, whoso believes,
> And get more faith, then shall you victors be
> Over ten thousand, else scarce over three.

So they went on, and Ignorance followed. They went then till they came at a place where they saw a way put itself* into their

---

* 'Put itself'—This way, which seemed as straight as the right way, and in entering on which there was no stile to be passed, must denote some very plausible and gradual deviation from the simplicity of the Gospel, in doctrine or practice. Peculiar circumstances may require the believer to determine how to act, when so much can be said in support of different measures, as to make him hesitate; and if he merely consider the subject in his own mind, or consult with his friends, without carefully examining the rule of Scripture, and praying for divine direction, he will very probably be seduced into the wrong path: and, if he listen to the Flatterer, he will certainly be misled. It is, therefore, requisite to inquire what is meant by the Flatterer. It would be a manifest impropriety to suppose these pilgrims hearkening to such as preach justification by the works of the law; or flatter men's self-complacency by harangues on the dignity of human nature, and the unbiassed freedom of the will; the sufficiency of reason in matters of religion, or the goodness of the heart; for experienced Christians cannot be thus imposed on. Nor would gross antinomianism engage the attention of those, who have been in Doubting Castle, for turning aside into By

way, and seemed withal to lie as straight as
the way which they should go ; and here they

path meadow. But the human mind is always accessible to
flattery, in one form or other ; and there have in every age
been teachers and professors, who have soothed men into a
good opinion of their state on insufficient grounds ; or fed
their spiritual pride by expressing too favourable thoughts of
their attainments, which is often mistaken for a very loving
spirit. This directly tends to unwatchfulness, and an unadvised way of deciding in difficult cases ; and thus men are
imperceptibly induced to consult their own inclination, ease,
or interest, instead of the will and glory of God. In the
mean time, such flatterers commend their prudence, in allowing themselves a little rest ; persuade them that they are entitled to distinction, and exempted from general rules ; insinuate that they are too well acquainted with Satan's devices
to be deceived ; and in short seem to make their opinion the
standard of right and wrong. Some excellent men, from a
natural easiness of temper, united with spiritual love and
genuine candour, thus undesignedly too much soothe their
brethren ; but the Flatterer is ' a black man in a white robe ;'
a designing hypocrite, who with plausibility, fluency of speech,
talents, eloquence, or polite accomplishments, and very evangelical views of religon, ' serves not our Lord Jesus Christ,
but his own belly ; and by good words and fair speeches de-
ceives the hearts of the simple.' Such a man will not shock
serious minds by gross antinomianism ; but he will insist
disproportionately and indiscriminately on privileges, promises, and consolatory topics ; and thus put his auditors into
good humour with themselves, and consequently with him, in
order to obtain advantages, not so easily acquired by other
means. There are many other flatterers : but this description, coming far more in the way of evangelical professors
than any other, seems emphatically to be intended. Satan
aims to lull men into a fatal security, wholly or in part ; flatterers of every kind are his principal agents ; and a smooth,
undistinguishing Gospel, united to a want of p ain dealing in
private, has immense influence in this respect. Too often, it
is to be feared, the preacher uses flattery in the pulpit and
the parlour, and is reciprocally flattered or rewarded :
and what wonder is it, if ungodly men take up the business
as a lucrative trade, and serve their own selfish purposes, by
quieting uneasy consciences into a false peace, misleading un-
wary souls, entangling incautious believers in a net, and thus

knew not which of the two to take, for both
seemed straight before them : therefore here
they stood still to consider. And as they
were thinking about the way, behold a man
of black flesh, but covered with a very light
robe, came to them, and asked them why
they stood there ? They answered, They
were a going to the Celestial city, but knew
not which of these ways to take. 'Follow

bringing a scandal on the Gospel ? 'Satan is transformed in
to an angel of light, and his ministers into ministers of righte
ousness :' and if this were the case in the apostles' days, in
the midst of terrible persecutions, it may well be expected
that the same attempts will be made at other times. Among
persons unacquainted with the Gospel a different method of
seduction will be employed ; in some places by vain philoso-
phy or pharisaical self-righteousness, in others by enthusiastic
imaginations or dreams of sinless perfection : but among established Christians, some plausible scheme, flattering men as
wise and strong in Christ, and as knowing their liberty and
priveleges, must be adopted ; such as were propagated among
the Corinthians, or those professors whom James, Peter, and
Jude successively addressed. In the present state of religious profession, a more important caution, I apprehend, cannot be given by the united voice of all those ministers, whom
the shepherds represent, than this, 'Beware of the Flatterer ;' of all teachers who address the self-preference of the
human heart, and thus render men forgetful of 'taking heed
to their way according to the word of God.' For if men
overlook the precepts of Scripture, and forsake practical distinguishing preachers, to follow such as bolster up their
hopes in some smoother way they will either be fatally deceived
or drawn out of the path of truth and duty, taken in the net
of error, and entangled among injurious connexions, and with
perplexing difficulties : at length indeed they will be unde-
ceived in respect of these fine-spoken men, but not till they
scarcely know what to do, or what will become of them
For when the Lord plucks their feet out of the net, he will
humble them in the dust for their sin and folly, and make
them thankful to be delivered, though with severe rebukes
and corrections

24*

me,' says the man, 'it is thither that I am going' So they followed him in the way that but now came into the road, which by degrees turned, and turned them so from the city that they desired to go to, that in a little time their faces were turned away from it: yet they followed him. But by and by, before they were aware, he led them both within the compass of a net, in which they were both so entangled that they knew not what to do; and with that the white robe fell off the black man's back: they then saw where they were. Wherefore there they lay crying some time, for they could not get themselves out.

Then said Christian to his fellow, Now do I see myself in an error. Did not the shepherds bid us beware of the flatterers? As is the saying of the wise man, so have we found it this day, 'A man that flattereth his neighbour spreadeth a net for his feet' (Prov. xxix. 5).

Hope. They also gave us a note of directions about the way, for our more sure finding thereof; but herein we have also forgotten to read, and have not kept ourselves from the 'paths of the destroyer.' Here David was wiser than we; for, saith he, 'concerning the works of men, by the word of thy lips I have kept me from the paths of the destroyer' (Ps. xvii. 4). Thus they lay bewailing themselves in the net. At last they spied a shining one coming towards them with a whip of small cord in his hand. When he was come to the place where they were, he asked them whence they came, and what they did there? They told him that they were poor pilgrims going to Zion, but were led out of their way by a black man clothed in white, who bid us, said they, follow him, for he was going thither too. Then said he with the whip, It is a flatterer, 'a false apostle, that hath transformed himself into an angel of light' (2 Cor. xi. 13, 14 ; Dan. xi. 32). So he rent the net, and let the men out. Then said he to them, Follow me, that I may set you in the way again, so he led them back to the way which they had left to follow the flatterer. Then he asked them, saying, Where did you lie the last night? They said, With the shepherds upon the Delectable Mountains. He asked them then if they had not a note of direction for the way? They answered, Yes. But did you, said he, when you were at a stand, pluck out and read your note? They answered, No. He asked them, Why? They said they forgot. He asked, moreover, If the shepherds did not bid them beware of the flatterer—Yes ; but we did not imagine, said they, that this fine-spoken man had been he (Rom. xvi. 12, 17).

Then I saw in my dream, that he commanded them to lie down (Deut. xxix. 2) ; which when they did, he chastised them sore, to teach them the good way wherein they should walk (2 Chron. vi. 26, 27) : and, as he chastised them, he said, 'As many as I love I rebuke and chasten ; be zealous, therefore, and repent' (Rev. iii. 19). This done, he bid them go on their way, and take good heed to the other directions of the shepherds. So they thanked him for all his kindness, and went softly along the right way, singing—

> Come hither, you that walk along the way,
> See how the pilgrims fare that go astray:
> They catched are in an entangling net,
> 'Cause they good counsel lightly did forget:
> 'Tis true, they rescu'd were, but yet you see
> They're scourg'd to boot: let this your caution be.

Now after a while they perceived, afar off, one coming softly, alone, all along the highway to meet them. Then said Christian to his fellow, yonder* is a man with his back towards Zion, and he is coming to meet us.

* ' Yonder'—Some false professors gradually renounce ' the truth as it is in Jesus ;' others openly set themselves against all kinds of religion, and turn scoffers and infidels. Indeed none are more likely to become avowed atheists, than such as have for many years professed the Gospel in hypocrisy: they often acquire an acquaintance with the several parts of religion, their connexion with each other, and the arguments with which they are supported ; so that they know not where to begin, if they would oppose any particular doctrine or precept of revelation : yet they hate the whole system ; and, having never experienced those effects from the truth, which the Scripture ascribes to it, they feel, that if there be any reality in religion, their own case is very dreadful, and wish to shake off this mortifying and alarming conviction : and, as they have principally associated with loose professors, and witnessed much folly and wickedness among them, they willingly take up a bad opinion of all who pretend to piety (as rakes commonly revile all women), and so they make a desperate plunge, and treat the whole of religion as imposture and delusion ; pretending, that upon a thorough investigation, they find it to be a compound of knavery, folly, and fanaticism. Thus God in awful judgment permits Satan to blind their eyes, because they ' obeyed not the truth,

Hope. I see him, let us take heed to ourselves now, lest he should prove a flatterer also. So he drew nearer and nearer, and at last came up to them. His name was Atheist; and he asked them whither they were going?

Chr. We are going to mount Zion.

Then Atheist fell into a very great laughter.

Chr. What is the meaning of your laughter?

Ath. I laugh to see what ignorant persons you are, to take upon you so ridiculous a journey; and yet are like to have nothing but your travel for your pains.

Chr. Why, man! do you think we shall not be received?

Ath. Received! there is no such place as you dream of in all the world.

Chr. But there is in the world to come.

Ath. When I was at home, in mine own country, I heard as you now affirm, and from that hearing went out to see, and have been seeking this city twenty years, but find no more of it than I did the first day I set out (Eccl. x. 15; Jer. xvii. 15).

but had pleasure in unrighteousness.' Men set out with a dead faith and a worldly heart, and at length occupy the seat of the scorner! The vain reasonings and contemptuous sneers of such apostates may turn aside other unsound characters, and perplex new converts; but the experience of established believers will fortify them against these manifest delusions; corrections for previous mistakes will render them jealous of themselves and one another; so that they will go on their way with greater circumspection. and pity the scorner who ridicules them.

Chr. We have both heard and believe that there is such a place to be found.

Ath. Had not I, when at home, believed, I had not come thus far to seek; but finding none (and yet I should, had there been such a place to be found, for I have gone to seek it farther than you) I am going back again, and will seek to refresh myself with the things that I then cast away for hopes of that which I now see is not.

Then said Christian to Hopeful his companion, Is it true which this man hath said?

Hope. Take heed, he is one of the flatterers: remember what it has cost us once already for our hearkening to such kind of fellows. What! no mount Zion? Did we not see from the Delectable Mountains the gate of the city? Also, are we not now to walk by faith? (2 Cor. v. 7.) Let us go on, said Hopeful, lest the man with the whip overtake us again. You should have taught me that lesson which I will round you in the ears withal: 'Cease, my son, to hear the instruction that causeth to err from the words of knowledge' (Prov. xix. 27; Heb. x. 39); I say, my brother, cease to hear him, and let us believe to the saving of the soul.

Chr. My brother, I did not put the question to thee for that I doubted of the truth of our belief myself, but to prove thee, and to fetch from thee a fruit of the honesty of thy heart. As for this man, I know that he is blinded by the god of this world. Let thee and I go on, knowing that we have belief of the truth, and 'no lie is of the truth' (1 John ii. 21).

Hope. Now I do rejoice in hope of the glory of God. So they turned away from the man, and he, laughing at them, went his way.

I saw then in my dream, that they went till they came into a certain country, whose air naturally tended to make one drowsy, if he came a stranger unto it. And here Hopeful began to be very dull and heavy of sleep · wherefore he said unto Christian, I now begin to grow so drowsy that I can scarcely hold up mine eyes; let us lie down here, and take one nap.

By no means, said the other, lest sleeping we never awake more.

Hope. Why, my brother? sleep is sweet to the labouring man; we may be refreshed if we take a nap.

Chr. Do you not remember, that one of the shepherds bid us beware of the Enchanted·

---

* ' Enchanted'—The Enchanted Ground may represent a state of exemption from peculiar trials, and of worldly prosperity, especially when Christians are unexpectedly advanced in their outward circumstances, or engaged in extensive flourishing business. A concurrence of agreeable dispensations sometimes succeed to long continued difficulties : the believer's peace is little interrupted, but he has not very high affections or consolations; he meets with respect and attention from his friends and acquaintance, and is drawn on by success in his secular undertakings. This powerfully tends, through remaining depravity, to produce a lethargic and indolent frame of mind : the man attends on religious ordinances, and the constant succession of duties, more from habit and conscience, than from delight in the service of God : and even they, who have acquitted themselves in a varied course of trials and conflicts, often lose much of their vigour, activity,

ground ? He meant by that, that we should beware of sleeping ; 'wherefore let us not sleep, as do others, but let us watch and be sober' (1 Thess. v. 6).

Hope. I acknowledge myself in a fault ; and, had I been here alone, I had by sleeping run the danger of death. I see it is true that the wise man saith, ' Two are better than one' (Eccl. iv. 9). Hitherto hath thy company been my mercy ; and thou shalt ' have a good reward for thy labour.'

Now then, said Christian, to prevent drowsiness in this place, let us fall into good discourse.

With all my heart, said the other.

Chr. Where shall we begin ?

Hope. Where God began with us : but do you begin, if you please.

Chr. I will sing you first this song—

> When saints do sleepy grow, let them come hither,
> And hear how these two pilgrims talk together :
> Yea, let them learn of them in any wise
> Thus to keep ope their drowsy slumb'ring eyes.
> Saints' fellowship, if it be manag'd well,
> Keeps them awake, and that in spite of hell.

Then Christian began, and said, I will ask

and vigilance, in these fascinating circumstances. No situation, in which a believer can be placed, requires so much watchfulness as this does : other experiences resemble storms, which keep a man awake almost against his will : this is a treacherous calm, which invites and lulls him to sleep. But pious discourse, the jealous cautions of faithful friends, and recollections of the Lord's dealings with us in times past, are admirably suited to counteract this tendency. The subsequent dialogue contains the author's own exposition of several particulars in the preceding allegory.

you a question ; how came you to think at first
of doing what you do now?

Hope. Do you mean, how came I at first to
look after the good of my soul ?

Chr. Yes, that is my meaning.

Hope. I continued a great while in the delight of those things which were seen and sold
at our fair ; things which I believe now would
have, had I continued in them still, drowned
me in perdition and destruction.

Chr. What things are they ?

Hope. All the treasures and riches of the
world.   Also I delighted much rioting, revel-
ling, drinking, swearing, lying, uncleanness,
sabbath-breaking, and what not, that tended
to destroy the soul.   But I found, at last, by
hearing and considering of things that are
divine, which indeed I heard of you, as also
of the beloved Faithful, that was put to death
for his faith and good living in Vanity-
fair, that 'the end of these things is death ;'
and that 'for these things' sake, the wrath of
God cometh upon the children of disobedience
(Rom. vi. 21—23 ; Eph. v. 6.)

Chr. And did you presently fall under the
power of this conviction ?

Hope. No, I was not willing presently to
know the evil of sin, nor the damnation that
follows upon the commission of it ; but endeavoured, when my mind at first began to be shak-
en with the word, to shut mine eyes against
the light thereof.

Chr. But what was the cause of your carrying of it thus to the first workings of God's blessed Spirit upon you ?"

Hope. The causes were—1. I was ignorant that this was the work of God upon me. I never thought, that by awakenings for sin God at first begins the conversion of a sinner. 2. Sin was yet very sweet to my flesh, and I was loth to leave it. 3. I could not tell how to part with my old companions, their presence and actions were so desirable unto me. 4. The hours in which convictions were upon me were such troublesome and such heart-affrighting hours, that I could not bear, no not so much as the remembrance of them upon my heart.

Chr. Then, it seems, sometimes you got relief of your trouble ?

Hope. Yes, verily, but it would come into my mind again, and then I would be as bad, nay worse than I was before.

Chr. Why, what was it that brought your sins to mind again ?

Hope. Many things ; as, if I did but meet a good man in the street ; or if I had heard any read in the Bible ; or if mine head did begin to ache ; or if I were told that some of my neighbours were sick ; or if I heard the bell toll for some that were dead ; or if I thought of dying myself ; or if I heard that sudden death happened to others ; but especially when I thought of myself, that I must quickly come to judgment.

Chr And could you at any time, with ease,

get off the guilt* of sin, when by any of
these ways it came upon you ?

Hope. No, not I ; for then they got faster
hold of my conscience ; and then if I did but
think of going back to sin (though my mind
was turned against it), it would be double torment to me.

Chr. And how did you do then ?

Hope. I thought I must endeavour to mend
my life ; for else, thought I, I am sure to be
damned.

Chr. And did you endeavour to amend ?

Hope. Yes : and fled from, not only my sins,
but sinful company too, and betook me to religious duties, as praying, reading, weeping
for sin, speaking truth to my neighbours, &c.
These things did I with many other, too much
here to relate.

Chr. And did you think yourself well then ?

Hope. Yes, for awhile ; but at the last my
trouble came tumbling upon me again, and
that over the neck of all my reformation.

Chr. How came that about, since you were
now reformed ?

---

* ' Guilt'—This word is used, here and in other places,
not to signify the evil of sin in the sight of God, and the transgressor's deserved liableness to punishment ; but the remorse
and fear of wrath, with which the convinced sinner is oppressed, and from which he often seeks relief by means which exceedingly increase his actual guilt. Nothing, except a free
pardon, by faith in the atoning sacrifice of Christ, can take
away guilt ; but the uneasiness of a man's conscience may be
for a time removed by various expedients. The words guilt
or guilty are often used in this latter sense by modern divines,
but it does not seem to be scripturally accurate, and may
produce misapprehensions.

Hope. There were several things brought it upon me ; especially such sayings as these —'All our righteousnesses are as filthy rags ; —' By the works of the law no man shall be justified ;'——When ye have done all these things, say, We are unprofitable' (Isa. lxiv. 6 ; Luke xvii. 10 ; Gal. ii. 16) : with many more such like. From whence I began to reason with myself thus : if all my righteousnesses are filthy rags ; if by the deeds of the law no man can be justified ; and if, when we have done all, we are unprofitable—then it is but a folly to think of heaven by the law. I farther thought thus——if a man runs a hundred pounds into the shopkeeper's debt, and after that shall pay for all that he shall fetch—yet, if this old debt stands still in the book un-crossed for that the shopkeeper may sue him, and cast him into prison till he shall pay the debt.

Chr. Well, and how did you apply this to yourself ?

Hope. Why, I thought with myself. I have by my sins run a great way into God's book, and that my now reforming will not pay off that score : therefore I should think still, under all my present amendments, But how shall I be freed from that damnation that I brought myself in danger of by my former transgressions ?

Chr. A very good application ; but pray go on.

Hope. Another thing that hath troubled me, ever since my late amendments, is, that if I look narrowly into the best of what I do now, I still see sin, new sin, mixing itself with the best of that I do ; so that now I am forced to conclude, that notwithstanding my former fond conceits of myself and duties, I have committed sin enough in one duty to send me to hell, though my former life had been faultless.

Chr. And what did you do then ?

Hope. Do ! I could not tell what to do, till I broke my mind to Faithful ; for he and I were well acquainted. And he told me, that unless I could obtain the righteousness of a man that never had sinned, neither my own, nor all the righteousness of the world, could save me.

Chr. And did you think he spake true ?

Hope. Had he told me so when I was pleased and satisfied with my own amendment, I had called him fool for his pains ; but now, since I see mine own infirmity, and the sin which cleaves to my best performance, I have been forced to be of his opinion.

Chr. But did you think, when at first he suggested it to you, that there was such a man to be found, of whom it might justly be said that he never committed sin ?

Hope. I must confess the words at first sounded strangely, but, after a little more talk and company with him, I had full conviction about it.

Chr. And did you ask him what man this was, and how you must be justified by him (Rom. iv ; Col. i ; Heb. x ; 2 Pet. i)

25*

Hope. Yes, and he told me it was the Lord Jesus, that dwelleth on the right hand of the Most High : And thus said he, you must be justified by him—even by trusting to what he hath done by himself in the day of his flesh, and suffered when he did hang on the tree. I asked him farther, how that man's righteousness could be of that efficacy to justify another before God ? And he told me he was the mighty God, and did what he did, and died the death also, not for himself, but for me, to whom his doing and the worthiness of them should be imputed, if I believed on him.

Chr. And what did you do then ?

Hope. I made my objections against my believing, for that I thought he was not willing to save me.

Chr. And what said Faithful to you then ?

Hope. He bid me go to him and see. Then I said it was presumption. He said, No, for I was invited to come (Matt. xi. 28). Then he gave me a book, of Jesus's inditing, to encourage me more freely to come ; and he said, concerning that book, that every jot and tittle thereof stood firmer than heaven and earth (Matt, xxiv. 35). Then I asked him what I must do when I came ? And he told me I must entreat upon my knees (Ps. xxv. 6 ; Jer. xxix. 12, 13 ; Dan. vi. 10), with all my heart and soul, the Father to reveal him to me. Then I asked him farther, how I must make my supplication to him ? And he said, Go, and thou shalt find him upon a mercy-seat (Exod. xxv, 22 ; Lev. xvi. 2 ; Heb. iv.

16) where he sits, all the year long, to give pardon and forgiveness to them that come. I told him that I knew not what to say when I came. And he bid me say to this effect— 'God be merciful to me a sinner,' and make me to know and believe in Jesus Christ, for I see, that if his righteousness had not been, or I have not faith in that righteousness, I am utterly cast away. Lord, I have heard that thou art a merciful God, and hast ordained that thy Son Jesus Christ should be the Saviour of the world ; and, moreover, that thou art willing to bestow him upon such a poor sinner as I am (and I am a sinner indeed) : Lord take therefore this opportunity, and magnify thy grace in the salvation of my soul, through thy son Jesus Christ. Amen.

Chr. And did you do as you were bidden ?

Hope. Yes, over, and over, and over.

Chr. And did the Father reveal the Son to you ?

Hope. Not at first, nor second, nor third, nor fourth, nor fifth, no, nor at the sixth time neither.

Chr. What did you do then ?

Hope. What ! why I could not tell what to do.

Chr. Had you not thoughts of leaving off praying ?

Hope. Yes, and a hundred times twice told.

Chr. And what was the reason you did not?

Hope. I believed that that was true which hath been told me, to wit, that without the righteousness of this Christ all the world could not save me : and therefore, thought I with myself, if I leave off, I die, and I can but die at the throne of grace. And withal this came into my mind, ' if it tarry, wait for it because it will surely come, and will not tarry') Hab. ii. 3). So I continued, until the Father shewed me his Son.

Chr. And how was he revealed unto you ?

Hope. I did not see him with my bodily eyes, but with the eyes of my understanding (Eph. i. 18, 19), and thus it was : one day I was very sad, I think sadder than at any one time of my life ; and this sadness was through a fresh sight of the greatness and vileness of my sins. And as I was then looking for nothing but hell, and the everlasting damnation of my soul, suddenly, as I thought, I saw the Lord Jesus look down from heaven upon me, and saying, ' Believe on the Lord Jesus Christ, and thou shalt be saved' (Acts xvi. 30, 31).

But I replied, Lord, I am a great, a very great sinner : and he answered, ' My grace is sufficient for thee.' Then I said, But Lord, what is believing ? And then I saw from that saying, ' He that cometh to me shall never hunger, and he that believeth on me shall never thirst' (John vi. 35), that believing and coming* was all one ; and that

* ' Coming'—Coming to Christ is properly the effect of faith : yet the language here used is warranted by Scripture. The word reveal and the vision of Christ conversing with Hopeful, seem to sanction such things as have been greatly mistaken and abused, and have occasioned many scandals and objections : yet it is evident that the author meant no-

he that came, that is, ran out in his heart and affection after salvation by Christ, he indeed believed in Christ. Then the water stood in mine eyes, and I asked farther, But, Lord, may such a great sinner as I am be indeed accepted of thee, and be saved by thee ? And I heard him say, ' And him that cometh to me, I will in no wise cast out (John vi. 37) Then I said, But how, Lord, must I consider of thee in my coming to thee, that my faith may be placed aright upon thee ? Then he said, ' Christ came into the world to save sinners ;' ' he is the end of the law for righteousness to every one that believes ;' ' he died for our sins, and rose again for our justification ;' ' he loved us, and washed us from our sins in his own blood ;' ' he is Mediator

thing contrary to the most sober statement of scriptural truth. Christ did not appear to Hopeful's senses, but to his understanding : and the words spoken are no other than texts of Scripture taken in that genuine meaning ; not informing him, as by a new revelation, that his sins were pardoned, but encouraging him to apply for this mercy, and all other blessings of salvation. So that, allowing for the nature of an allegory, the whole account for substance exactly coincides with the experience of the most sober Christians; who, having been deeply humbled, and ready to sink under discouragement, have had such views of the love of Christ, of his glorious salvation, the freeness of the invitations, the largeness of the promises, and the nature of justifying faith, as have 'filled them with peace and joy in believing :' and these have been followed by those abiding effects afterwards described, which completely distinguish them from all the false joys of hypocrites and enthusiasts. Others indeed cannot relate so orderly an account of their convictions and comforts ; yet they are brought (though by varied methods) to the same reliance on Christ, and the same devoted obedience.

betwixt God and us ;' 'he ever liveth to make intercession for us' (1 Tim. i. 15 ; Rom. x. 4 ; Heb. vii. 24, 25). From all which I gathered, that I must look for righteousness in his person, and for satisfaction for my sins by his blood ; that which he did in obedience to his Father's law, and in submitting to the penalty thereof, was not for himself, but for him that will accept it for his salvation, and be thankful. And now was my heart full of joy, mine eyes full of tears, and mine affections running over with love to the name, people, and ways of Jesus Christ.

Chr. This was a revelation of Christ to your soul indeed : but tell me particularly what effect this had upon your spirit.

Hope. It made me see that all the world, notwithstanding all the righteousness thereof, is in a state of condemnation : It made me see that God the Father, though he be just, can justly justify the coming sinner : it made me greatly ashamed of the vileness of my former life, and confounded me with the sense of mine own ignorance ; for there never came thought into my heart before now, that shewed so the beauty of Jesus Christ : it made me love a holy life, and long to do something for the honour and glory of the Lord Jesus ; yea, I thought, that had I now a thousand gallons of blood in my body, I could spill it all for the sake of the Lord Jesus.

I saw then in my dream, that Hopeful looked back and saw Ignorance, whom they had left behind, coming after : Look, said he to Christian, how far yonder youngster loitereth behind.

Chr. Ay, ay, I see him : he careth not for our company.

Hope. But I trow it would not have hurt him, had he kept pace with us hitherto

Chr. That is true ; but I'll warrant you he thinketh otherwise.

Hope. That I think he doth : but however, let us tarry for him. So they did.

Then Christian said to him, Come away, man, why do you stay so behind ?

Ignor. I take* my pleasure in walking alone ; even more a great deal than in company ; unless I like it better.

Then said Christian to Hopeful (but softly), Did I not tell you he cared not for our company ? But, however, said he, come up and let us talk away the time in this solitary place. Then, directing his speech to Ignorance, he said, Come, how do you do ? how stands it between God and your soul now ?

Ignor. I hope well, for I am always full of good motions, that come into my mind to comfort me as I walk.

Chr. What good motions ? pray tell us.

Ignor. Why, I think of God and heaven.

Chr. So do the devils and damned souls.

* ' I take'—In the following dialogue Ignorance speaks exactly in character ; and the answers of the pilgrims are conclusive against such absurd and unscriptual grounds of confidence as are continually maintained by many who would be ought pious Christians.

Ignor. But I think of them and desire* them.

Chr. So do many that are never like to come there. 'The soul of the sluggard desires, and hath nothing' (Prov. xiii. 4).

Ignor. But I think of them, and leave all for them.

Chr. That I doubt : for leaving of all is a hard matter ; yea, a harder matter than many are aware of. But why, or by what, art thou persuaded that thou hast left all for God and heaven ?

Ignor. My heart tells me so.

Chr. The wise man says, 'He that trusts his own heart is a fool' (Prov. xxviii. 26).

Ignor. This is spoken of an evil heart, but mine is a good one.

Chr. But how dost thou prove that ?

Ignor. It comforts† me in hopes of heaven.

---

* 'Desire'—The desire of heavenly felicity, when the real nature of it is not understood, the proper means of obtaining it are neglected, other objects are preferred to it, or sloth and procrastination intervene, is no proof that a man will be saved. In like manner this expression, ' the desire of grace is grace,' must be owned to be very fallacious and ambiguous. Men may be notionally convinced that without grace they must perish, and mere selfishness my excite some feeble desires after it ; though worldly affections predominate, and the real value of the spiritual good is not perceived. But to hunger and thirst for God and his righteousness, his favour, image, and service, as the supreme good, so that no other object can satisfy the earnest desire of the heart, and every thing is renounced that interferes with the pursuit of it, is grace indeed, and shall be completed in glory.

† 'Comforts'—It is exceedingly dangerous to make comfort a ground of confidence ; unless the nature, source, concomitants, and effect of that comfort be considered ; for it may result entirely from ignorance and self-flattery, in a variety of ways

Chr. That may be through its deceitfulness, for a man's heart may minister comfort to him, in the hopes of that thing for which he yet has no ground to hope.

Ignor. But my heart and life agree together; and therefore my hope is well grounded.

Chr. Who told thee that thy heart and life agree together?

Ignor. My heart tells me.

Chr. 'Ask my fellow if I be a thief?' Thy heart tells thee so! except the word of God beareth witness in this matter, other testimony is no value.

Ignor. But is it not a good heart that has good thoughts? and is not that a good life that is according to God's commandments?

Chr. Yes, that is a good heart that hath good thoughts, and that is a good life that is according to God's commandments; but it is one thing indeed to have these, and another thing only to think so.

Ignor. Pray what count you good thoughts, and a life according to God's commandments?

Chr. There are good thoughts of divers kinds; some respecting ourselves, some—God, some—Christ, and some—other things

Ignor. What be good thoughts respecting ourselves?

Chr. Such as agree with the word of God

Ignor. When do our thoughts of ourselves agree with the word of God?

Chr. When we pass the same judgment

upon ourselves which the word passes. To explain myself: the word of God saith of persons in a natural* condition. 'There is none righteous, there is none that doeth good.' It saith also, that 'every imagination of the heart of man is only evil, and that continually' (Gen vi. 5; Rom. iii.). And again, 'The imagination of man's heart is evil from his youth.' Now then, when we think thus of ourselves, having sense thereof then are our thoughts good ones, because according to the word of God.

Ignor. I will never believe that my heart is thus bad.

Chr. Therefore thou never hadst one good thought concerning thyself in thy life. But let me go on. As the word passeth a judgment upon our heart, so it passeth a judgment upon our ways; and when the thoughts of our hearts and ways agree with the judgment which the word giveth of both, then are both good, because agreeing thereto.

Ignor. Make out your meaning.

Chr. Why, the word of God saith that man's ways are crooked ways, not good, but perverse: it saith they are naturally out of the good way; that they have not known it (Ps. cxxv. 5; Prov. ii. 15). Now when a man

* 'Natural'—'That which is born of the flesh is flesh;' 'the carnal mind is enmity against God; is not subject to his law, neither indeed can be; so then they that are in the flesh cannot please God;' for 'they are by nature the children of wrath.' 'Ye are not in the flesh, but in the spirit:' 'for that which is born of the Spirit is spirit;' and to such persons the texts adduced do not apply.

thus thinketh of his ways, I say when he doth sensibly, and with heart humiliation, thus think, then hath he good thoughts of his own ways, because his thoughts now agree with the judgment of the word of God.

Ignor. What are good thoughts concerning God?

Chr. Even, as I have said concerning ourselves, when our thoughts of God do agree with what the word saith of him; and that is when we speak of his being and attributes as the word hath taught; of which I cannot now discourse at large. But to speak of him in reference to us; then we have right thoughts of God when we think that he knows us better than we know ourselves, and can see sin in us when and where we can see none in ourselves: when we think he knows our inmost thoughts, and that our heart, with all its depths, is always open unto his eyes: also when we think that all our righteousness stinks* in his nostrils, and that therefore he

'Stinks'—The external services performed by unregenerate persons from selfish motives, being scanty and partial, and made the ground of self-complacency, and the pride of self-righteousness, 'are abomination in the sight of God,' however 'highly esteemed among men:' for men 'look at the outward appearance, but the Lord looketh at the heart.' Even the obedience of a true believer, though it springs from right principles, and has some spiritual excellency in it, is yet so defective and defiled by sin, that if it were not accepted as the fruit of the Spirit, through the mediation of Christ, it would be condemned by the holy law, and rejected with abhorrence by a God of infinite purity. Men may allow this in words, and yet not know what it is to come, as condemned sinners, for a free justification and salvation, by faith in Christ The way of being justified by faith, for which

cannot abide to see us stand before him in any confidence, even in all our best performances.

Ignor. Do you think that I am such a fool as to think God can see no farther than I ? or that I would come to God in the best of my performances ?

Chr. Why, how dost thou think in this matter ?

Ignor. Why, to be short, I think I must believe in Christ for justification.

Chr. How ! think thou must believe in Christ, when thou seest not thy need of him ! Thou neither seest thy original nor actual infirmities ; but hast such an opinion of thyself, and of what thou doest, as plainly renders thee to be one that did never see a necessity of Christ's personal righteousness to justify thee before God. How then dost thou say, I believe in Christ ?

Ignor. I believe well enough for all that.

Chr. How dost thou believe ?

Ignor. I believe that Christ died for sinners ; and that I shall be justified before God from the curse, through his gracious acceptance of my obedience to his laws. Or thus, Christ makes my duties, that are religious, acceptable to his Father by virtue of his merits, and so shall I be justified.

Ignorance pleads, may well be called ' fantastical, as well as ' false ;' for it is nowhere laid down in Scripture : and it not only changes the way of acceptance, but it takes away the rule and standard of righteousness, and substitutes a vague notion, called sincerity, in its place, which never was, or can be, defined with precision.

Chr. Let us give an answer to this confession of thy faith.

1. Thou believest with a fantastical faith for this faith is no where described in the word.

2. Thou believest with a false faith ; because thou takest justification from the personal righteousness of Christ, and appliest it to thy own.

3. This faith maketh not Christ a justifier of thy person, but of thy actions ; and of thy person for thy actions' sake, which is false.

4. Therefore this faith is deceitful, even such as will leave thee under wrath in the day of God Almighty : for true justifying faith puts the soul, as sensible of its lost condition by the law, upon fleeing for refuge unto Christ's righteousness (which righteousness of his is not an act of grace by which he maketh, for justification, thy obedience accepted of God, but his personal obedience to the law, in doing and suffering for us what that required at our hands) ; this righteousness, I say, true faith accepteth ; under the skirt of which the soul being shrouded, and by it presented as spotless before God, it is accepted, and acquits from condemnation.

Ignor. What, would you have us trust to what Christ in his own person hath done without us ? This conceit would loosen the reins of our lust, and tolerate us to live as we list : for what matter how we live, if we may be justified by Christ's personal righteousness for all, when we believe it ?

26*

Chr. Ignorance is thy name, and as thy name is so art thou; even this thy answer demonstrateth what I say. Ignorant thou art of what justifying righteousness is and as ignorant how to secure thy soul, through the faith of it, from the heavy wrath of God. Yea, thou also art ignorant of the true effect of saving faith in this righteousness of Christ, which is to bow and win over the heart to God in Christ, to love his name, his word, ways, and people, and not as thou ignorantly imaginest.

Hope. Ask him if ever he had Christ revealed to him from heaven?

Ignor. What! you are a man for revelations! I do believe that what both you and all the rest of you say about that matter is but the fruit of distracted brains.

Hope. Why, man! Christ is so hid* in God from the natural apprehensions of the flesh, that he cannot by any man be savingly known, unless God the Father reveals him to them.

Ignor. That is your faith, but not mine: yet mine, I doubt not, is as good as yours, though I have not in my head so many whimsies as you.

Chr. Give me leave to put in a word:— you ought not to speak so slightly of this mat-

* 'Hid'—Pride, unbelief, and carnal prejudices or affections, so close the mind of a sinner against the spiritual glory of the person and redemption of Christ, that nothing, but the illumination of the Spirit removing this veil can enable him to understand and receive the revelation of the sacred oracles on these important subjects.

ter ; for this I boldly affirm (even as my good companion hath done), that no man can know Jesus Christ but by the revelation of the Father ; yea, and faith too, by which the soul layeth hold upon Christ (if it be right), must be wrought by the exceeding greatness of his mighty power (Matt. xi. 27 ; 1 Cor. xii. 3 ; Eph. i. 18, 19) ; the working of which faith, I perceive, poor Ignorance, thou art ignorant of. Be awakened then, see thine own wretchedness, and flee to the Lord Jesus ; and by his righteousness, which is the righteousness, of God (for himself is God), thou shalt be delivered from condemnation.

Ignor. You go so fast I cannot keep pace with you : do you go on before ; I must stay awhile behind.

Then they said—

> Well, Ignorance, wilt thou yet foolish be
> To slight good counsel, ten times given thee ?
> And if thou yet refuse it, thou shalt know,
> Ere long, the evil of thy doing so.
> Remember, man, time in ; stop, do not fear,
> Good counsel taken well saves ; therefore hear ;
> But if thou yet shall slight it, thou wilt be
> The loser, Ignorance, I'll warrant thee.

Then Christian addressed himself thus to his fellow :

Chr. Well, come, my good Hopeful, I perceive that thou and I must walk by ourselves again.

So I saw in my dream, that they went on apace before, and Ignorance, he came hobbling after. Then said Christian to his companion, it pities me much for this poor man; it will certainly go ill with him at last.

Hope. Alas! there are abundance in our town in this condition, whole families, yea, whole streets, and that of pilgrims* too; and if there be so many in our parts, how many, think you, must there be in the place where he was born?

Chr. Indeed the word saith, 'He hath blinded their eyes, lest they should see,' &c.

But, now we are by ourselves, what do you think of such men? have they at no time, think you, convictions of sin, and so consequently fear that their state is dangerous?

Hope. Nay, do you answer that question yourself, for you are the elder man.

Chr. Then I say, sometimes (as I think) they may; but they,† being naturally igno-

---

* 'Pilgrims'—If such numbers of ignorant persons may be found among the apparently religious, what must be the case of those who are left without instruction to their native pride and self-conceit!

† 'But they'—Fears of wrath are too generally ascribed to unbelief, and deemed prejudicial: but this arises from ignorance and mistake; for belief of God's testimony must excite fears in every heart, till it is clearly perceived how that wrath may be escaped; and doubts mingled with hopes must arise from faith, till a man is conscious of having experienced a saving change. These fears and doubts excite men to self-examination, watchfulness, and diligence, and thus tend to the believer's establishment, and 'the full assurance of hope unto the end:' while the want of them often results from unbelief and stupidity of conscience, and terminates in carnal security and abuse of the Gospel. They may indeed be excessive and unreasonable, and the effect of unbelief: but it is better to mark the extreme, and caution men against it, than by declaiming indiscriminately against all doubts and fears,

rant, understand not that such convictions tend
to their good ; and therefore they do desper
ately seek to stifle them, and presumtuously
continue to flatter themselves in the way of
their own hearts.

Hope. I do believe, as you say, that fear
tends much to men's good, and to make them
right at their beginning to go on pilgrimage.

Chr. Without all doubt it doth, if it be right :
for so says the word, 'The fear of the Lord is
the beginning of wisdom' (Job xxviii. 28 ; Ps.
cxi. 10 ; Prov. i. 7 ; ix. 10).

Hope. How will you describe right fear ?

Chr. True or right fear is discovered by
three things : 1. By its rise : it is caused by
saving convictions for sin. 2. It driveth the
soul to lay fast hold of Christ for salvation. 3.
It begetteth and continueth in the soul a great
reverence of God, his word, and ways, keeping
it tender, and making it afraid to turn from
them, to the right hand or to the left, to any
thing that may dishonour God, break its peace,
grieve the spirit, or cause the enemy to speak
reproachfully.

Hope. Well said ! I believe you have said
the truth. Are we now almost got past the
Enchanted ground ?

Chr. Why ? art thou weary of this discourse ?

Hope. No verily, but that I would know
where we are.

to help sinners to deceive themselves, and discourage weak
believers from earnestly using the scriptual means of ' making their calling and election sure.'

Chr. We have not now above two miles farther to go thereon. But let us return to our matter. Now the ignorant know not that such convictions, that tend to put them in fear, are for their good, and therefore they seek to stifle them.

Hope. How do they seek to stifle them?

Chr. 1. They think that those fears are wrought by the devil (though indeed they are wrought by God); and, thinking so, they resist them, as things that directly tend to their overthrow. 2. They also think that these fears tend to the spoiling of their faith; when alas for them, poor men that they are, they have none at all!—and therefore they harden their hearts against them. 3. They presume they ought not to fear, and therefore in despite of them wax presumptuously confident. 4. They see that those fears tend to take away from them their pitiful* oldself-holiness, and herefore they resist them with all their might.

Hope. I know something of this myself: before I knew myself it was so with me.

Chr. Well, we will leave, at this time our neighbour Ignorance by himself, and fall up-on another profitable question.

Hope. With all my heart: but you shall still begin.

* ' Pitiful'—The expression, ' pitiful old self-holiness,' de-notes the opinion that ignorant persons entertain of their hearts as good and holy; while the term ' self-righteousness' relates to their supposed good lives: but nothing can be farther from our author's meaning, than to speak against ' sanctification by the Spirit unto obedience,' as eviden-tial of our union with Christ, and acceptance in his righteous-ness.

Chr. Well, then, did you* know about ten years ago, one Temporary in your parts, who was a forward man in religion then ?

Hope. Know him ! yes, he dwelt in **Grace-less**, a town about two miles off of **Honesty**, and he dwelt next door to one **Turnback**.

Chr. Right, he dwelt under the same roof with him. Well, that man was much awakened once ; I believe that then he had some sight of his sins, and of the wages that were due thereto.

Hope. I am of your mind, for (my house not being above three miles from him) he would oft-times come to me, and that with many tears. Truly I pitied the man, and was not altogether without hope of him : but, one may see, it is not every one that cries Lord, Lord.

Chr. He told me once that he was resolv-

' Did you'—Temporary was doctrinally acquainted with the Gospel, but a stranger to its sanctifying power. Such men have been forward in religion, but that is now past ; for they were always graceless, and came short of honesty in their profession, if not in their moral conduct, and were ever ready to turn back into the world at a convenient season. They have indeed been alarmed : but terror without humiliation will never subvert self-confidence : and of the numbers with whom some ministers converse under trouble of conscience, and of whom they hope well, how many disappoint their expectations, and after a time plunge deeper into sin than ever ! Such convictions resemble the blossoms of the fruit-tree, which precede the ripe fruit, but did not always produce it ; so that we cannot say, ' the more blossoms there are, the greater abundance will there be of fruit ;' though we may be assured that there can be no fruit if there be no blossoms. The reasons and the manner of such men's declensions and apostacy are very justly and emphatically stated ; though perhaps not with sufficient delicacy to suit the taste of this fastidious age.

ed to go on pilgrimage, as we go now : but all of a sudden he grew acquainted with one Saveself, and then he became a stranger to me.

Hope. Now, since we are talking about him, let us a little inquire into the reason of the sudden backsliding of him and such others.

Chr. It may be very profitable ; but do you begin.

Hope. Well, then, there are in my judgment four reasons for it.

First, Though the consciences of such men are awakened, yet their minds are not changed : therefore, when the power of guilt weareth away, that which provoketh them to be religious ceaseth : wherefore they naturally return to their old course again ; even as we see the dog that is sick of what he hath eaten, so long as his sickness prevails he vomits and casts all up : not that he does this of free mind (if we may say a dog has a mind), but because it troubleth his stomach : but now, when his sickness is over, and so his stomach eased, his desires being not at all alienated from his vomit, he turns him about, and licks up all : and so it is true which is written, 'The dog is turned to his own vomit again' (2 Pet. ii. 22). Thus I say being hot for heaven, by virtue only of the sense and fear of the torments of hell, as their sense of hell and fear of damnation chills and cools, so their desires for heaven and salvation cool also. So then it comes to pass, that, when their guilt and fear is gone, their desires for hea-

when their guilt and fear is gone, their desires for heaven and happiness die, and they return to their course again.

Second, Another reason is, they have slavish fears that do over-master them :—I speak now of the fears that they have of men : ' for the fear of men bringeth a snare' (Prov. xx. 25). So then, though they seem to be hot for heaven so long as the flames of hell are about their ears, yet, when that terror is a little over, they betake themselves to second thoughts namely, that it is good to be wise, and not to run (for they know not what) the hazard of losing all, or at least of bringing themselves into unavoidable and unnecessary troubles ; and so they fall in with the world again.

Third, The shame that attends religion lies also as a block in their way : they are proud and haughty, and religion in their eye is low and contemptible : therefore, when they have lost their sense of hell and wrath to come, they return again to their former course.

Fourth, Guilt, and to meditate terror, are grievous to them ; they like not to see their misery before they come into it ; though perhaps the sight of it first, if they loved that sight, might make them flee whither the righteous flee and are safe ; but because they do, as I hinted before, even shun the thoughts of guilt and terror, therefore, when once they are rid of their awakenings about the terrors and wrath of God, they harden their hearts gladly, and choose such ways as will harden them more and more.

Chr. You are pretty near the business, for the bottom of all is, for want of a change in their mind and will. And therefore they are but like the felon that standeth before the judge; he quakes and trembles, and seems to repent most heartily: but the bottom of all is, the fear of the halter; not that he hath any detestation of the offences; as it is evident, because, let but this man have his liberty, and he will be a thief, and so a rogue still; whereas, if his mind was changed, he would be otherwise.

Hope. Now I have shewed you the reason of their going back, do you shew me the manner thereof.

Chr. So I will willingly. They draw off their thoughts, all that they may, from the remembrance of God, death, and judgment to come :—then they* cast off by degrees

* 'Then'—The hypocrite will not pray always; nor can he ever pray, with faith or sincerity, for spiritual blessings: but he may deprecate misery, and beg to be made happy, and continue to observe a form of private religion. But when such men begin to shun the company of lively Christians, to neglect public ordinances, and to excuse their conduct by imitating the devil, the accuser of the brethren, in calumniating pious persons, magnifying their imperfections, insinuating suspicions of them, and aiming to confound all distinction of character among men; we may safely conclude their state to be perilous in the extreme. While professors should be exhorted carefully to look to themselves, and to watch against the first incursions of this spiritual declension, it should also be observed, that the lamented infirmities and dulness of those who persist in using the means of grace, and striving against sin, who decidedly prefer th

private duties and closet-prayers, curbing
their lusts, watching, sorrow for sin, &c :—
then they shun the company of lively and
warm Christians :—after that they grow cold
to public duty ; as hearing, reading, godly
conference, and the like :—then they begin
to pick holes, as we say, in the coats of some
of the godly, and that devilishly, that they
may have a seeming colour to throw religion
(for the sake of some infirmities they have
spied in them) behind their backs :—then
they begin to adhere to, and associate themselves with, carnal, loose, and wanton men :—
then they give way to carnal and wanton discourses in secret ; and glad are they if they
can see such things in any that are counted
honest, that they may the more boldly do it
through their example. After this, they begin to play with little sins openly :—and then,
being hardened, they shew themselves as
they are. Thus being launched again into
the gulf of misery, unless a miracle of grace
prevent it, they everlastingly perish in their
own deceivings.

Now I saw in my dream that by this time
the pilgrims were got over the Enchanted
ground, and entering into the country* of

company of believers, and deem them the excellent of the
earth, and who are severe in judging themselves, but candid
to others ; are of a contrary nature and tendency to the
steps of Temporary's apostacy.

* 'Country'—The word Beulah signifies married ; and
the prophet, in the passage whence it is quoted, predicted a
very flourishing state of religion, which is yet in futurity:
but the author accomodates it to the sweet peace and confi-

Beulah (Cant. ii. 10—12 ; Isa. lxii. 4—12),
whose air was very sweet and pleasant, the
way lying directly through it, they solaced
themselves there for a season.   Yea, here
they heard continually the singing of birds,
and saw every day the flowers appear in the
earth, and heard the voice of the turtle in the
land.   In this country the sun shineth night
and day : wherefore this was beyond the valley of the Shadow of Death, and also out of
the reach of giant Despair ; neither could
they from this place so much as see Doubting Castle.   Here they were within sight of

dence which tried believers commonly experience towards
the close of their lives.   This general rule admits indeed of
exceptions ; but the author having witnessed many of these
encouraging scenes, was willing to animate himself and his
afflicted brethren with the hope of similar triumphant joys.
The communion of saints in prayer, praises, and thanksgivings, with liberty and ardour, and hearts united in cordial
love ; the beauties of holiness, and the consolations of the
Holy Spirit ; the healing beams of the sun of righteousness,
shining by the sweet light of divine truth upon the soul,
exemption from darkening temptations and harassing doubts ;
lively earnests and near prospects of heavenly felicity ; a
cheering sense of union of spirit with the heavenly host, in
their fervent adorations, and a realizing apprehension of
their ministering care over the heirs of salvation : a comfortable renewal of the acceptances of Christ, sealed with
the tokens, pledges, and assurances of his love ; gratitude,
submission, confidence in God, hope, and the sweet exercise
of tenderness, sympathy, meekness, and humility, but little interrupted by the working of the contrary evils ; these
things seem to constitute the happy state here represented.
It is remarkable, that the Psalms (which were intended,
among other uses, to regulate the devotions and experience
of believers) abound at first with confessions, complaints,
fears, and earnest cries of distress ; but towards the close become more and more the language of confidence, gratitude and
joy, and conclude with unmingled praises and thanksgi-ings-

the city they were going to ; also here met them some of the inhabitants thereof ; for in this land the shining ones commonly walked, because it was upon the borders of heaven. In this land also the contract between the bride and the bridegroom was renewed ; yea, here, ' as the bridegroom rejoiceth over the bride, so did their God rejoice over them. Here they had no want of corn and wine ; for in this place they met abundance of what they had sought for in all their pilgrimage. Here they heard voices from out of the city, loud voices, saying, ' Say ye to the daughter of Zion, Behold, thy salvation cometh ! Behold, his reward is with him !' Here all the inhabitants of the country called them ' the holy people, the redeemed of the Lord, sought out,' &c.

Now, as they walked in this land, they had more rejoicing than in parts more remote from the kingdom to which they were bound ; and drawing near to the city they had yet a more perfect view thereof. It was builded of pearls and precious stones, also the streets thereof were paved with gold ; so that, by reason of the natural glory of the city, and the reflection of the sun-beams upon it, Christian with desire* fell sick ; Hopeful also

* ' Desire'—In the immediate] view of heavenly felicity, Paul ' desired to depart hence and be with Christ, as far better' than life ; and David ' fainted for God's salvation.' In the lively exercise of holy affections, the believer grows weary of this sinful world, longs to have his faith changed for sight, his hope swallowed up in enjoyment, and his love perfected, and secured from all interruption and abatement.

27*

had a fit or two of the same disease; wherefore here they lay by it awhile crying out because of their pangs, 'If you see my beloved, tell him that I am sick of love.'

But, being a little strengthened, and better able to bear their sickness, they walked on their way, and came nearer and nearer, where were orchards, vineyards, and gardens, and their gates opened into the highway. Now, as they came up to these places, behold the gardener stood in the way; to whom the pilgrims said, Whose* goodly vineyards and gardens are these? He answered, They are the King's, and are planted here for his own delight, and also for the solace of pilgrims. So the gardener had them into the vineyards, and bid them refresh themselves with the dainties (Deut. xxiii. 24); he also shewed them there the King's walks and arbours, where he delighted to be; and here they tarried and slept.

Now I beheld in my dream, that they talked more in their sleep at this time than ever they did in all their journey; and, being in a

Were this frame of mind habitual, it might unfit men for the common concerns of life, which appear very trifling to the soul when employed in delightful admiring contemplation of heavenly glory.

* 'Whose'—Attendance on the public ordinances is always the believer's duty and privilege; yet he cannot at all times delight in them: but when holy affections are in lively exercise, he sweetly rests in these earnests of heavenly joy; and speaks freely and fervently of the love of Christ and the blessings of salvation, to the edification of those around him; who often wonder at witnessing such a change, from reserve and diffidence to boldness and earnestness in urging others to mind the one thing needful.

muse thereabout, the gardener said even to
me, Wherefore musest thou at the matter ? it
is the nature of the fruit of the grapes of
these vineyards 'to go down so sweetly as
to cause the lips of them that are asleep to
speak.'

So I saw that when they awoke they ad
dressed themselves to go up to the city. For
as I said, the reflection of the sun upon the
city (for the city was pure gold, Rev. xxi. 18 ;
2 Cor. iii. 18), was so extremely glorious,
that they could not as yet with open face behold it, but through an instrument made for
that purpose. So I saw, that as they went on
there met them two men in raiment that
shone like gold, also their faces shone as the
light.

These* men asked the pilgrims whence
they came ? and they told them. They also
asked them where they had lodged, what difficulties and dangers, what comforts and
pleasures, they had met with in the way ? and
they told them. Then said the men that met
them, You have but two difficulties more to
meet with, and then you are in the city.

Christian then and his companion asked the
men to go along with them ; so they told them
they would. But, said they, you must obtain
it by your own faith. So I saw in my dream

---

* ' These'—Perhaps the author here alluded to those pre-
intimations of death that some persons seem to receive ; and
he appears to have referred them to the common opinion of
guardian angels watching over every individual believer.
Death and admission into the city were the only difficulties
that awaited the pilgrims.

that they went on together till they came in sight of the gate.

Now* I farther saw, that betwixt them and the gate was a river; but there was no bridge

* 'Now'—Death is aptly represented by a deep river without a bridge, separating the believer from his heavenly inheritance; as the Jordan flowed between Israel and the promised land. From this river nature shrinks back, even when faith, hope, and love are in lively exercise; but when these decline, alarm and consternation may unite with reluctance. The dreaded pangs that precede the awful separation of those intimate associates, the soul and body; the painful parting with dear friends and every earthly object; the gloomy ideas of the dark, cold, and noisome grave; and the solemn thought of launching into an unseen eternity, render Death the king of terrors. Faith in a crucified, buried, risen, and ascended Saviour; experience of his faithfulness and love in times past; hope of an immediate entrance into his presence, where temptation, conflict, sin, and suffering, will find no admission; and the desire of perfect knowledge, holiness, and felicity, will reconcile the mind to the inevitable stroke, and sometimes give a complete victory over every fear: yet if faith and hope be weakened, through the recollection of any peculiar misconduct, the withholding of divine light and consolation, or some violent assault of the tempter, the believer will be peculiarly liable to alarm and distress. His reflecting mind, having long been accustomed to consider the subject in its important nature and consequences, has very different apprehensions of God, of eternity, of judgment, of sin, and of himself, than other men have. Sometimes experienced saints are more desponding in these circumstances than their junior brethren; constitution has considerable effect upon their mind; and some men (like Christian) are, in every stage of their profession, more exposed to temptations of a discouraging nature, than to ambition, avarice, or fleshly lusts. It has before been suggested, that the author probably meant to describe the peculiarities of his own experience, in the character of Christian; and he may perhaps here have intimated his apprehension lest he should not meet death with becoming fortitude. A conscientious life indeed is commonly favoured with a peaceful close, even when forebodings to the contrary have troubled men during their whole lives: this is so far general, that they best provide for a comfortable death,

to go over : the river was very deep. At the sight therefore of this river, the pilgrims were much stunned ; but the men that went with them, said You must go through, or you cannot come at the gate.

The pilgrims began to inquire if there was no other way to the gate ? to which they answered, Yes ; but there hath not any, save two, to wit, Enoch and Elijah, been permitted to tread that path since the foundation of the world, nor shall until the last trumpet shall sound. The pilgrims then (especially Christian) began to despond in their minds, and looked this way and that, but no way could be found by them, by which they might escape the river. Then they asked the men if the waters were all of a depth ? they said, no ; yet they could not help them in that case ; For, said they, you shall find it deeper or shallower, as you believe in the king of the place.

They then addressed themselves to the water, and, entering, Christian began to sink, and crying out to his good friend Hopeful, he said, 'I sink in deep waters ; the billows

who most diligently attend to the duties of their station and the improvement of their talents, from evangelical principles ; whereas they who live negligently, and yield to temptation, make, as it were, an assignation with terror to meet them on their death-bed, a season when comfort is more desirable than at any other. The Lord, however, is no man's debtor ; none can claim consolation as their due ; and, though a believer's experience and the testimony of his conscience may evidence the sincerity of his faith and love, yet he must disclaim to the last every other dependance than the righteousness and blood of Christ, and the free mercy of God in him

g⁊ over my head, all his waves go over me.
Selah.'

Then said the other, be of good cheer, my
brother ; I feel the bottom and it is good.
Then said Christian, Ah ! my friend, the sorrow of death hath compassed me about, I shall
not see the land that flows with milk and honey   And with that a great darkness and horror fell upon Christian, so that he could not
see before him.   Also he* in a great measure
lost his senses, so that he could neither remember nor orderly talk of any of those sweet
refreshments, that he had met with in the way
of his pilgrimage.   But all the words he spake
still tended to discover that he had horror of
mind, and heart fears that he should die
in that river, and never obtain entrance in at
the gate.   Here also, as they that stood by
perceived, he was much in the troublesome
thoughts of the sins that he had committed,
both since and before he began to be a pilgrim.   It was also observed, that he was
troubled with apparitions of hobgoblins and
evil spirits ; for ever and anon he would in-

---

* ' Also he'—The temporary distresses of dying believers
often arise from bodily disease, which interrupt the free exercise of their intellectual powers.   Of this Satan will be sure
to take advantage, as far as he is permitted ; and will suggest gloomy imaginations, not only to distress them, but to
dishearten others by their example.   What may in this state
be painted before the fancy we cannot tell ; but it is generally observed, that such painful conflicts terminate in renewed
hope and comfort, frequently by means of the conversation
and prayers of Christians and ministers ; so that they, who
for a time have been most distressed, have at length died most
triumphantly.

timate so much by words. Hopeful therefore here had much ado to keep his brother's head above water; yea, sometimes he would be quite gone down, and then, ere a while, would rise up again half dead. Hopeful did also endeavour to comfort him, saying, Brother, I see the gate, and men standing by to receive us; but Christian would answer, It is you, it is you they wait for; you have been Hopeful ever since I knew you. And so have you, said he to Christian. Ah, brother, said he, surely if I was right, he would now rise to help me; but for my sins he hath brought me into the snare, and hath left me. Then said Hopeful, My brother, you have quite forgot the text where it is said of the wicked, ' There are no bands in their death, but their strength is firm; they are not troubled as other men, neither are they plagued like other men.' These troubles and distresses that you go through in these waters are no sign that God hath forsaken you; but are sent to try you, whether you will call to mind that which heretofore you have received of his goodness, and live upon him in your distresses.

Then I saw in my dream that Christian was in a muse awhile. To whom also Hopeful added these words, ' Be of good cheer, Jesus Christ maketh thee whole.' And with that Christian brake out with a loud voice, Oh, I see him again! and he tells me, ' When thou passest through the waters, I will be with thee; and through the rivers,

they shall not overflow thee' (Isa. xliii. 2).
Then they both took courage, and the enemy
was after that as still as a stone, until they
were gone over. Christian therefore presently found ground to stand upon, and so it
followed, that the rest of the river was but
shallow ; but thus they got over. Now upon
the bank of the river, on the other side, they saw
the two* shining men again, who there waited for them. Wherefore, being come out of
the river, they saluted them, saying, ' We are
ministering spirits, sent forth to minister for
those that shall be heirs of salvation.' Thus
they went along towards the gate. Now you
must note that the city stood upon a mighty
hill ; but the pilgrims went up the hill with
ease, because they had these two men to lead
them up by the arms : also they had left their
mortal garments behind them in the river ; for
though they went in with them, they came out
without them. They therefore went up here
with much agility and speed, though the foundation upon which the city was framed was
higher than the clouds : they therefore went
up through the region of the air, sweetly
talking as they went, being comforted, be-

' The two'—When ' Lazarus died, he was carried by angels into Abraham's bosom ;' and we have every reason to
believe, that the services of these friendly spirits to the souls
of departed saints are immediate and sensible ; and that their
joy is such as is here described. The beautiful description
that follows admits of no elucidation ; some of the images indeed are taken from modern customs ; but in all other respects
it is entirely scriptural, and very intelligible and animating to
the spiritual mind.

cause they safely got over the river and had such glorious companions to attend them.

The talk that they had with the shining ones was about the glory of the place ; who told them, that the beauty and glory of it was inexpressible. There, said they, is 'Mount Zion, the heavenly Jerusalem, the innumerable company of angels, and the spirits of just men made perfect' (Heb. xii. 22—24). You are going now, said they, to the Paradise of God, wherein you shall see the tree of life, and eat of the never-fading fruits thereof ; and when you come there you shall have white robes given you, and your walk and talk shall be every day with the King, even all the days of eternity (Rev. ii. 7 ; iii. 4 ; xxii. 5). There you shall not see again such things as you saw when you were in the lower region upon the earth, to wit, sorrow, sickness, affliction, and death, 'for the former things are passed away' (Isa. lxv. 16). You are going now to Abraham, to Isaac, and to Jacob, and to the prophets, men that God hath taken away from the evil to come, and that are now 'resting upon their beds, each one walking in his righteousness.' The men then asked, What must we do in the holy place ? To whom it was answered, You must there receive the comforts of all your toil, and have joy for all your sorrow ; you must reap what you have sown, even the fruit of all your prayers, and tears, and sufferings for the King by the way (Gal. vi. 7, 8). In that place you must wear crowns of gold, and en

joy the perpetual sight and vision of the Holy One, for there you shall see him as he is'
(1 John iii. 2). There also you shall serve
him continually with praise, with shouting,
and thanksgiving, whom you desired to serve
in the world, though with much difficulty,
because of the infirmity of your flesh. There
your eyes shall be delighted with seeing and
your ears with hearing the pleasant voice of
the Mighty One. There you shall enjoy
your friends again, that are gone thither before you ; and there you shall with joy receive even every one that follows into the holy places after you. There also you shall be
clothed with glory and majesty, and put into
an equipage fit to ride out with the King of
Glory. When he shall come with sound of
trumpet in the clouds, as upon the wings of
the wind, you shall come with him ; and
when he shall sit upon the throne of judgment, you shall sit by him ; yea, and when
he shall pass sentence upon all the workers
of iniquity, let them be angels or men, you
also shall have a voice in that judgment, because they were his and your enemies. Also
when he shall again return to the city, you
shall go too with sound of trumpet, and be
ever with him (1 Thess. iv. 13—17 ; Jude
14, 15 ; Dan. vii. 9, 10 ; 1 Cor. vi. 2, 3).

Now, while they were thus drawing towards the gate, behold a company of the heavenly host came out to meet them ; to whom
it was said by the other two shining ones,
These are the men that have loved our Lord

when they were in the world, and that have left all for his holy name, and he hath sent us to fetch them ; and we have brought them thus far on their desired journey, that they may go in and look their Redeemer in the face with joy. Then the heavenly host gave a great shout, saying, ' Blessed are they that are called to the marriage-supper of the Lamb' (Rev. xix. 9). There came out also at this time to meet them several of the King's trumpeters, clothed in white and shining raiment, who with melodious noises and loud made even the heavens to echo with their sound. These trumpeters saluted Christian and his fellow with ten thousand welcomes from the world ; and this they did with shouting and sound of trumpet.

This done, they compassed them round on every side ; some went before, some behind, and some on the right-hand, some on the left (as it were to guard them through the upper region), continually sounding as they went, with melodious noise, in notes on high ; so that the very sight was, to them that could behold it, as if heaven itself was come down to meet them. Thus therefore they walked on together ; and, as they walked, ever and anon these trumpeters, even with joyful sound, would, by mixing their music with looks and gestures, still signify to Christian and his brother how welcome they were into their company, and with what gladness they came to meet them. And now were these two men, as it were, in heaven, before they

came at it, being swallowed up with the sight
of angels, and with hearing their melodious
notes. Here also they had the city itself in
view ; and they thought they heard all the
bells therein to ring, to welcome them thereto. But, above all, the warm and joyful
thoughts that they had about their own dwelling there with such company, and that for ever and ever, oh ! by what tongue or pen can
their glorious joy be expressed ! Thus they
came up to the gate.

Now, when they were come up to the gate,
there was written over it in letters of gold,
'Blessed* are they that do his commandments, that they may have right to the tree of
life, and may enter in through the gates into
he city (Rev. xxii. 14).

Then I saw in my dream that the shining
men bid them call at the gate ; the which
when they did, some from above looked over
the gate, to wit, Enoch, Moses, and Elias,
&c. to whom it was said, These pilgrims are
come from the city of Destruction, for the
ove that they bear to the King of this place ;
and then the pilgrims gave in unto them each

* 'Blessed'—The commandments of God, as given to
sinners under a dispensation of mercy, call them to repentance, faith in Christ, and the obedience of faith and love ;
the believer habitually practices according to these commandments, from the time of his receiving Christ for salvation ; this evidences his interest in all the blessings of the
new covenant, and proves that he has a right through grace
to the heavenly inheritance. May the writer of these remarks, and every reader, have such ' an abundant entrance'
as is here described ' into the everlasting kingdom of our
Lord and Saviour Jesus Christ!'

man his certificate, which they had received
in the beginning ; these therefore were carri
ed in unto the King, who, when he had read
them, said, Where are the men ? to whom it
was answered, they are standing without the
gate. The King then commanded to open the
gate, ' that the righteous nation,' said he,
' that keepeth truth may enter in' (Isa. xxvi.
2).

Now I saw in my dream that these two men
went in at the gate ; and, lo ! as they entered they were transfigured ; and they had raiment put on that shone like gold. There
were also that met them with harps and
crowns, and gave them to them ; the harps
to praise withal, and the crowns in token of
honour. Then I heard in my dream that all
the bells in the city rang again for joy, and
that it was said unto them, 'Enter ye into
the joy of your Lord.' I also heard the men
themselves, that they sang with a loud voice,
saying, ' Blessing, honour, and glory, and
power, be to him that sitteth upon the throne,
and to the Lamb for ever and ever' (Rev. v.
13, 14).

Now, just as the gates were opened to let
in the men, I looked in after them, and behold the city shone like the sun ; the streets
also were paved with gold ; and in their
walked many men with crowns on their heads
palms in their hands, and golden harps to
sing praises withal.

There were also of them that had wings,
and they answered one another without inter-

mission, saying, 'Holy, holy, holy, is the
Lord.' And after that they shut up the gates :
which when I had seen, I wished myself
among them.

Now, while I was gazing upon all these
things, I turned my head to look back, and
saw* Ignorance come up to the river side ;
but he soon got over, and that without half
the difficulty which the other two men met
with. For it happened that there was then in
that place one Vain-hope, a ferryman, that
with his boat helped him over : so he, as the
other I saw, did ascend the hill, to come up

* 'And saw'—We frequently hear of persons that have
lived strangers to evangelical religion, and the power of godliness, dying with great composure and resignation ; and such
instances are brought forward as an objection to the necessity of faith, or of a devoted life. But what do they prove ?
What evidence is there, that such men are saved ? Is it not
far more likely that they continued to the end under the power of ignorance and self-conceit; that Satan took care not to
disturb them ; and that God gave them over to a strong delusion, and left them to perish with a lie in their right hand ?
Men, who have neglected religion all their lives, or have habitually for a length of years disgraced an evangelical profession, being when near death visited by pious persons,sometimes
obtain a sudden and extraordinary measure of peace and joy,
and die in this frame. This should in general be considered
as a bad sign ; for deep humiliation, yea, distress, united wit
some trembling hope in God's mercy through the Gospel
is far more suited to their case, and more likely to be the
effect of spiritual illumination. But when a formal visit
from a minister of any sect, a few general questions, and a
prayer, with or without the sacrament, calm the mind of a
dying person, whose life has been unsuitable to the Christian profession ; no doubt, could we penetrate the veil, we
should see him wafted across the river in the boat of
Vain-hope, and meeting with the awful doom that is here
described. From such delusions good Lord deliver us
Amen

to the gate; only he came alone; neither did any man meet him with the least encouragement. When he was come up to the gate, he looked up to the writing that was above, and then began to knock, supposing that entrance should have been quickly administered to him: but he was asked by the man that looked over the top of the gate, Whence come you? And what would you have? He answered 'I have eat and drank in the presence of the King, and he has taught in our streets.' Then they asked him for his certificate, that they might go in and shew it to the King: so he fumbled in his bosom for one, and found none. Then said they, You have none; but the man answered never a word. So they told the King, but he would not come down to see him, but commanded the two shining ones, that conducted Christian and Hopeful to the city, to go out and take Ignorance, and bind him hand and foot, and have him away. Then they took him up, and carried him through the air to the door that I saw in the side of the hill, and put him in there. Then I saw that there was a way to hell, even from the gates of heaven, as well as from the city of Destruction. So I awoke, and beheld it was a dream.

END OF VOL. I.

THE

PILGRIM'S PROGRESS.

PART II.

COURTEOUS* COMPANIONS,

SOME time since, to tell you a dream that I had of Christian, the pilgrim, and of his dangerous journey towards the celestial country, was pleasant to me and profitable to you. I told you then also, what I saw concerning his wife and children, and how unwilling they

---

* ' Courteous'—It has been before observed, that the ' first part of the Pilgrim's Progress' is in all respects the most complete : yet there are many things in the second, well worthy of the pious reader's attention ; nor can there be any doubt, but it was penned by the same author. It is not however, necessary that the annotator should be so copious upon it as upon the more interesting instructions of the preceding part. In some places, it is not easy to discover the precise meaning of the allegory ; in others, it does not seem sufficiently important to demand so large a measure of attention as would be required to the explanation of every minute circumstance : and, in general, the leading incidents may be considered as the author's own exposition of his meaning in the former part, or as his delineation of some varieties, that occur in events of a similar nature. In things of this kind, brevity must here be observed : but some particulars will demand a more copious elucidation

were to go with him on pilgrimage : insomuch
that he was forced to go on his progress with
out them, for he durst not run the danger of
that destruction, which he feared would come
by staying with them in the city of Destruction ; wherefore, as I then shewed you, he
left them and departed.

Now it hath so happened, through the multiplicity of business, that I have been much
hindered and kept back from my wonted travels into those parts where he went, and so
could not, till now, obtain an opportunity to
make farther inquiry after whom he left behind, that I might give you an account of
them. But having had some concerns that
way of late, I went down again thitherward.
Now having taken up my lodging in a wood,
about a mile off the place, as I slept I dreamed again.

And, as I was in my dream, behold, an
aged gentleman came by where I lay ; and
because he was to go some part of the way
that I was travelling, methought I got up and
went with him. So, as we walked, and as
travellers usually do, I was as if we fell into
a discourse, and our talk happened to be
about Christian and his travels, for thus I began with the old man :

Sir, said I, what town is that there below,
that lieth on the left-hand of our way ?

Then said Mr. Sagacity (for that was his
name), It is the city of Destruction, a populous place, but possessed with a very ill con-
ditioned and idle sort of people.

I thought that was that city, quoth I ; I went once myself through that town ; and therefore I know that this report you give of it is true.

Sag. Too true ! I wish I could speak truth in speaking better of them that dwell therein.

Well, Sir, quoth I, then I perceive you to be a well-meaning man, and so one that takes pleasure to hear and tell of that which is good : pray did you never hear what happened to a man some time ago in this town (whose name was Christian), that went on a pilgrimage up towards the higher regions ?

Sag. Hear of him ! Ay, and I also heard of the molestations, troubles, wars, captivities, cries, groans, frights, and fears, that he met with, and had on his journey. Besides, I must tell you, all our country rings of him ; there are but few houses, that have heard of him and his doings, but have sought after and got the records of his pilgrimage : yea, I think I may say, that this hazardous journey has got many well-wishers to his ways ; for though, when he was here, he was fool in every man's mouth, yet now he is gone he is highly commended of all. For it is said he lives bravely where he is : yea, many of them that are resolved never to run his hazards, yet have their mouths water at his gains.

They may, quoth I, well think, if they think any thing that is true, that he liveth well where he is ; for he now lives at and in the Fountain of Life, and has what he has without labour and sorrow, for there is no

1*

grief mixed therewith. But pray, what talk have the people about him ?

Sag. Talk ! the people talk strangely about him : some say, that he now walks in white (Rev. iii. 4 ; vi. 11) ; and that he has a chain of gold about his neck ; that he has a crown of gold, beset with pearls, upon his head : others say, that the shining ones, that sometimes shewed themselves to him in his journey, are become his companions, and that he is as familiar with them in the place where he is, as here one neighbour is with another (Zech. iii. 7). Besides it is confidently affirmed concerning him, that the King of the place where he is has bestowed upon him already a very rich and pleasant dwelling at court, and that he every day eateth, and drinketh, and walketh, and talketh with him, and receiveth the smiles and favours of him that is judge of all there. Moreover,* it is expected of some, that his prince, the lord of

---

* ' Moreover'—Christians are the representatives on earth of the Saviour and Judge of the world ; and the usage they meet with whether good or bad, commonly originates in men's love to him, or contemptuous enmity against him. The decisions of the great day therefore will be made with an especial reference to this evidence of men's faith or unbelief ; faith works by love of Christ, and of his people for his sake, which influences men to self-denying kindness towards the needy and distressed of the flock. Where these fruits are totally wanting, it is evident there is no love of Christ, and consequently no faith in him, or salvation by him. And as true believers are the excellent of the earth, no man can have any good reason for despising, hating, and injuring them ; so that this usage will be adduced as a proof of positive enmity to Christ, and expose the condemned sinner to more aggravated misery. Indeed, it often appears after the death of consis

that country, will shortly come into these parts, and will know the reason, if they can give any, why his neighbours, set so little by him, and had him so much in derision, when they perceived that he would be a pilgrim (Jude 14, 15).

. For they say, that now he is so in the affections of his prince, and that his sovereign is so much concerned with the indignities that were cast upon Christian when he became a pilgrim, that he will look upon all as if done to himself : and no marvel, for it was for the love that he had to his prince, that he ventured as he did (Luke x. 16).

I dare say, quoth I ; I am glad of it ; I am glad for the poor man's sake, for that now he has rest from his labour (Rev. xiv. 13), and for that he now reaps the benefits of his tears with joy (Ps. cxxvi. 5, 6) ; and for that he has got beyond the gun-shot of his enemies, and is out of the reach of them that hate him. I also am glad, for that a rumour of these things is noised abroad in this country ; who can tell but that it may work some good effect on some that are left behind ? But pray, Sir, while it is fresh in my mind, do you hear any thing of his wife and children ? Poor hearts, I wonder in my mind what they do.

Sag. Who ? Christiana and her sons ?

tent Christians, that the consciences of their most scornful opposers secretly favoured them : it must then surely be deemed the wisest conduct by every reflecting person, to let these men alone, lest haply he should be found to fight against God.'

They are like to do as well as did Christian himself; for, though they all played the fool at first, and would by no means be persuaded by either the tears or entreaties of Christian, yet second thoughts have wrought wonderfully with them; so they have packed up, and are also gone after him

Better and better, quoth I : but, what !* wife and children and all ?

Sag. It is true : I can give you an account of the matter, for I was on the spot at the instant, and was thoroughly acquainted with the whole affair.

Then, said I, may a man report it for a truth ?

Sag. You need not fear to affirm it : I mean, that they are all gone on pilgrimage, both the good woman and her four boys. And being we are, as I perceive, going some

---

* ' But what !'—If the allegory should here be thought to deviate from the exact rule of propriety; it may be said, that the author was intent on encouraging pious persons to persevere in using all means for the spiritual good of their children, even when they see no effect produced by them. The Scripture teaches us to expect a blessing on such endeavours : the dying testimony and counsels of exemplary believers frequently make a deeper impression than all their previous instructions : the death of near relations, who have behaved well to such as despised them, proves a heavier loss than was expected : the recollection of unkind behaviour to such valuable friends, and of the pains to harden the heart against their affectionate admonitions, sometimes lies heavy on the conscience ; thus the prayers of the believer for his children or other relatives are frequently answered after his death, and when some of them begin to inquire ' what they must do to be saved ?' they will become zealous instruments in seeking the conversion of those whom before they endeavoured to prejudice against the ways of God.

considerable way together, I will give you an account of the whole matter.

This Christiana (for that was her name from the day that she with her children betook themselves to a pilgrim's life), after her husband was gone over the river (Part i. p. 322—329), and she could hear of him no more, her thoughts began to work in her mind. First, for that she had lost her husband, and for that the loving bond of that relation was utterly broken betwixt them. For you know, said he to me, nature can do no less but entertain the living with many a heavy cogitation, in the remembrance of the loss of loving relations. This, therefore, of her husband, did cost her many a tear. But this was not all, for Christiana did also begin to consider with herself, whether her unbecoming behaviour towards her husband was not one cause that she saw him no more ; and that in such sort he was taken away from her. And upon this came into her mind, by swarms, all her unkind, unnatural, and ungodly carriage to her dear friend, which also clogged her conscience, and did load her with guilt. She was, moreover, much broken with calling to remembrance the restless groans, the brinish tears, and self-bemoaning of her husband, and how she did harden her heart against all his entreaties, and loving persuasions, of her and her sons to go with him ; yea, there was not any thing that Christian either said to her, or did before her, all the while that his burthen did hang on his back,

but it returned upon her like a flash of lightning, and rent the caul of her heart in sun-
der ; especially that bitter outcry of his,
' What shall I do to be saved ?' did ring in
her ears most dolefully (Part i. p. 33—35).

Then said she to her children, Sons, we
are all undone. I have sinned away your
father, and he is gone ; he would have had us
with him, bu I would not go myself : I also
have hindered you of life. With that the
boys fell into tears, and cried to go after their
father. Oh ! said Christiana, that it had
been but our lots to go with him ; then it had
fared well with us, beyond what it is like to
do now. For, though I formerly foolishly
imagined concerning the troubles of your
father, that they proceeded of a foolish fancy
that he had, or for that he was overrun with
melancholy humours ; yet now it will not out
of mind, but that they sprang from another
cause, to wit, for that the light of life was given
him (John viii. 12) ; by the help of which,
as I perceive, he has escaped the snares of
death. Then they wept all again, and cried
out, Oh, woe worth the day !

The next night Christiana had a dream ;*
and behold, she saw as if a broad parchment

* ' Dream'—The mind during sleep, is often occupied about
those subjects that have most deeply engaged the waking
thoughts : and it sometimes pleases God to make use of
ideas, thus suggested, to influence the conduct, by exciting
fears or hopes. Provided an intimation be scriptural, and
the effect salutary, we need not hesitate to consider it as a
divine monition, however it was brought to the mind : but, if
men attempt to draw conclusions in respect of their acceptance

was opened before her, in which were recorded the sum of her ways, and the crimes, as
she thought, looked very black upon her.
Then she cried out aloud in her sleep, ' Lord
have mercy upon me a sinner' (Luke xviii.
13) : and the little children heard her.

After this, she thought she saw two very
ill-favoured ones standing by her bed-side, and
saying, What shall we do with the woman ?
for she cries out for mercy waking and sleeping : if she be suffered to go on as she begins,
we shall lose her as we have lost her husband. Wherefore we must, by some way,
seek to take her off from the thoughts of what
shall be hereafter, else all the world cannot
help but she will become a pilgrim.

Now she awoke in a great sweat ; also a
trembling was upon her : but after awhile she
fell to sleeping again. And then she thought
she saw Christian, her husband, in a place of
bliss among many immortals, with a harp in
his hand, standing and playing upon it before
one that sat on a throne, with a rainbow about
his head. She saw also, as if he bowed his
head with his face towards the paved work
that was under his Prince's feet, saying, I

or duty, to determine the truth of certain doctrines, to prophesy,
or to discover hidden things by dreams or visions of any kind ;
they then become a very dangerous and disgraceful species
of enthusiasm. Whatever means are employed, conviction
of sin, and a disposition earnestly to cry for mercy, are the
work of the Holy Spirit in the heart : and, on the other hand,
the powers of darkness will surely use every effort and stratagem to take off inquirers from thus earnestly seeking the salvation of God.

heartily thank my Lord and King for bringing me into this place. Then shouted a company of them that stood round about and harp-
ed with their harps ; but no man living could
tell what they said, but Christian and his companions.

Next morning, when she was up, had prayed to God, and talked with her children
awhile, one knocked hard at the door ; to
whom she spake out, saying, If thou comest
in God's name, come in. So he said Amen ·
and opened the door, and saluted her with
Peace on this house. The which, when he
had done, he said, Christiana, knowest thou
wherefore I am come ? Then she blushed and
trembled ; also her heart began to wax warm
with desires to know from whence he came,
and what his errand was to her. So he said
unto her, My name* is Secret ; I dwell with

* ' My name'—' The secret of the Lord is with them that
fear him.' The silent influences of the Holy Spirit bring the
encouragement of Scripture to the convinced sinner's remembrance, who thus learns that the way of salvation is yet open
to him. The general invitations of the Gospel may be considered as a message sent to the broken-hearted penitent, more
fragrant and refreshing than the most costly ointment, and
more precious than the gold of Ophir. It is observable, that
Secret does not inform Christiana that her sins were forgiven,
or that Christ and the promises belonged to her ; but merely
that she was invited to come, and that, coming in the appointed way, she would be accepted, notwithstanding her
pertinacious unbelief in the preceding part of her life. Thus,
without seeming to have intended it, the author hath stated
the scriptual medium between the extremes, which have been
contended for, with great eagerness and immense mischief, in
modern days ; while some maintain, that sinners should not
be invited to come to Christ, or commanded to repent and
believe the Gospel : and others that they should be urged to

those that are high. It is talked of, where I dwell, as if thou hadst a desire to go thither : also, there is a report, that thou art aware of the evil thou hast formerly done to thy husband, in hardening of thy heart against his way, and in keeping of these babes in their ignorance. Christiana, the Merciful One has sent me to tell thee, that he is a God ready to forgive, and that he taketh delight to multiply the pardon of offences. He also would have thee to know, that he inviteth thee to come into his presence, to his table, and that he will feed thee with the fat of the house, and with the heritage of Jacob thy father.

There is Christian, thy husband that was, with legions more, his companions, ever beholding that face that doth minister life to the beholders ; and they will all be glad, when they shall hear the sound of thy feet step over thy father's threshold.

Christiana at this was greatly abashed in herself, and bowed her head to the ground. This vision proceeded, and said, Christiana, here is also a letter for thee, which I have brought from thy husband's King ; so she took it and opened it, but it smelt after the manner of the best perfume (Song i. 3). Also it was written in letters of gold. The con tents of the letter were these : that the King

believe at once, with full assurance, that all the blessings of salvation belong to them, previous to repentance, or works meet for repentance. For the intimations of Secret represent the teaching of the Holy Spirit, by which the sinner understands the real meaning of the sacred Scriptures.

would have her do as did Christian her husband; for that was the only way to come to
his city, and to dwell in his presence with joy
for ever. At this the good woman was quite
overcome : so she cried out to her visitor
Sir, will you carry me and my children with
you, that we may also go and worship the
King ?

Then said the visitor, Christiana, the bitter
is before the sweet. Thou must through
troubles, as he did that went before thee, enter this Celestial city. Wherefore I advise
thee to do as did Christian, thy husband : go
to the wicket-gate yonder, over the plain, for
that stands in the head of the way up which
thou must go, and I wish thee all good speed.
Also, I advise thee, that thou put this letter
in thy bosom ; that thou read therein to thyself, and to thy children, until they have got
it by heart ; for it is one of the songs that
thou must sing while thou art in this house
of thy pilgrimage (Ps. cxix. 54) : also this
thou must deliver in at the far gate.

Now I saw in my dream, that this old gentleman, as he told me this story, did himself
seem to be greatly affected therewith. He
moreover proceeded, and said, So Christiana
called her sons together, and began thus to
address herself unto them : My sons, I have,
as you may perceive, been of late under
much exercise in my soul about the death of
your father ; not for that I doubt at all of his
happiness, for I am satisfied now that he is
well. I have been also much affected with

the thoughts of mine own estate and yours which I verily believe is by nature miserable. My carriage also to your father in his distress is a great load to my conscience ; for I hardened both my heart and yours against him, and refused to go with him on pilgrimage.

The thoughts of these things would now kill me out-right, but for that a dream which I had last night, and but for that the encouragement this stranger has given me this morning. Come, my children, let us pack up, and be gone to the gate that leads us to that Celestial country, that we may see your father and be with him and his companions in peace, according to the laws of that land.

Then did her children burst out into tears, for joy that the heart of their mother was so inclined. So the visitor bid them farewell ; and they began to prepare to set out for their journey.

But while they were thus about to be gone, two of the women that were Christiana's neighbours came up to her house, and knocked at her door. To whom she said as before. At this the women were stunned ; for this kind of language they used not to hear, or to perceive to drop from the lips of Christiana. Yet they came in : but behold, they found the good woman a preparing to be gone from her house.

So they began and said, Neighbour, pray what is your meaning by this ?

Christiana answered and said to the eldest of them, whose name was Mrs. Timorous, I am preparing for a journey (this Timorous, was daughter to him that met Christian upon the hillof Difficulty, and would have had him gone back for fear of the lions, Part i. 101).

Tim. For what journey, I pray you ?

Chr. Even to go after my old husband. And with that she fell a weeping.

Tim. I hope not so, good neighbour ; pray, for your poor children's sake, do not so unwomanly cast away yourself.

Chr. Nay, my children shall go with me, not one of them is willing to stay behind.

Tim. I wonder in my heart what, or who, has brought you into this mind !

Chr. Oh, neighbour, knew you but as much as I do, I doubt not but that you would go along with me.

Tim. Pr'ythe, what new knowledge hast thou got, that so worketh off thy mind from thy friends, and that tempteth thee to go nobody knows where ?

Then Christiana replied, I have been sorely afflicted since my husband's departure from me ; but especially since he went over the river. But that which troubleth me most is my churlish carriage to him, when he was under his distress. Besides, I am now as he was then ; nothing will serve me, but going on pilgrimage. I was a dreaming last night that I saw him. O that my soul was with him ! He dwelleth in the presence of the King of the country ; he sits and eats with him at his table ; he is become a companion of immortals, and has a house now given him to dwell in, to which the best palaces on earth if compared, seem to me but as a dunghill (2 Cor. v. 1—4). The Prince of the palace has also sent for me, with promises of entertainment, if I shall come to him : his messenger was here even now, and brought me a letter, which invites me to come. And with that she plucked out her letter, and read it, and said to them, What now will you say to this ?

Tim. Oh, the madness that has possessed thee and thy husband ! to run yourselves upon such difficulties ! You have heard, I am sure, what your husband did meet with, even in a manner at the first step that he took on his way, as our neighbour Obstinate can yet testify, for he went along with him ; yea, and Pliable too, until they, like wise men, were afraid to go any farther (Part i. p. 39—48). We also heard, over and above, how he met with the lions, Apollyon, the Shadow of Death, and many other things. Nor is the danger that he met with at Vanity fair to be forgotten by thee. For if he, though a man, was so hard put to it, what canst thou being but a poor woman, do ? Consider also, that these four sweet babes are thy children, thy flesh, and thy bones. Therefore, though thou shouldest be so rash as to cast away thyself, yet, for the sake of the fruit of thy body, keep them at home.

But Christiana said unto her, Tempt me not my neighbour : I have now a price put into my hand to get a gain, and I should be a fool of the greatest sort, if I should have

2*

no heart to strike in with the opportunity. And for that you tell me of all these troubles that I am like to meet with in the way, they are so far from being to me a discouragement, that they shew I am in the right. 'The bitter* must come before the sweet,' and that also will make the sweet the sweeter. Wherefore since you came not to my house in God's name, as I said, I pray you begone, and do not disquiet me farther.

Then Timorous also reviled her, and said to her fellow, Come, neighbour Mercy, let us leave her in her own hands, since she scorns our counsel and company. But Mercy was at a stand, and could not so readily comply with her neighbour; and that for a two-fold reason. First, Her bowels yearned over Christiana. So she said within herself, If my neighbour will needs be gone, I will go a little way with her, and help her.

---

* 'The bitter'—' Through much tribulation we must enter into the kingdom of God.' Self-denial, mortification of our sinful inclinations, inward conflicts, the renunciation of worldly interests and connexions, the scorn and hatred of the world, sore temptations, and salutary chastisements, are very bitter to our natural feelings. Habits and situations often render some of them extremely painful, like ' cutting off a right hand, or plucking out a right eye :' and deep poverty, persecution, or seasons of public calamity, may enhance these tribulations. If a man, therefore, meet with nothing bitter, in consequence of his religious profession, he has great reason to suspect, that he is not in the narrow way : yet many argue against themselves, on account of those very trials, which are a favourable token in their behalf. But on the other hand, the believer has ' a joy that a stranger meddleth not with,' which counterbalanceth all his sorrows, so that, even in this life he possesses more solid satisfaction than they do, who choose the road to destruc-

Secondly, Her bowels yearned over her own soul ; for what* Christiana had said had taken some hold upon her mind. Wherefore she said within herself again, I will yet have more talk with this Christiana ; and if I find truth and life in what she shall say, myself with my heart shall also go with her. Wherefore Mercy began thus to reply to her neighbour Timorous.

Mer. Neighbour, I did indeed come with you to see Christiana this morning ; and since she is, as you see, a taking her last farewell of the country, I think to walk this sun-shiny morning a little with her, to help her on her way. But she told her not of her second reason, but kept it to herself.

Tim. Well, I see you have a mind to go a fooling too ; but take heed in time, and be

tion from fear of the difficulties attending the way of life, Satan is however, peculiarly successful in persuading men, that religion, the very essence of heavenly happiness, will make them miserable on earth ; and that sin, the source of all the misery in the universe, will make them happy ! By such manifest lies does this old murderer support his cause !

* 'For what'—The very things, which excite the rage and scorn of some persons, penetrate the hearts and consciences of others. Thus the Lord makes one to differ from another, by preparing the heart to receive the good seed of divine truth, which is sown in it : yet every one willingly chooses the way he takes, without any constraint or hinderance, except his own prevailing dispositions. This consideration gives the greatest encouragement to the use of all proper means, in order to influence sinners to choose the good part : for who knows, but the most obvious truth, warning, or exhortation, given in the feeblest manner, may reach the conscience of a child, relative, neighbour, enemy, or persecutor ; even when the most convincing and persuasive discourses of eloquent and learned teachers produce no effect ?

wise ; while we are out of danger, we are
out : but, when we are in we are in. So Mrs
Timorous returned to her house, and Christiana betook herself to her journey. But,
when Timorous was got home to her house,
she sends for some of her neighbours, to wit,
Mrs. Bat's-eyes, Mrs. Inconsiderate, Mrs.
Light-mind, and Mrs. Know-nothing. So,
when they were come to her house she falls
to telling of the story of Christiana, and of
her intended journey. And thus she began
her tale :*—

Neighbours, having but little to do this
morning, I went to give Christiana a visit ;
and, when I came at the door, I knocked, as
you know it is our custom ; and she answered,
If you come in God's name, come in. So in

* ' Tale'—The following dialogue, by the names, arguments, and discourse introduced into it, shews what kind
of persons despise and revile all those that fear God and
seek the salvation of their souls ; from what principles, affections, and conduct such opposition springs ; and on what
grounds it is maintained. Men of the most profligate characters, who never studied, or practised religion in their
lives, often pass sentence on the sentiments and actions of
pious persons, and decide in the most difficult controversies,
without the least hesitation ; as if they knew the most ab-
truse subjects by instinct or intuition, and were acquainted
with the secrets of men's hearts ! These presumers should
consider, that they must be wrong, let who will be right ;
that any religion is as good as open impiety and profligacy ;
and that it behoves them to ' cast out the beam out of their own
eye, before they attempt to pull out the mote from their brother's eye.' Believers also, recollecting the vain conversation
from which they have been redeemed, and the obligations that
have been conferred upon them, should not disquiet themselves about the scorn and censure of such persons, but learn
to pray for them, as entitled to their compassion, even more
than their detestation.

I went, thinking all was well : but, when I came in, I found her preparing herself to depart the town ; she, and also her children. So I asked her, what was her meaning by that ? And she told me in short, that she was now of a mind to go on pilgrimage, as did her husband. She told me also a dream that she had, and how the king of the country where her husband was had sent her an inviting letter to come thither.

Then said Mrs. Know-nothing, And what do you think she will do ?

Tim. Ay, go she will, whatever come on't ; and methinks I know it by this ; for that which was my great argument to persuade her to stay at home (to wit, the troubles she was like to meet with in the way), is one great argument with her, to put her forward on her journey. For she told me in so many words, ' The bitter goes before the sweet ;' yea, and for as much as it doth, it makes the sweet the sweeter.

Mrs. Bat's eyes. Oh this blind and foolish woman ! and will she not take warning by her husband's afflictions ? For my part, I see if he were here again, he would rest him content in a whole skin, and never run so many hazards for nothing.

Mrs. Inconsiderate also replied, saying, Away with such fantastical fools from the town : a good riddance, for my part, I say of her ; should she stay where she dwells, and retain this mind, who could live quietly by her ? for she will either be dumpish or un neighbourly, to talk of such matters as no wise body can abide : wherefore, for my part, I shall never be sorry for her departure ; let her go, and let better come in her room : it was never a good world since these whimsical fools dwelt in it.

Then Mrs. Light-mind added as followeth : Come, put this kind of talk away. I was yesterday at Madam Wanton's (Part i. p. 151), where we were as merry as the maids. For who do you think should be there, but I and Mrs. Love-the-flesh, and three or four more, with Mr. Lechery, Mrs. Filth, and some others : so there we had music and dancing, and what else was meet to fill up the pleasure. And, I dare say, my lady herself is an admirable well-bred gentlewoman, and Mr. Lechery is as pretty a fellow.

By this time Christiana was got on her way, and Mercy went along with her : so as they went, her children being there also, Christiana began to discourse. And, Mercy, said Christiana, I take this as an unexpected favour, that thou shouldest set foot out of doors with me to accompany me a little in my way.

Then said young Mercy (for she was but young), If I thought it would be to purpose to go with you, I would never go near the town.

Well, Mercy, said Christiana, cast in thy lot with me. I well know what will be the end of our pilgrimage : my husband is where he would not but be for all the gold in the Spanish mines. Nor shalt thou be rejected, though thou goest but upon my invitation.* The King, who hath sent for me and my children, is one that delighteth in mercy. Besides, if thou wilt, I will hire thee, thou shalt go along with me as my servant. Yet we will have all things in common betwixt thee and me : only go along with me.

Mer. But how shall I be ascertained that I also shall be entertained ? Had I this hope from one that can tell, I would make no stick at all, but would go, being helped by him that can help, though the way was never so tedious.

Chr. Well, loving Mercy, I will tell thee what thou shalt do : go with me to the wicket-gate, and there I will farther inquire for thee ; and, if there thou shalt not meet with encouragement, I will be content that thou shalt return to thy place ; I also will pay thee for thy kindness which thou shewest to me and my

---

* ' Invitation'—There are remarkable circumstances attending the conversion of some persons, with which others are wholly unacquainted. The singular dispensations of Providence, and the strong impressions made by the word of God upon their minds, seem to amount to a special invitation : whereas others are gradually and gently brought to think on religious subjects, and to embrace the proposals of the Gospel ; who are, therefore, sometimes apt to conclude, that they have never been truly awakened to a concern about their souls. This discouragement is often increased by the discourse of such professors as lay great stress on the circumstances attending conversion : these misapprehensions, however, are best obviated, by shewing that ' the Lord delighteth in mercy,' that Christ ' will in no wise cast out any that come to him,' and that they who leave all earthly pursuits to seek salvation, and renounce all other confidence to trust in the mercy of God through the redemption of his Son, shall assuredly be saved.

children, in the accompanying of us in our way as thou dost.

Mer. Then will I go thither, and will take what shall follow ; and the Lord grant that my lot may there fall, even as the King of heaven shall have his heart upon me.

Christiana was then glad at heart ; not only that she had a companion ; but also for that she had prevailed with this poor maid to fall in love with her own salvation. So they went on together, and Mercy began to weep. Then said Christiana, Wherefore weepeth my sister so ?

Alas ! said she, who can but lament, that shall but rightly consider what a state and condition my poor relations are in, that yet remain in our sinful town : and that which makes my grief the more is, because they have no instruction, nor any to tell them what is to come.

Chr. Bowels become pilgrims : and thou doest for thy friends, as my good Christian did for me when he left me ; he mourned for that I would not heed nor regard him ; but his Lord and ours did gather up his tears, and put them into his bottle ; and now both I and thou, and these my sweet babes, are reaping the fruit and benefit of them. I hope, Mercy, that these tears of thine will not be lost ; for the truth hath said, that ' they that sow in tears, shall reap in joy' and singing. And ' he that goeth forth and weepeth, bearing precious seed, shall doubtless come again with rejoicing, bringing his sheaves with him' (Psal cxxvi 5, 6).

Then said Mercy,

> Let the most Blessed be my guide,
>   If 't be his blessed will,
> Unto his gate, into his fold,
>   Up to his holy hill :
> And let him never suffer me
>   To swerve or turn aside
> From his free-grace and holy ways,
>   Whate'er shall me betide,
> And let him gather them of mine,
>   That I have left behind ;
> Lord, make them pray they may be thine,
>   With all their heart and mind.

Now my old friend proceeded, and said, But, when Christiana came to the slough of Despond (Part. i. p. 43—46), she began to be at a stand ; For, said she, this is the place in which my dear husband had like to have been smothered with mud. She perceived also, that notwithstanding the command of the king to make this place for pilgrims good ; yet it was rather worse* than

* 'Worse'—The author seems to have observed a declension of evangelical religion, subsequent to the publication of his original Pilgrim. Probably he was grieved to find many renounce or adulterate the Gospel, by substituting plausible speculations, or moral lectures in its stead ; by narrowing and confining it within the limits of a nice system, which prevents the preacher from freely inviting sinners to come unto Christ ; by representing the preparation of heart, requisite to a sincere acceptance of free salvation, as a legal condition of being received by him ; or by condemning all diligence, repentance, and tenderness of conscience, as interfering with an evangelical frame of spirit. By these, and various other misapprehensions, the passage over the slough is made worse ; and they occasion manifold discouragements to awakened sinners, even to this day : for, as the promises, strictly speaking, belong only to believers, if invitations and exhortations be not freely given to sinners in general, a kind of gulph will

formerly. So I asked if that was true ?
Yes, said the old gentleman, too true : for
many there be, that pretend to be the king's
labourers, and say they are for mending the
king's highways, that bring dirt and dung instead of stones, and so mar instead of mending. Here Christiana, therefore, and her boys,
did make a stand. But, said Mercy, Come,
let us venture ; only let us be wary. Then
they looked well to their steps, and made a
shift to get staggering over.

Yet Christiana had like to have been in,
and that not once or twice. Now they had
no sooner got over, but they thought they
heard words that said unto them, ' Blessed is
she that believeth, for there shall be a perfor
mance of what has been told her from the Lord'
(Luke i. 45).

Then they went on again ; and said Mercy to Christiana, had I as good ground to
hope for a loving reception at the wicket-
gate as you, I think no slough of Despond
could discourage me.

formed, over which no way can be seen, except as men take
it for granted, without any kind of evidence, that they are
true believers, which opens the door to manifold delusions and
enthusiastic pretensions. But if all be invited, and encouraged to ask, that they may receive, the awakened sinner will
be animated to hope in God's mercy, and use the means of
grace, and thus giving diligence to make his calling and election sure, he will be enabled to rise superior to the discouragements, by which others are retarded. Labourers enough,
indeed, are ready to lend their assistance, in mending the
road across this slough ; but let them take care that they
use none but scriptural materials, or they will make bad
worse.

Well, said the other, you know your sore,* and I know mine ; and, good friend, we shall all have enough evil before we come to our journey's end. For it cannot be imagined, that the people that design to attain such excellent glories as we do, and that are so envied that happiness as we are ; but that we shall meet with what fears and snares, with what troubles and afflictions, they can possibly assault us with, that hate us.

And now, Mr. Sagacity left me to dream out my dream by myself. Wherefore, methought I saw Christiana, and Mercy, and the boys, go all of them up to the gate ; to which when they came, they betook themselves to a short debate, about how they must manage their calling at the gate ; and what should be said unto him that did open unto them ; so it was concluded, since Christiana was the eldest, that she should knock for entrance, and that she should speak to him that did open, for the rest. So Christiana began to knock, and, as her poor husband did, she knocked and knocked again (P. i. p. 66). But instead of any that answered, they all thought they heard as if a

* ' Your sore'—Some persons are discouraged by recollecting past si s, and imagining them too heinous to be forgiven ; while others disquiet themselves by the apprehension, that they have never been truly humbled and converted. Indeed, all the varieties in the experience of those, who, upon the whole, are walking in the same path, can never be enumerated, and some of them are not only unreasonable, but unaccountable, through the weakness of the human mind, the abiding effects of peculiar impressions, the remains of unbelief and the artifices of Satan.

dog came barking upon them ; a dog, and a great one too ; and this made the women and children afraid. Nor durst* they for awhile to knock any more, for fear the mastiff should fly upon them. Now therefore they were greatly tumbled up and down in their minds, and knew not what to do ; knock they durst not for fear of the dog ; go back they durst not, for fear the keeper of that gate should spy them as they so went, and be offended with them ; at last they thought of knocking again, and knocking more vehemently than they did at first. Then said the keeper of the gate, ' Who is there ?' So the dog left off to bark, and he opened upon them.

Then Christiana made low obeisance, and said, Let not our Lord be offended with his handmaidens, for that we have knocked at his princely gate. Then said the keeper, Whence come ye ? And what is it that you would have ?

Christiana answered, We are come from whence Christian did come, and upon the same errand as he ; to wit, to be, if it shall

---

* ' Nor durst'—The greater fervency new converts manifest in prayer for themselves and each other, the more violent opposition will they experience from the powers of darkness. Many have felt such terrors, whenever they attempted to pray, that they have for a time been induced wholly to desist ; and doubtless numbers, whose convictions were superficial, have thus been finally driven back to their former course of ungodliness. But when the fear of God, and a real belief of his word, possess the heart ; such disturbances cannot long prevent earnest cries for mercy but will eventually render them more fervent and importunate than ever.

please you, graciously admitted, by this gate, into the way that leads unto the celestial city. And I answer, my Lord, in the next place, that I am Christiana, once the wife of Christian, that now is gotten above.

With that the keeper of the gate did marvel, saying, What, is she now become a pilgrim, that but awhile ago abhorred that life? Then she bowed her head, and said, Yea; and so are these my sweet babes also.

Then he took her by the hand, and let her in, and said also, ' Suffer the little children to come unto me,' and with that he shut up the gate. This done, he called to a trumpeter that was above, over the gate, to entertain Christiana with shouting, and sound of trumpet, for joy. So he obeyed, and sounded, and filled the air with his melodious notes.

Now all this while poor Mercy did stand without, trembling and crying for fear that she was rejected. But when Christiana had gotten admittance for herself and her boys, then she began to make intercession for Mercy.

And she said, my Lord, I have a companion of mine that stands yet without, that is come hither upon the same account as myself; one that is much dejected in her mind, for that she comes, as she thinks, without sending for; whereas I was sent to by my husband's King to come.

Now Mercy began to be very impatient, and each minute was as long to her as an hour; wherefore she prevented Christiana

3*

from a fuller interceding for her, by knocking at the gate herself. And she knocked then so loud, that she made Christiana to start. Then said the keeper of the gate, Who is there? and Christiana said, It is my friend.

So he opened the gate and looked out, but Mercy was fallen down without in a swoon, for she fainted, and was afraid that no gate would be opened to her.

Then he took her by the hand, and said, ' Damsel, I bid thee arise.'

O sir, said she, I am faint ; there is scarce life left in me. But he answered, that one said, ' When my soul fainted within me, I remembered the Lord, and my prayer came unto thee, into thy holy temple' (Jonah ii. 7). Fear not, but stand upon thy feet, and tell me wherefore thou art come.

Mer. I am come for that unto which I was never invited, as my friend Christiana was. Hers was from the King, and mine was but from her. Wherefore I presume.

Good. Did she desire thee to come with her to this place ?

Mer. Yes ; and, as my Lord sees, I am come : and, if there is any grace and forgiveness of sins to spare, I beseech that thy poor handmaid may be partaker thereof.

Then he took her again by the hand, and led her gently in, and said, I pray for all them that believe on me, by what means soever they come unto me. Then said he to those that stood by, Fetch something, and give it Mer-

cy to smell on, thereby to stay her faintings
So they fetched her a bundle of myrrh
Awhile after she was revived.

And now was Christiana, and her boys,
and Mercy, received of the Lord at the head
of the way, and spoke kindly unto by him.
Then said they yet farther unto him, We are
sorry for our sins, and beg of our Lord his
pardon, and farther information what we must
do.

I grant pardon, said he, by word* and
deed ; by word in the promise of forgiveness ;
by deed in the way I obtained it. Take the
first from my lips with a kiss, and the other
as it shall be revealed (Cant. i. 2 ; John xx.
19).

Now I saw in my dream, that he spake
many good words unto them, whereby they
were greatly gladded. He also had them up
to the top of the gate, and shewed them by
what deed they were saved ; and told them
withal, that that sight they would have again

---

* ' By word'—' Pardon by word' denotes the general discovery of free salvation by Jesus Christ to all that believe ;
which, being depended on by the humbled sinner, is sealed by
transient comforts and lively affections. ' Pardon by deed'
relates to the manner in which the blessing was purchased by
the Saviour ; and when this is clearly understood, the believer
attains to stable peace and hope. This coincides with the explanation already given of the Gate, the Cross, and the Sepulchre ; and it will be farther confirmed in the sequel. The
' pardon by deed' must be waited for ; yet the pilgrims obtained a distant glimpse of the deed by which they were saved,
for some general apprehensions of redemption by the cross of
Christ commonly connect with the believers' first comforts ;
though the nature and glory of it be more fully perceived as
they proceed.

as they went along in the way, to their comfort.

So he left them awhile in a summer parlour below, where they entered into talk by themselves; and thus Christiana began : O Lord, how glad am I that we are got in hither !

Mer. So you well may ; but I of all have cause to leap for joy.

Chr. I thought one time as I stood at the gate (because I had knocked and none did answer), that all our labour had been lost ; especially when that ugly cur made such a heavy barking at us.

Mer. But my worst fear was, after I saw that you was taken into his favour, and that I was left behind. Now, thought I, it is fulfilled which is written, 'Two women shall be grinding together, the one shall be taken and the other left' (Matt. xxiv. 41). I had much ado to forbear crying out, Undone ! And afraid I was to knock any more ; but, when I looked up to what was written* over the

* 'Written'—The express words of such invitations, exhortations, and promises prove more effectual to encourage those who are ready to give up their hopes, than all the consolatory topics that can possibly be substituted in their place. It is, therefore, much to be lamented, that pious men, by adhering to a supposed systematical exactness of expression, should clog such scriptural addresses with exceptions and limitations, which the Spirit of God did not see good to insert. They will not say that the omission was an oversight in the inspired writers ; or admit the thought for a moment, that they can improve on their plan ; why then cannot they be satisfied to 'speak according to the oracles of God,' without affecting a more entire consistency ? Great mischief has thus been done by very different descriptions of men, who unde-

gate (P. i. p. 65), I took courage. I also
thought, that I must either knock again or
die; so I knocked, but I cannot tell how;
for my spirit now struggled between life and
death.

Chr. Can you not tell how you knocked?
I am sure your knocks were so earnest, that
the very sound made me start : I thought I
never heard such knocking in all my life : I
thought you would come in by a violent
hand, or take the kingdom by storm (Matt.
xi. 12).

Mer. Alas, to be in my case! who that so
was could but have done so? You saw that
the door was shut upon me, and that there
was a most cruel dog thereabout. Who, I
say, that was so fainthearted as I, would not
have knocked with all their might? But
pray, what said my Lord unto my rudeness?
Was he not angry with me?

Chr. When he heard your lumbering
noise, he gave a wonderful innocent smile : I
believe what you did pleased him well, for he
shewed no sign to the contrary. But I marvel in my heart why he keeps such a dog :
had I* known that before, I should not have

signedly concur in giving Satan an occasion of suggesting to
the trembling inquirer, that perhaps he may persevere in asking, seeking, and knocking, with the greatest earnestness and
importunity, and yet finally be a cast-away. When the sinner prays under the urgent fear of perishing, he is excited
to peculiar fervency of spirit ; and the more fervant our
prayers are, the better are they approved by the Lord, how
much soever men may object to the manner or expressions of
them.

* ' Had I'—Could soldiers, when they enlist, foresee all the

had heart enough to have ventured myself in this manner. But now we are in, we are in, and I am glad with all my heart.

Mer. I will ask, if you please, next time he comes down, why he keeps such a filthy cur in his yard : I hope he will not take it amiss.

Do so, said the children, and persuade him to hang him, for we are afraid he will bite us when we go hence.

So at last he came down to them again, and Mercy fell to the ground on her face before him, and worshipped, and said, Let my Lord accept the sacrifice of praise which I now offer unto him with the calves of my lips.

So he said unto her, ' Peace be to thee ; stand up.' But she continued upon her face, and said, ' Righteous art thou, O Lord, when I plead with thee, yet let me talk with thee of thy judgments' (Jer. xii. 1, 2) : wherefore dost thou keep so cruel a dog in thy yard, at the sight of which such women and children as we are ready to flee from the gate for fear ?

dangers and hardships to be encountered ; or could mariners, when about to set sail, be fully aware of all the difficulties of the voyage : their reluctancy or discouragement would be increased by the prospect. But, when they have engaged, they find it impossible to recede ; and thus they press forward through one labour and peril after another, till the campaign or voyage be accomplished. Thus it is with the Christian : but they strive for corruptible things, which they may never live to obtain ; while he seeks for an incorruptible crown of glory, of which no event can deprive him. If he knew all from the first, it would be his only wisdom to venture ; whereas the case with them is commonly very different.

He answered and said, That dog has another owner: he is also kept close in another man's, ground, only my pilgrims hear his barking: he belongs to the castle which you see there at a distance (P. i. p. 67); but can come up to the walls of this place. He has frightened many an honest pilgrim from worse to better, by the great voice of his roaring. Indeed, he that owneth him doth not keep him out of any good-will to me or mine, but with intent to keep the pilgrims from coming to me, and that they may be afraid to come and knock at this gate for entrance. Sometimes also he has broken out, and has worried some that I loved; but I take all at present patiently. I also give my pilgrims timely help, so that they are not delivered up to his power, to do to them what his doggish nature would prompt him to. But what! my purchased one, I trow, hadst thou known never so much beforehand, thou wouldest not have been afraid of a dog. The beggars that go from door to door will, rather than they will lose a supposed alms, run the hazard of the bawling, barking, and biting too, of a dog: and shall a dog in another man's yard, a dog whose barking I turn to the profit of pilgrims, keep any from coming to me? I deliver them from the lions, and 'my darling from the power of the dog.'

Then said Mercy, I confess my ignorance: I speak what I understand not: I acknowledge that thou doest all things well.

Then Christiana began to talk of their

journey, and to inquire after the way (P. i p 70). So he fed them and washed their feet, and set them in the way of his steps, according as he had dealt with her husband before

So I saw in my dream, that they went on their way ; and the weather was comfortable to them.

Then Christiana began to sing, saying :

> Bless'd be the day that I began
>   A pilgrim for to be ;
> And blessed also be that man
>   That thereunto mov'd me.
> 'Tis true, 'twas long ere I began
>   To seek to live for ever (Matt. xx. 16) ;
> But now I run fast as I can ;
>   'Tis better late, than never.
> Our tears to joy, our fears to faith
>   Are turned, as we see ;
> That our beginning (as one saith)
>   Shews what our end will be.

Now there was on the other side of the wall, that fenced in the way, up which Christiana and her companions were to go, a garden, and that belonged to him, whose was that barking dog, of whom mention was made before. And some of the fruit trees, that grew in the garden, shot their banches over the wall ; and being mellow, they that found them did gather them up and eat of them to their hurt. So Christiana's boys (as boys* are apt

* ' As boys'—The terrifying suggestions of Satan give believers much present uneasiness ; yet they often do them great good, and never eventually hurt them : but the allurements of those worldly objects, which he throws in their way, are far more dangerous and pernicious. Many of these, for which the aged have no relish, are very attractive to young persons :

to do), being pleased with the trees, and with the fruit that did hang thereon, did pluck them, and began to eat. Their mother did also chide them for so doing, but still the boys went on.

Well, said she, my sons, you transgress, for that fruit is none of ours: but she did not know that they did belong to the enemy: I'll warrant you, if she had, she would have been ready to die for fear. But that passed, and they went on their way. Now, by that they were gone about two bows-shot from the place that led them into the way, they spied two*

but, instead of conniving at their indulging themselves, from an idea that allowance must be made for youth; all who love the souls of their children should use their influence and authority to restrain them from such vain pleasures as 'war against the soul,' and are most dangerous when least suspected. This fruit may be found in the pilgrim's path; but it grows in Beelzebub's garden, and should be shunned as poison. Many diversions and pursuits, both in high and low life, are of this nature, though often pleaded for as innocent by some persons who ought to know better.

* 'Two'—Satan designs, by every means, to take off awakened sinners from the great concern of eternal salvation; and he makes use of ungodly men for that purpose, among his manifold devices against the female sex. These are very ill-favoured to the gracious mind; however alluring their persons, circumstances, or proposals may be to the carnal eye. As such vile seducers are too often successful, they are emboldened to attempt even those who profess to be religious: nor are they always by them, for many, of whom favourable hopes were once entertained, have thus awfully been again entangled and overcome, so that their last state has been worse than the first. But when such proposals are repulsed with decided abhorrence, and earnest prayers, the Lord will give deliverance and victory. The faithful admonitions and warnings of a stated pastor are especially intended by the conductor. The reliever seems to represent the occasional direction and counsel of some able minister; for he

very ill-favoured ones coming down apace to meet them. With that Christiana and Mercy, her friend, covered themselves with their veils, and kept also on their journey : the children also went on before : so that at last they met together. Then they that came down to meet them came just up to the women, as if they would embrace them : but Christiana said, Stand back, or go peaceably as you should. Yet these two, as men that are deaf, regarded not Christiana's words, but began to lay hands upon them : at that Christiana waxed very wroth, and spurned at them with her feet. Mercy also, as well as she could, did what she could to shift them. Christiana again said to them, Stand back, and be gone, for we have no money to lose, being pilgrims, as you see, and such too as live upon the charity of our friends.

Then said one of the two men, We make no assault upon your money, but are come out to tell you, that if you will but grant one small request which we shall ask, we will make women of you for ever.

Now Christiana, imagining what they should mean, made answer again, We will neither hear nor regard, nor yield to what you shall ask. We are in haste, and cannot stay ; our business is of life and death. So again she and her companions made a fresh essay to go past them : but they letted them in their way.

speaks of Christ as his Lord, and must therefore be considered as one of the servants by whom help is sent to the distressed.

And they said, We intend no hurt to your lives ; 'tis another thing we would have.

Ay, quoth Christiana, you would have us body and soul, for I know 'tis for that you are come ; but we will die rather upon the spot, than to suffer ourselves to be brought into such snares as shall hazard our well-being hereafter. And with that they both shrieked out, and cried, murder ! murder ! and so put themselves under those laws that are provided for the protection of women (Deut. xxii. 23—27). But the men still made their approach upon them, with design to prevail against them. They therefore cried out again.

Now they being, as I said, not far from the gate, in at which they came, their voice was heard from where they were thither : wherefore some of the house came out, and, knowing that it was Christiana's tongue, they made haste to her relief. But by that they were got within sight of them, the women were in a very great scuffle : the children also stood crying by. Then did he that came in for their relief call out to the ruffians, saying, What is that thing you do ? Would you make my Lord's people to transgress ? He also attempted to take them but they did make their escape over the wall into the garden of the man to whom the great dog belonged : so the dog became their protector. This reliever then came up to the women, and asked them how they did. So they answered, We hank thy prince pretty well ; only we have been somewhat affrighted : we thank thee also, that thou camest in to our help, for otherwise we had been overcome.

So after a few more words, this reliever said as followeth : I marvelled much, when you were entertained at the gate above, being ye know that ye were but weak women, that you petitioned not the Lord for a conductor : then you might have avoided these troubles and dangers : he would have granted you one.

Alas ! said Christiana, we were so taken with our present blessing, that dangers to come were forgotten by us : beside, who could have thought, that so near the king's palace, there should have lurked such naughty ones ! Indeed it had been well for us, had we asked our Lord for one ; but, since our Lord knew it would be for our profit, I wonder he sent not one along with us.

Rel. It is not always necessary to grant things not asked for, lest by so doing they become of little esteem ; but, when the want of a thing is felt, it then comes under, in the eyes of him that feels it, that estimate that properly is its due ; and so consequently will be hereafter used. Had my Lord granted you a conductor, you would not, neither so have bewailed that oversight of yours in not asking for one, as now you have occasion to do. So all things work for good, and tend to make you more wary.

Chr. Shall we go back again to my Lord, and confess our folly, and ask one ?

Rel. Your confessions of your folly will I present him with : to go back again, you need not ; for in all places where you shall come you will find no want at all ; for at every of my Lord's lodgings, which he has prepared for the reception of his pilgrims, there is sufficient to furnish them against all attempts whatsoever. But as I said, 'he will be inquired of by them, to do it for them' (Ezek xxxvi. 37). And it is a poor thing that is not worth asking for. When he had thus said, he went back to his place, and the pilgrims went on their way.

Then said Mercy, What a sudden blank is here ! I made account we had been past all danger, and that we should never sorrow more.

Thy innocency, my sister, said Christiana to Mercy, may excuse thee much ; but, as for me, my fault is so much the greater, for that I saw this danger before I came out of the doors, and yet did not provide for it where provision might have been had. I am much to be blamed.

Then said Mercy, How knew you this before you came from home ? Pray open to me this riddle.

Chr. Why, I will tell you. Before I set foot out of doors, one night as I lay in my bed, I had a dream about this : for methought I saw two men, as like these as ever the world they could look, stand at my bed's feet, plotting how they might prevent my salvation. I will tell you their very words: they said (it was

4*

when I was in my troubles), ' What shall we do with this woman ? for she cries out waking and sleeping for forgiveness : if she be suffered to go on as she begins, we shall lose her as we have lost her husband.' This you know might have made me take heed, and have provided when provision might have been had.

Well, said Mercy, as by this neglect we have an occasion ministered unto us to behold our imperfections, so our Lord has taken occasion thereby to make manifest the riches of his grace : for he, as we see, has followed us with unasked kindness, and has delivered us from their hands that were stronger than we, of his mere good pleasure.

Thus now, when they had talked away a little more time, they drew near to a house that stood in the way ; which house was built for the relief of pilgrims ; as you will find more fully related in the first part of the records of the Pilgrim's Progress (P. i. p. 73—88). So they drew on towards the house (the house of the Interpreter) ; and, when they came to the door, they heard a great talk in the house : then they gave ear, and heard, as they thought, Christiana mentioned by name. For you must know, that there went along, even before her, a talk of her and her children going on pilgrimage. And this was the more pleasing to them, because they had heard that she was Christian's wife, that woman who was some time ago so unwilling to hear of going on pilgrimage.

Thus therefore, they stood still, and heard the good people within commending her who they little thought stood at the door. At last Christiana knocked; as she had done at the gate before. Now, when she had knocked, there came to the door a young damsel, named Innocent, and opened the door, and looked, and, behold, two women were there.

Then said the damsel to them, With whom would you speak in this place?

Christiana answered, We understand that this is a privileged place for those that are become pilgrims, and we now at this door are such; wherefore we pray that we may be partakers of that for which we at this time are come; for the day, as thou seest, is very far spent and we are loath to-night to go any farther.

Dam. Pray what may I call your name, that I may tell it to my Lord within?

Chr. My name is Christiana; I was the wife of that pilgrim that some years ago did travel this way; and these be his four children. This maiden is also my companion, and is going on pilgrimage too.

Then ran Innocent in (for that was her name), and said to those within, Can you think who is at the door? there is Christiana and her children, and her companion, all waiting for entertainment here! Then they leaped for joy, and went and told their master. So he came to the door, and, looking upon her, he said, Art thou that Christiana whom Christian the good man left behind him when he betook himself to a pilgrim's life?

Chr. I am that woman that was so hard hearted as to slight my husband's troubles, and that left him to go on his journey alone ; and these are his four children ; but now I also am come, for I am convinced that no way is rig^t but this.

ter. Then is fulfilled that which is written of the man that said to his son, 'Go work to-day in my vineyard ; and he said to his father, I will not ; but afterwards repented and went' (Matt. xxi. 28, 29).

Then said Christiana, So be it : Amen. God make it a true saying upon me, and grant that I may be found at the last ' of him in peace, without spot, and blameless !'

Inter. But why standest thou at the door ? Come in, thou daughter of Abraham : we were talking of thee but now, for tidings have come to us before, how thou art become a pilgrim. Come, children, come in : come maiden, come. So he had them all into the house.

So, when they were within, they were bidden to sit down and rest them ; the which when they had done, those that attended upon the pilgrims in the house came into the room to see them. And one smiled, and another smiled, and another smiled, and they all smiled, for joy that Christiana was become a pilgrim : they also looked upon the boys ; they stroked them over their faces with their hands in token of their kind reception of them : they also carried it lovingly to Mercy, and bid them all welcome into their Master's house.

After awhile, because supper was not ready, the Interpreter took them into his significant rooms, and shewed them what Christian, Christiana's husband, had seen some time before. Here therefore they saw the man in the cage, the man and his dream, the man that cut his way through his enemies, and the picture of the biggest of all ; together with the rest of those things that were then so profitable to Christian.

This done,* and after those things had been somewhat digested by Christiana and her company, the Interpreter takes them apart again, and has them first into a room where was a man that could look no way but downwards, with a muck-rake in his hand : there stood also one over his head with a celestial crown in his hand, and proffered him that crown for his muck-rake ; but the man did neither look up nor regard, but rake to himself the straws, the small sticks, and dust of the floor.

Then said Christiana, I persuade myself that I know somewhat the meaning of this ; for this is the figure of a man in this world : is it not, good Sir ?

* ' This done'—The emblematical instruction at the Interpreter's house, in the former part, was so important and comprehensive, that no other selection equally interesting could be expected : some valuable hints, however, are here adduced. The first emblem is very plain ; and so apposite, that it is wonderful any person should read it without lifting up a prayer to the Lord, and saying, ' Oh ! deliver me from this muck-rake.' Yet alas, it is to be feared, such prayers are still little used even by professors of the Gospel ; at least they are contradicted by the habitual conduct of numbers among them : and this may properly lead us to weep over others and tremble for ourselves.

Thou hast said right, said he, and his muck-rake doth shew his carnal mind. And whereas thou seest him rather give heed to rake up straws and sticks, and the dust of the floor, than do what he says that calls to him from above, with the celestial crown in his hand; it is to shew, that heaven is but as a fable to some, and that things here are counted the only things substantial. Now, whereas it was also shewed thee, that the man could look no way but downwards, it is to let thee know, that earthly things, when they are with power upon men's minds, quite carry their hearts away from God.

Then said Christiana, Oh! deliver me from this muck-rake.

That prayer, said the Interpreter has lain by till it is almost rusty; 'Give me not riches,' is scarce the prayer of one of ten thousand (Pov. xxx. 8). Straws, and sticks, and dust, with most, are the great things now looked after.

With that Mercy and Christiana wept, and said, It is alas! too true.

When the Interpreter had shewed them this, he had them into the very best room in the house (a very brave room it was): so he bid them look round about, and see if they could find any thing profitable there. Then they looked round and round; for there was nothing to be seen but a very great spider* on the wall; and that they overlooked.

* 'Spider'—The instruction grounded on accommodation of Scriptural quotations, though solid and important, is not

Then said Mercy, Sir, I see nothing ; but Christiana held her peace.

But, said the Interpreter, Look again : she therefore looked again, and said, ' Here is not any thing but an ugly spider, who hangs by her hands upon the wall. Then, said he, Is there but one spider in all this spacious room ? Then the water stood in Christiana's eyes, for she was a woman quick of apprehension ; and she said, Yes, Lord, there is more here than one. Yea, and spiders whose venom is far more destructive than that which is in her. The Interpreter then looked pleasantly on her, and said, Thou hast said the truth. This made Mercy blush, and the boys to cover their faces, for they all began now to understand the riddle.

Then said the Interpreter again, ' The spider taketh hold with her hands (as you see), and is in king's palaces.' And wherefore is this recorded, but to shew you, that

so convincing to the understanding as that which results from the obvious meaning of the words, though many persons are for the time more excited to attention by a lively exercise of the imagination, and the surprise of unexpected inferences This method, however, should be used with great caution by the friends of truth ; for it is a most formidable engine in the hands of those, who endeavour to pervert or oppose it. The author did not mean by the emblem of the spider, that the sinner might confidently assure himself of salvation by the blood of Christ, while he continued full of the poison of sin, without experiencing or evidencing any change : but only, that no consciousness of inward pollution or actual guilt need discourage any one from applying to Christ, and fleeing for refuge to ' lay hold on the hope set before him,' that thus he may be delivered from condemnation, and cleansed from pollution, and so made meet for those blessed mansions, into which no unclean thing can find admission.

how full of the venom of sin soever you be, yet you may, by the hand of faith, lay hold of, and dwell in the best room that belongs to the king's house above ?

I thought, said Christiana, of something of this ; but I could not imagine it all. I thought, that we were like spiders, and that we looked like ugly creatures, in what fine rooms soever we were ; but that by this spider, this venomous and ill-favoured creature, we were to learn how to act faith, that came not into my thoughts ; that she worketh with hands ; and, as I see, dwells in the best room in the house. God has made nothing in vain.

Then they seemed all to be glad ; but the water stood in their eyes : yet they looked one upon another, and also bowed before the Interpreter.

He had them into another room, where was a hen* and chickens, and bid them observe awhile. So one of the chickens went to the trough to drink, and every time she

* 'A hen'--Our Lord hath, in immense condescension, employed this emblem, to represent his tender love to his people, for whom he bear the storm of wrath himself, that they might be safe and happy under the shadow of his wings (Matt. xxiii. 37). The common call signifies the general invitations of the Gospel, which should be addressed without restriction to all men that come under the sound of it : ' as many as ye find, bid to the marriage.' The special call denotes those influences of the Spirit, by which the heart is sweetly made willing to embrace the invitation, and apply for the blessing, in the use of the appointed means, by which sinners actually experience the accomplishment of the promises, as their circumstances require. The brooding note was

drank she lifted up her head and her eyes towards heaven. See, said he, what this little chick doeth, and learn of her to acknowledge, whence your mercies come, by receiving them with looking up. Yet again, said he, observe and look ; so they gave heed, and perceived that the hen did walk in a fourfold method towards her chickens. 1. She had a common call, and that she had all the day long. 2. She had a special call, and that she had but sometimes. 3. She had a brooding note. And 4. She had an out cry (Matt. xxiii. 37).

Now, said he, compare this hen to your King, and these chickens to his obedient ones. For, answerable to her, himself has his methods, which he walketh in towards his people ; by his common call he gives nothing ; by his special call he always has something to give ; he has also a brooding voice for them that are under his wing ; and he has an out-cry, to give the alarm when he seeth the enemy come. I choose, my darlings, to lead you into the room where such things are, because you are women, and they are easy for you.

And, Sir, said Christiana, pray let us see some more. So he had them into the slaug-

intended to represent that communion with God, and those consolations of the holy Spirit, which the Scriptures encourage us to expect, and by which the believer is trained up for eternal felicity ; whilst the out-cry refers to the warnings and cautions, by which believers are excited to vigilance, circumspection, and self-examination, and to beware of all deceivers and delusions.

ter-house, where was a butcher killing of sheep ; and behold the sheep was quiet, and took her death patiently. Then, said the Interpreter, you must learn of this sheep to suffer, and to put up wrongs without murmurings and complaints. Behold how quietly she takes her death, and, without objecting, she suffereth her skin to be pulled over her ears. Your King doth call you his sheep.

After this he led them into his garden,* where was great variety of flowers ; and he said, Do you see all these ? So Christiana said, Yes. Then said he again, Behold the flowers are diverse in stature, in quality, and colour, and smell, and virtue ; and some are better than some ; also where the gardener hath set them, there they stand, and quarrel not one with another.

Again, he had them into his field,† which he had sown with wheat and corn : but when

---

* ' Garden'—We ought not to be contented (so to speak), with a situation among the useless and noxious weeds of the desert; but if we be planted among the ornamental and fragrant flowers of the Lord's garden, we may deem ourselves sufficiently distinguished and honoured. We should, therefore, watch against envy and ambition, contempt of our brethren, and contention. We ought to be satisfied in our place, doing ' nothing through strife or vain-glory,' or ' with murmurings and disputings :' but endeavouring, in the meekness of wisdom, to diffuse a heavenly fragrance around us, and ' to adorn the doctrine of God our Saviour in all things.'

' † Field'—The labour and expense of the husbandman are not repaid by the straw or the chaff, but by the corn. The humiliation and sufferings of Christ, the publication of the Gospel, the promises and instituted ordinances, and the labours of ministers, were not intended merely to bring men to profess certain doctrines, or observe certain forms ; or

they beheld, the tops of all were cut off, only the straw remained. He said again, This ground was dunged, and sowed; but what shall we do with the crop? Then said Christiana, Burn some, and make muck of the rest. Then said the Interpreter again, Fruit, you see, is that thing you look for, and for want of that you condemn it to the fire, and to be trodden under foot of men; beware that in this you condemn not yourselves.

Then, as they were coming in from abroad, they spied a robin with a great spider in his mouth; so the Interpreter said, Look here So they looked, and Mercy wondered, but Christiana said, What a disparagement is it to such a little pretty bird as the robin-redbreast is! he being also a bird above many, that loveth to maintain a kind of sociableness with men: I had thought they had lived upon crumbs of bread, or upon other such harmless matter; I like him worse than I did.

The Interpreter then replied, this robin is an emblem, very apt to set forth some professors by; for to sight they are, as this robin, pretty of note, colour, and carriage; they seem also to have a very great love for professors that are sincere; and above all other

even to produce convictions, affections, or comforts, in any order or degree whatsoever; but to render men fruitful in good works, by the influences of the Spirit of Christ, and through his sanctifying truth; and all profession will terminate in everlasting contempt and misery, which is not productive of this good fruit, whatever men may pretend, or however they may deceive themselves and one another.

to desire to associate with them, and to be in their company ; as if they could live upon the good man's crumbs. They pretend also, that therefore it is that they frequent the house of the godly, and the appointments of the Lord ; but when they are by themselves, as the robin, they catch and gobble up spiders, they can change their diet, drink and swallow down sin like water.

So when they were come again into the house, because supper as yet was not ready, Christiana again desired that the Interpreter would either shew or tell some other things that are profitable.

Then the Interpreter began, and said . The fatter the sow is, the more she desires the mire ; the fatter the ox is, the more gamesomely he goes to the slaughter ; and the more healthy the lusty man is, the more prone is he unto evil.

There is a desire in women to go neat and fine ; and it is a comely thing to be adorned with that, which in God's sight is of great price.

'Tis easier watching a night or two, than to sit up a whole year together ; so 'tis easier for one to begin to profess well, than to hold out as he should to the end.

Every shipmaster, when in a storm, will willingly cast that overboard that is of the smallest value in the vessel : but who will throw the best out first ? None but he that feareth not God.

One leak will sink a ship ; and one sin* will destroy a sinner.

He, that forgets his friend is ungrateful unto him : but he that forgets his Saviour, is unmerciful to himself.

He that lives in sin, and looks for happiness hereafter, is like him that soweth cockle, and thinks to fill his barn with wheat or barley.

If a man would live well, let him fetch his last day to him, and make it always his company-keeper.

Whispering and change of thought prove that sin is in the world.

If the world, which God sets light by, is counted a thing of that worth with men ; what is heaven, that God commendeth ?

If the life, that is attended with so many troubles, is so loath to be let go by us, what is the life above ?

Every body will cry up the goodness of men ; but who is there, that is, as he should be, affected with the goodness of God ?

We seldom sit down to meat, but we eat and leave : so there is in Jesus Christ more merit† and righteousness than the whole world has need of.

* 'One sin'—By repentance and faith in Christ, the leaks that sin hath made are, as it were, stopped : but one sin, habitually committed with allowance, proves a man's profession hypocritical, however plausible it may be in all other respects ; as one leak unstopped will assuredly at length sink the ship.

† 'More merit'—This observation is grounded on the good old distinction, that the merit of Christ's obedience unto death

5*

When the Interpreter had done, he takes them out into his garden again, and had them to a tree, whose inside was all rotten and gone, and yet it grew and had leaves. Then said Mercy, What means this?—This tree, said he, whose outside is fair, and whose inside is rotten, is it, to which many may be compared that are in the garden of God : who with their mouths speak high in behalf of God, but indeed will do nothing for him ; whose leaves are fair, but their heart good for nothing, but to be tinder for the devil's tinder-box.

Now supper was ready, the table spead, and all things set on board ; so they sat down and did eat, when one had given thanks. And the Interpreter did usually entertain those that lodged with him, with music at meals ; so the minstrels played. There was also one that did sing, and a very fine voice he had His song was this—

> ' The Lord is only my support,
>   And he that doth me feed ;
> How can I then want any thing
>   Whereof I stand in need ?'

When the song and music were ended, the

is sufficient for all, though only effectual to some, namely, in one view of the subject, to the elect, in another to all who by faith apply for an interest in it. This makes way for general invitations, and shews it to be every one's duty to repent and believe the Gospel ; as nothing but pride, the carnal mind, and enmity to God and religion, influence men to neglect so great a salvation : and, when the regenerating power of the Holy Spirit accompanies the word, sinners are made willing to except the proffered mercy, and encouraged by the general invitations, which before they sinfully slighted.

Interpreter asked Christiana, what it was that at first did move her thus to betake herself to a pilgrim's life ? Christiana answered, First the loss of my husband came into my mind, at which I was heartily grieved : but all that was but natural affection. Then, after that, came the troubles and pilgrimage of my husband into my mind, and also how like a churl I had carried it to him as to that. So guilt took hold of my mind, and would have drawn me into the pond ; but that opportunely I had a dream of the well-being of my husband, and a letter sent me by the King of that country where my husband dwells, to come to him. The dream and the letter together so wrought upon my mind, that they forced me to this way.

Inter. But met you with no opposition before you set out of doors ?

Chr. Yes, a neighbour of mine, one Mrs Timorous (she was kin to him that would have persuaded my husband to go back, for fear of the lions), she also so befooled me, for, as she called it, my intended desperate adventure ; she also urged what she could to dishearten me from it ; the hardship and troubles that my husband met with in the way ; but all this I got over pretty well. But a dream that I had of two ill-looked ones, that I thought did plot how to make me miscarry in my journey, that hath troubled me : yea, it still runs in my mind, and makes me afraid of every one that I meet lest they should meet me to do me a mischief, and to turn me out of the way. Yea, I may tell my Lord, though I would not every body knew it, that between this and the gate by which we got into the way, we were both so sorely assaulted, that we were made to cry out murder ; and the two, that made this assult upon us, were like the two that I saw in my dream.

Then said the Interpreter, Thy beginning is good, thy latter end shall greatly increase. So he addressed him to Mercy, and said unto her, And what moved thee to come hither, sweetheart ?

Then Mercy blushed and trembled, and for awhile continued silent.

Then said he, Be not afraid, only believe, and speak thy mind.

Then she began, and said, Truly, Sir, my want of experience is that which makes me covet to be in silence, and that also that fill-eth me with fears of coming short at last. I cannot tell of visions and dreams, as my friend Christiana can : nor know I what it is to mourn for my refusing of the counsel of those that were good relations.

Inter. What was it then, dear heart, that hath prevailed with thee to do as thou hast done ?

Mercy. Why, when our friend here was packing up to be gone from our town, I and another went accidentally to see her. So we knocked at the door, and went in. When we were within, and seeing what she was doing, we asked her what she meant ? She said, she was sent for to go to her husband ; and then she up and told us how she had seen him in a dream, dwelling in a curious place, among immortals, wearing a crown, playing upon a harp, eating and drinking at his Prince's table, and singing praises to him for the bringing him thither, &c. Now methought while she was telling these things unto us, my heart burned within me. And I said in my heart if this be true, I will leave my father and my mother, and the land of my nativity, and will, if I may, go along with Christiana.

So I asked her farther of the truth of these things, and if she would let me go with her : for I saw now, that there was no dwelling, but with the danger of ruin, any longer in our town. But yet I came away with a heavy heart ; not for that I was unwilling to come away, but for that so many of my relations were left behind. And I am come with all my heart, and will, if I may, go with Christiana to her husband, and his King.

Inter. Thy setting out is good, for thou hast given credit* to the truth ; thou art a Ruth,

---

* 'Given credit'—This is a most simple definition of faith ; it is 'the belief of the truth,' as the sure testimony of God, relative to our most important concerns. When we thus credit those truths that teach us the peril of our situation as justly condemned sinners, we are moved with fear, and humbled in repentance ; when we thus believe the report of a refuge provided for us, our hopes are excited ; those truths that relate to inestimable blessings attainable by us, when really credited, kindle our fervent desires ; while such as shew us the glory, excellency, and mercy of God our Saviour, and our obligations to his redeeming grace, produce, and work by, love, gratitude, and every fervent affection. This living faith influences a man's judgment, choice, and conduct ; and especially induces him to receive Jesus Christ for all the

who did for the love she bare to Naomi, and
to the Lord her God, leave father and mother, and the land of her nativity, to come out
and go with a people that she knew not before. 'The Lord recompense thy work, and
a full reward be given thee of the Lord God
of Israel, under whose wings thou art come to
trust' (Ruth ii. 11, 12).

purposes of salvation, and to yield himself to his service, as
constrained by love of him and zeal for his glory. We need
no other ground for this faith than the authenticated word of
God. This may be brought to our recollection by means of
distress or danger, or even in a dream, or with some very
strong impression on the the mind; yet true faith rests only
on the word of God, according to its meaning as it stands in
the Bible; and not on the manner in which it occurs to the
thoughts, or according to any new sense put upon it in a
dream, or by an impression; as this would be a new revelation. For if the words, 'Thy sins are forgiven thee,' should
be impressed on my mind; they would contain a declaration
nowhere made in Scripture concerning me; consequently the
belief of them on this ground would be a faith not warranted
by the word of God. Now as we have no reason to expect
such new revelations, and as Satan can counterfeit any of
these impressions; we must consider every thing of this kind
as opening a door to enthusiasm, and the most dangerous delusions; though many, who rest their confidence on them,
have also scriptural evidence of their acceptance, which they
overlook. On the other hand, should the following words be
powerfully impressed on my mind, 'Him that cometh to me
I will in no wise cast out,' or, 'He that confesseth and for-
saketh his sin shall find mercy;' I may deduce encouragement from the words, according to the genuine meaning of
them as they stand in Scripture, without any dread of delusion,
or any pretence to new revelations; provided I be conscious
that I do come to Christ, and confess my sins with the sincere purpose of forsaking them. But there are so many
dangers in this matter, that the more evidently our faith and
hope are grounded wholly on the plain testimony of God, and
confirmed by our subsequent experience and conduct; the
safer will our course be, and the less occasion will be given
to the objections of our despisers.

Now supper was ended, and preparation
was made for bed : the women were laid
singly alone, and the boys by themselves.
Now when Mercy was in bed, she could not
sleep for joy, for that now her doubts of missing at last were removed farther from her
than ever they were before. So she lay
blessing and praising God, who had such favour for her.

In the morning they arose with the sun,
and prepared themselves for their departure ;
but the Interpreter would have them tarry
awhile ; for, said he, you must orderly go
from hence. Then said he to the damsel
that first opened unto them, Take them and
have them into the garden to the Bath,* and
there wash them and make them clean from
the soil which they have gathered by travel-

---

* 'Bath'—The author calls this ' the bath of sanctification'
in a marginal note : whence we may infer, that he specially
meant to intimate, that believers should constantly seek fresh
supplies of grace from the Holy Spirit, to purify their hearts
from the renewed defilement of sin, which their intercourse
with the world will continually occasion ; and to revive and
invigorate those holy affections, which in the same manner
are apt to grow languid. Yet he did not intend to exclude
their habitual reliance on the blood of Christ for pardon and
acceptance : for in both respects we need daily washing.
The sanctification of the Spirit unto obedience, warrants the
true Christian's ' peace and joy in believing :' it gives him
beauty in the sight of his brethren ; it strengthens him for every
conflict and service ; and the image of Christ, discernible in
his spirit and conduct, seals him as a child of God and an
heir of glory ; while the inward consciousness of living by
faith in the Son of God for all the blessings of salvation, and
of experiencing all filial affections toward God as his reconciled Father, inspires him with humble joy and confidence in
his love

ling. Then Innocent the damsel took them,
and led them into the garden, and brought
them to the Bath; so she told them, that
there they must wash and be clean, for so her
Master would have the women to do, that
called at his house as they were going on
pilgrimage. Then they went in and washed,
yea, they and the boys and all; and they
came out of that Bath not only sweet and
clean, but also much enlivened and strengthened in their joints. So when they came in,
they looked fairer a deal than when they
went out to the washing.

When they were returned out of the garden from the Bath, the Interpreter took them,
and looked upon them, and said unto them,
' Fair as the moon.' Then he called for the
seal, wherewith they used to be sealed that
were washed in his Bath. So the seal was
brought, and he set his mark upon them, that
they might be known in the places whither
they were yet to go. Now the seal was the
contents and sum of the passover which the
children of Israel did eat when they came
out of the land of Egypt (Exod. xiii. 8—10) ;
and the mark was set between their eyes.
This seal greatly added to their beauty, for
it was an ornament to their faces. It also
added to their gravity, and made their countenances more like them of angels.

Then said the Interpreter again to the damsel that waited upon the women, ' Go into the
vestry, and fetch out garments for these people : so she went and fetched out white rai

ment,* and laid it down before him : so he
commanded them to put it on : it was 'fine
linen, white and clean.' When the women
were thus adorned, they seemed to be a terror one to the other ; for that they could not
see that glory each one in himself, which
they could see in each other. Now therefore
they began to esteem each other better than
themselves. For you are fairer than I am,
said one ; and you are more comely than I
am, said another. The children also stood
amazed, to see into what fashion they were
brought.

The Interpreter then called for a man-
servant of his, one Great-heart,† and bid
him take a sword, and helmet, and shield ;

---

* 'White raiment'—The pilgrims are supposed to have
been justified on their admission at the gate ; the Interpreter
is the emblem of the Holy Spirit ; and the raiment here
mentioned rendered those who are adorned with it comely in
the eyes of their companions. We cannot, therefore, with
propriety explain it to signify the righteousness of Christ imputed to the believer, but the renewal of the soul to holiness ;
for this alone is visible to the eyes of men. They, who have
put on this raiment, are also ' clothed with humility :' so that
they readily perceive the excellences of other believers, but
cannot discern their own, except when they look in the glass
of God's word. At the same time they become very obser-
vant of their own defects, and severe in animadverting on
them, but proportionably candid to their brethren : and thus
they learn the hard lesson of ' esteeming others better than
themselves.'

† 'Great heart'—The stated pastoral care of a vigilant
minister, who is strong in faith, and courageous in the cause
of God, is represented by the conductor of the pilgrims. We
shall have repeated opportunities of shewing how desirous the
author was to recommend this advantage to his readers, to
excite them to be thankful for it, and to avail themselves of
't when graciously afforded them.

and take these my daughters, said he, conduct them to the house called Beautiful, at
which place they will rest next.   So he took
his weapons, and went before them; and the
Interpreter said, God speed.   Those also
that belonged to the family sent them away
with many a good wish. So they went on their
way, and sang

> This place has been our second stage
>   Here we have heard and seen
> Those good things, that from age to age
>   To others hid have been.
> The dunghill-raker, spider, hen,
>   The chicken too, to me
> Hath taught a lesson; let me then
>   Conformed to it be.
> The butcher, garden, and the field,
>   The robin and his bait,
> Also the rotten tree doth yield
>   Me argument of weight;
> To move me for to watch and pray,
>   To strive to be sincere:
> To take my cross up day by day,
>   And serve the Lord with fear.

Now I saw in my dream, that those went
on, and Great-heart before them; so they
went and came to the place where Christian's
burthen fell of his back, and tumbled into a
sepulchre (P. i. p. 90).   Here then they
made a pause; here also they blessed God.
Now, said Christiana, it comes to my mind
what was said to us at the gate, to wit,
that we should have pardon by word and
deed; by word, that is, by the promise; by
deed, to wit, in the way it was obtained.
What the promise is, of that I know something; but what it is to have pardon by deed,

or in the way it was obtained, Mr. Great-
heart, I suppose you know; which, if you
please, let us hear your discourse thereof.

Gr.-h. Pardon* by the deed done, is pardon obtained by some one, for another that

* 'Pardon'—The subsequent discourse, on 'Pardon by
the deed done,' confirms the interpretation that hath been
given of the cross, and of Christian's deliverance from his
burthen. The doctrine is, however, here stated in a manner
to which some may object, and indeed it is needlessly systematical and rather obscure. By the righteousness of Christ
as God, his essential divine attributes of justice and holiness
must be intended: his righteousness as man denotes his human nature as free from all the defilement of sin. The righteousness of his person, as he hath the two natures joined in
one, can only mean the perfection of his mysterious person
in all respects; and his capacity of acting as our surety, by
doing and suffering in our nature all that was requisite, while
his divine nature stamped an infinite value on his obedience
unto death. The eternal Word, the only-begotten Son of
God, was under no obligation to assume our nature: and
when he had seen good to asume it, he was not bound to live
a number of years here on earth, obedient to the law, both
in its ceremonial and moral requirements, amidst hardships,
sufferings, and temptations of every kind; except as he had
undertaken to be our surety. In this sense he himself had
no need of that righteousness which he finished for our justification. And assuredly he was under no obligation, as a
perfectly holy man, to suffer even unto the violent, torturing,
and ignominious death upon the cross. That part of his
obedience, which consisted in enduring agony, and pain in
body and soul, was only needful as he bare our sins, and gave
himself a sacrifice to God for us. Indeed, his righteousness
is not the less his own, by being imputed to us: for we are
considered as one with him by faith, and thus 'made the
righteousness of God in him,' and we are justified in virtue
of this union. He was able by his temporal sufferings and
death to pay our debt and ranson or inheritance, thus delivering us from eternal misery, which else had been inevitable,
and bringing us to eternal life, which had otherwise been un-
attainable; and the law of love, to which as a man he became subject, required him to do this: for if we loved our
'neighbour as ourselves,' we should be willing to submit to

hath need thereof; not by the person pardoned, but in the way, saith another, in which I have obtained it. So then (to speak to the question more at large), the pardon that you, and Mercy, and these boys have attained by another; to wit, by him that let you in at that gate: and he hath obtained in this double way; he hath performed righteousness to cover you, and spilt blood to wash you in.

Chr. But if he parts with his righteousness to us, what will he have for himself.

Gr.-h. He has more righteousness than you have need of, or than he needeth himself.

Chr. Pray make that appear.

Gr.-h. With all my heart: but first I must premise, that he, of whom we are now about to speak, is one that has not his fellow. He has two natures in one person, plain to be distinguished, impossible to be divided. Unto each of these natures a righteousness belongeth, and each righteousness is essential to that nature. So that one may as easily cause the natures to be extinct, as to separate its justice or righteousness from it. Of these righteousnesses, therefore we are not made partakers, so that they, or any of them, should be put upon us, that we might be made just, and live thereby. Besides these, there is a righteousness which this person has, as these two natures are joined in one. And this is

any inferior loss, hardship, or suffering, to rescue an enemy or stranger from a greater and more durable misery, which he hath no other way of escaping; or to secure to him a more valuable and permanent advantage, which can no otherwise be obtained.

not the righteousness of the Godhead, as distinguished from the manhood, nor the righteousness of the manhood, as distinguished from the Godhead ; but a righteousness which standeth in the union of both natures, and may properly be called the righteousness that is essential to his being prepared of God to the capacity of the mediatory office, which he was entrusted with. If he parts with his first righteousness, he parts with his Godhead : if he parts with his second righteousness, he parts with the purity of his manhood : if he parts with his third, he parts with that perfection which capacitates him to the office of mediation. He has therefore another righteousness, which standeth in performance, or obedience to a revealed will : and that is what he puts upon sinners, and that by which their sins are covered. Wherefore he saith, 'As by one man's disobedience, many were made sinners : so by the obedience of one, shall many be made righteous' (Rom. v. 19).

Chr. But are the other righteousnesses of no use to us ?

Gr.-h. Yes ; for though they are essential to his natures and office, and cannot be communicated unto another, yet it is by virtue of them that the righteousness that justifies is for that purpose efficacious. The righteousness of his Godhead gives virtue to his obedience : the righteousness of his manhood giveth capability to his obedience to justify ; and the righteousness, that standeth in the union of these two natures to his office,

6*

giveth authority to that righteousness to do the work for which it was ordained.

So then here is a righteousness that Christ, as God, has no need of : for he is God without it : here is a righteousness that Christ, as man, has no need of to make him so, for he is perfect man without it : again, here is a righteousness that Christ, as God and as God-man, has no need of, with reference to himself, therefore he can spare it ; a justifying righteousness, that he for himself wanteth not, and therefore giveth it away. Hence it is called 'the gift of righteousness' (Rom. v. 17). This righteousness, since Christ Jesus the Lord has made himself under the law, must be given away ; for the law doth not bind him that is under it, to do justly, but to use charity. Wherefore he must, or ought by the law, if he hath two coats, to give one to him that has none. Now our Lord indeed hath two coats, one for himself, and one to spare ; wherefore he freely bestows one upon those that have none. And thus, Christiana and Mercy, and the rest of you that are here, doth your pardon come by deed, or by the work of another man. Your Lord Christ is he tha worked, and hath given away what he wrought for, to the next poor beggar he meets.

But again, in order to pardon by deed, there must something be paid to God as a price, as well as something prepared to cover us withal Sin has delivered us up to the just course of a righteous law ; now from this course we must be justified by way of redemption, a price being paid for the harms we have done ; and this is by the blood of your Lord, who came and stood in your place and stead, and died your death for your transgressions. Thus has he ransomed you from your transgressions, by blood, and covered your polluted and deformed souls with righteousness (Rom. viii. 34 ; Gal. iii. 13) ; for the sake of which, God passeth by you, and will not hurt you, when he comes to judge the world.

Chr. This is brave ; now I see that there was something to be learned by our being pardoned by word and deed. Good Mercy, let us labour to keep this in mind ; and my children, do you remember it also. But, Sir, was not this it that made my good Christian's burthen fall from off his shoulder, and that made him give three leaps for joy ?

Gr.-h. Yes, it was the belief of this that cut of those strings, that could not be cut by other means ; and it was to give him a proof of the virtue of this, that he was suffered to carry his burthen to the cross.

Chr. I thought so ; for though my heart was lightful and joyous before, yet it is ten times more lightsome and joyous now. And I am persuaded by what I have felt (though I have felt but little as yet), that if the most burthened man in the world was here, and did see and believe as I now do, it would make his heart the more merry and blithe.

Gr.-h. There is not only one comfort, and the ease of a burthen brought to us, by the sight and consideration of these, but an endeared affection begot in us by it ; for who can (if he does but once think that pardon comes not only by promise, but thus) but be affected with the way and means of redemption, and so with the man that hath wrought it for him ?

Chr. True ; methinks it makes my heart bleed to think, that he should bleed for me. Oh ! thou loving One ! Oh ! thou blessed One ! Thou deservest to have me ; thou hast bought me ; thou deservest to have me all ; thou hast paid for me ten thousand times more than I am worth ! No marvel that this made the water stand in my husband's eyes, and that it made him trudge so nimbly on ; I am persuaded he wished me with him ; but vile wretch that I was ! I let him come all alone. O Mercy, that thy father* and mo-

---

* ' Thy father'—When believers, ' in the warmth of their affections,' feel the humbling, melting, endearing, and sanctifying effects of contemplating the glory of the cross, and the love of Christ in dying for sinners, and considering themselves as the special objects of that inexpressible compassion and kindness, they are apt to conclude that the belief of the propositions, that Christ loves them and died for them, and that God is reconciled to them, produces the change by its own influence ; and would affect the most carnal hearts in the same manner, could men be persuaded to believe it : for they vainly imagine, that apprehensions of God's severi.y, and dread of his vengeance, are the sources of the enmity which sinners manifest against him. Hence very lively and affectionate Christians have frequently been prone to sanction the unscriptural tenet, that the justifying act of faith consists in assuredly believing that Christ died for me in particular, and that God loves me ; and to consider this appropriation as preceding repentance and every other gracious disposition ; and in some sense the cause of regeneration, win-

ther were here ; yea, and Mrs. Timorous also ; nay, I wish with all my heart, that here

ning the heart to love God, and to rejoice in him and in
obeying his commandments. From this doctrine others
have inferred, that if all men, and even devils too, believed
the love of God to them, and his purpose at length to make
them happy, they would be won over from their rebellion
against him, which they persist in from a mistaken idea,
that he is their implacable enemy ; and they make this one
main argument, in support of the salutary tendency of the
final restitution scheme. But all these opinions arise from
a false and flattering estimate of human nature ; for the
carnal mind hates the scriptural character of God, and the glory displayed in the cross, even more than that which shines
forth in the fiery law. Indeed, if we take away the offensive
part of the Gospel, the honour it puts upon the law and its
awful sanctions, and the exhibition it makes of the divine
justice and holiness, it will give the proud carnal heart but
little umbrage : if we admit that men's aversion to God and
religion arise from misapprehension, and not desperate wickedness, many will endure the doctrine. A reconciliation,
in which God assures the sinner that he has forgiven him,
even before he has repented of his sins, will suit men's pride ;
and if he have been previously frighted, a great flow of affections will follow ; but the event will prove, that they differ essentially from spiritual love of God, gratitude, holy
joy, and genuine humiliation, which arise from a true per-
ception of the glorious perfections of God, the righteousness
of his law and government, the real nature of redemption,
and the odiousness and desert of sin. In short, all such
schemes render regeneration needless ; or substitute something else in its stead, which is effected by a natural process,
and not by the new-creating power of the Holy Spirit. But
when this divine agent has communicated life to the soul,
and a capacity is produced of perceiving and relishing spiritual excellency, the enmity against God receives a mortal
wound ; from that season the more his real character and
glory are known, the greater affection will be excited, and
a proportionable transformation into the same holy image
effected. Then the view of the cross, as the grand display
of all the harmonious perfections of the Godhead, will soft-
en, humble, and meliorate the heart ; while the persuasion
of an interest in these blessings, and an admiring sense of
having received such inconceivable favours from this glori-

was Madam Wanton too. Surely, surely, their hearts would be affected ; nor could the fear of the one, nor the powerful lusts of the other, prevail with them to go home again, and refuse to become good pilgrims.

Gr.-h. You speak now in the warmth of your affections ; will it, think you, be always thus with you ? Besides, that is not communicated to every one, nor to every one that did see your Jesus bleed. There were that stood by, and that saw the blood run from the heart to the ground, and yet were so far off this, that, instead of lamenting, they laughed at him ; and, instead of becoming his disciples, did harden their hearts against him. So that all that you have, my daughters, you have by peculiar impression made by a divine contemplating upon what I have spoken to you. Remember that it was told you, that the hen, by her common call, gives no meat to her chickens. This you have, therefore, by a special grace.

ous and holy Lord God, will still farther elevate the soul above all low pursuits, and constrain it to the most unreserved and self-denying obedience. But while the heart remains unregenerate, the glory of God and the Gospel will either be misunderstood, or hated in proportion as it is discovered. Such views and affections therefore as have been described spring from special grace ; are not produced by the natural efficacy of any sentiments, but by the immediate influences of the Holy Spirit ; so that even true believers, though they habitually are persuaded of their interest in Christ, and the love of God to them, are only at times thus filled with holy affections : nor will the same contemplations constantly excite similar exercises ; but they often bestow much pains to get their minds affected by them in vain ; while at other times a single glance of thought fills them with the most fervent emotions of holy love and joy.

Now I saw still in my dream, that hey
went on until they were come to the place
that Simple, and Sloth, and Presumption,
lay and slept in, when Christian went by on
pilgrimage ; and behold they were hanged*
up in irons a little way off on the other side.
Then said Mercy to him that was their guide
and conductor, What are these three men ?
and for what are they hanged there ?

Gr.-h. These three men were men of bad
qualities ; they had no mind to be pilgrims
themselves, and whomsoever they could they
hindered ; they were for sloth and folly themselves, and whomsoever they could persuade,
they made so too ; and withal taught them
to presume that they should do well at last.
They were asleep when Christian went by ;
and now you go by they are hanged.

Mer. But could they persuade one to be
of their opinion ?

Gr.-h. Yes, they turned several out of the

---

* 'Hanged'—The dreadful fall and awful deaths of some
professors are often made notorious, for a warning to others,
and to put them upon their guard against superficial, slothful,
and presumptuous men, who draw aside many from the holy
ways of God. The names of the persons thus deluded shew
the reasons why men listen to deceivers ; for these are only
the occasions of their turning aside, the cause lies in the
concealed lusts of their own hearts. The transition is very
easy from orthodox notions and profession without experience, to false and loose sentiments, and then to open ungodliness. These lines are here inserted under a plate :—

' Behold here how the slothful are a sign
Hung up 'cause holy ways they did decline :
See here too, how the child doth play the man,
And weak grows strong, when Great-heart leads the van.'

way. There was Slow-pace they persuaded to do as they. They also prevailed with one Short-wind, with one No-heart, with one Linger-after-lust, and with one Sleepy-head, and with a young woman, her name was Dull, to turn out of the way and become as they. Besides, they brought up an ill report of your Lord, persuading others that he was a hard taskmaster. They also brought up an evil report of the good land, saying it was not half so good as some pretended it was. They also began to villify his servants, and to count the best of them meddlesome, troublesome, busy-bodies : farther, they would call the bread of God, husks ; the comforts of his children, fancies ; the travail and labour of pilgrims, things to no purpose.

Nay, said Christiana, if they were such they should never be bewailed by me : they have but what they deserve ; and I think it well that they stand so near the highway, that others may see and take warning. But had it not been well if their crimes had been engraven on some pillar of iron or brass, and left here where they did their mischiefs, for a caution to other bad men ?

Gr.-h. So it is as you may well perceive, if you will go a little to the wall.

Mer. No, no ; let them hang, and their names rot, and their crimes live forever against them ; I think it is a high favour that they are hanged before we came hither ; who knows else what they might have done to such poor women as we are ? Then she turned it into a song, saying :—

Now then you three hang there, and be a sign
To all that shall against the truth combine,
And let him that comes after fear this end,
  f unto pilgrims he is not a friend.
And thou, my soul, of all such men beware,
That unto holiness opposers are.

Thus they went on, till they came at the
foot of the hill Difficulty, where again their
good friend, Mr. Great-heart, took an occasion to tell them what happened there when
Christian himself went by (P. i. p. 98, 100).
So he had them first to the spring : Lo, saith
he, this is the spring that Christian drank of
before he went up this hill ; and then it was
clear* and good, but now it is dirty with the
feet of some, that are not desirous that pilgrims here should quench their thirst (Ezek.
xxxiv. 18).   Thereat Mercy said, And why
so envious, trow ? But said the guide, it will
do, if taken up and put into a vessel that is
sweet and good ; for then the dirt will sink to
the bottom, and the water come out by itself
more clear.   Thus, therefore, Christiana and
her companions were compelled to do. They
took it up, and put into an earthen pot, and

* ' Clear'—This passage shows, that the preaching of the
Gospel was especially intended by the spring, in the former
part of the work. Since that had been published, the author had witnessed a departure from the simplicity of the
Gospel, as has been before observed (note. p. 26). This
might be done unadvisedly in those immediately concerned ;
but it originated from the devices of evil men, and the subtlety of Satan. Nevertheless they who honestly and carefully aimed to distinguish between the precious and the vile,
might separate the corrupt part from the truths of God, and
from the latter derive comfort and establishment.

so let it stand till the dirt was gone to the
bottom, and then they drank thereof.

Next he shewed them the two by-ways that
were at the foot of the hill, where Formality
and Hypocrisy lost themselves. And, said
he, there are dangerous paths : two were
here cast away when Christian came by.
And although you see these ways are since
stopped* up with chains, posts, and a ditch,
yet there are they that will choose to adventure here, rather than take the pains to go up
this hill.

Chr. 'The way of transgressors is hard'
(Prov. xiii. 15): it is a wonder that they can
get into those ways without danger of breaking their necks.

Gr.-h. They will venture ; yea, if at any
time any of the King's servants do happen to
see them, and doth call upon them, and tell
them that they are in the wrong ways, and do
bid them beware of the danger, then they rail-
ingly return them answer, and say, 'As for
the word that thou hast spoken unto us in the
name of the King, we will not hearken unto

---

* 'Stopped'—The express declarations, commandments,
and warnings of Scripture, and the heart-searching doctrine
and distinguishing application of faithful ministers, sufficiently hedge up all those by-ways, into which professors are
tempted to turn aside : but carnal self-love and desire of ease
to the flesh, which always opposes its own crucifixion, induce numbers to break through all obstacles, and to risk
their eternal interests rather than deny themselves and endure hardship in the way to heaven. Nor will teachers be
wanting to flatter them with the hope of being saved by notionally believing certain doctrines, while they practically
treat the whole word of God as a lie.

thee : but we will certainly do whatsoever
thing goeth out of our mouths' (Jer. xliv. 16,
17). Nay, if you look a little farther, you
shall see that these ways are made cautiona-
ry enough, not only by these posts, and ditch,
and chain, but also by being hedged up ; yet
they will choose to go there.

Chr. They are idle ; they love not to take
pains ; uphill way is unpleasant to them. So it
is fulfilled unto them as it is written, 'The
way of the slothful man is as a hedge of thorns'
(Prov. xv. 19). Yea, they will rather choose
to walk upon a snare, than to go up this hill,
and the rest of this way to the city.

Then they set forward, and began to go
up the hill, and up the hill they went ; but
before they got up to the top, Christiana began to pant, and said, I dare say this is a
breathing hill ; no marvel if they that love
their ease more than their souls choose to
themselves a smoother way. Then said Mercy, I must sit down ; also the least of the
children began to cry : Come, come, said
Great-heart, sit not down here, for a little
above is the Prince's arbour. Then he took
the little boy by the hand, and led him thereto.

When they were come to the arbour, they
were very willing to set down, for they were all
in a pelting heat. Then said Mercy, How
sweet is rest to them that labour (Matt. xi
28); and how good is the Prince of pilgrims,
to provide such resting-places for them ! Of
this arbour I have heard much ; but I never
saw it before. But here let us beware of

stopping : for, as I have heard, for that it cost poor Christian dear.

Then said Mr. Great-heart to the little ones, Come, my pretty boys, how do you do ? What think you now of going on pilgrimage ? Sir, said the least, I was almost beat out of heart ; but I thank you for leading me a hand at my need. And I remember now what my mother hath told me, namely, that the way to heaven is as a ladder, and the way to hell is as down a hill. But I had rather go up the ladder to life, than down the hill to death.

Then said Mercy, But the proverb is, ' To go down the hill is easy :' but James said (for that was his name), The day is coming when, in my opinion, going down the hill will be the hardest of all. 'Tis a good boy, said his master, thou hast given her a right answer. Then Mercy smiled, but the little boy did blush.

Come, said Christiana, will you eat a bit, to sweeten your mouths, while you sit here to rest your legs ? For I have here a piece of pomegranate, which Mr. Interpreter put into my hand just when I came out of his doors ; he gave me also a piece of an honey-comb, and a little bottle of spirits. I thought he gave you something, said Mercy, because he called you aside. Yes, so he did, said the other. But, said Christiana, it shall be still as I said it should, when at first we came from home ; thou shalt be a sharer in all the good that I have, because thou so willingly didst become my companion. Then she

gave to them, and they did eat, both Mercy
and the boys. And said Christiana to Mr
Great-heart, Sir, will you do as we? But he
answered, You are going on pilgrimage, and
presently I shall return: much good may
what you have do to you. At home I eat
the same every day. Now when they had
eaten and drunk, and had chatted a little
longer, their guide said to them, The day
wears away; if you think good, let us prepare to be going. So they got up to go, and
the little boys went before: but Christiana
forgot to take her bottle of spirits with her;
so she sent her little boy back to fetch it.
Then said Mercy, I think this is a losing
place. Here Christian lost his roll; and
here Christiana left her bottle behind her;
Sir, what is the cause of this? So their
guide made answer and said, The cause is
sleep or forgetfulness; some sleep when
they should keep awake; and some forget
when they should remember; and this is
the very cause, why often at the resting-
places some pilgrims in some things come off
losers. Pilgrims should watch, and remember what they have already received under
their greatest enjoyments; but for want of
doing so, oftentimes their rejoicing ends in
tears, and their sunshine in a cloud: witness
the story of Christian at this place.

When they were come to the place where
Mistrust and Timorous met Christian to persuade him to go back for fear of the lions,
they perceived as it were a stage, and before

7*

it, towards the road, a broad plate, with a copy of verses written thereon, and underneath, the reason of raising up of that stage in that place rendered, The verses were—

> Let him that sees that stage, take heed
> Upon his heart and tongue :
> Lest if he do not, here he speed
> As some have long agone.

The words underneath the verses were, This stage was built to punish such upon, who, through timorousness or mistrust, shall be afraid to go farther on pilgrimage : also on this stage both Mistrust and Timorous were burnt through the tongue with a hot iron, for endeavouring to hinder Christian on his journey.

Then said Mercy, This is much like to the saying of the Beloved,* ' What shall be given unto thee, or what shall be done unto thee, thou false tongue ? sharp arrows of the mighty, with coals of juniper' (Ps. cxx. 3, 4).

So they went on, till they came within sight of the lions (P. i. p. 106). Now Mr. Greatheart was a strong man, so he was not afraid of a lion : but yet when they were come up

---

* ' Beloved'—The word David signifies beloved. We should be very cautious, not to speak any thing, which may discourage such as seem disposed to a religious life ; lest we should be found to have abetted that enemy, who spares no pains to seduce them back again into the world. Even the unbelieving fears and complaints of weak and tempted Christians should be repressed before persons of this description : how great then will be the guilt of those who stifle their own convictions, and act contrary to their conscience, from fear of reproach or persecution, and then employ themselves in dissuading others from serving God !

to the place where the lions were, the boys
that went before were glad to cringe behind,
for they were afraid of the lions : so they
stept back and went behind.   At this their
guide smiled, and said, How now, my boys,
do you love to go before when no danger
doth approach, and love to come behind so
soon as the lions appear ?

Now as they went on, Mr. Great-heart
drew his sword, with intent to make a way
for the pilgrims in spite of the lions.   Then
there appeared one, that it seems had taken
upon him to back the lions : and he said to
the pilgrims' guide, what is the cause of
your coming hither ? Now the name of that
man was Grim* or Bloodyman, because of
his slaying of pilgrims ; and he was of the
race of the giants.

Then said the pilgrims' guide, These wo-

---

* 'Grim'—It is not very easy to determine the precise idea
of the author, in each of the giants, who assault the pilgrims,
and are slain by the conductor and his assistants.   Some
have supposed that unbelief is here meant ; but Grim, or
Bloodyman, seem not to be apposite names for this inward
foe ; nor can it be conceived, that unbelief should more violently assult those who were under the care of a valiant conductor, than it had done the solitary pilgrims.   I apprehend
therefore that this giant was intended for the emblem of certain active men, who busied themselves in framing and executing persecuting statutes ; which was done at this time
more violently than before.   Thus the temptation to fear
man, which at all times assaults the believer, when required
to make an open profession of his faith, was exceedingly increased : and, as heavy fines, and severe penalties, in ac-
cession to reproach and contempt, deterred men from joining
themselves in communion with dissenting churches, that way
was almost unoccupied, and the travellers went through by-
paths, according to the author's sentiments on that subject.

men and children are going on pilgrimage
and this is the way they must go, and go it
they shall, in spite of thee and the lions.

Grim. This is not their way, neither shall
they go therein. I am come forth to withstand them, and to that end will back the
lions.

Now, to say the truth, by reason of the
fierceness of the lions, and of the grim carriage of him that did back them, this way
had of late lain much unoccupied, and was
all grown over with grass.

Then said Christiana, Though the highways have been unoccupied heretofore, and
though the travellers have been made in
times past to walk through by-paths, it must
not be so now I am risen, 'Now I am risen a
mother in Israel' (Judg. v. 6, 7).

Then he swore by the lions but it should :
and therefore bid them turn aside, for they
should not have passage there. But their
guide made first his approach unto Grim, and
laid so heavily on him with his sword, that he
forced him to retreat.

But the preaching of the Gospel, by which the ministers of
Christ wielded the sword of the Spirit, overcame this enemy :
for the example and exhortations of such courageous comba-
tants animated even weak believers to overcome their fears,
and to act according to their consciences, leaving the event to
God. This seems to have been the author's meaning ; and
perhaps he also intended to encourage his brethren boldly to
persevere in resisting such persecuting statutes, in confidence of prevailing for the repeal of them ; by which, as by
the death of the giant, the pilgrims might be freed from additional terror, in acting consistently with their avowed prin
ciples.

Then said he that attempted to back the lions, Will you slay me upon mine own ground ?

Gr.-h. It is the king's highway that we are in, and in this way it is that thou hast placed the lions ; but these women and these children, though weak, shall hold on their way in spite of the lions. And with that he gave him again a downright blow, and brought him upon his knees. With this blow he also broke his helmet, and with the next cut off an arm. Then did the giant roar so hideously, that his voice frighted the women ; and yet they were glad to see him lie sprawling upon the ground. Now the lions were chained, and so of themselves could do nothing. Wherefore, when old Grim, that intended to back them, was dead, Great-heart said to the pilgrims, Come now and follow me, and no hurt shall happen to you from the lions They therefore went on, but the women trembled as they passed by them ; the boys also looked as if they would die, but they all got by without farther hurt.

Now, when they were within sight of the Porter's lodge, they soon came up unto it ; but they made the more haste after this to go thither, because it is dangerous travelling there in the night. So when they were come to the gate, the guide knocked, and the porter cried, Who is there ? But as soon as the guide had said, It is I, he knew his voice, and came down (for the guide had oft before that come thither as a conductor of pilgrims)

When he was come down, he opened the gate, and, seeing the guide standing just before it (for he saw not the women, for they were behind him), he said unto him, How now, Mr. Great-heart, what is your business here so late at night? I have brought, said he, some pilgrims hither, where, by my Lord's commandment, they must lodge: I had been here some time ago, had I not been opposed by the giant that used to back the lions. But I, after a long and tedious combat with him, have cut him off, and have brought the pilgrims hither in safety.

Por. Will not you go in, and stay till morning?

Gr.-h. No. I will return to my Lord to-night.

Chr. Oh, Sir, I know not how to be willing you should leave us in our pilgrimage, you have been so faithful and so loving to us, you have fought so stoutly for us, you have been so hearty in counselling of us, that I shall never forget your favour towards us.

Then said Mercy, O that we might have thy company to our journey's end! How can such poor women as we hold out in a way so full of troubles as this way is, without a friend or defender?

Then said James, the youngest of the boys, Pray, Sir, be persuaded to go with us and help us because we are so weak, and the way so dangerous as it is.

Gr.-h. I am at my Lord's commandment: if he shall allot me to be your guide quite

through, I will willingly wait upon you. But
here you failed* at first; for when he bid me
come thus far with you, then you should have
begged me of him to have gone quite through
with you, and he would have granted your
request. However, at present I must withdraw; and so, good Christiana, Mercy, and
my brave children, Adieu.

Then the porter, Mr. Watchful, asked
Christiana of her country, and of her kindred:
and she said, I came from the city of Destruction; I am a widow woman, and my husband
is dead: his name was Christian, the pilgrim.
How! said the porter, was he your husband?
Yes, said she; and these his children; and
this (pointing to Mercy) is one of my town's-
women. Then the porter rang his bell, as at
such time he is wont, and there came to the
door one of the damsels, whose name was
Humble-mind. And to her the porter said,
Go, tell it within, that Christiana, the wife of
Christian, and her children, are come hither
on pilgrimage. She went in, therefore, and told
it. But, oh, what noise for gladness was therein, when the damsel did but drop that out of
her mouth!

---

* 'Failed'—We are repeatedly reminded, with great propriety, that we ought to be very particular and explicit in all
our prayers; especially in every thing pertaining to our spiritual advantage. The removal of faithful ministers, or the fear
of losing them, may often remind Christians that ' here they
have failed:' they have not sufficiently valued and prayed for
them; or, making sure of their continuance from apparent
probabilities, they have not made that the subject of their
peculiar requests, and therefore are rebuked by the loss of
them.

So they came with haste to the porter, for Christiana stood still at the door. Then some of the most grave said unto her, Come in, Christiana, come in, thou wife of that good man, come in, thou blessed woman, come in, with all that are with thee. So she went in, and they followed her that were her children and her companions. Now when they were gone in, they were had into a large room, and bid to sit down: so they sat down, and the chief of the house were called to see and welcome* the guest. Then they came in, and, understanding who they were, did salute each other with a kiss, and said, Welcome, ye vessels of

---

* 'Welcome'—'Angels rejoice over one sinner that repenteth :' and all, who truly love the Lord, will gladly welcome such as appear to be true believers into their most endeared fellowship : yet there are certain individuals, who, being related to those that have greatly interested their hearts, or having long been remembered in their prayers, are welcomed with singular joy and satisfaction, and whose profession of faith ⸺ᵐates them in a peculiar manner. The passover was a pᵣₑᵣiguration of the sufferings of Christ, and the believer's acceptance of him ; of his professed reliance on the atoning sacrifice, preservation from wrath, and deliverance from the bondage of Satan, to set out on his heavenly pilgrimage ; and the Lord's supper is a commemorative ordinance of a similar import ; representing the body of Christ broken for our sins, and his blood shed for us ; our application of these blessings to our souls by faith, our profession of this faith, and of love to him and his people, influencing us to devoted, self-denying obedience : and the effects which follow from thus ' feeding on Christ in our hearts by faith with thanksgiving,' in strengthening us for every conflict and service to which we are called. 'The unleavened bread of sincerity and truth,' and ' the bitter herbs' of godly sorrow, deep repentance, mortification of sin, and bearing the cross, accompany the spiritual feast ; and even render it more relishing to the true believer, as endearing to him Christ and his salvation

the grace of God, welcome unto us who are
your faithful friends.

Now, because it was somewhat late, and
because the pilgrims were weary with their
journey, and also made faint with the sight of
the fight, and the terrible lions, they desired as
soon as might be, to prepare to go to rest.
Nay, said those of the family, refresh yourselves with a morsel of meat : for they had
prepared for them a lamb, with the accustomed sauce thereto (Exod. xii. 3). For the porter had heard before of their coming, and had
told it to them within. So when they had
supped, and ended their prayer with a psalm,
they desired they might go to rest. But let
us, said Christiana, if we may be so bold as
to choose, be in that chamber* that was my
husband's when he was here. So they had
them up thither, and they all lay in a room
(John i. 29). When they were at rest Christiana and Mercy entered into discourse about
things that were convenient.

Chr. Little did I think once, when my husband went on pilgrimage, that I should ever
have followed him.

Mer. And you as little thought of lying in
his bed, and his chamber to rest, as you do
now.

Chr. And much less did I ever think of

* ' Chamber'—A marginal note here says, ' Christ's bosom is for all pilgrims.' The sweet peace arising from calm
confidence in the Saviour, the consolations of his Spirit, submission to his will, and the cheerful obedience of fervent love,
give rest to the soul, as if we were reclining on his bosom
with the beloved disciple P. i. p. 119).

seeing his face with comfort, and of worship-ing the Lord the King with him ; and yet now I believe I shall !

Mer. Hark, don't you hear a noise ?

Chr. Yes, 'tis, as I believe, a noise of mu sic, for joy that we are here.

Mer. Wonderful! Music in the house, music in the heart, and music also in heaven, for joy that we are here !

Thus they talked awhile, and then betook themselves to sleep. So in the morning, when they were awaked, Christiana said to Mer-cy, What was the matter that you did laugh in your sleep to-night ? I suppose you was in a dream.

Mer. So I was, and a sweet dream it was ; but are you sure I laughed ?

Chr. Yes ; you laughed heartily ; but pray thee, Mercy, tell me thy dream.

Mer. I was dreaming that I sat all alone in a solitary place, and was bemoaning of the hardness of my heart. Now I had not sat there long, but methought many were gather-ed about me to see me, and to hear what it was that I said. So they hearkened, and I went on bemoaning the hardness of my heart. At this some of them laughed at me, some called me fool, and some began to thrust me about. With that, methought I looked up, and saw one coming with wings towards me So he came directly to me, and said, Mercy what aileth thee ? Now when he had heard me make my complaint, he said, Peace be to thee ; he also wiped mine eyes with his hand.

kerchief, and clad me in silver and gold. He put a chain upon my neck, and ear-rings in mine ears, and a beautiful crown upon my head (Ezek. xvi. 8—13). Then he took me by the hand, and said, Mercy, come after me. So he went up, and I followed, till we came at a golden gate. Then he knocked ; and, when they within had opened, the man went in, and I followed him up to a throne, upon which one sat, and he said to me, Welcome, daughter. The place looked bright and twinkling, like the stars, or rather like the sun, and I thought that I saw your husband there. So I awoke from my dream. But did I laugh ?

Chr. Laugh ! ay, and well you might, to see yourself so well. For you must give me leave to tell you, that it was a good dream ; and that as you* have begun to find the first part true, so you shall find the second at last. ' God speaks once, yea twice, yet man perceiveth it not ; in a dream, in a vision of the night, when deep sleep falleth upon men, in slumbering upon the bed' (Job xxxiii. 14 —16). We need not, when a-bed, to lie awake to talk with God ; he can visit us while we sleep, and cause us then to hear

---

* ' As you'—They who feel and lament the hardness of their hearts, and earnestly pray that they may be humbled, softened, and filled with the love of Christ, may be assured that their sorrow shall be turned into joy : though they must expect to be ridiculed by such as know not their own hearts. The assurance, that the dream should be accomplished, is grounded on the effects produced upon Mercy's heart ; and there is no danger of delusion, when so scriptural an encouragement is inferred even from a dream.

his voice. Our heart oft-times wakes when we sleep; and God can speak to that, either by words, by proverbs, by signs and similitudes, as well as if one was awake.

Mer. Well, I am glad of my dream, for I hope ere long to see it fulfilled, to the making me laugh again.

Chr. I think it is now high time to rise, and to know what we must do.

Mer. Pray, if they advise us to stay awhile, let us willingly accept of the proffer. I am the willinger to stay awhile here, to grow better acquainted with these maids; methinks Prudence, Piety, and Charity have very comely and sober countenances.

Chr. We shall see what they will do So when they were up and ready, they came down, and they asked one another of their rest, and if it was comfortable or not.

Very good, said Mercy; it was one of the best night's lodgings that ever I had in my life.

Then said Prudence and Piety, if you will be persuaded to stay here awhile, you shall have what the house will afford.

Ay, and that with a very good will, said Charity. So they consented, and staid there about a month or above, and became very profitable one to another. And, because Prudence would see how Christiana had brought up her children, she asked leave of her to catechise them; so she gave her free consent. Then she began with the youngest whose name was James. And she said

Come James, canst thou tell me who made thee ?

Jam. God the Father, God the Son, and God the Holy Ghost.

Prud. Good boy. And canst thou tell who saved thee ?

Jam. God the Father, God the Son, and God the Holy Ghost.

Prud. Good boy still. But how doth God the Father save thee ?

Jam. By his grace.*

Prud. How doth God the Son save thee ?

Jam. By his righteousness, and blood, and death, and life.

Prud. And how doth God the Holy Ghost save thee ?

Jam. By his illumination, by his renovation, and by his preservation.

Then said Prudence to Christiana, You are to be commended for thus bringing up your children. I suppose I need not ask the rest these questions, since the youngest of them can answer them so well. I will therefore now apply myself to the next youngest

---

* ' Grace'—Grace, in this connexion, signifies unmerited mercy or favour, from which all the blessings of salvation flow ; while the Father freely gave his Son to be our redeemer, and freely communicates his Spirit, through the merits and mediation of the Son, to be our Sanctifier ; and thus, with Christ, freely gives all things to those, who are enabled truly to believe in him. The important, but much neglected, duty of catechising children is here very properly inculcated ; without attention to which, the minister's labours, both in public preaching and private instruction, will be understood in a very imperfect degree ; and any revival of religion that takes place, will probably die with the generation to which it is vouchsafed.

8*

Then she said, Come Joseph (for his name was Joseph), will you let me catechise you?

Jos. With all my heart.

Prud. What is man?

Jos. A reasonable creature, made so by God, as my brother said.

Prud. What is supposed by this word, saved?

Jos. That man by sin has brought himself into a state of captivity and misery.

Prud. What is supposed by his being saved by the Trinity?

Jos. That sin is so great and mighty a tyrant, that none can pull us out of its clutches, but God; and that God is so good and loving to man, as to pull him indeed out of this miserable state.

Prud. What is God's design in saving poor man?

Jos. The glorifying of his name, of his grace, and justice, &c. and the everlasting happiness of his creature.

Prud. Who are they that must be saved?

Jos. Those that accept* of his salvation.

* 'Accept'—The young pupil is not here taught to answer systematically, 'all the elect;' but practically, 'those that accept of his salvation;' this is perfectly consistent with the other; but it is suited to instruct and encourage the learner, who would be perplexed, stumble, or misled by the other view of the same truth. Thus our Lord observed to his disciples, 'I have many things to say unto you, but ye cannot bear them now;' and Paul fed the Corinthians 'with milk, and not with meat; for they were not able to bear it.' How beneficial would a portion of the same heavenly wisdom prove to the modern friends evangelical truth; How absurd is it to teach the hardest lessons to the youngest scholars in the school of Christ!

Prud. Good boy, Joseph; thy mother hath taught thee well, and thou hast hearkened to what she has said unto thee.

Then said Prudence to Samuel (who was the eldest son but one), Come, Samuel, are you willing that I should catechise you also ?

Sam. Yes, forsooth, if you please.

Prud. What is heaven ?

Sam. A place and state most blessed, because God dwelleth there.

Prud. What is hell ?

Sam. A place and state most woeful, because it is the dwelling place of sin, the devil, and death.

Prud. Why wouldest thou go to heaven ?

Sam. That I may see God, and serve without weariness; that I may see Christ, and love him everlastingly ; that I may have that fulness of the Holy Spirit in me, that I can by no means here enjoy.

Prud. A very good boy, and one that has learned well. Then she addressed herself to the eldest, whose name was Matthew ; and she said to him, Come, Matthew, shall I also catechise you ?

Mat. With a very good will.

Prud. I ask, then, if there was ever any thing that had a being antecedent to, or before, God ?

Mat. No ; for God is eternal ; nor is there any thing, excepting himself, that had a being until the beginning of the first day : 'For in six days the Lord made heaven and earth, the sea, and all that in them is.'

Prud. What do you think of the Bible ?

Mat It is the holy word of God.

Prud. Is there nothing written therein but what you understand ?

Mat. Yes, a great deal.

Prud. What do you do when you meet with places therein, that you do not understand ?

Mat. I think God is wiser* than I. I pray also that he will please to let me know all therein that he knows will be for my good.

Prud. How believe you as touching the resurrection of the dead ?

Mat. I believe they shall rise, the same that was buried ; the same in nature, though not in corruption. And I believe this upon a double account : First, Because God has promised it : Seeondly, Because he is able to perform it.

Then said Prudence to the boys, You must still hearken to your mother, for she can learn you more. You must also diligently give ear to what good talk you shall hear from others ; for your sakes do they speak

* ' Wiser'—We ought not to think ourselves capable of comprehending all the mysteries of revelation, or informed of all that can be known concerning them : yet we should not make our incapacity a reason for neglecting those parts of Scripture, which we do not at present understand ; but, uniting humble diligence with fervent prayer, we should wait for farther light and knowledge, in all things conducive to our good. There may be many parts of Scripture, which would not be useful to us, if we could understand them ; though they have been, are, or will be useful to others : and our inability to discover the meaning of these passages may teach us humility, and submission to the decisions of our infallible instructor.

good things. Observe also, and that with carefulness, what the heavens and the earth do teach you : but especially be much in the meditation of that book, that was the cause of your father's becoming a pilgrim. I, for my part, my children, will teach you what I can while you are here, and shall be glad if you will ask me questions that tend to godly edifying.

Now by that these pilgrims had been at this place a week, Mercy had a visitor,* that pretended some good will unto her, and his name was Mr. Brisk, a man of some breeding, and that pretended to religion ; but a man that stuck very close to the world. So he came once or twice, or more, to Mercy, and offered love unto her. Now Mercy was of fair countenance, and therefore the more alluring. Her mind also was, to be always busying of herself in doing ; for when she had nothing to do for herself, she would be making of hose and garments for others, and

* ' A visitor'---Designing men will often assume an appearance of religion, in order to insinuate themselves into the affections of such pious young women, as are on some accounts agreeable to them : and thus many are drawn into a most dangerous snare. This incident, therefore, is very properly introduced, and is replete with instruction. At the same time an important intimation is given, concerning the manner, in which those, who are not taken up with the care of a family, may profitably employ their time, adorn the Gospel, and be useful in the church and the community. It is much better to imitate Dorcas, who through faith obtained a good report, in making garments for the poor, than to waste time and money in frivolous amusements, or needless decorations ; or even in the more elegant and fashionable accomplishments.

would bestow them upon them that had need. And Mr. Brisk, not knowing where or how she disposed of what she made, seemed to be greatly taken, for that he found her never idle. I will warrant her a good housewife, quoth he to himself.

Mercy then revealed* the business to the maidens that were of the house, and inquired of them concerning him, for they did know him better than she. So they told her, that he was a very busy young man, and one that pretended to religion ; but was, as they feared, a stranger to the power of that which is good.

* ' Revealed'---Young people ought not wholly to follow their own judgment in this most important concern, on which the comfort and usefulness of their whole future lives in a great measure depend : and yet it is equally dangerous to advise with impoper counsellors. The names of the maidens shew what kind of persons should be consulted : and, when such friends are of opinion that there is danger of a clog instead of a helper in the way to heaven, all who love their own souls will speedily determine to reject the proposal, however agreeable in all other respects. The apostolical rule, ' only in the Lord,' is absolute ; the most upright and cautions may indeed be deceived ; but they, who neglect to ask, or refuse to take, counsel, will be sure to smart for their folly, if they be indeed the children of God. An unbelieving partner must be a continual source of anxiety and uneasiness, a thorn in the side ; and an hinderance to all family religion, and the pious education of children, who generally adhere to the maxims and practices of the ungodly party. Nothing tends more, than such marriages, to induce a declining state of religion ; or indeed more plainly shews that it is already in a very unprosperous state. But, when Christians plainly avow their principles, purposes, and rules of conduct, they may commonly detect and shake off such selfish pretenders : while the attempts made to injure their character will do them no material detriment, and will render them the more thankful for having escaped the snare.

Nay then, said Mercy, I will look no more on him; for I purpose never to have a clog to my soul.

Prudence then replied, that there needed no great matter of discouragement to be given to him; for continuing so, as she had begun, to do for the poor, would quickly cool his courage.

So the next time he comes he finds her at her old work, a making of things for the poor. Then said he, What, always at it? Yes, said she, either for myself or for others. And what canst thou earn a day? quoth he. I do these things, said she, that I may be rich in good works, laying a good foundation against the time to come, that I may lay hold of eternal life (1 Tim. vi. 17—19). Why pry'thee, what dost thou do with them? said he. Clothe the naked, said she. With that his countenance fell. So he forbore to come at her again. And when he was asked the reason why, he said, that Mercy was a pretty lass, but troubled with ill conditions.

When he had left her, Prudence said, Did I not tell thee, that Mr. Brisk would soon forsake thee? yea, he will raise up an ill report of thee: for, notwithstanding his pretence to religion, and his seeming love to mercy, yet mercy and he are of tempers so different, that I believe they will never come together.

Mer. I might have had husbands before now, though I spoke not of it to any; but they were such as did not like my conditions, though never did any of them find fault with my person. So they and I could not agree.

Prud. Mercy in our days is little set by, any farther than as to its name : the practice, which is set forth by the conditions, there are but few that can abide.

Well, said Mercy, if nobody will have me I will die a maid, or my conditions shall be to me as a husband : for I cannot change my nature ; and to have one that lies cross to me in this, that I purpose never to admit of as long as I live. I had a sister, named Bountiful, married to one of these churls : but he and she could never agree ; but, because my sister was resolved to do as she had begun, that is, to shew kindness to the poor, therefore her husband first cried her down at the cross, and then turned her out of his doors.

Prud And yet he was a professor, I warrant you !

Mer. Yes, such a one as he was, and of such as the world is now full : but I am for none of them all.

Now Matthew, the eldest son of Christiana, fell sick,* and his sickness was sore upon him,

---

* 'Fell sick'—Sin, heedlessly or wilfully committed, after the Lord has spoken peace to our souls, often produces great distress long afterwards, and sometimes darkness and discouragement oppress the mind, when the special cause of them is not immediately recollected : for we have grieved the Holy Spirit and he withholds his consolations. In this case we should adopt the prayer of Job, ' Do not condemn me ; shew me wherefore thou contendest with me :' and this inquiry will often be answered by the discourse of skilful ministers, and the faithful admonitions of our fellow Christians. When hopeful professors are greatly cast down, it is not wise

for he was much pained in his bowels, so that
he was with it, at times, pulled, as it were,
both ends together. There dwelt also not
far from thence, one Mr. Skill, an ancient and
well-approved physician. So Christiana desired it, and they sent for him, and he came :
when he was entered the room, and had a
little observed the boy, he concluded that he
was sick of the gripes. Then he said to his
mother, What diet has Matthew of late fed
upon ? Diet ! said Christiana, nothing but
what is wholesome. The physician answered, This boy has been tampering with something that lies in his maw undigested, and
that will not away without means. And I
tell you he must be purged or else he will
die.

Then said Samuel, Mother, what was that
which my brother did gather and eat, so soon
as we were come from the gate that is at the
head of this way ? You know, that there was
an orchard on the left hand, on the other
side of the wall, and some of the trees hung
over the wall, and my brother did pluck and
did eat.

True, my child, said Christiana, he did
take thereof, and did eat ; naughty boy as

to administer cordials to them immediately : but to propose
such questions, as may lead to discovery of the concealed
cause of their distress. Thus it will often be found, that they
have been tampering with forbidden fruit ; which discovery
may tend to their humiliation, and produce a like effect on
those who have neglected their duty, by suffering them to go
on without warning or reproof.

he was, I chid him, and yet he would eat thereof.

Skill. I knew he had eaten something that was not wholesome food; and that food, to wit, that fruit, is even the most hurtful of all. It is the fruit of Beelzebub's orchard. I do marvel that none did warn you of it; many have died thereof.

Then Christiana began to cry; and she said, O naughty boy! and O careless mother! what shall I do for ny son?

Skill. Come, do not be too dejected; the boy may do well again, but he must purge and vomit.

Chr. Pray, Sir, try the utmost of your skill with him, whatever it costs.

Skill. Nay, I hope I shall be reasonable. So he made him a purge, but it was too weak; it was said, it was made of the blood of a goat, the ashes of a heifer, and with some of the juice of hyssop, &c. (Heb. ix. 13--19; x. 1 --4). When Mr. Skill had seen that that purge was too weak, he made him one to the purpose; it was made 'Ex Carne* et San-

* 'Ex carne'—To support the allegory, the author gives the physician's prescription in Latin; but he adds, in the margin, with admirable modesty, 'The Latin I borrow.' Without the shedding of blood, there is no remission of sins,' or true peace of conscience; 'the blood of bulls and goats cannot take away sin:' nothing, therefore, can bring health and cure, in this case, but the 'body and blood of Christ,' as broken and shed for our sins. These blessings are made ours by faith exercised on the promises of God; sanctifying grace of the Holy Spirit, which seasons our words and actions as with salt, always connects with living faith; and godly sorrow, working genuine repentance, is renewed every time we look to the Saviour, whom we have pierced by our recent

guine Christi' (John vi. 54—57 ; Heb. ix. 14 :
—you know, physicians give strange medi-
cines to their patients), and it was made up
into pills, with a promise or two, and a proportionable quantity of salt (Mark ix. 49).
Now he was to take them three at a time, fasting, in half a quarter of a pint of the tears of repentance (Zech. xii. 10). When this potion was
prepared, and brought to the boy, he was loath
to take it, though torn with the gripes, as if
he should be pulled in pieces. Come, come,
said the physician, you must take it. It goes
against my stomach, said the boy. I must
have you take it, said his mother. I shall
vomit it up again, said the boy. Pray, Sir,
said Christiana to Mr. Skill, how does it taste ?
It has no ill taste, said the doctor ; and with
that she touched one of the pills with the tip
of her tongue. Oh, Matthew, said she, this
potion is sweeter than honey. If thou lovest
thy mother, if thou lovest thy brothers, if thou
lovest Mercy, if thou lovest thy life, take it.
So with much ado, after a short prayer for the
blessing of God upon it, he took it, and it
wrought kindly with him. It caused him to
purge, to sleep, and to rest quietly ; it put him
into a fine heat and breathing sweat, and rid
him of his gripes.

offences, and of whom we again seek forgiveness. The natural pride, stoutness, and unbelief of our hearts, render us
very reluctant to this humiliating method of recovering
our peace and spiritual strength ; and this often prolongs
our distress ; yet nothing yields more unalloyed comfort,
than thus abasing ourselves before God, and relying on his
mercy through the atonement and mediation of his beloved
Son.

So in a little time he got up, and walked about with a staff, and would go from room to room, and talk with Prudence, Piety, and Charity, of his distemper, and how he was healed.

So when the boy was healed, Christiana asked Mr. Skill, saying, Sir, what will content you for your pains and care to me and of my child ? And he said, You must pay the master of the college of physicians, according to rules made in that case and provided (Heb, xiii. 11 —15).

But, Sir, said she, what is this pill good for else ?

Skill. It is a universal pill ; it is good against all diseases that pilgrims are incident to ; and, when it is well prepared, will keep good time out of mind.

Chr. Pray, Sir, make me up twelve boxes of them ; for, if I can get these, I will never take other physic.

Skill. The pills are good to prevent diseases, as well as to cure when one is sick. Yea I dare say it, and stand to it, that if a man will but use this physic as he should, it will make him live for ever (John vi. 58). But good Christiana, thou must give these pills no other way* but as I have prescribed ; for

---

* 'No other way'—This hint should be carefully noted. Numbers abuse the doctrine of free salvation, by the merits and redemption of Christ, and presume on forgiveness, when they are destitute of genuine repentance, and give no evidence of sanctification. But this most efficacious medicine in that case will ' do no good ;' or rather the perverse abuse of it will increase their guilt, and tend to harden their hearts in sin.

if you do, they will do no good. So he gave unto Christiana physic for herself, and her boys, and for Mercy ; and bid Matthew take heed how he eat any more green plums ; and kissed him and went his way.

It was told you before, that Prudence bid the boys, that, if at any time they would, they should ask her some questions that might be profitable, and she would say something to them.

Then Matthew, who had been sick, asked her, Why, for the most part, physic should be bitter to our palates ?

Prud. To shew how unwelcome the word of God, and the effects thereof, are to a carnal heart.

Mat. Why does physic, if it does good, purge, and cause to vomit ?

Prud. To shew, that the word, when it works effectually, cleanseth the heart and mind For, look, what the one doeth to the body, the other doeth to the soul.

Mat. What should we learn by seeing the flame of our fire go upwards ? and by seeing the beams and sweet influences of the sun strike downwards ?

Prud. By the going up of the fire we are taught to ascend to heaven, by fervant and hot desires. And by the sun his sending his heat, beams, and sweet influences downwards, we are taught that the Saviour of the world, though high, reaches down with his grace and love to us below.

Mat. Where have the clouds their water ?

Prud. Out of the sea.

Mat. What may we learn from that ?

Prud. That ministers should fetch their doctrine from God.

Mat. Why do they empty themselves on the earth ?

Prud. To shew that ministers should give out what they know of God to the world.

Mat. Why is the rainbow caused by the sun ?

Prud. To shew that the covenant of God's grace is confirmed to us in Christ.

Mat. Why do the springs come from the sea to us through the earth ?

Prud. To shew, that the grace of God comes to us through the body of Christ.

Mat. Why do some of the springs rise out of the top of high hills ?

Prud. To shew, that the Spirit of grace shall spring up in some that are great and mighty, as well as in many that are poor and ow

Mat. Why doth the fire fasten upon the candlewick ?

Prud. To shew, that, unless grace doth kindle upon the heart, there will be no true light of life in us.

Mat. Why is the wick, and tallow, and all, spent to maintain the light of the candle ?

Prud. To shew, that body and soul, and all, should be at the service of, and spend themselves to maintain in good condition, that grace of God that is in us.

Mat. Why doth the pelican pierce her own breast with her bill ?

Prud. To nourish her young ones with her blood, and thereby to shew that Christ the blessed so loveth his young, his people, as to save them from death by his blood.

Mat. What may one learn by hearing of the cock crow ?

Prud. Learn to remember Peter's sin and Peter's repentance. The cock's crowing shews also, that day is coming on ; let then the crowing of the cock put thee in mind of that last and terrible day of judgment.

Now about this time their month was out ; wherefore they signified to those of the house, that it was convenient for them to up and be going. Then said Joseph to his mother, It is convenient that you forget not to send to the house of Mr. Interpreter, to pray him to grant that Mr. Great-heart should be sent unto us, that he may be our conductor the rest of our way. Good boy, said she, I had almost forgot. So she drew up a petition,* and prayed Mr. Watchful, the porter, to it send by some fit man, to her good friend Mr. Interpreter ; who, when it was come, and he had seen the contents of the petition, said to the messenger, Go tell them that I will send him.

---

* ' Petition'—This may be applied to the case of persons who are unavoidably removed from those places, where they first made an open profession of the faith. The vigilant pastor, who can no longer watch for their souls, will earnestly recommend them to the care of some other minister, and join with them in prayer, that the same faithful services, or better, may be rendered them by some other servant of their common Lord.

When the family, where Christiana was, saw that they had a purpose to go forward, they called the whole house together, to give thanks to their King, for sending of them such profitable guests as these. Which done, they said unto Christiana, And shall we not shew thee something according as our custom is to do to pilgrims, on which thou mayest meditate when thou art on the way ? So they took Christiana, her children, and Mercy, into the closet, and shewed them one of the apples that Eve ate of, and that she also did give to her husband, and that for the eating of which they were both turned out of Paradise ; and asked her, What she thought that was ? Then Christiana said, It is food or poison, I know not which. So they opened* the matter to her, and she held up her hands and wondered (Gen. iii. 1—6 ; Rom. vii. 24).

Then they had her to a place, and shewed her Jacob's ladder †   Now at that time there

---

* ' Opened'—The nature of the first transgression, the ambiguous insinuations by which the tempter seduced Eve, and by her Adam ; the motives from which they ate the forbidden fruit ; and the dreadful disappointment that followed ; with all the aggravations and consequences of that most prolific offence, which contained in it, as in miniature and embryo, all future sins ; are very instructive to the pious mind. For the enemy still proceeds against us according to the same general plan ; suggesting hard thoughts of God, doubts about the restrictions and threatenings of his word, proud desires of independence or useless knowledge, hankerings after forbidden indulgence, and hopes of enjoying the pleasures of sin, without feeling the punishment denounced against transgressors.

† ' Ladder'—Christ, in his person and offices, is the medium of communication between heaven and earth, between

were some angels ascending upon it. So
Christiana looked and looked to see the angels go up ; so did the rest of the company
(Gen. xxviii. 12). Then they were going into another place, to shew them something
else ; but James said to his mother. Pray
bid them stay a little longer, for this is a curious sight. So they turned again, and stood
feeding their eyes on this so pleasant a prospect. After this, they had them into a place,
where there did hang up a golden anchor, so
they bid Christiana take it down ; for, said
they, you shall have it with you, for it is of
absolute necessity that you should, that you
may lay hold of that within the veil, and
stand steadfast in case you should meet with
turbulent weather : So they were glad thereof
(Joel iii. 16 ; Heb. vi. 19). Then they took
them, and had them to the mount upon which
Abraham our father had offered up Isaac his
son, and shewed them the altar, the wood,

God and man ; by him sinners come to God with acceptance,
and God dwells with them and is glorified ; through him they
present their worship and services, and receive supplies of all
heavenly blessings ; and for his sake angels delight in ' min
istering to the heirs of salvation,' as instruments of his providential care over them and all their concerns. This was
represented or typified by Jacob's ladder. The hope of glory,
or of the fulfilment of all God's promises to our souls, is the
golden or precious anchor, by which we must be kept steadfast in the faith, and encouraged to abide in our proper station, amidst the storms of temptation, affliction, and persecution. This it will certainly effect ; provided it be genuine
and living, grounded on the word of God, springing from faith
in his Son, warranted by the experience of his grace, accompanied by prevailing desires of a holy felicity, in the presence,
favour, and service of the Lord.

the fire, and the knife ; for they remain to be seen to this very day. When they had seen it, they held up their hands, and blessed themselves, and said, Oh what a man for love to his Master, and for denial to himself, was Abraham ! After they had shewed them all these things, Prudence took them into a dining-room, where stood a pair of excellent virginals ; so she played upon them, and turned what she had shewed them into this excellent song, saying,

> Eve's apple we have shewed you ;
>   Of that be you aware ;
> You have seen Jacob's ladder too,
>   Upon which angels are ;
> An anchor you received have ;
>   But let not this suffice,
> Until with Abraham you have gave
>   Your best of sacrifice.

Now about this time one knocked at the door ; so the porter, opened, and, behold, Mr. Great-heart was there ! But when he was come in, what joy was there ! for it came now fresh again into their minds, how but awhile ago he had slain old Grim Bloody-man the giant, and had delivered them from the lions.

Then said Mr. Great-heart, to Christiana and to Mercy, My Lord has sent each of you a bottle of wine, and also some parched corn, together with a couple of pomegranates ; he also sent the boys some figs and raisins, to refresh you in your way.

Then they addressed themselves to their journey ; and Prudence and Piety went

along with them. When they came at the
gate, Christiana asked the porter, if any of
late went by. He said, No, only one, some
time since, who also told me, that of late
there had been a great robbery committed on
the King's high-way, as you go; but, said
he, the thieves are taken, and will shortly be
tried for their lives. Then Christiana and
Mercy were afraid; but Matthew said, Mother, fear nothing, as long as Mr. Great-heart
is to go with us, and to be our conductor.

Then said Christiana to the porter, Sir, I
am much obliged to you for all the kindness
that you have shewed to me since I came
hither; and also that you have been so loving and kind to my children; I know not how
to gratify your kindness; wherefore, pray,
as a token of my respects to you, accept of
this small mite; so she put a gold angel in
his hand; and he made her a low obeisance,
and said, Let thy garments be always white,
and let thy head want no ointment. Let
Mercy live and not die, and let not her works
be few. And to the boys he said, Do you flee
youthful lusts, and follow after godliness with
them that are grave and wise; so shall you
put gladness in your mother's heart, and obtain praise of all that are sober-minded. So
they thanked the porter, and departed.

Now I saw in my dream, that they went
forward until they were come to the brow of
the hill, where Piety bethinking herself, cried
out, Alas! I have forgot what I intended to
bestow upon Christiana and her companions;

I will go back and fetch it. So she ran and fetched it. When she was gone, Christiana thought she heard in a grove, a little way off on the right hand, a most curious melodious note, with words much like these :—

'Through all my life thy favour is
    So frankly shew'd to me,
That in thy house for evermore
    My dwelling-place shall be.'

And listening still she thought she heard another answer it, saying,

'For why ? The Lord our God is good,
    His mercy is for ever sure ;
His truth at all times firmly stood,
    And shall from age to age endure.'

So Christiana asked Prudence what it was that made those curious notes. They are, said she, our country birds ; they sing these notes but seldom, except it be at the spring, when the flowers appear, and the sun shines warm, and then you may hear them all the day long. I often, said she, go to hear them ; we also oft-times keep them tame in our house. They are very fine company for us when we are melancholy ; also they make the woods and groves, and solitary places, places desirous to be in (Sol. Song ii. 11, 12).

By this time Piety was come again ; so she said to Christiana, Look here, I have brought thee a scheme of all those things that thou hast seen at our house, upon which thou may-est look when thou findest theyself forgetful,

and call those things again to remembrance,
for thy edification and comfort.

Now they began to go down the hill to the
valley of Humiliation. It was a steep hill,
and the way was slippery ; but they were ve
ry careful ; so they got down pretty well.
When they were down in the valley, Piety
said to Christiana, This is the place where
your husband met with the foul fiend Apollyon, and where they had the great fight that
they had ; I know you cannot but have heard
thereof. But be of good courage, as long
as you have here Mr. Great-heart to be
your guide and conductor, we hope you will
fare the better. So when these two had committed the pilgrims unto the conduct of their
guide, he went forward, and they went after.

Then said Mr. Great-heart, We need not
be so afraid of this valley, for here is nothing
to hurt us, unless we procure it ourselves. It
is true, Christian did here meet with Apollyon, with whom he had also a sore combat ;
but that fray was the fruit of those slips*

* ' Slips'—As the author here alluded to some particulars
n his own experience, a more explicit account of these slips
would have been very interesting and instructive ; but as it
is, we can only conjecture his meaning. He probably alluded to some erroneous conclusions, which he had formed, concerning the measure of the Lord's dealings with his people,
and the nature of their situation in this world. Having
therefore obtained peace and comfort, and enjoyed sweet satisfaction in communion with his brethren, he expected the
continuance of this happy frame, and considered it as the evidence of his acceptance ; so that afflictions and humiliating
discoveries of the evils of his heart, by interrupting his comforts, induced him to conclude that his past experience was a
delusion, and that God was become his enemy : and this un

that he got in his going down the hill; for they that get slips there, must look for combats here (P. i. p. 140—143). And hence it is that this valley has got so hard a name. For the common people, when they hear that some frightful thing has befallen such a one, in such a place, are of opinion that that place is haunted with some foul fiend, or evil spirit; when, alas! it is for the fruit of their doing, that such things do befal them there.

This valley of Humiliation is of itself as fruitful a place as any the crow flies over; and I am persuaded, if we could hit upon it, we might find somewhere here-about something that might give us an account, why Christian was so hardly beset in this place.

Then James said to his mother, Lo, yonder stands a pillar, and it looks as if something was written thereon? let us go and see what it is. So they went, and found there written, Let Christian's slips, before he came hither,

scriptural way of judging concerning his state seems to have made way for the dark temptations that followed. Were it not for such mistakes, humiliating dispensations and experiences would not have any necessary connexion with terror; and they would give less occasion to temptations than prosperity and comfort do; while a lowly condition is exempted from the numberless snares, incumbrances, and anxieties of a more exalted station; and humility is the parent of patience, meekness, and contentment, thankfulness, and every holy disposition that can enrich and adorn the soul. A far greater proportion of believers are found in inferior circumstances, than among the wealthy; and they who are kept low commonly thrive the best, and are most simple and diligent. Without poverty of spirit we cannot possess ' the unsearchable riches of Christ;' and more promises are made to the humble, than to any other character whatsoever.

and the burthen that he met with in this place, be a warning to those that come after. Lo, said their guide, did I not tell you that there was something hereabouts that would give intimation of the reason why Christian was so hard beset in this place. Then, turning to Christiana, he said, No disparagement to Christian, more than to many others whose hap and lot it was. For it is easier going up than down this hill, and that can be said but of few hills in all these parts of the world But we will leave the good man, he is at rest, he also had a brave victory over his enemy; let Him grant that dwelleth above, that we fare no worse, when we come to be tried, than he!

But we will come again to this valley of Humiliation. It is the best and most fruitful piece of ground in all these parts. It is a fat ground ; and, as you see, consisteth much in meadows : and if a man was to come here in the summer-time,* as we do now, if he

* 'Summer time'—The consolations of humble believers, even in their lowest abasement, when favoured by the exhilarating and fertilizing beams of the Sun of Righteousness, are represented under this emblem. The lilies are the harmless and holy disciples of Christ who adorn a poor and obscure condition of life ; and who are an ornament to religion, being clothed with humility.' Many grow rich in faith and good works in retirement and obscurity ; and become averse, even at the call of duty, to emerge from it, lest any advancement should lead them into temptation, stir up their pride, or expose them to envy and contention. Perhaps the shepherd's boy may refer to the obscure but quiet station of some pastors over small congregations, who live almost unknown to their brethren, but are in a measure useful, and very comfortable.

knew not any thing before thereof, and if he also delighted himself in the sight of his eyes, he might see that which would be delightful to him. Behold, how green this valley is; also how beautiful with lilies (Sol. Song ii. 1; James iv. 6; 1 Peter v. 5). I have also known many labouring men that have got good estates in this valley of Humiliation; (for 'God resisteth the proud, but giveth more grace to the humble;') for indeed it is a very fruitful soil, and doth bring forth by handfuls. Some also have wished, that the next way to their Father's house were here, that they might be troubled no more with either hills or mountains to go over: but the way is the way, and there is an end.

Now as they were going along, and talking, they spied a boy feeding his father's sheep. The boy was in very mean clothes, but of a fresh and well-favoured countenance; and as he sat by himself he sung. Hark, said Mr. Great-heart, to what the shepherd's boy saith: so they hearkened, and he said,

> He that is down, needs fear no fall;
>   He that is low no pride:
> He that is humble ever shall
>   Have God to be his guide.
> I am content with what I have,
>   Little be it or much:
> And, Lord, contentment still I crave,
>   Because thou savest such.
> Fulness to such a burden is
>   That go on pilgrimage:
> Here little, and hereafter bliss,
>   Is best from age to age. (Heb. xiii. 5.)

Then said the guide, Do you hear him ? I will dare to say, this boy lives a merrier life, and wears more of the herb called heart's-ease in his bosom, than he that is clad in silk and velvet. But we will proceed in our discourse.

In this valley our Lord formerly had his country house ;* he loved much to be here : he loved also to walk in these meadows, and he found the air was pleasant. Besides, here a man shall be free from the noise and from the hurryings of this life : all states are full of noise and confusion, only the valley of Humiliation is that empty and solitary place. Here a man shall not be let and hindered in his contemplation, as in other places he is apt to be. This is a valley that nobody walks in, but those that love a pilgrim's life. And though Christian had the hard hap to meet with Apollyon, and to enter with him a brisk encounter ; yet I must tell you, that in former times men have met with angels here,

* ' Country house'—Our Lord chose retirement, poverty, and an obscure station, as the rest and delight of his own mind ; as remote from bustle and contention, and favourable to contemplation and devotion : so that his appearance in a public character, and in crowded scenes, for the good of man kind and the glory of the Father, was a part of his self-denial, in which ' he pleased not himself.'—Indeed there is a pe culiar congeniality between a lowly mind and a lowly condition : and as much violence is done to the inclinations of the humble, when they are rendered conspicuous and advanced to high stations, as to those of the haughty, when they are thrust down into obscurity and neglect. Other men seem to be banished into this valley ; but the poor in spirit love to walk in it : and, though some believers here struggle with distressing temptations, others in passing through it enjoy much communion with God.

10*

have found pearls here, and have in this place found the words of life (Hos. xii. 4, 5).

Did I say our Lord had here in former days his country-house, and that he loved here to walk ? I will add, in this place, and to the people that live and trace these grounds he has left a yearly revenue, to be faithfully paid them at certain seasons for their maintenance by the way, and for their further encouragement to go on their pilgrimage.

Now, as they went on, Samuel said to Mr. Great-heart ; Sir, I perceive that in this valley my father and Apollyon had their battle ; but whereabout was the fight ? for I perceive this valley is large.

Gr.-h. Your father had the battle with Apollyon, at a place yonder before us, in a narrow passage, just beyond* Forgetful Green. And indeed that place is the most dangerous place in all these parts : for if at any time pilgrims meet with any brunt, it is when they forget what favours they have received, and how unworthy they are of them. This is the place also, where others have been hard put to it. But more of the place

* 'Beyond'—When consolations and privileges betray us into forgetfulness of our entire unworthiness of such special favours, humiliating dispensations will commonly ensue : and these sometimes reciprocally excite murmurs and forgetfulness of past mercies. Thus Satan gains an opportunity of assaulting the soul with dreadful temptations ; and, while at one moment hard thoughts of God, or doubts concerning the truth of his word, are suggested to our minds, at the next we may be affrighted by our own dreadful rebellion and ingratitude, prompted to condemn ourselves as hypocrites, and almost driven to despair.

when we are come to it ; for I persuade myself, that to this day there remains either
some sign of the battle, or some monument
to testify that such a battle there was fought.

Then said Mercy, I think I am as well in
this valley as I have been anywhere else in
all our journey : the place, methinks, suits
with my spirit. I love to be in such places
where there is no rattling with coaches, nor
rumbling with wheels : methinks, here one
may, without much molestation, be thinking
what he is, whence he came, what he has
done, and to what the King has called him .
here one may think, and break at heart, and
melt in one's spirit, until one's eyes become
' as the fish-pools of Heshbon.' They that
go rightly through this ' valley of Baca,'
make it ' a well ; the rain,' that God sends
down from heaven upon them that are here,'
' also filleth the pools.' This valley is that
from whence also the King will give to them
their vineyards (Sol. Song vii. 4 ; Ps. lxxxiv
5—7 ; Hos. li. 15) : and they that go through
it shall sing as Christian did, for all he met
with Apollyon.

It is true, said the guide, I have gone
through this valley many a time, and never
was better than when here. I have also
been a conductor to several pilgrims, and
they have confessed the same. ' To this man
will I look,' (saith the King) ' even to him
that is poor, and of a contrite spirit, and that
trembleth at my word.'

Now they were come to the place where

the aforementioned battle was fought. Then said the guide to Christiana, her children, and Mercy, This is the place : on this ground Christian stood, and up there came Apollyon against him : and, look,* did I not tell you, here is some of your husband's blood upon these stones to this day : behold, also, how here and there are yet to be seen upon the place some of the shivers of Apollyon's broken darts : see also, how they did beat the ground with their feet as they fought, to make good their places against each other ; how also, with their by-blows, they did split the very stones in pieces : verily Christian did here play the man, and shewed himself as stout as Hercules could, had he been there, even he himself. When Apollyon was beat, he made his retreat to the next valley, that is called the valley of the Shadow of Death, unto which we shall come anon. Lo, yonder also stands a monument, on which is engraven this battle, and Christian's victory, to his fame throughout all ages.

* 'And look'—We ought carefully to study the records left us of the temptations, conflicts, faith, patience, and victories of former believers ; we should mark well what wounds they received, and by what misconduct they were occasioned, that we may watch and pray lest we fall in like manner : we ought carefully to observe, how they succesfully repelled the various assaults of the tempter, that we may learn to resist him, steadfast in the faith : and, in general, their triumphs should animate us, to ' put on,' and keep on, ' the whole armour of God, that we may be enabled to withstand in the evil day.' On the other hand, such as have been rendered victorious should readily speak of their experiences among those that fear God, that they may be cautioned, instructed, and encouraged by their example.

So, because it stood, just on the way-side before them, they stepped to it, and read the writing, which word for word was this—

> Hard by here was a battle fought,
>   Most strange, and yet most true ;
> Christian and Apollyon sought
>   Each other to subdue.
> The man so bravely play'd the man,
>   He made the fiend to fly ;
> Of which a monument I stand,
>   The same to testify.

When they had passed by this place, they came upon the borders of the Shadow* of Death, and this valley was longer than the other ; a place also most strangely haunted with evil things, as many are able to testify : but these women and children went the better through it, because they had day-light,

* ' Shadow'—The meaning of this valley hath been stated in the notes on the first part of the work ; and the interpretation there given is here confirmed. As it relates chiefly to the influence, which ' the prince of the power of the air' possesses over the imagination ; it must vary exceedingly, according to the constitution, animal spirits, health, education, and the strength of mind or judgment of different persons. They who are happily incapable of understanding either the allegory or the explanation, should beware of despising or condemning such as have been thus harassed. And, on the other hand, these should take care not to consider such temptations as proofs of spiritual advancement ; or to yield to them, as if they were essential to maturity of grace and experience ; by which means Satan often obtains dreadful advantages. It is most advisable for tempted persons to consult some able judicious minister, or compassionate and established Christian, whose counsel and prayers may be singularly useful in this case ; observing the assistance which Great-heart gave to the pilgrims, in passing through the valley.

and because Mr. Great-heart was their conductor.

When they were entered upon this valley, they thought that they heard a groaning, as of dead men ; a very great groaning. They thought also that they did hear words of lamentation, spoken as of some in extreme torment. These things made the boys to quake, the women also looked pale and wan ; but their guide bid them be of good comfort.

So they went on a little farther, and they thought that they felt the ground begin to shake under them, as if some hollow place was there ; they heard also a kind of hissing, as of serpents, but nothing as yet appeared. Then said the boys, Are we not yet at the end of this doleful place ? But the guide also bid them be of good courage, and look well to their feet, lest haply, said he, you be taken in some snare.

Now James began to be sick, but I think the cause thereof was fear : so his mother gave him some of that glass of spirits that she had given her at the Interpreter's house, and three of the pills that Mr. Skill had prepared, and the boy began to revive. Thus they went on till they came to about the middle of the valley ; and then Christiana said Methinks, I see something yonder upon the road before us ; a thing of a shape such as I have not seen. Then said Joseph, Mother, what is it ? An ugly thing, child ; an ugly thing, said she. But, mother, what is it like ? said he. 'Tis like, I cannot tell what, said she. And

now it is but a little way off.   Then said she,
It is nigh.

Well, said Mr. Great-heart, Let them that
are most afraid, keep close to me.   So the
fiend came on, and the conductor met it ; but
when it was just come to him, it vanished to
all their sights : then remembered they what
had been said some time ago ; 'Resist the
devil, and he will flee from you.'

They went therefore on, as being a little
refreshed ; but they had not gone far, before
Mercy, looking behind her saw as she thought,
something almost like a lion,* and it came a
great padding pace after ; and it had a hol
low voice of roaring ; and every roar that it
gave, it made the valley echo, and all their
hearts to ache, save the heart of him that was
their guide.   So it came up, and Mr. Great-
heart went behind, and put the pilgrims all
before him.   The lion also came on apace, and
Mr. Great-heart addressed himself to give

* ' A lion'—Whatever attempt Satan may make to terrify
the believer, resolute resistance by faith in Christ will drive
him away ; but if fear induce men to neglect the means of
grace, he will renew his assults on the imagination, whenever they attempt to pray, read the Scripture, or attend on any
duty ; till for a time, or finally, they gave up their religion.
In this case, therefore determined perseverance in opposition to every terrifying suggestion is our only safety.   Yet
sometimes temptations may be so multiplied and varied, that
it may seem impossible to proceed any farther, and the mind
of the harassed believer is enveloped in confusion and dismay,
as if an horrible pit were about to swallow him up, or the
prince of darkness to seize upon him.   But the counsel of
some experienced friend or minister, exciting confidence in
the power, mercy, and faithfulness of God, and encouraging
him to ' pray without ceasing,' will at length make way for
his deliverance.

him battle. But when he saw, that it was de-
.ermined that resistance should be made, he
also drew back, and came no farther (1 Pet
v. 8).

Then they went on again, and their conductor did go before them, till they came at
a place where was cast up a pit the whole
breadth of the way ; and, before they could
be prepared to go over that, a great mist and
a darkness fell upon them, so that they could
not see. Then said the pilgrims, Alas ! now
what shall we do ? But their guide made answer, Fear not, stand still, and see what an end
will be put to this also. So they staid there, because their path was marred. They then also
thought they did here more apparently the
noise and rushing of the enemies ; the fire
also, and smoke of the pit was much easier to
be discerned. Then said Christiana to Mercy, Now I see what my poor husband went
through ; I have heard much of this place,
but I never was here before now : poor man !
he went here, all alone, in the night ; he had
night almost quite through the way : also
these fiends were busy about him, as if they
would have torn him in pieces. Many have
spoke of it, but none tell what the valley of the
Shadow of Death should mean until they
come in themselves.   'The heart knows its
own bitterness ; a stranger intermeddleth
not with its joy.' To be here is a fearful
thing.

Gr.-h. This is like doing business in great
waters, or like going down into the deep ;

this is like being in the heart of the sea, and
like going down to the bottoms of the mountains ; now it seems as if the earth, with its
bars, were about us for ever. ' But let them
that walk in darkness, and have no light, trust
in the name of the Lord, and stay upon their
God.' For my part, as I have told you already, I have gone often through this valley ;
and have been much harder put to it than I
now am ; and yet you see I am alive. I
would not boast, for that I am not mine own
Saviour. But I trust we shall have a good
deliverance. Come, pray for light to him
that can lighten our darkness, and that can
rebuke, not only these, but all the Satans in
hell.

So they cried and prayed, and God sent
light and deliverance ; for there was now no
let in their way, no not there where but now
they were stopt with a pit. Yet they were not
got through the valley : so they went on till,
and behold great stinks and loathsome smells,
to the great annoyance of them. Then said
Mercy to Christiana, There is not such pleasant being here as at the gate, or at the Interpreter's, or at the house where we lay last.

O but,* said one of the boys, it is not so bad
to go through here, as it is to abide here al-

* ' O but'—Should any one by hearing the believer say,
The sorrows of death compassed me, and the pains of hell
get hold upon me,' be tempted to avoid all religious duties,
company, and reflections, lest he should experience similar
terrors, let him well weigh this observation. It is not so
bad to go through here, as to abide here always. Nothing
can be more absurd than to neglect religion, lest the fear

ways ; and, for aught I know, one reason why
we must go this way to the house prepared for
us is, that our home might be made the sweeter to us.

Well said, Samuel quoth the guide, thou
hast now spoke like a man. Why, if ever I
get out here again, said the boy, I think I
shall prize light and good way, better than ever
I did in all my life. Then said the guide, We
shall be out by-and-by.

So on they went, and Joseph said, Cannot
we see to the end of this valley as yet ? Then
said the guide, Look to* your feet, for we
shall presently be among snares. So they
looked to their feet, and went on ; but were

---

of hell should discompose a man's mind, when such neglect
exposes him to the eternal endurance of it ; whereas the
short taste of distress, which may be experienced by the
tempted believer, will make redemption more precious,
and render peace, comfort, and heaven, at last doubly delightful.

* ' Look to'—The discouragement of dark temptations is
not so formidable in the judgment of experienced Christians,
as the snares connected with them ; for, while numbers renounce their profession to get rid of their disquietude, many
are seduced into some false doctrine that may sanction negligence, and quiet their consciences by assenting to certain
notions, without regarding the state of their hearts, or what
passes in their experience ; and others are led to spend all
their time in company, or even to dissipate the gloom by engaging in worldly amusements, because retirement exposes
them to these suggestions. In short the enemy endeavours to
terrify the professor, that he may drive him away from God,
entangle him in heresy, or draw him into sin ; in order to
destroy his soul, or at least ruin his credit and prevent his
usefulness. But circumspection and prayer constitute our
best preservative ; through which, they who take heed to
their steps escape, while the heedless are taken and destroyed for a warning to those that come after.

troubled much with the snares Now when they were come among the snares, they spied a man cast into the ditch on the left hand, with his flesh all rent and torn. Then said the guide, That is one Heedless, that was going this way; he has lain there a great while. There was one Take-heed with him when he was taken and slain, but he escaped their hands. You cannot imagine how many are killed here-abouts, and yet men are so foolishly venturous, as to set out lightly on pilgimage, and to come without a guide. Poor Christian, it was a wonder that he here escaped! but he was beloved of his God: also he had a good heart of his own, or else he could never have done it. (P. i. p. 146).

Now they drew towards the end of the way, and just there, where Christian had seen the cave when he went by, out thence came forth Maul* a giant. This Maul did use to spoil young pilgrims with sophistry; and he called Great-heart by his name, and said unto him, How many times have you been forbidden to

---

* 'Maul'—This giant came out of the cave, where Pope and Pagan had resided. He is therefore the emblem of those formal superstitious teachers, and those speculating moralists, who in protestant countries have too generally succeeded the Romish priests and the heathen philosophers, in keeping men ignorant of the way of salvation, and in spoiling by their sophistry such as seem to be seriously disposed. These persons often represent faithful ministers, who draw off their auditors, by preaching 'repentance towards God, and faith towards our Lord Jesus Christ,' as robbers and kidnappers; they terrify many (especially when they have the power of enforcing penal statutes) from professing or hearing the Gospel, and acting according to their consciences; and put the faith of God's servants to a severe trial. Yet perseverance,

do these things ? Then said Great-heart,
What things ? What things ! quoth the giant ;
you know what things ! but I will put an end
to your trade But pray, said Mr. Great-
heart, before we fall to it, let us understand
wherefore we must fight. (Now the women
and children stood trembling, and knew not
what to do.) Quoth the giant, You rob the
country, and rob it with the worst of thieves.
These are but generals, said Mr. Great-heart,
come to particulars, man.

Then said the giant, Thou practisest the
craft of a kidnapper, thou gatherest up women and children, and carriest them into a
strange country, to the weakening of my master's kingdom. But now Great-heart replied,
I am a servant of the God of heaven ; my business is to persuade sinners to repentance ;
I am commanded to do my endeavour to turn
men, women, and children, ' from darkness to
light, and from the power of Satan to God ;'
and if this be indeed the ground of thy quarrel, let us fall to it as soon as thou wilt.

Then the giant came up, and Mr. Great-
heart went to meet him : and as he went he
drew his sword ; but the giant had a club.*

patience, and prayer, will obtain the victory ; and they that
are strong will be instrumental in animating the feeble to
go on their way rejoicing and praising God. But though
these enemies may be baffled, disabled, or apparently slain,
it will appear that they have left a posterity on earth to revile,
injure, and oppose the spiritual worshippers of God in every
generation.

* ' Club'—This seems to mean the secular arm, or power,
by which opposers of the Gospel are generally desirous of enforcing their arguments and persuasions. ' We have a law,

So without more ado, they fell to it, and at the first blow the giant struck Mr. Great-heart down upon one of his knees ; with that the women and children cried : so Mr. Great-heart, recovering himself, laid about him in a full lusty manner, and gave the giant a wound in his arm ; that he fought for the space of an hour, to that hight of heat, that the breath came out of the giant's nostrils, as the heat doth out of a boiling caldron.

Then they sat down to rest them, but Mr. Great-heart betook himself to prayer ; also the women and children did nothing but sigh and cry all the time that the battle did last.

When they had rested them, and taken breath, they both fell to it again ; and Mr. Great-heart with a full blow fetched the giant down to the ground. Nay, hold, let me recover, quoth he : so Great-heart let him fairly get up. So to it they went again, and the giant missed but little of breaking Mr. Great-heart's scull with his club.

Mr. Great-heart seeing that, runs to him in the full heat of his spirit, and pierced him under the fifth rib ; with that the giant began to faint, and could hold up his club no longer. Then Mr. Great-heart seconded his blow, and smote the head of the giant from his shoulders.   Then the women and children rejoiced,

and by our law he ought to die :' this decision, like a heavy club, seems capable of bearing all down before it ; nor can any withstand its force, but those who rely on him that is stronger than all.

11*

and Mr. Great-heart also praised God for the deliverance he had wrought.

When this was done, they among them erected a pillar, and fastened the giant's head thereon, and wrote under it in letters that passengers might read :

> He that did wear this head, was one
>   That pilgrims did misuse ;
> He stopp'd their way, he spared none,
>   But did them all abuse :
> Until that I, Great-heart arose,
>   The pilgrims' guide to be ;
> Until that I did him oppose,
>   That was their enemy.

Now I saw that they went to the ascent, that was a little way off cast up to be a prospect for pilgrims (that was the place from whence Christian had the first sight of Faithful, his brother ; P. i. p. 147). Wherefore here they sat down and rested ; they also here did eat and drink, and make merry, for that they had gotten deliverance from this so dangerous an enemy. As they sat thus and did eat, Christiana asked the guide if he had got no hurt in the battle ? Then said Mr. Great-heart, No, save a little on my flesh ; yet that also shall be so far from being to my detriment, that it is at present a proof of my love to my Master and you, and shall be a means, by grace, to increase my reward at last.

Chr. But was you not afraid, good Sir, when you saw him come with his club.

It is my duty, said he, to distrust my own

ability, that I may have reliance on him that is stronger than all (2 Cor. iv).

Chr. But what did you think, when he fetched you down to the ground at the first blow?

Why, I thought, quoth he, that so my master himself was served, and yet he it was that conquered at last.

Mat. When you all have thought what you please, I think God has been wonderful good unto us, both in bringing us out of this valley, and in delivering us out of the hand of this enemy; for my part, I see no reason why we should distrust our God any more, since he has now, and in such a place as this, given us such testimony of his love as this.

Then they got up and went forward. Now a little before them stood an oak; and under it, when they came to it, they found an old pilgrim* fast asleep: they knew that he was a pilgrim by his clothes, and his staff, and his girdle.

So the guide, Mr. Great-heart awaked him; and the old gentleman, as he lifted up

* 'Old pilgrim'—The allegory requires us to suppose that there were some places in which the pilgrims might safely sleep: so that nothing disadvantageous to the character of this old disciple seems to have been intended. An avowed dependance on Christ for righteousness, a regard to the word of God, and an apparent sincerity in word and deed, mark a man to be a pilgrim, or constitute a professor of the Gospel; but we should not too readily conclude every professor to be a true believer. The experienced Christian will be afraid of new acquaintance; in his most unwatchful seasons he will be fully convinced that no enemy can hurt him, unless he is induced to yield to temptation and commit sin.

his eyes, cried out, What's the matter ? Who are you ? and what is your business here ?

Gr.-h. Come, man, be not so hot, here is none but friends. Yet the old man gets up, and stands upon his guard, and will know of them what they were. Then said the guide, My name is Great-heart ; I am the guide of these pilgrims, which are going to the Celestial country.

Then said Mr. Honest, I cry your mercy ; I feared that you had been of the company of those that some time ago did rob Littlefaith of his money ; but now I look better about me, I perceive you are honester people.

Gr.-h. Why, what would, or could you have done, or helped yourself, if we indeed had been of that company ?

Hon. Done ! why I would have fought as long as breath had been in me ; and had I so done, I am sure you could never have given me the worst on't ; for a Christian can never be overcome unless he should yield himself.

Well said, farther Honest, quoth the guide ; for by this I know thou art a cock of the right kind, for thou hast said the truth.

Hon. And by this also I know that thou knowest what true pilgrimage is : for all others do think, that we are the soonest overcome of any.

Gr.-h. Well, now we are happily met, let me crave your name, and the name of the place you came from ?

Hon. My name I cannot: But I came from the town of Stupidity : it lieth about four degrees beyond the city of Destruction.

Gr.-h. Oh ! are you that countryman then ? I deem I have half a guess of you ; your name is old Honesty, is it not ? So the old gentleman blushed, and said, Not Honesty in the abstract ;* but Honest is my name, and I wish that my nature may agree to what I am called.

But, Sir, said the old gentleman, how could you guess that I am such a man, since I came from such a place.

Gr.-h. I have heard of you before, by my master, for he knows all things that are done on the earth ; but I have often wondered that any should come from your place, for your town is worse than is the city of Destruction itself.

Hon. Yes, we lie more off from the sun,† and so are more cold and senseless ; but was

---

* 'Abstract'—Honesty in the abstract seems to mean sinless perfection. The pilgrim was a sound character, but conscious of many imperfections, of which he was ashamed, and from which he sought deliverance. The nature of faith, hope, love, patience, and other holy dispositions, is described in Scripture, as a man would define gold by its essential properties. This shews what they are in the abstract ; but as exercised by us, they are always mixed with considerable alloy ; and we are richer or poorer in this respect, in proportion to the degree of the gold or of the alloy which is found in our affections and character.

† 'Sun'.—The Lord sometimes calls those sinners, whose character, connexions, and situation, seem to place at the greatest distance from him ; that the riches of his mercy and the power of his grace may be thus rendered the more conspicuous and illustrious.

a man in a mountain of ice, yet if the Sun of Righteousness will arise upon him, his frozen heart shall feel a thaw. And thus it has been with me.

Gr.-h. I believe it, father Honest, I believe it; for I know the thing is true.

Then the old gentleman saluted all the pilgrims with a holy kiss of charity; and asked them of their names, and how they had fared since they had set out on their pilgrimage.

Then said Christiana, My name, I suppose you have heard of: good Christian was my husband, and these four were his children. But can you think how the old gentleman was taken, when she told him who she was! He skipped, he smiled, and blessed them with a thousand good wishes; saying, I have heard much of your husband, and of his travels and wars, which he underwent in his days. Be it spoken to your comfort, the name of your husband rings all over these parts of the world; his faith, his courage, his enduring, and his sincerity under all, has made his name famous. Then he turned him to the boys, and asked of them their names, which they told him. And then said he unto them, Matthew, be thou like Matthew the publican, not in vice but in virtue. Samuel, saith he, be thou like Samuel the prophet, a man of faith and prayer. Joseph, said he, be thou like Joseph in Potiphar's house, chaste, and one that flees from temptation. And James, be thou like James the Just, and like James the brother of our Lord (Matt. x. 3 ; Ps. xcix. 6 ; Gen. xxxix ; Acts i. 13, 14). Then they told him of Mercy, and how she had left her town and her kindred to come along with Christiana and with her sons. At that the old honest man said, Mercy is thy name ; by mercy shalt thou be sustained, and carried through all those difficulties that shall assault thee in thy way, till thou shalt come thither, where thou shalt look the fountain of mercy in the face with comfort.

All this while the guide, Mr. Great-heart, was very well pleased, and smiled upon his companions.

Now, as they walked together, the guide asked the old gentleman if he did not know one Mr. Fearing, that came on pilgrimage out of his parts ?

Yes, very well, said he.   He was* a man that had the root of the matter in him ; but he was one of the most troublesome pilgrims that I ever met with in all my days.

---

* ' He was'—The character and narrative of Fearing has been generally admired by experienced readers, as drawn and arranged with great judgment, and in a very affecting manner.   Little-faith in the first part was faint-hearted and distrustful, and thus he contracted guilt and lost his comfort ; but Fearing dreaded sin, and coming short of heaven, more than all that flesh could do unto him.   He was alarmed at the appearance or report of opposition ; but this arose more from conscious weakness, and the fear of being overcome by temptation, than from a reluctance to undergo derision or persecution.   The peculiarity of this description of Christians must be traced back to constitution, habit, first impressions, disproportionate and partial views of truth, and improper instructions : these, concurring with weakness of faith, and the common infirmities of human nature, give a

Gr.-h. I perceive you knew him, for you have given a very right character of him.

Hon. Knew him; I was a great companion of his; I was with him most an end; when he first began to think of what would come upon us hereafter, I was with him.

Gr.-h. I was his guide, from my master's house to the gate of the Celestial city.

Hon. Then you knew him to be a troublesome one.

Gr.-h. I did so but I could very well bear it; for men of my calling are oftentimes intrusted with the conduct of such as he was.

Hon. Well then, pray let us hear a little of him, and how he managed himself under your conduct.

Gr.-h. Why, he was always afraid that he should come short whither he had a desire to go. Every thing frighted him that he heard any body speak of, that had but the least appearance of opposition in it. I hear that he lay roaring* at the slough of Despond for

cast to their experience and character, which renders them uncomfortable to themselves, and troublesome to others; yet no competent judges doubt but they have the root of the matter in them; and none are more entitled to the patient, sympathizing, and tender attention of ministers and Christians.

* ' Roaring'—Professors of this description are greatly retarded in their progress by discouraging fears; they are apt to spend too much time in unavailing complaints; they do not duly profit by the counsel and assistance of their brethren, and often neglect the proper means of getting relief from their terrors: yet they cannot think of giving up their feeble hopes, or returning to their forsaken worldly pursuits and pleasures. They are, indeed, helped forward, through the mercy of God, in a very extraordinary manner: yet they

above a month together ; nor durst he, for all he saw several go over before him, venture, though they many of them offered to lend him their hand. He would not go back again neither. The Celestial city ! he said, he should die if he came not to it ; and yet was dejected at every difficulty, and stumbled at every straw that any body cast in his way. Well, after he had lain at the slough of Despond a great while, as I have told you, one sunshine morning, I don't know how, he ventured, and so got over ; but when he was over, he would scarce believe it. He had, I think, a slough of despond in his mind, a slough that he carried every where with him, or else he could never have been as he was. So he came up to the gate (you know what I mean), that stands at the head of this way ; and there also he stood a good while, before he would venture to knock. When the gate was opened, he would give back, and give

still remain exposed to alarms and discouragements, in every stage of their pilgrimage : nor can they ever habitually rise superior to them. They are afraid even of relying on Christ for salvation ; because they have confused views of his love, and the methods of his grace, and imagine some other qualification to be necessary besides the willingness to seek, knock, and ask for the promised blessings, with a real desire of obtaining them. They imagine, that there has been something in their past life, or that there is some peculiarity in their present habits and propensities, and way of applying to Christ, which may exclude them from the general benefit : so that they pray with diffidence ; and being consciously unworthy, can hardly believe that the Lord regards them, or will grant their requests. They are also prone to overlook the most decisive evidences of their reconciliation to God ; and to persevere in arguing with perverse ingenuity against their own manifest happiness.

place to others, and say, that he was not worthy ; for all he got before some to the gate,
yet many of them went in before him. There
the poor man would stand shaking and shrink-
ing ; I dare say it would have pitied one's
heart to have seen him ; nor would he go
back again. At last he took the hammer
that hanged at the gate in his hand, and
gave a small rap or two ; then one opened to
him, but he shrunk back as before. He that
opened, stepped out after him, and said,
Thou trembling one, what wantest thou ?
With that he fell down to the ground He
that spake **to him, wondered** to see him so
faint. He said to him, Peace to thee ; up,
for I have set open the door to thee ; come in,
for thou art blessed. With that he got up,
and went in trembling ; and when that he
was in, he was ashamed to shew his face.
Well, after he had been entertained there
awhile (as you know the manner is), he was
bid go on his way, and also told the way he
should take. So he went till he came to our
house ; but as he behaved himself at the
gate, so he did at my master the Interpreter's
door. He lay* thereabout in the cold a good

* ' He lay'—The same mixture of humility and unbelief
renders persons of this description backward in associating
with their brethren, and in frequenting those companies in
which they might obtain farther instruction : for they are
afraid of being considered as believers, or even serious inquirers : so that affectionate and earnest persuasion is requisite
to prevail with them to join in those religious exercises, by
which Christians especially receive the teaching of the Holy
Spirit. Yet this arises not from disinclination, but diffidence ; and though they are often peculiarly favoured with

while, before he would adventure to call ; yet
he would not go back : and the nights were
long and cold then. Nay, he had a note of
necessity in his bosom to my master, to receive him, and grant him the comfort of his
house, and also to allow him a stout and valiant conductor, because he was himself so
chicken-hearted a man ! and yet, for all that,
he was afraid to call at the door. So he lay
up and down thereabouts, till, poor man, he
was almost starved ; yea, so great was his dejection, that, though he saw several others
for knocking got in, yet he was afraid to venture. At last, I think, I looked out of the
window, and perceiving a man to be up and
down about the door, I went out to him, and
asked what he was ; but, poor man, the water stood in his eyes ; so I perceived what he
wanted. I went therefore in, and told it in
the house, and we shewed the things to our

seasons of great comfort, to counterbalance their dejections,
yet they never hear or read of false professors, who have
drawn back to perdition, but they are terrified with the idea,
that they shall shortly resemble them ; so that every warning given against hypocrisy or self-deception seems to point
them out by name, and every new discovery of any fault or
mistake in their views, temper, or conduct, seems to decide
their doom. At the same time, they are often remarkably
melted into humble admiring gratitude, by contemplating the
love and sufferings of Christ, and seem to delight in hearing
of that subject above all others. They do not peculiarly fear
difficulties, self-denial, reproaches, or persecution, which deter numbers from making an open profession of religion ; and
yet they are more backward in this respect than others ; because they deem themselves unworthy to be admitted to such
privileges, and into such society ; or else are apprehensive of
being finally separated from them, or becoming a disgrace to
religion

Lord; so he sent me out again to entreat him to come in; but, I dare say, I had hard work to do it. At last he came in; and I will say that for my Lord, he carried it wonderful loving to him. There were but a few good bits at the table, but some of it was laid upon his trencher. Then he presented the note; and my Lord looked thereon, and said his desire should be granted. So when he had been there a good while, he seemed to get some heart, and to be a little more comforted. For my master, you must know, is one of very tender bowels, especially to them that are afraid; wherefore he carried it so towards him as might tend most to his encouragement. Well, when he had a sight of the things of the place, and was ready to take his journey to go to the city, my Lord, as he did to Christian before, gave him a bottle of spirits, and some comfortable things to eat. Thus we set forward, and I went before him; but the man was but of few words, only he would sigh aloud.

When we were come to where the three fellows were hanged, he said, that he doubted that that would be his end also. Only he seemed glad when he saw the cross and the sepulchre. There I confess he desired to stay a little to look, and he seemed for a while after to be a little comforted. When we came at the hill Difficulty, he made no stick at that, nor did he much fear the lions; for you must know, that his trouble was not about such things as these; his fear was about his acceptance at last.

I got him in at the house Beautiful, I think,
before he was willing ; also, when he was in,
I brought him acquainted with the damsels
that were of the place, but he was ashamed
to make himself much for company ; he desired much to be alone, yet he always loved
good talk, and often would get behind the
screen to hear it ; he also loved much to see
ancient things, and to be pondering them in
his mind. He told me afterwards, that he
loved to be in those two houses from which
he came last, to wit, at the gate, and that of the
Interpreter, but he durst not be so bold as to
ask.

When we went also from the house Beautiful, down the hill, into the valley* of Humiliation, he went down as well as ever I saw a
man in my life ; for he cared not how mean he
was so he might be happy at last.   Yea, I
think there was a kind of sympathy betwixt
that valley and him, for I never saw him bet-

* 'Valley'—A low and obscure situation suits the disposition of the persons here described : they do not object to the
most humiliating views of their own hearts, of human nature,
or of the way of salvation ; they are little tempted to covet
eminence among their brethren, and find it easier ' to esteem
others better than themselves,' than persons of a different
frame of mind can well conceive. On the other hand, their imaginations are peculiarly susceptible of impressions, and of the
temptations represented by the valley of the Shadow of Death :
so that in this respect they need more than others the tender
and patient instructions of faithful ministers: while they repeat
the same complaints, and urge the same objections against
themselves, that have already been obviated again and again ;
but the tender compassion of the Lord to them should suggest
an useful instruction to his servants, on this part of their
work.

ter in all his pilgrimage, than he was in that valley.

Here he would lie down, embrace the ground, and kiss the very flowers that grew in this valley (Lam. iii. 27—29). He would now be up every morning by break of day, tracing and walking to and fro in the valley.

But, when he was come to the entrance of the valley of the Shadow of Death, I thought I should have lost my man; not for that he had inclination to go back (that he always abhorred), but he was ready to die for fear. O the hobgoblings will have me, the hobgoblins will have me! cried he, and I could not beat him out on't. He made such a noise, and such an outcry here, that, had they but heard him, it was enough to encourage them to come and fall upon us. But this I took very great notice of, that this valley was as quiet when he went through it, as ever I knew it before or since. I suppose those enemies here had now a special check from our Lord, and a command not to meddle until Mr. Fearing was passed over it.

It would be too tedious to tell you of all; we will therefore only mention a passage or two more. When* he was come to Vanity

* 'When'—No Christians are more careless about the opinion of the world, or more zealous against its vanities, than persons of this description: or more watchful in times of ease and prosperity: but the prospect of death is often a terror to them, especially when they suppose it to be at hand; yet they often die with remarkable composure and comfort. Few ministers, who have had an opportunity of carefully ob-

Fair, I thought he would have fought with all the men in the fair ; I feared there we should both have been knocked on the head, so hot was he against their fooleries. Upon the Enchanted ground, he also was very wakeful. But, when he was come at the river where was no bridge, there again he was in a heavy case : Now, now, he said, he should be drowned for ever, and so never see that face with comfort, that he had come so many miles to behold. And here also I took notice of what was very remarkable, the water of that river was lower at this time than ever I saw it in all my life ; so he went over at last, not much above wet-shod. When he was going up to the gate, Mr. Great-heart began to take his leave of him, and to wish him a good reception above ; so he said, I shall, I shall ; then parted we asunder, and I saw him no more.

serving the people intrusted to their pastoral care, can help thinking of some individual, who might seem to have been the original of this admirable portrait : which is full of instruction both to them, and the timid, but conscientious part of their congregations. Indeed numbers, who are not characteristically Fearfuls, have something of the same disposition in many particulars. But such as fear reproach and self-denial more than those things, which this good man dreaded, bear a contrary character, and are travelling the road to an opposite place ; and even they, whose confidence of an interest in Christ far exceeds the degree of their humiliation, conscientiousness, abhorrence of sin, and victory over the world, may justly be suspected of having begun their religion in a wrong manner : as they more resemble the stony ground hearers, who ' received the word with joy, but had no root in themselves ;' than those who ' sow in tears, to reap in joy.' For ' godly sorrow worketh repentance unto salvation, not to be repented of.'

Hon. Then, it seems, he was well at last ?

Gr.-h. Yes, yes, I never had doubt about him ; he was a man of a choice spirit ; only he was always kept very low, and that made his life so burthensome to himself, and so very troublesome to others (Ps. lxxxviii). He was, above many, tender of sin ; he was so afraid of doing injuries to others, that he would often deny himself of that which was lawful, because he would not offend (Rom. xiv. 21 ; 1 Cor. vii. 13).

Hon. But what should be the reason that such a good man should be all his days so much in the dark ?

Gr.-h. There are two sorts of reasons for it ; one is, the wise God will have it so ; some must pipe, and some must weep (Matt. xi. 16. 18) : now Mr. Fearing was one that played upon the bass. He and his fellows sound the sackbut, whose notes are more doleful than notes of other music are ; though indeed, some say, the bass is the ground of music. And, for my part, I care not at all for that profession, that begins not in heaviness of mind. The first string that the musician usually touches is the bass, when he intends to put all in tune ; God also plays upon this string first when he sets the soul in tune for himself. Only there was the imperfection of Mr. Fearing, he could play upon no other music but this, till towards his latter end.

[I make bold to talk thus metaphorically, for the ripening of the wits of young readers ; and because, in the book of revelation, the saved are compared to a company of musicians, that played upon their trumpets and harps, and sing their songs before the throne.—Rev. viii xiv. 2, 3.]

Hon. He was a very zealous man, as one may see by what relation you have given of him. Difficulties, lions, or Vanity Fair, he feared not at all ; it was only sin, death, and hell, that were to him a terror, because he had some doubts about his interest in that Celestial country.

Gr.-h. You say right ; those were things that were his troubles ; and they, as you have well observed, arose from the weakness of his mind thereabout, not from weakness of spirit, as to the practical part of a pilgrim's life. I dare believe, that, as the proverb is, He could have bit a firebrand, had it stood in his way ; but those things with which he was oppressed, no man ever yet could shake off with ease.

Then said Christiana, This relation of Mr. Fearing has done me good ; I thought nobody had been like me, but I see there was some semblance betwixt this good man and I ; only we differ in two things ; his troubles were so great that they brake out, but mine I kept within. His also lay so hard upon him, they made him that he could not knock at the houses provided for entertainment ; but my troubles were always such, as made me knock the louder.

Mer. If I might also speak my mind, I must say, that something of him has also dwelt in me ; for I have ever been more afraid of the lake, and the loss of a place in Paradise, than I have been at the loss of other things. O ! thought I, may I have the happiness to have a habitation there, it is enough, though I part with all the world to win it.

Then said Matthew, Fear was one thing that made me think that I was far from having that within me that accompanies salvation ; but if it was so with such a good man as he, why may it not also go well with me ?

No fears, no grace, said James. Though there is not always grace where there is the fear of hell ; yet, to be sure there is no grace where there is no fear of God.

Gr.-h. Well said, James ; thou hast hit the mark, for 'the fear of God is the beginning of wisdom ;' and, to be sure, they that want the beginning have neither middle nor end. But we will here conclude our discourse of Mr. Fearing, after we have sent after him his farewell.

> Whilst, master Fearing, thou didst fear
>   Thy God, and wast afraid
> Of doing any thing, while here,
>   That would have thee betray'd ;
> And didst thou fear the lake and pit ?
>   Would others did so too !
> For as for them, they want thy wit,
>   They do themselves undo.

Now I saw that they all went on in their talk ; for, after Mr. Great-heart had made an end with Mr. Fearing, Mr. Honest began

to tell them of another, but his name* was Mr.
Selfwill.   He pretended himself to be a pilgrim, said Mr. Honest; but I persuade myself, he never came in at the gate that stands
at the head of the way.

Gr.-h. Had you ever any talk with him
about it ?

Hon. Yes, more than once or twice ; but
he would always be like himself, self-willed

* ' Name'—The author peculiarly excels in contrasting his
characters, of which a striking instance here occurs. The
preceding episode relates to a very conscientious Christian,
who through weak faith and misapprehension carried his self-
suspicion to a troublesome and injurious extreme ; and we
have next introduced a false professor who, pretending to
strong faith, made his own obstinate self-will the only rule of
his conduct. But, in fact, this arises from total unbelief :
for the word of God declares such persons to be unregenerate,
under the wrath of God, in the gall of bitterness and the bond
of iniquity. It would hardly be imagined, that men could be
found maintaining such detestable sentiments as are here
stated, did not facts most awfully prove it. We need not, spend
however, time in exposing such a character : a general expression of the deepest detestation may suffice; for none, who
have been given up to such strong delusion, can reasonably
be supposed accessible to the words of truth and soberness ;
nor can they succeed in perverting others to such palpable
and gross absurdities and abominable tenets ; except they
meet with those, that have long provoked God, by endeavouring to reconcile a wicked life with the hope of salvation.
But it may properly be observed, that several expressions,
which seem to represent faith as an assurance of a personal
interest in Christ ; or to intimate, that believers have nothing to do with the law, even as the rule of their conduct ,
with many unguarded assertions concerning the liberty of the
Gospel, and indiscriminate declamations against doubts,
fears, and a legal spirit, have a direct tendency to prepare
the mind of impenitent sinners to receive the poisonous principles of avowed antinomians. Much harm has been done
in this way, and great disgrace brought upon the Gospel ;
for ' there are many of this man's mind, who have not this
man's mouth.'

He neither cared for man, nor argument, nor example ; what his mind prompted him to, that he would do ; and nothing else could he be got to.

Gr.-h. Pray what principles did he hold ? for I suppose you can tell.

Hon. He held, that a man might follow the vices as well as the virtues of the pilgrims ; and that if he did both, he should be certainly saved.

Gr.-h. How ! if he had said, it is possible for the best to be guilty of the vices, as well as partake of the virtues of pilgrims, he could not much have been blamed. For indeed, we are exempted from no vice absolutely, but on condition that we watch and strive. But this, I perceive, is not the thing : but if I understand you right, your meaning is, that he was of that opinion, that it was allowable so to be.

Hon. Ay, ay, so I mean ; and so he believed and practised.

Gr.-h. But what grounds had he for so saying ?

Hon. Why, he said he had the Scripture for his warrant.

Gr.-h. Pr'ythee, Mr. Honest, present us with a few particulars.

Hon. So I will. He said, to have to do with other men's wives had been practised by David, God's beloved ; and therefore he could do it. He said, to have more women than one, was a thing that Solomon practised ; and therefore he could do it. He said, that

Sarah and the godly midwives of Egypt lied,
so did Rahab ; and therefore he could do it
He said that the disciples went, at the bid-
ding of their Master, and took away the owner's ass and therefore he could do so too.
He said that Jacob got the inheritance of his
father a way of guile and dissimulation ; and
therefore he could do so too.

Gr.-h. High base indeed and are you sure
he was of this opinion ?

Hon. I have heard him plead for it, bring
Scripture for it bring arguments for it, &c.

Gr.-h. An opinion that is not fit to be with
any allowance in the world !

Hon. You must understand me rightly ; he
did not say that any man might do this ; but
that those that had the virtues of those that
did such things, might also do the same.

Gr.-h. But what was more false than such
conclusion ? for this is as much as to say,
that, because good men heretofore have sinned of infirmity, therefore he had allowance
to do it of a presumptuous mind : or if, because a child, by the blast of wind, or for
that it stumbled at a stone, fell down, and defiled itself in mire, therefore he might will-
fully lie down and wallow like a boar therein.
Who could have thought that any one could
so far have been blinded by the power of
lust ? But what is written must be true ,
'they stumbled at the word, being disobedi-
ent ; where unto also they were appointed'
(Pet. ii. 8). His supposing that such may
have the godly man's virtues, who addict

themselves to his vices, is also a delusion as strong as the other. It is just as if the dog should say I have, or may have the qualities of a child, because I lick up its stinkling excrements. 'To eat up the sin of God's people' (Hos. iv. 8), is no sign of one that is possessed with their virtues. Nor can I believe, that one that is of this opinion can at present have faith or love in him. But I know you have made strong objections against him; pr'ythee what can he say for himself?

Hon. Why, he says, to do this by way of opinion, seems abundance more honest than to do it and yet hold contrary to it in opinion.

Gr.-h. A very wicked answer; for, though to let loose the bridles to lusts, while our opinions are against such things, is bad; yet to sin, and plead a toleration so to do, is worse; the one stumbles beholders accidentally, the other leads them unto the snare.

Hon. There are many of this man's mind, that have not this man's mouth; and that makes going on pilgrimage of so little esteem as it is.

Gr.-h. You have said the truth, and it is to be lamented; but he that feareth the King of Paradise shall come out of them all.

Chr. There are strange opinions in the world; I know one who said it was time enough to repent when he came to die.

Gr.-h. Such are not over-wise; that man would have been loath, might he have had a week to run twenty miles for his life, to have deferred that journey to the last hour of that week.

Hon. You say right ; and yet the generality of them that count themselves pilgrims do indeed do thus. I am, as you see an old man, and have been a traveller in this road many a day ; and I have taken notice of many things.

I have seen some, that set out as if they would drive all the world afore them, who yet have, in a few days, died as they in the wilderness, and so never got sight of the promised land. I have seen some, that have promised nothing, at first setting out to be pilgrims, and that one would have thought could not have lived a day, that have yet proved very good pilgrims. I have seen some who have run hastily forward, that again have, after a little time, run as fast just back again. I have seen some who have spoken very well of a pilgrim's life at first, that after a while have spoken as much against it. I have heard some, when they first set out for Paradise, say positively, There is such a place ; who, when they have been almost there, have come back again, and said, There is none. I have heard some vaunt what they would do, in case they should be opposed, that have even at a false alarm, fled faith, the pilgrim's way, and all.

Now as they were thus in their way, there came one running to meet them, and said, Gentlemen, and you of the weaker sort, if you love life, shift for yourselves, for the robbers are before you.

Then said Mr. Great-heart, They be the three that set upon Little-faith heretofore. Well, said he, we are ready for them. So they went on their way. Now they looked at every turning, when they should have met with the villains ; but, whether they heard of Mr. Great-heart, or whether they had some other game, they came not up to the pilgrims.

Christiana then wished for an inn* for herself and her children, because they were weary. Then said Mr. Honest, There is one a little before us, where a very honourable disciple, one Gaius, dwells (Rom. xvi. 23). So they all concluded to turn in thither, and the rather, because the old gentleman gave him so good a report. So when they came to the door, they went in, not knocking ; for folks use not to knock at the door of an inn. Then they called for the master of the house, and he came to them. So they asked if they might lie there that night ?

Gai. Yes, gentlemen, if you be true men, for my house is for none but pilgrims. Then was Christiana, Mercy, and the boys, more

* 'An inn'—The spiritual refreshment, arising from experimental and affectionate conversation with Christian friends, seems to be here more especially intended : yet the name of Gaius suggests also the importance of the apostle's exhortation, 'Use hospitality without grudging.' This ought to be attended to, even in respect of those with whom we have hitherto had no acquaintance, provided their characters are properly certified to us : for we are all brethren in Christ.

glad, for that the innkeeper was a lover of
pilgrims. So they called for rooms, and he
shewed them one for Christiana and her children, and Mercy, and another for Mr. Great-
heart and the old gentleman.

Then said Mr. Great-heart, Good Gaius,
what hast thou for supper? for these pilgrims have come far to-day, and are weary.

It is late, said Gaius, so we cannot conve-
niently go out to seek food, but such as I
have you shall be welcome to, if that will
content you.

Gr.-h. We will be content with what thou
hast in the house : forasmuch as I have proved thee, thou art never destitute of that which
is convenient.

Then he went down and spake to the
cook, whose name was Taste-that-which-is-
good, to get ready supper for so many pil
grims. This done, he comes up again, saying, Come, my good friends, you are welcome
to me, and I am glad that I have a house to
entertain you ; and while supper is making
ready, if you please, let us entertain one another with some good discourse : so they all
said, Content.

Then said Gaius, Whose wife is this aged
matron? and whose daughter is this young
damsel?

Gr.-h. The woman is the wife of one
Christian, a pilgrim in former times ; and
these are his four children. The maid is one
of her acquaintance ; one that she hath persuaded to come with her on pilgrimage. The

13*

boys take all after their father, and covet to
tread in his steps : yea, if they do but see
any place where the old pilgrim had lain,
or any print of his foot, it ministereth joy to
their hearts, and they covet to lie or tread in
the same.

Then said Gaius, Is this Christian's wife,
and are these Christian's children ? I knew
your husband's father, yea, also his father's
father.   Many have been good of this stock ;
their ancestors first dwelt at Antioch (Acts
xi. 26).   Christian's progenitors (I suppose
you have heard your husband talk of them)
were very worthy men.   They have, above
any that I know, shewed themselves men of
great virtue and courage for the Lord of the
pilgrims, his ways, and them that loved him.
I have heard of many of your husband's relations, that have stood all trials for the sake
of the truth.   Stephen, that was one of the
first of the family from whence your husband
sprang, was knocked on the head with stones
(Acts vii. 59, 60).   James, another of this
generation was slain with the edge of the
sword (Acts xii. 2).   To say nothing of Paul
and Peter, men anciently of the family from
whence your husband came, there was Igna-
tius, who was cast to the lions ; Romanus,
whose flesh was cut by pieces from his bones ;
and Polycarp, that played the man in the fire.
There was he that was hanged up in a basket
in the sun, for the wasps to eat ; and he
whom they put into a sack, and cast him into
the sea to be drowned.   It would be impos-

ible utterly to count up all that family, that
have suffered injuries and death for the love
of a pilgrim's life.   Nor can I but be glad,
to see that thy husband has left behind him
four such boys as these.   I hope they will
bear up their father's name, and tread in their
father's steps, and come to their father's end.

Gr.-h. Indeed, Sir, they are likely lads :
they seem to choose heartily their father's
ways.

Gai. That is what I said; wherefore
Christian's family is like still to spread
abroad upon the face of the ground, and yet
to be numerous upon the face of the earth :
wherefore let Christiana look out some damsels for her sons, to whom they may be be-
trothed, &c , that the name of their father
and the house of his progenitors may never
be forgotten in the world.

Hon. It is pity his family should fall and be
extinct.

Gai. Fall it cannot, but be diminished it
may : but let Christiana take my advise, and
that's the way to uphold it.

And, Christiana, said this innkeeper, I am
glad to see thee and thy friend Mercy together here, a lovely couple.   And may I advise,* Take Mercy into a nearer relation to

* 'Advise'—The author availed himself of the opportunity
here presented him, of giving his opinion on a very important
subject, about which religious persons often hold different sentiments.   He evidently intended to say, that he deemed it
generally most safe and advantageous to the parties themselves, and most conducive to the spread and permanency of
true religion, for young professors to marry ; provided it be

thee : if she will, let her be given to Matthew, thy eldest son : it is the way to preserve a prosterity in the earth. So this match was concluded, and in process of time they were married : but more of that hereafter.

Gaius also proceeded, and said, I will now speak on the behalf of women, to take away their reproach. For as death and the curse came into the world by a woman, so also did life and health : 'God sent forth his Son, made of a woman (Gen. iii. ; Gal. iv. 4).' Yea, to shew how much those that came after did abhor the act of the mother, this sex in the Old Testament coveted children, if happily this or that woman might be the mother of the Saviour of the world. I will say again, that when the Saviour was come,

done in the fear of God, and according to the rules of his word. Yet we cannot suppose but he would readily have allowed of exceptions to this rule : for there are individuals, who, continuing single, employ that time and those talents in assiduously doing good, which in the married state must have been greatly abridged or preoccupied; and thus they are more extensively useful than their brethren. Yet, in common cases, the training up of a family, by the combined efforts of pious parents, in honesty, sobriety, industry, and the principles of true religion : when united with fervent prayer, and the persuasive eloquence of a good example, is so important a service to the church and to the community, that few persons are capable of doing greater or more permanent good in any other way. But this requires strict attention to the rules of Scripture, in every step of these grand concerns ; for children brought up in ungodliness and ignorance, among those who are strangers to the Gospel, are far more hopeful than such as have received a bad education, witnessed bad examples, and imbibed worldly principles, in the families of evangelical professors.

women rejoiced in him, before either man or
angel (Luke ii.) I read not, ever man did
give unto Christ so much as one groat : but
the women followed him, and ministered to
him of their substance. It was a woman
that washed his feet with tears, and a woman
that anointed his body to the burial. They
were women that wept, when he was going
to the cross ; and women that followed him
from the cross, and that sat by his sepulchre
when he was buried. They were women
that were first with him at his resurrection
morn ; and women that brought tidings first
to his disciples, that he was risen from the
dead (Luke vii. 37—50 ; viii. 2, 3 ; xxiv. 22,
23 ; John ii. 3 ; xi. 2 ; Matt. xxvii. 55, 56—
61). Women therefore are highly favoured,
and shew by these things, that they are sharers with us in the grace of life.

Now the cook sent up to signify that supper was almost ready : and sent one to lay
the cloth, and the trenchers, and to set the
salt and bread in order.

Then said Matthew, the sight of this cloth,
and of this forerunner of the supper, begetteth in me a greater appetite to my food than
I had before.

Gai. So let all ministering doctrines to
thee, in this life, beget in thee a greater desire to sit at the supper of the great king in
his kingdom ; for all preaching, books, and
ordinances here, are but as the laying of the
trenchers, and as sitting of salt upon the
board, when compared with the feast that our

Lord will make us when we come to his house.

So supper* came up: and first a heave-shoulder and a wave-breast were set on the table before them; to show that they must begin the meal with prayer and praise to God (Lev. vii. 32—34; x. 14, 15; Ps. xxv. 1; Heb. xiii. 15.) The heave-shoulder, David lifted his heart up to God with; and with the wave-breast, where his heart lay, with that he used to lean upon his harp, when he play-

* ' Supper'—The different parts of social worship and christian fellowship are here allegorically described. The heave-shoulder and wave-breast seem to have typified the power and love of our great High Priest; and to have conveyed an instruction to the priests to do their work with all their might, and with their whole heart: but they are here supposed to be also emblems of fervent prayer and grateful praise. The wine represents the exhilarating remembrance of the love of Christ in shedding his blood for us, and the application of the blessing to ourselves by living faith. The milk is the emblem of the plain, simple, and important instructions of Scripture, as brought forward by believers, when they meet together for their edification. The butter and honey may denote those animating views of God, and realizing anticipations of heavenly joy, which tend greatly to establish the judgment, instruct the understanding, and determine the affections, in cleaving to the good part that the believer hath chosen. The apples represent the promises and privileges which believers possess by communion with Christ in this ordinance, (Cant. ii. 3) and the nuts signify such difficult subjects as experience and observation enable mature Christians to understand; and which amply repay the pains of endeavouring to penetrate their meaning; though they are not proper for the discussions of young converts. Whatever unbelievers may think, a company of Christians, employing themselves in the manner here described, have far sweeter enjoyments, than they ever experienced when engaged in the mirth, diversions, and pleasures, of the world: for these are merely the shadow of joy but religion puts us in possession of the substance.

ed. These two dishes were very fresh and good, and they all ate heartily thereof.

The next they brought up was a bottle of wine, as red as blood. So Gaius said to them, Drink freely, that is the true juice of the vine, that makes glad the heart of God and man. So they drank and were merry (Deut. xxxii. 14 ; Judg. ix. 13 ; John xv. 5). The next was a dish of milk well crumbled: but Gaius said, Let the boys have that, that they may 'grow thereby' (1 Pet. ii. 1, 2). Then they brought up in course a dish of butter and honey. Then said Gaius, Eat freely of this, for this is good to cheer up and strengthen your judgments and understandings. This was our Lord's dish when he was a child : ' Butter and honey shall he eat, that he may know to refuse the evil, and choose the good' (Isaiah vii. 15) Then they brought him up a dish of apples, and they were very good tasted fruit. Then said Matthew, May we eat apples, since they were such, by and with which the serpent beguiled our first mother ?

Then said Gaius,

> Apples were they with which we were beguil'd,
> Yet sin, not apples, hath our souls defil'd:
> Apples forbid, if eat, corrupt the blood,
> To eat such, when commanded, does us good :
> Drink of his flagons, then, thou, church his dove,
> And eat his apples, who are sick of love.

Then said Matthew, I made the scruple, because awhile since, I was sick with eating of fruit

Gai. Forbidden fruit will make you sick, put not what our Lord has tolerated.

While they were thus talking, they were presented with another dish, and it was a dish of nuts (Sol. Song vi. 11). Then said some at the table, Nuts spoil tender teeth, especially the teeth of the children. Which when Gaius heard, he said :

> Hard texts are nuts (I will not call them cheaters),
> Whose shell do keep their kernels from the eaters;
> Open then the shells, and you shall have the meat;
> They here are brought for you to crack and eat.

Then they were very merry, and sat at the table a long time, talking of many things. Then said the old gentleman, My good landlord, while ye are cracking your nuts, if you please, do you open this riddle :

> A man there was (though some did count him mad),
> The more he cast away, the more he had.

Then they all gave good heed, wondering what good Gaius would say ; so he sat still awhile, and then thus replied :—

> He who thus bestows his goods upon the poor,
> Shall have as much again, and ten times more.

Then said Joseph, I dare say, Sir, I did not think you could have found it out.

Oh ! said Gaius, I have been trained up in this way a great while : nothing teaches like experience : I have learned of my Lord to be kind ; and have found by experience, that I have gained thereby. 'There is that scattereth, yet increaseth ; and there is that withholdeth more than is meet, but it tendeth to poverty : There is that maketh himself rich, yet hath nothing : there is that maketh him-self poor, yet hath great riches' (Prov. xi. 24 ; xiii. 7).

Then Samuel whispered to Christiana, his mother, and said, Mother, this is a very good man's house ; let us stay here a good while, and let my brother Matthew be married here to Mercy, before we go any farther.

The which Gaius the host overhearing, said, With a very good will, my child.

So they staid here more than a month ; and Mercy was given to Matthew to wife.

While they staid here, Mercy, as her cus tom was, would be making coats and garments to give to the poor, by which she brought up a very good report* upon pilgrims.

But to return again to our story. After supper, the lads desired a bed, for they were weary with travelling : then Gaius called to shew them their chamber ; but said Mercy, I will have them to bed. So he had them to bed, and they slept well : but the rest sat up all night ; for Gaius and they were such suitable company, that they could not tell how to part. Then after much talk of their Lord,

* ' Report'—If our love to sinners be only shewn by seeking their spiritual good, it will be considered as a mere bigoted desire to proselyte them to our sect or party : but uniform, diligent, and expensive endeavours to relieve their temporal wants are intelligible to every man, and brings a good report on the profession of the Gospel (Matt v. 16).

hemselves, and their journey, old Mr. Honest (he that put forth the riddle to Gaius) began to nod. Then said Great-heart, What, Sir, you begin to be drowsy? come, rub up, now here is a riddle for you. Then said Mr Honest, let us hear it.

Then said Mr. Great-heart,

> He that will kill, must first be overcome :
> Who live abroad would, first must die at home.

Ha! said Mr. Honest, it is a hard one, hard to expound, and harder to practise. But come, landlord, said he, I will if you please, leave my part to you ; do you expound it and I will hear what you say.

No, said Gaius, it was put to you, and it is expected you should answer it.

Then said the old gentleman,

> He first by grace* must conquer'd be,
>   That sin would mortify :
> Who, that he lieves, would convince me,
>   Unto himself must die.

It is right, said Gaius ; good doctrine and experience teaches this. For, until grace displays itself, and overcomes the soul with its glory, it is altogether without heart to oppose sin : besides, if sin is Satan's cords, by which the soul lies bound, how should it make resistance, before it is loosed from that infir-

---

* 'Grace'—The gracious operations of the Holy Spirit are here meant : these overcome our natural pride, love of sin, and aversion to God and religion; and then we repent, believe in Christ, are justified by faith, mortify sin, die to ourselves, and live to God in righteousness and true holiness.

mity ? Nor will any, that knows either reason
or grace, believe that such a man can be a
living monument of grace, that is a slave to
his own corruption. And now it-comes in my
mind I will tell you a story worth the hearing
There were two men that went on pilgrimage,
the one began when he was young the other
when he was old ; the young man had strong
corruptions to grapple with, the old man's
were weak with the decays of nature : the
young man trode his steps as even as did the
old one, and was every way as light as he :
who now, or which of them, had their graces
shining clearest, since both seemed to be
alike ?

Hon. The young man's, doubtless. For
that which heads it against the greatest opposition gives best demonstration that it is
strongest ; especially when it also holdeth
pace with that that meets not with half so
much ; as to be sure old age* does not. Be-

* ' Old age'—Old age affords a man great advantage in
overcoming some corrupt propensities : yet habits of indulgence, often more than counterbalance the decays of nature ;
and avarice, suspicion, and peevishness, with other evils,
gather strength as men advance in years. It is therefore in
some particulars only, that age has the advantage over youth ;
and some old men imagine that they have renounced sin, because they are no longer capable of committing the crimes in
which they once lived : so there are young men, who presume that they shall live to be old, and imagine that repentance
will then be comparatively easy to them : whereas, sin, in one
form or other, gathers strength and establishes its dominion,
as long as it is permitted to reign in the soul. The instruction, however, that is here conveyed, is very important ; provided it be properly understood : for if we do not estimate
the advantages of our situation, we cannot determine how

sides, I have observed, that old men have blessed themselves with this mistake ; namely, taking the decays of nature for a gracious conquest over corruptions, and so have been apt to beguile themselves. Indeed, old men, that are gracious, are best able to give advice to them that are young, because they have seen most of the emptiness of things : but yet, for an old and a young man to set out both together, the young one has the advantage of the fairest discovery of a work of grace within him, though the old man's corruptions are naturally the weakest.

Thus they sat talking till break of day. Now when the family was up, Christiana bid her son James that he should read a chapter ; so he read the fifty-third of Isaiah. When he had done, Mr. Honest, asked, why it was said that the Saviour is said to come out of a dry ground ; and also that he had no form or comeliness in him ?

Then said Mr. Great-heart, To the first, I answer, because the church of the Jews, of which Christ came, had then lost almost all

far external amendment results from internal renovation. During tedious diseases, or in the immediate prospect of death, men often feel very indifferent to the world, set against sin, disinclined to former indulgences, and earnest about salvation : yet returning health, business, company, and temptation terminate such promising appearances. Many suppose themselves to be very good-tempered, while every one studies to oblige them ; yet provocation excites vehement anger and resentment in their breast : nay, riches and honour seem at a distance to have no charms for those, who are powerfully attracted by their magentical influence when placed within their reach.

the sap and spirit of religion. To the second, I say, the words are spoken in the person of the unbeliever, who, because they want the eye that can see into our Prince's heart, therefore they judge of him by the meanness of his outside. Just like those that know not that precious stones are covered over with a homely crust; who when they have found one, because they know not what they have found, cast it again away, as men do a common stone.

Well, said Gaius, now you are here, and since, as I know, Mr. Great-heart is good at his weapons, if you please, after we have refreshed ourselves, we will walk into the fields, to see if we can do any good. About a mile*

* 'A mile'—The refreshment of divine consolations and Christian fellowship is intended to prepare us for vigorously maintaining the good fight of faith; not only against the enemies of our own souls, but also against the opposers of our holy religion, according to the talents entrusted to us, and the duties of our several stations. We are soldiers belonging to the great army under the command of the captain of our salvation; and we ought to strive against sin, and 'contend for the faith once delivered to the saints,' by our profession, example, prayers, converse, and every other method authorised by the word of God. All that love the Lord are our brethren; and every thing that can mislead, dismay, or hinder any of them, should be considered as an adversary to the common cause; and we should counteract with meekness, but with firmness and decision, all the endeavours of those who obstruct men in the ways of the Lord, or turn them aside into by-paths. It does not however clearly appear what particular description of opposers were represented by Slay-good: whether the author had in view certain selfish and malignant persecutors, who intimidated professors by fines and imprisonment, to the hazard of their lives, or of their souls; or some plausible heretics, who 'taught things which they ought not, for filty lucre's sake,' to the total ruin

14*

from hence there is one Slay-good, a giant, that does much annoy the king's highway in these parts : and I know whereabout his haunt is : he is master of a number of thieves ; ıt would be well if we could clear these parts of him.

So they consented, and went, Mr. Great-heart with his sword, helmet, and shield, and the rest with spears and staves.

When they came to the place where he was, they found him with one Feeble-mind in his hand, whom his servants had brought unto him, having taken him in the way : now the giant was rifling him, with a purpose, after that, to pick his bones ; for he was of the nature of flesh-eaters.

Well, so soon as he saw Mr. Great-heart and his friends at the mouth of the cave, with their weapons, he demanded what they wanted.

Gr.-h. We want thee, for we are come to revenge the quarrels of the many that thou hast slain of the pilgrims, when thou hast dragged them out of the king's highway ; wherefore come out of thy cave. So he armed himself and came out ; and to the battle they went, and fought for above an hour, and then stood still to take wind.

of many that seemed hopeful, and the great detriment of others, who were weak in faith and confused in judgment. The conflict seems merely to denote the efforts which Christians should make, to prevent the effects of such opposition and delusion, and to remove such occasions of mischief out of the way : as also to shew, that the strong in faith are peculiarly called to these services, and ought not to shrink from hardship, danger, and suffering in so good a cause.

Then said the giant, Why are you here on my ground ?

Gr.-h. To revenge the blood of pilgrims, as I also told thee before. So they went to it again, and the giant made Mr. Great-heart give back ; but he came up again, and in the greatness of his mind he let fly with such stoutness at the giant's head and sides, that he made him let his weapon fall out of his hand ; so he smote and slew him, and cut off his head, and brought it away to the inn. He also took Feeble-mind the pilgrim, and brought him with him to his lodgings. When they were come home, they shewed his head to the family, and set it up, as they had done others before, for a terror to those that shall attempt to do as he, hereafter.

Then they asked Mr. Feeble-mind, how he fell into his hands ?

Then said the poor man,* I am a sickly man, as you see, and because death did usu- ally once a day knock at my door, I thought I should never be well at home ; so I betook

* ' Poor man'—The character of Feeble-mind seems to coincide in some things with that of Fearing : and in others with the description of Little-faith. Constitutional timidity and lowness of spirits, arising from a feeble frame and fre- quent sickness, while they are frequently the means of excit- ing men to religion, give also a peculiar cast to their views and the nature of their profession ; tend to hold them under perpetual discouragements ; and unfit them for hard and per- ilous services. This seems implied in the name given to the native place of Feeble-mind : his uncertainty or hesitation in his religious profession was the effect of his natural turn of mind, which was opposite to the sanguine and confident. Yet this timid and discouraged irresolution often connects with evident sincerity and remarkable perseverance in the ways of

myself to a pilgrim's life ; and have travelled hither from the town of Uncertain, where I and my father were born. I am a man of no strength at all of body, nor yet of mind ; but would, if I could, though I can but crawl, spend my life in the pilgrim's way. When I came at the gate that is at the head of the way, the Lord of that place did entertain me freely : neither objected he against my weakly looks, nor against my feeble mind ; but gave me such things that were necessary for my journey, and bid me hope to the end. When I came to the house of the Interpreter, I received much kindness there ; and because the hill of Difficulty was judged too hard for me, I was carried up that by one of his servants. Indeed I have found much relief from pilgrims, though none was willing to go softly as I am forced to do : yet still as they came on, they bid me be of good cheer, and said, that it was the will of their Lord, that ' comfort' should be given to ' the feebleminded ;' and so went on their own pace. When I was come to Assault-lane, then this giant met with me, and bid me prepare for an encounter ; but, alas ! feeble one that I was ! I had more need of a cordial : so he came up and took me. I conceived he should not kill me : also when he had got me into his den,

God. The principle difference between Feeble-mind and Fearing seems to be this :—that the former was more afraid of opposition, and the latter more doubtful about the event : which perhaps may intimate, that Slay-good rather represents persecutors than deceivers.

since I went not with him willingly, I believed I should come out alive again; for I have heard, that not any pilgrim, that is taken captive by violent hands, if he keeps heartwhole towards his Master, is, by the laws of Providence, to die by the hand of the enemy. Robbed I looked to be, and robbed to be sure I am; but I am, as you see, escaped with life, for the which I thank my King as author, and you as the means. Other brunts I also look for; but this I have resolved on, to wit, to run when I can, to go when I cannot run, and to creep when I cannot go. As to the main, I thank him that loved me, I am fixed; my way is before me, my mind is beyond the river that has no bridge; though I am, as you see, but of a feeble mind.

Then said old Mr. Honest, Have not you some time ago been acquainted with one Mr. Fearing, a pilgrim?

Feebl. Acquainted with him! yes; he came from the town of Stupidity, which lies four degrees northward of the city of Destruction, and as many off of where I was born; yet we were well acquainted, for indeed he was my uncle, my father's brother; he and I have been much of a temper; he was a little shorter than I, but yet we were much of a complexion.

Hon. I perceive you know him; and I am apt to believe also, that you were related one to another, for you have his whitely look, a cast like his with your eye, and your speech is much alike

Feebl. Most have said so, that have known us both ; and, besides, what I have read in him, I have for the most part found in myself.

Come, Sir, said good Gaius, be of good cheer, you are welcome to me, and to my house ; and what thou hast a mind to, call for freely ; and what thou wouldest have my servants do for thee, they will do it with a ready mind.

Then said Mr. Feeble-mind, This is an unexpected favour, and as the sun shining out of a very dark cloud. Did giant Slay-good intend me this favour when he stopt me, and resolved to let me go no farther ? Did he intend, that after he had rifled my pocket, should go to ' Gaius mine host ?' Yet so it is.

Now just as Mr Feeble-mind and Gaius were thus in talk, there comes one running, and called at the door, and told, that about a mile and a half off there was one Mr. Notright, a pilgrim, struck dead upon the place where he was, with a thunder-bolt.

Alas !* said Mr Feeble-mind, is he slain ? He overtook me some days before I came so

---

* ' Alas !'—Here again we meet with a contrast between a feeble believer and a specious hypocrite. The latter eludes persecution by time-serving, yet perishes in his sins: the former suffers and trembles, yet hopes; is delivered and comforted, and finds his trials terminate in his greater advantage. The frequency with which this difference is introduced, and the variety of character by which it is illustrated, shows us, how important the author deemed it to warn false professors at the same time that we comfort the feeble minded, and to mark as exactly as we can the discriminating peculiarities of their aim and experience.

far as hither, and would be my company-keeper ; he also was with me when Slay-good the giant took me, but he was nimble of his heels, and escaped ; but, it seems, he escaped to die, and I was took to live

> What, one would think, doth seek to slay outright.
> Oft-times delivers from the saddest plight.
> That very providence, whose face is death,
> Doth oft-times, to the lowly, life bequeath.
> I taken was, he did escape and flee ;
> Hands cross'd give death to him, and life to me.

Now about this time Matthew and Mercy were married ; also Gaius gave his daughter Phebe to James, Matthew's brother, to wife After which time they staid about ten days at Gaius's house ; spending their time, and the seasons, like as pilgrims used to do.

When they were to depart, Gaius made t em a feast, and they did eat and drink, and were merry. Now the hour was come that they must be gone ; wherefore Mr. Great-heart called for a reckoning. But Gaius told him, that at his house it was not the custom of pilgrims to pay for their entertainment. He boarded them by the year, but looked for his pay from the Good Samaritan, who had promised him, at his return, whatsoever charge he was at with them, faithfully to re-pay him (Luke x. 34, 35). Then said Mr. Great-heart to him, ' Beloved, thou dost faithfully, whatsoever thou doest to the brethren and to strangers, which have borne witness of thy charity before the church, whom if thou yet bring forward on their jour-

ney, after a godly sort, thou shalt do well
(3 John 5, 6).

Then Gaius took his leave of them all,
and his children, and particularly of Mr.
Feeble-mind : he also gave him something
to drink by the way.

Now Mr. Feeble-mind, when they were
going out at the door, made as if he intended
to linger. The which when Mr. Great-heart
spied, he said, Come, Mr. Feeble-mind, pray
do you go along with us, I will be your conductor, and you shall fare as the rest.

Fee. Alas ! I want a suitable companion ;
you are all lusty and strong ; but I, as you
see am weak ; I choose therefore rather to
come behind, lest by reason of my many in
firmities, I should be both a burthen to myself and to you.   I am, as I said, a man of a
weak and feeble mind, and shall be offended*

---

* ' Offended'—Weak believers are conscientious, even to
scrupulosity : so far from allowing themselves in the practice
of known sin, or the omission of evident duty, they are prone
to abridge themselves in things which are indifferent, they
often impose rules on themselves, which they do not expect
others to observe ; and sometimes are sensible that their uneasiness, at the liberty used by their brethren, arises from ignorance and low attainments ; and therefore they deem it
better to live retired, than to burthen others with their peculiarities, or be grieved with things which everywhere meet their
observation. But there are persons, that expect to be encouraged as weak believers, who are far removed from such
scrupulousness ; and whose weakness consists merely in an
inability to maintain an unwavering confidence, while they
live in a loose and negligent manner. These seem more to
resemble Not-right than Feeble-mind. They that are indeed
weak believers should learn from this passage to beware of
censoriousness, and of making themselves a standard for others : and their stronger brethren should be reminded not to

and made weak at that which others can bear.
I shall like no laughing ; I shall like no gay
attire ; I shall like no unprofitable questions.
Nay, I am so weak a man, as to be offended
with that which others have a liberty to do. I
do not know all the truth ; I am a very ignorant
Christian man ; sometimes, if I hear some
rejoice in the Lord, it troubles me, because I
cannot do so too. It is with me, as it is with
a weak man among the strong, or as a lamp
despised. 'He, that is ready to slip with his
feet, is a lamp despised in the thought of him
that is at ease' (Job xiii. 5) ; so that I know
not what to do.

But, brother, said Mr. Great-heart, I have
it in commission to ' comfort the feeble-mind-
ed,' and to support the weak. You must
needs go along with us ; we will wait for
you ; we will lend you our help ; we will deny ourselves of some things, both opiniona-
tive and practical, for your sake ; we will not
enter into ' doubtful disputations' before you ;
we will be made all things to you, rather than
you shall be left behind (Rom. xiv ; 1 Cor.
viii ; ix. 22).

Now all this while they were at Gaius's
door ; and behold, as they were thus in the
heat of their discourse, Mr. Ready-to-halt
came by, with his crutches in his hand, and

despise or grieve them, by an inexpedient use of their liberty.
[The author, in a marginal note, has marked Great-heart's
answer as a christian spirit.]   They will, however, commonly find associates, in some measure, of their own turn who
are often more useful to them, than such as cannot entirely
sympathize with their feelings.

he also was going on pilgrimage (Psalm
xxxviii. 17).

Then said Mr. Feeble-mind to him, How
camest thou hither ? I was but now complain
ing that I had not a suitable companion ; but
thou art according to my wish. Welcome,
welcome, good Mr. Ready-to-halt, I hope
thou and I may be some help.

Ready-to-halt. I shall be glad of thy company, said the other ; and, good Mr. Feeble-
mind, rather than we will part, since we are
thus happily met, I will lend thee one of my
crutches.

Fee. Nay, said he, though I thank thee for
thy good-will, I am not inclined to halt before I am lame. Howbeit, I think, when occasion is, it may help me against a dog.

Ready-to-halt. If either myself or my
crutches can do thee a pleasure, we are both
at thy command, good Mr Feeble-mind.

Thus therefore they went on. Mr. Great-
heart and Mr. Honest went before, Christiana
and her children went next, and Mr. Feeble-
mind and Mr. Ready-to-halt came behind
with his crutches. Then said Mr. Honest,
Pray, Sir, now we are upon the road, tell us
some profitable things of some that have gone
on pilgrimage before us.

Gr.-h. With a good will. I suppose you
have heard how Christian of old did meet
with Apollyon in the valley of Humiliation,
and also what hard work he had to go through
the valley of the Shadow of Death. And I
think you cannot but have heard how Faithful

was put to it by Madam Wanton, with Adam the First, with one Discontent and Shame : four as deceitful villains as a man can meet with upon the road.

Hon Yes, I believe I heard of all this ; but indeed good Faithful was hardest put to it with Shame ; he was an unwearied one.

Gr.-h. Ay : for, as the pilgrim well said, he of all men had the wrong name.

Hon. But pray, Sir, where was it that Christian and Faithful met Talkative ? that same was a notable one.

Gr.-h. He was a confident fool ; yet many follow his ways.

Hon. He had like to have beguiled Faithful.

Gr.-h. Ay, but Christian put him into a way quickly to find him out.

Thus they went on till they came to the place where Evangelist met with Christian and Faithful, and prophesied to them what they should meet with at Vanity-fair.

Then said their guide, Hereabouts did Christian and Faithful meet with Evangelist, who prophesied to them of what troubles they should meet with at Vanity-fair.

Hon. Say you so ? I dare say it was a hard* chapter that then he did read unto them

* 'Hard'—The near prospect of persecution is formidable even to true believers, notwithstanding all the encouragements of God's word. It is therefore very useful to realize such scenes to our minds, and to consider how we should feel were they actually present ; that we may be preserved from self-confidence, excited to diligence in every thing connected

Gr.-h. It was so, but then he gave them
encouragement withal. But what do we talk
of them ? they were a couple of lion-like-men ;
they had set their faces like flints. Do not you
remember how undaunted they were when
they stood before the judge ?

Hon. Well, Faithful bravely suffered.

Gr.-h. So he did, and as brave things came
on't : for Hopeful and some others, as the story relates, were converted by his death (P. i.
p. 138—209).

Hon. Well, but pray go on ; for you are
well-acquainted with things.

Gr.-h. Above all that Christian met with
after he had passed through Vanity-fair, one
By-ends was the arch one.

Hon. By-ends ! What was he ?

Gr.-h. A very arch fellow, a downright
hypocrite ; one that would be religious, which
way ever the world went : but so cunning,
that he would be sure never to lose or suffer
for it. He had his mode of religion for every
fresh occasion, and his wife was as good at it
as he. He would turn and change from opinion to opinion : yea, and plead for so doing
too. But, as far as I could learn, he came to
an ill-end with his by-ends : nor did I ever
hear, that any of his children were ever of any

with the assurance of hope, put on our guard against every
action or engagement which might weaken our confidence
in God ; and pray without ceasing, for that measure of
wisdom, fortitude, patience, meekness, faith, and love
which might be sufficient for us, should matters come to the
worst.

esteem with any that truly fear God (P. i. p. 212—230).

Now by this time they were come within sight of the town of Vanity, where Vanity-fair is kept. So when they saw that they were so near the town, they consulted with one another how they should pass through the town : and some said one thing, and some another. At last Mr. Great-heart said, I have, as you may understand, often been a conductor of pilgrims through this town : now I am acquainted with one Mr. Mnason, a Cyprusian by nation, and an old disciple, at whose house we may lodge. If you think good, said he, we will turn in there.

Content, said old Honest ; Content, said Christiana ; Content, said Mr. Feeble-mind ; and so they said all. Now you must think it was even-tide by that they got to the outside of the town ; but Mr. Great-heart knew the way to the old man's house. So thither they came ; and he called at the door ; and the old man within knew his tongue so soon as ever he heard it ; so he opened, and they all came in. Then said Mnason, their host, How far have you come to-day ? So they said, From the house of Gaius our friend. I promise you, said he, you have done a good stitch ; you may well be weary : sit down. So they sat down.

Then said their guide, Come, what cheer, good Sirs ? I dare say you are welcome to my friend

I also, said Mr. Mnason, do bid you wel
15*

come; and whatever you want, do but say, and we will do what we can to get it for you.

Hon. Our great want, awhile since, was harbour and good company, and now I hope we have both.

Mnas. For harbour, you see what it is: but for good company, that will appear in the trial.

Well said Mr. Great-heart, will you have the pilgrims into their lodging?

I will, said Mr. Mnason. So he had them to their respective places; and also shewed them a very fair dining-room, where they might be, and sup together, until time was come to go to rest.

Now when they were set in their places, and were a little cheery after their journey, Mr. Honest asked his landlord, if there were any store of good people in the town?

Mnas. We have a few; for indeed they are but a few, when compared with them on the other side.

Hon. But how shall we do to see some of them? for the sight* of good men, to them that are going on pilgrimage, is like to the appearing of the moon and stars to them that are going a journey.

Then Mr. Mnason stamped with his foot, and his daughter Grace came up: so he said

* 'The sight'—Even in those populous cities, where vanity most prevails, and where persecution at some seasons has most raged, a remnant of real Christians will generally reside: and believers will in every place inquire after such persons, associate with them (Ps. cxix. 63; 1 John i. 14).

unto her, Grace, go you tell my friends, Mr.
Contrite, Mr. Holyman, Mr. Lovesaints,
Mr. Dare-not-lie, and Mr. Penitent, that I
have a friend or two at my house that have a
mind this evening to see them.

So Grace went to call them, and they came,
and, after salutation made, they sat down together at the table.

Then said Mr. Mnason, their landlord, My
neighbours, I have, as you see, a company
of strangers come to my house : they are
pilgrims ; they come from afar, and are going
to Mount Sion. But who, quoth he, do you
think this is ? (pointing his fingers at Christiana.) It is Christiana, the wife of Christian,
that famous pilgrim, who, with Faithful his
brother, were so shamefully handled in our
town. At that they stood amazed, saying,
We little thought to see Christiana, when
Grace came to call us ; wherefore this is a
very comfortable surprise. Then they asked
her about her welfare, and if these young
men were her husband's sons. And when
she had told them they were, they said, The
King whom you love and serve, make you
as your father, and bring you where he is in
peace !

Then, Mr. Honest, when they were all sat
down, asked Mr. Contrite, and the rest, in
what posture their town was at present ?

Cont. You may be sure we are full of hurry
in fairtime It is hard keeping our hearts
and spirits in good order, when we are in a
cumbered condition. He that lives in such

a place as this, and that has to do with such
as we have, has need of an item, to caution
him to take heed every moment of the day.

Hon. But how are your neighbours now
for quietness?

Cont. They are much more moderate now
than formerly.   You know how Christian and
Faithful were used at our town : but of late,
I say, they have been far more moderate.   I
think the blood of Faithful lieth with load upon them till now ; for since they burned him,
they have been ashamed to burn any more :
in those days we were afraid to walk the
streets, but now we can shew our heads.
Then the name of a professor was odious ;
now, especially in some parts of our town
(for you know our town is large), religion is
counted honourable.

Then said Mr. Contrite to them, Pray how
fareth it with you in your pilgrimage ? How
stands the country affected towards you ?

Hon. It happens to us, as it happeneth to
wayfaring men : sometimes our way is clean,
sometimes foul, sometimes up hill, sometimes
down hill ; we are seldom at a certainty : the
wind is not always on our backs, nor is every
one a friend that we meet with in the way.
We have met with some notable rubs already,
and what are yet behind we know not ; but,
for the most part, we find it true that has
been talked of old ; ' A good man must suffer
trouble.'

Cont. You talk of rubs : what rubs have
you met withal ?

Hon. Nay, ask Mr. Great-heart our guide, for he can give the best account of that.

Gr.-h. We have been beset three or four times already.   First, Christiana and her children were beset with two ruffians, that they feared would take away their lives.   We were beset with giant Bloodyman, giant Maul, and giant Slaygood.   Indeed we did rather beset the last, than were beset of him.   And thus it was : after we had been some time at the house of Gaius, ' mine host, and of the whole church,' we were minded upon a time to take our weapons with us, and to go see if we could light upon any of those that were enemies to pilgrims ; for we heard that there was a notable one thereabouts.   Now Gaius knew his haunt better than I, because he dwelt thereabout ; so we looked and looked, till at last we discerned the mouth of his cave ; then were we glad, and plucked up our spirits.   So we approached up to his den ; and lo, when we came there, he had dragged, by mere force, into his net, this poor man, Mr. Feeble-mind, and was about to bring him to his end.   But when he saw us, supposing, as we thought, he had another prey, he left the poor man in his house, and came out.   So we fell to it full sore, and he lustily laid about him ; but in conclusion, he was brought down to the ground, and his head cut off, and set up by the way-side, for a terror to such as should after practise such ungodliness.   That I tell you the truth here is the man himself to affirm it, who was as a lamb taken out of the mouth of the lion.

Then said Mr. Feeble-mind, I found this true, to my cost and comfort ; to my cost, when he threatened to pick my bones every moment ; and to my comfort, when I saw Mr. Great-heart and his friends, with their weapons, approach so near for my deliverance.

Then said Mr. Holyman, There are two things that they have need to be possessed of, that go on pilgrimage ; courage, and an unspotted life. If they have not courage, they can never hold on their way ; and, if their lives be loose, they will make the very name of a pilgrim stink.

Then said Mr. Lovesaint, I hope this caution is not needful among you ; but truly there are many that go upon the road, that rather declare themselves strangers to pilgrimage, than strangers and pilgrims in the earth.

Then said Mr. Dare-not-lie, It is true, they neither have the pilgrim's weed, nor the pilgrim's courage ; they go not uprightly, but all awry with their feet ; one shoe goeth inward, another outward, and their hosen out behind ; here a rag, and there a rent, to the disparagement of their Lord.

These things, said Mr. Penitent, they ought to be troubled for ; nor are the pilgrims like to have that grace upon them and their pilgrims' progress as they desire, until the way is cleared of such spots and blemishes.

Thus they sat talking and spending the time until supper was set upon the table ; unto which they went and refreshed their weary bodies : so they went to rest. Now they stayed in the fair a great while, at the house of Mr. Mnason, who in process of time, gave his daughter Grace unto Samuel, Christiana's son, and his daughter Martha to Joseph.

The time, as I said, that they lay here was long ; for it was not now as in former times. Wherefore the pilgrims grew acquainted with many of the good people of the town, and did them what service they could. Mercy, as she was wont, laboured much for the poor ; wherefore their bellies and backs blessed her, and she was there an ornament to her profession. And, to say the truth for Grace, Phœbe, and Martha, they were all of a very good nature, and did much good in their places. They were also all of them very fruitful ; so that Christian's name, as was said before, was like to live in the world.

While they lay here, there came a monster* out of the woods, and slew many of the

* Monster'—This refers to the prevalence of popery for some time before the revolution in 1688 ; by which many nominal Protestants were drawn aside, and numbers of children educated in the principles of that dark superstition. The favour or frown of the prince and his party operated so powerfully, that worldly men in general yielded to the imposition ; but several persons among the nonconformists, as well as in the established church, did eminent service at that crisis by their preaching and writings, in exposing the delusions and abominations of that monstrous religion ; and these endeavours were eventually the means of overturning the plan forma-

people of the town. It would also carry away
their children, and teach them to suck its
whelps. Now no man in the town durst so
much as face the monster; but all men fled
when they heard of the noise of his coming
The monster was like unto no one beast upon
the earth : its body was 'like a dragon, and
it had seven heads and ten horns' (Rev. xii
3). It made a great havoc of children, and
yet it was governed by a woman. This monster propounded conditions to men ; and such
men as loved their lives more than their souls
accepted of those conditions.

Now Mr. Great-heart, together with those
who came to visit the pilgrims at Mr. Mnason's
house, entered into a covenant to go and engage this beast, if perhaps they might deliver
the people of this town from the paws and
mouth of this so devouring a serpent.

Then did Mr. Great-heart, Mr. Contrite,
Mr. Holyman, Mr. Dare-not-lie, and Mr.
Penitent, with their weapons, go forth to meet
him. Now the monster, at first, was very
rampant, and looked upon these enemies with
great disdain ; but they so belaboured him,
being sturdy men of arms, that they made him
make a retreat : so they came home to Mr.
Mnason's house again.

The monster, you must know, had his certain

---

ed for the re-establishment of popery in Britain. The disinterested and bold decided conduct of many dissenters on this
occasion procured considerable favour both to them and their
brethren, with the best friends of the nation ; but the prejudices of others prevented them from reaping all the advantag
from it that they ought to have done.

seasons to come out in, and to make his attempts upon the children of the people of the town : also these seasons did these valiant worthies watch him in, and did continually assault him ; insomuch that in process of time he became not only wounded, but lame ; also he had not made the havoc of the townmen's children as formerly he has done   And it is verily believed by some, that this beast will certainly die of his wounds.   This therefore made Mr. Great-heart and his fellows of great fame in this town ; so that many of the people, that wanted their taste of things, yet had a reverent esteem and respect for them. Upon this account therefore it was, that these pilgrims got not much hurt here.   True, there were some of the baser sort, that could see no more than a mole, nor understand no more than a beast ; these had no reverence for these men, nor took they notice of their valour and adventures.

Well, the time drew on that the pilgrims must go on their way ; therefore they prepared for their journey.   They sent for their friends ; they conferred with them ; they had some time set apart therein, to commit each other to the protection of their Prince. There were again that brought them of such things as they had, that were fit for the weak and the strong, for the women and the men, and so laded them with such things as were necessary (Acts xxviii. 10).   Then they set forward on their way ; and their friends accompanying them so far as was convenient, they again committed each other to the protection of their King, and departed.

They, therefore, that were of the pilgrims' company, went on, and Mr. Great-heart went before them ; now the women and children being weakly, they were forced to go as they could bear ; by this means Mr. Ready-to-halt and Mr. Feeble-mind had more to sympathize with their condition.

When they were gone from the townsmen, and when their friends had bid them farewell, they quickly came to the place where Faithful was put to death ; therefore they made a stand and thanked Him that had enabled him to bear his cross so well ; and the rather, because they now found, that they had a benefit by such a man's sufferings as he was They went on, therefore, after this a good way farther, talking of Christian and Faithful ; and how Hopeful joined himself to Christian, after that Faithful was dead (P. i. 210).

Now they were come up with the hill Lucre, where the silver mine was, which took Demas off from his pilgrimage, and into which, as some think, By-ends fell and perished ; wherefore they considered that. But when they were come to the old monument that stood over against the hill Lucre, to wit to the pillar of salt, that stood also within view of Sodom and its stinking lake (P. i. p. 230), they marvelled as did Christian before, that men of that knowledge and ripeness of wit, as they were, should be so blind as to turn

aside here. Only they considered again,
that nature is not affected with the harms that
others have met with, especially if that thing,
upon wnich they look, has an attracting virtue upon the foolish eye.

I saw now that they went on till they came
to the river that was on this side of the Delectable Mountains (P. i. p. 234). To the
river where the fine trees grow on both sides ;
and whose leaves if taken inwardly, are good
against surfeits (Ps. xxiii), where the meadows are green all the year long, and where
they might lie down safely.

By this river side, in the meadows, there
were cotes and folds for sheep, a house built
for the nourishing and bringing up of those
lambs, the babes of those women that go on
pilgrimage. Also there was here one that
was entrusted with them, who could have
compassion, and that could gather these
lambs with his arm, and carry them is his
bosom, and that could gently lead those that
were with young (Heb. v. 2 ; Isa. lxiii).
Now to the care* of this man Christiana ad-
monished her four daughters to commit their

* ' Care'—Under this emblem we are taught the importance of early recommending our children to the faithful care
of the Lord Jesus, by fervent prayer, with earnest desires of
their eternal good, above all secular advantages whatsoever :
consequently we ought to keep them at a distance from such
places, connexions, books, and companies, as may corrupt
their principles and morals ; to instil such pious instructions
as they are capable of receiving ; to bring them early under
the preaching of the Gospel and to the ordinances of God ;
and to avail ourselves of every help, in thus ' training them
up in the nurture and admonition of the Lord.' For deprav-

little ones, that by these waters they might be
housed, harboured, succoured, and nourished,
and that none of them might be lacking in
time to come. This man, if any of them go
astray, or be lost, he will bring them again :
he will also bind up that which was broken,
and will strengthen them that are sick (Jer.
xxiii. 4 ; Ezek. xxxiv. 11—16). Here they
will never want meat, drink, and clothing ;
here they will be kept from thieves and robbers ; for this man will die before one of
those committed to his trust shall be lost.
Besides, here they shall be sure to have
good nurture and admonition ; and shall be
taught to walk in right paths ; and that
you know is a favour of no small account
Also here, as you see, are delicate waters,
pleasant meadows, dainty flowers, variety of
trees, and such as bear wholesome fruit ;
fruit not like that which Matthew eat of, that
fell over the wall out of Beelzebub's garden ;
but fruit that procureth health where there
is none, and that continueth and increaseth
where it is.

So they were content to commit their little
ones to him ; and that which was also an en-

---

and natural propensities, the course of the world, the artifices
of Satan, the inexperience, credulity, and sanguine expectations of youth, the importance of the case, and the precepts
of Scripture, concur in requiring this conduct of us. Yet, after all, our minds must be anxious about the event, in proportion as we value their souls, except as we find relief, by
commending them to the faithful care of that tender Shepherd,
who ' gathers the lambs with his arm, and carries them in
his bosom.'

couragement to them so to do was, for that
all this was to be at the charge of the King ;
and so was an hospital to young children and
orphans.

Now they went on : and when they were
come to By-path meadow, to the stile over
which Christian went with his fellow Hopeful, when they were taken by giant Despair,
and put into Doubting-castle, they sat down
and consulted what was best to be done ; to
wit, now they were so strong, and had got
such a man as Mr. Great-heart for their conductor, whether they had not best to make an
attempt upon the giant, demolish his castle,
and if there were any pilgrims in it, to set
them at liberty, before they went any farther
(P. i. p. 243—254).   So one said one thing,
and another said to the contrary.   One questioned if it was lawful to go upon unconsecra-
ted ground ; another said they might, provided their end was good.   But Mr. Great-
heart said, Though that assertion offered
last cannot be universally true, yet I have a
commandment to resist sin, to overcome evil,
to fight the good fight of faith : and I pray,
with whom should I fight this good fight, if
not with giant Despair ? I will therefore attempt the taking away of his life, and the demolishing of Doubting-castle.   Then said he,
Who will go with me ? Then said old Honest, I will.   And so we will too, said Christiana's four sons, Matthew, Samuel, James,
and Joseph : for they were young men and
strong (1 John ii. 13, 14).

16*

So they left the women on the road, and with them Mr. Feeble-mind and Mr. Ready-to-halt, with his crutches, to be their guard, until they came back ; for in that place, though giant Despair dwelt so near, they keeping in the road, a little child might lead them (Isa. xi. 6).

So Mr. Great-heart, old Honest, and the four young men went to go up to Doubting-castle, to look for giant Despair. When they came to the castle gate, they knocked for entrance with an unusual noise. With that the old giant comes to the gate, and Diffidence his wife follows. Then said he, Who and what is he that is so hardy, as after this manner to molest the giant Despair ? Mr. Great-heart replied, It is I, Great-heart, one of the King of the celestial country's conductors of pilgrims to their place : and I demand of thee, that thou open thy gates for my entrance : Prepare thyself also to fight, for I am come to take away thy head, and to demolish Doubting-castle.

Now giant Despair, because he was a giant, thought no man could overcome him, and again, thought he, Since heretofore I have made a conquest of angels, shall Great-heart make me afraid ? So he harnessed himself, and went out ; he had a cap of steel upon his head, a breast-plate of fire girded to him, and he came out in iron shoes, with a great club in his hand. Then these six men made up to him, and beset him behind and before : also when Diffidence the giantess

came up to help him, old Mr. Honest cut her
down at one blow. Then they fought for
their lives, and giant Despair was brought
down to the ground, but was very loath to
die : he struggled hard, and had, as they say,
as many lives as a cat ; but Great-heart was
his death ; for he left him not till he had sev-
ered his head from his shoulders.

Then they fell to demolishing Doubting-
castle, and that you know might with ease be
done, since giant Despair was dead. They
were seven days in destroying of that : and in
it, of pilgrims they found Mr. Despondency,
almost starved to death, and one Much-afraid,
his daughter ; these two they saved alive.
But it would have made you have wondered
to have seen the dead bodies that lay here
and there in the castle yard, and how full of
dead men's bones the dungeon was.

When Mr. Great-heart and his companions had performed this exploit, they took Mr.
Despondency, and his daughter Much-afraid,
into their protection ; for they were honest
people, though they were prisoners in Doubting-castle to that giant Despair. They therefore, I say, took with them the head of the
giant (for his body they had buried under a
heap of stones), and down to the road and
to their companions they came, and shewed
them what they had done. Now when
Feeble-mind and Ready-to-halt saw that it
was the head of giant Despair indeed, they
were very jocund and merry. Now Christiana, if need was could play upon the viol,

and her daughter Mercy upon the lute: so, since they were so merry disposed, she played them a lesson, and Ready-to-halt would dance. So he took Despondency's daughter, named much afraid by the hand, and so dancing they went in the road. True, he could not dance without one crutch in his hand; but I promise you he footed it well: also the girl was to be commended, for she answered the musick handsomely.

As for Mr. Despondency, the musick was not much to him: he was for feeding rather than dancing; for that he was almost starved So Christiana gave him some of her bottle of spirits, for present relief, and then prepared him something to eat; and in a little time the old gentleman came to himself, and began to be finely revived.

Now I saw in my dream, when all these things were finished, Mr. Great-heart took the head of giant Despair, and set it upon a pole by the highway-side, right over against the pillar that Christian erected for a caution to pilgrims that came after, to take heed of entering into his grounds.

Then he writ under it, upon a marble stone, these verses following :—

'This is the head* of him, whose name only
In former time, did pilgrims terrify.

.* 'The head'—These lines are here added, as in other places,

'Though Doubting-castle be demolished,
And giant Despair too has lost his head;
Sin can rebuild the castle, make 't remain,
And make Despair the giant live again.'

His castle's down, and Diffidence, his wife,
Brave master Great-heart has bereft of Life.
Despondency, his daughter Much-afraid,
Great-heart for them also the man has play'd.
Who hereof doubts, if he'll but cast his eye
Up hither, may his scruples satisfy.
This head also, when doubting cripples dance,
Doth shew from fears they have deliverance.

When those men had thus bravely shewed
themselves against Doubting-castle, and had
slain giant Despair, they went forward, and
went on till they came to the Delectable
Mountains, where Christian and Hopeful
refreshed themselves with the varieties of the

Indeed they seem to be much wanted; for the exploit of
destroying Doubting-castle, and killing giant Despair, is
more liable to exception, than any incident in the whole
work. To relieve the minds of such as are discouraged in
the path of duty, or when inquiring the way of salvation, is
doubtless a most important service in the cause of Christ;
this is represented by the attempts made to mend the road
over the slough of Despond: but By-path meadow ought to
lead to Doubting-castle; such inward distresses are as useful
to Christians as any other rebukes and corrections, by which
their loving Friend renders them watchful and circumspect.
Could this order be reversed, it would give strength to temptation; and tend to embolden men to seek relief from difficulties by transgression; for the apprehension of subsequent
distress is one grand preventative, even to the true believer,
when such measures are suggested to his mind. Indeed this
is the Lord's method of performing his covenant to his people; 'I will,' says he, ' put my fear in their hearts, that they
shall not depart from me' (Jer. xxxii. 40). If therefore love
be not in lively exercise, he has so ordered it, that fear should
intervene, to prevent worse consequences. So that, when
believers have not only departed from the way, but have also
fallen asleep on forbidden ground, their alarms and doubts
are salutary, though often groundless and extreme: and
should any man, by preaching or writing, be able to prevent
all the despondings of such persons, previous to their repentance and its happy effects, he would subserve the design of
the tempter, and counteract the Lord's plan. We can, with

place. They also acquainted themselves with the shepherds there, who welcomed them, as they had done Christian before, unto the Delectable Mountains.

Now the shepherds seeing so great a train follow Mr. Great-heart (for with him they were well-acquainted), they said unto him, Good Sir, you have got a goodly company here : pray where did you find all these ?

> *Gr.-h.* First, here is Christiana and her train,
> Her sons, and her sons' wives, who, like the wain,
> Keep by the pole, and do by compass steer
> From sin to grace, else they had not been here.
> Next, here's old Honest come on pilgrimage ;
> Ready-to-halt too, who, I dare engage,
> True-hearted is, and so is Feeble-mind,
> Tho willing was not to be left behind.
> Despondency, good man, is coming after,
> And so also is Much-afraid his daughter.
> May we have entertainment here, or must
> We farther go ? Let's know whereon to trust.

Then said the shepherds, This is a comfortable company ; you are welcome to us, for we have for the feeble, as for the strong : our Prince has an eye to what is done to the least of these (Matt. xxv. 40) : therefore in-

propriety, do no more in this case, than encourage the fallen to repent and seek forgiveness, by the general truth, invitations, and promises of Scripture ; and comfort them when penitent, by suitable topics, that they may not be swallowed up for over-much sorrow. But though this part of the allegory may be deemed liable to some objection, or capable of being abused, yet it is probable, that the author only intended to shew, that the labours of faithful ministers, with the converse and prayers of such believers as are strong in faith, may be very useful in recovering the fallen, and relieving them that are ready to despond ; and of thus preventing the more durable and dreadful effects of the weak believer's transgressions.

firmity must not be a block to our entertainment. So they had them to the palace-doors, and then said unto them, Come in, Mr. Feeble-mind ; come in, Mr. Ready-to-halt ; come in, Mr. Despondency, and Mrs. Much-afraid his daughter. These, Mr. Great-heart, said the shepherds to the guide, we call in by name, for that they are most subject to draw back ; but as for you, and the rest that are strong, we leave you to your wonted liberty. Then said Mr. Great-heart, This day I see that grace doth shine in your faces, and that you are my Lord's shepherds indeed ; for that you have not pushed these diseased neither with side nor shoulder, but have rather strewed their way into the palace with flowers, as you should (Ezek. xxxiv. 21).

So the feeble and weak went in, and Mr. Great-heart and the rest did follow. When they were also sat down, the shepherds said to those of the weaker sort, What is it that you would have ? For, said they, all things must be managed here to the supporting of the weak, as well as the warning of the unruly.

So they made them a feast of things easy of digestion, and that were pleasant to the palate and nourishing : the which when they had received, they went to their rest, each one respectively unto his proper place. When morning was come, because the mountains were high, and the day clear ; and because it was the custom of the shepherds to shew the pilgrims before their departure some rarities; therefore, after they were ready, and had refreshed themselves, the shepherds took them out into the fields, and shewed them firs what they had shewed to Christian before (P. i. p. 257—263).

Then they had them to some new places. The first was mount Marvel,* where they looked, and beheld a man at a distance, that tumbled the hills about with words. Then they asked the shepherds, what that should mean? So they told them, that that man was the

---

* ' Marvel'—Faith exercised on the promises, and according to the warrants, of Scripture, engages the arm of Omnipotence on our side, as far as our duty or advantage, and the glory of God are concerned: so that strong faith will remove out of our way every obstacle which prevents our progress. But many things seem to us to be insurmountable obstacles, which are merely trials of our patience, or ' thorns in the flesh' to keep us humble: no degree of faith, therefore, will remove them; but believing prayer will be answered by inward strength communicated to our souls. The grace of the Lord Jesus be sufficient for us: his strength will be perfected in our weakness: the burning bush shall not be consumed: and we shall be enabled to proceed, though in great weakness, and with many trembling apprehensions. On the other hand, real hinderances frequently obstruct our path, because of our unbelief, and because we neglect the proper means of increasing our faith (Matt. xvii. 19—21). The other emblems are sufficiently explained, and only require to be duly considered, with reference to their practical import. It may however be observed, that some godly men are durably suspected of crimes, charged upon them by prejudiced persons, of which they are entirely innocent: yet, perhaps, this will be found to have originated from some misconduct in other respects, or from want of circumspection in ' avoiding the appearance of evil:' so that the general rule may be allowed to be valid; and they who feel themselves to be exceptions to it will do well to examine, whether they have not by indiscretions, at least, exposed themselves to this painful trial. I apprehend most of us have cause enough in this respect for humiliation and patience.

son of Mr. Great-grace [of whom you read in the first part of the records of the Pilgrim's Progress] : and he is set there to teach pilgrims how to believe down, or to tumble out of their ways, what difficulties they should meet with, by faith (Mark xi. 23, 24).   Then said Mr. Great-heart, I know him ; he is a man above many.

Then they had them to another place, called mount Innocence : and there they saw a man clothed all in white ; and two men, Prejudice and Ill-will, continually casting dirt upon him.   Now behold, the dirt, whatsoever they cast at him, would in a little time fall off again, and his garment would look as clear as if no dirt had been cast thereat.   Then said the pilgrims, What means this ?   The shepherds answered, This man is named Godlyman, and the garment is to shew the innocency of his life.   Now those that throw dirt at him are such as hate his well-doing ; but as you see the dirt will not stick upon his clothes, so it shall be with him that lives truly innocently in the world.   Whoever they be that would make such men dirty, they labour all in vain ; for God, by that a little time is spent, will cause that their innocence shall break forth as the light, and their righteousness as the noon-day.

Then they took them, and had them to mount Charity, where they shewed them a man that had a bundle of cloth lying before him, out of which he cut coats and garments for the poor that stood about him ; yet his bundle or roll of cloth was never the less. Then said they, What should this be? This is, said the shepherds, to shew you, that he that has a heart to give of his labour to the poor, shall never want wherewithal. 'He that watereth, shall be watered himself.' And the cake, that the widow gave to the prophet, did not cause that she had ever the less in her barrel.

They had them also to the place, where they saw one Fool, and one Want-wit, washing of an Ethiopian, with an intention to make him white; but the more they washed him, the blacker he was. Then they asked the shepherds, what that should mean? So they told them, saying, Thus shall it be with the vile persons; all means used to get such a one a good name, shall in conclusion tend but to make him more abominable. Thus it was with the Pharisees, and so it shall be with all hypocrites.

Then said Mercy, the wife of Matthew, to Christiana her mother, I would, if it might be, see the hole in the hill, or that commonly called the Bye-way to hell. So her mother brake her mind to the shepherds (P. i. p. 261). Then they went to the door (it was on the side of a hill); and they opened it, and bid Mercy hearken awhile. So she hearkened, and heard one saying, Cursed be my father, for holding of my feet back from the way of peace and life: And another said, O that I had been torn in pieces, before I had, to save my life, lost my soul! And another said, If I were to live again, how would I deny myself, rather than come to this place! Then there was as if the very earth groaned and quaked under the feet of this young woman for fear; so she looked white, and came trembling away, saying, Blessed be he and she that is delivered from this place.

Now when the shepherds had shewn them all these things, then they had them back to the palace, and entertained them with what the house would afford: but Mercy being a young and breeding woman, longed for something that she saw there, but was ashamed to ask. Her mother-in-law then asked her what she ailed, for she looked as one not well? Then said Mercy, There is a looking-glass hangs up in the dining room, off which I cannot take my mind; if therefore I have it not, I think I shall miscarry. Then said her mother, I will mention thy wants to the shepherds, and they will not deny it thee. But she said, I am ashamed that these men should know that I longed. Nay, my daughter, said she, it is no shame, but a virtue, to long for such a thing as that. So Mercy said, Then, mother, if you please, ask the shepherds if they are willing to sell it.

Now the glass* was one of a thousand. It

* 'The glass'—The holy Scriptures, revealing to us the mysteries and perfections of God, shewing us our own real character and condition, and discovering Christ and his salvation to our souls, are represented under this emblem. Every true believer longs to be more completely acquainted with them from day to day, and to look into them continually.

would present a man, one way, with his own features exactly; and turn it but another way, and it would shew one the very face and similitude of the Prince of the pilgrims himself. Yes, I have talked with them that can tell, and they have seen the very crown of thorns upon his head, by looking in that glass; they have therein also seen the holes in his hands, in his feet, and his side. Yea, such an excellency is there in that glass, that it will shew him to one where they have a mind to see him; whether living or dead, whether in earth or in heaven; whether in a state of humiliation, or in his exaltation; whether coming to suffer, or coming to reign (James i. 23—25; 1 Cor. xiii. 12; 2 Cor iii. 18).

Christiana therefore went to the shepherds apart (now the names of the shepherds were Knowledge, Experience, Watchful, and Sincere—P. 1 p. 257), and said unto them, There is one of my daughters, a breeding woman, that, I think, doth long for something that she hath seen in this house, and she thinks she shall miscarry, if she should by you be denied.

Exper. Call her, call her: she shall assuredly have what we can help her to. So they called her, and said to her, Mercy, what is that thing thou wouldest have? Then she blushed, and said, The great glass that hangs up in the dining-room. So Sincere ran and fetched it, and with a joyful consent it was given her. Then she bowed her head, and gave thanks, and said, By this I know that I have obtained favour in your eyes.

They also gave to the other young women such things as they desired, and to their husbands great commendations, for that they had joined with Mr. Great-heart, to the slaying of giant Despair, and the demolishing of Doubting Castle. About Christiana's neck the shepherds put a bracelet, and so they did about the necks of her four daughters; also they put ear-rings in their ears, and jewels on their foreheads.

When they were minded to go hence, they let them go in peace, but gave not to them those certain cautions which before were given to Christian and his companion. The reason* was, for that these had Great-

---

* ' Reason'—The author embraces every opportunity of shewing the important advantages of the pastoral office, when faithfully executed : by which he meant, the regular care of a stated minister over a company of professed Christians, who are his peculiar charge, have voluntarily placed themselves under his instructions, seek counsel from him in all their difficulties, and pay regard to his private admonitions ; being convinced that he uprightly seeks their spiritual welfare, and is capable of promoting it.   Nothing so much tends to the establishment and consistent conduct of believers, or the permanent success of the Gospel, as a proper reciprocal attention of pastors and their flocks to each other.   A general way of preaching and hearing, with little or no connexion, cordial unreserved intercourse, or even acquaintance between ministers and their congregations ; with continual changes from one place to another, may tend to spread a superficial knowledge of evangelical truth more widely ; but through the want of seasonable reproof, counsel, encouragement, or admonition, the general directions delivered from the pulpit will seldom be recollected when they are most wanted.   Hence it is that professors so often miss their way, are taken in the Flatterer's net, and fall asleep on the enchanted ground : and a faith-

17*

heart to be their guide, who was one that
was well acquainted with things, and so could
give them their cautions more seasonable ; to
wit, even then when the danger was nigh the
approaching. What cautions Christian and
his companion had received of the shepherds
(P. i. p. 263), they had also lost by that the
time was come that they had need to put them
in practice. Wherefore, here was the advantage that this company had over the other.

From hence they went on singing, and they
said,

> Behold, now fitly are the stages set
> For their relief that pilgrims are become,
> And how they us receive without one let,
> That make the o'ner life the mark and home.

> What novelties they have, to us they give,
> That we though pilgrims, joyful lives may live.
> They do upon us, too, such things bestow,
> That shew we pilgrims are, where'er we go.

When they were gone from the shepherds,
they quickly came to the place where Christian had met with one Turn-away, that dwelt
in the town of Apostacy (P. i. p. 266).
Wherefore of him Mr. Great-heart, their

ful guide, ever at hand, to give the caution or direction at
the time, is the proper remedy, for which no adequate substitute can be found. But as it is much easier to preach at
large on general topics ; and after a few sermons delivered
in one congregation, to go over the same ground again in another place than to perform duly the several parts of the ar-
duous office, which is sustained by the stated pastor of a regular congregation : and as it is far more agreeable to nature,
to be exempted from private admonitions than to be troubled
with them : it may be feared, that this important subject will
not at present be duly attended to.

guide, did now put them in mind, saying, This
is the place where Christian met with one
Turn-away, who carried with him the character of his rebellion at his back. And this
I have to say concerning this man ; he
would hearken to no counsel, but, once a-fall-
ing, persuasion could not stop him. When
he came to the place where the cross and the
sepulchre was, he did meet with one that did
bid him look there ; but he gnashed with his
teeth, and stamped, and said, he was resolved to go back to his own town. Before he
came to the gate, he met with Evangelist,
who offered to lay hands on him to turn him
into the way again. But this Turn-away resisted him, and having done much despite unto him, he got away over the wall, and so escaped his hand.

Then they went on ; and just at the place
where Little-faith formerly was robbed, there
stood a man with his sword drawn, and his
face all bloody. Then said Mr. Great-heart,
What art thou ? The man* made answer,

* 'The man'—From the names afterwards given to the
opponents, with whom this pilgrim fought, we may infer,
that the author meant to represent by them certain wild en-
thusiast, who, not having ever duly considered any religious
subject, officiously intrude themselves in the way of professors ; to perplex their minds, and persuade them, that unless
they adopt their reveries or superstitions, they cannot be saved. An ungovernable imagination, a mind incapable of sober
reflection, and a dogmatizing spirit, characterize these enemies of the truth, they assault religious persons with specious
reasonings, cavilling objections, confident assertions, bitter
reproaches, proud boastings, sarcastical censures, and rash
judgments : they endeavour to draw them over to their party,
or to deprive them from attending to religion at all ; or to

saying, I am one whose name is Valiant-for-truth. I am a pilgrim, and am going to the Celestial city. Now, as I was in my way, there were three men that did beset me, and propounded unto me these three things: Whether I would become one of them: or go back from whence I came; or die upon the place? To the first I answered, I had been a true man a long season, and therefore it could not be expected that I now should cast in my lot with thieves (Prov. i. 10—19). Then they demanded what I would say to the second. So I told them, the place from whence I came, had I not found incommodity there, I had not forsaken it at all; but finding it altogether unsuitable to me, and very unprofitable for me, I forsook it for this way. Then they asked me what I said to the third? And I told them, My life cost more dear far, than that I should lightly give it away: besides, you have nothing to do to put things to my choice; wherefore at your peril be it if you meddle. Then the three, to wit, Wild-head, Inconsiderate, and Pragmatick, drew upon me, and I also drew upon them. So

terrify them with the fears of damnation, in their present endeavours to serve God, and find his salvation. Whatever company of persons we suppose that the author had in view, we may learn from the passage what our strength, hope, and conduct ought to be, when we are thus assaulted. The word of God used in faith, and with fervent and persevering prayer, will at length enable us to silence such dangerous assailants: and if we be valiant for the truth, and meekly contend for it, amidst revilings, menaces, and contempt, we may hope to confirm others also, and to promote the common cause.

we fell to it, one against three, for the space of three hours. They have left upon me, as you see, some of the marks of their valour, and have also carried away with them some of mine. They are but just now gone; I suppose they might, as the saying is, hear your horse dash, and so they betook themselves to flight.

Gr.-h. But here was great odds, three against one.

Val. 'Tis true, but little or more are nothing to him that has the truth on his side: 'Though an host should encamp against me,' said one, 'my heart shall not fear: though war shall rise against me, in this will I be confident,' &c. Besides, said he, I have read in some records, that one man has fought an army; and how many did Samson slay with the jaw-bone of an ass?

Then said the guide, Why did you not cry out, that some might have come in for your succour?

Val. So I did to my King, who I knew could hear me, and afford invisible help, and that was enough for me.

Then said Great-heart to Mr. Valiant-for-truth, Thou hast worthily behaved thyself; let me see thy sword: so he shewed it him. When he had taken it into his hand, and looked thereon awhile, he said, Ha! it is a right Jerusalem blade.

Val. It is so. Let a man have one of these blades, with a hand to wield it, and skill to use it, and he may venture upon an angel with it. He need not fear its holding, if he can but tell how to lay on. Its edge will never blunt. It will cut flesh and bones, and soul and spirit and all.

Gr.-h. But you fought a great while; I wonder you was not weary.

Val. I fought till my sword did cleave to my hand, and then they were joined together, as if a sword grew out of my arm; and when the blood run through my fingers, then I fought with most courage.

Gr.-h. Thou hast done well; thou hast ' resisted unto blood, striving against sin;' thou shalt abide by us, come in and go out with us, for we are thy companions.

Then they took him, and washed his wounds, and gave him of what they had to refresh him; and so they went together. Now as they went on, because Mr. Great-heart, was delighted in him (for he loved one greatly that he found to be a man of his hands), and because there were in company them that were feeble and weak, therefore he questioned with him about many things; as, first, what countryman he was.

Val. I am of Dark-land, for there I was born, and there my father and mother are still.

Dark-land! said the guide: doth not that lie on the same coast with the city of Destruction?

Val. Yes, it doth. Now that which caused me to come on pilgrimage was this: we had Mr Tell-true came into our parts, and he told it about what Christian had done, that went from the city of Destruction ; namely, how he had forsaken his wife and children, and had betaken himself to a pilgrim's life. It was also confidently reported, how he had killed a serpent, that did come out to resist him in his journey ; and how he got through to whither he intended. It was also told, what welcome he had to all his Lord's lodgings, especially when he came to the gates of the Celestial city ; for there, said the man, he was received with sound of trumpet, by a company of shining ones. He told it also, how all the bells in the city did ring for joy at his reception, and what golden garments he was clothed with ; with many other things that now I shall forbear to relate. In a word, that man so told the story of Christian and his travels, that my heart fell into a burning heat to be gone after him ; nor could father or mother stay me. So I got from them, and am come thus far on my way.

Gr.-h. You came in at the gate, did you not ?

Val. Yes, yes ; for the same man also told us, that all would be nothing, if we did not begin to enter this way at the gate.

Look you, said the guide to Christiana the pilgrimage of your husband, and what he has gotten thereby, is spread abroad far and near.

Val. Why, is this Christian's wife ?

Gr.-h. Yes, that it is ; and these are also her four sons.

Val. What ! and going on pilgrimage too ?

Gr.-h. Yes, verily, they are following after.

Val. It glads me at heart ; good man, how joyful will he be, when he shall see them, that would not go with him, to enter before him in at the gates into the Celestial city !

Gr.-h. Without doubt it will be a comfort to him ; for, next to the joy of seeing himself there, it will be a joy to meet there his wife and children.

Val. But, now you are upon that, pray let me hear your opinion about it.   Some make a question, whether we shall know one another when we are there.

Gr.-h. Do they think they shall know themselves then, or that they shall rejoice to see themselves in that bliss ? and if they think they shall know and do these, why not know others, and rejoice in their welfare also ? Again, since relations are our second self, though that state will be dissolved, yet why may it not be rationally concluded that we shall be more glad to see them there, than to see they are wanting ?

Val. Well, I perceive whereabouts you are to this.   Have you any more things to ask me about my beginning to come on pilgrimage ?

Gr.-h. Yes ; was your father and mother willing that you should become a pilgrim *?*

Val. Oh no ! they used all means imaginable to persuade me to stay at home.

Gr.-h. What could they say against it

Val. They said, it was an idle* life ; and, if I myself were not inclined to sloth and laziness, I would never countenance a pilgrim's condition.

Gr.-h. And what did they say else ?

Val. Why, they told me that it was a dangerous way ; Yea, the most dangerous way in the world, say they, is that which the pilgrims go.

Gr.-h. Did they shew you wherein this way is dangerous ?

Val. Yes ; and that in many particulars.

Gr.-h. Name some of them.

Val. They told me of the slough of Despond, where Christian was well nigh smoth-

---

* ' Idle'—This hath been the reproach cast on religion in every age. Pharaoh said to Moses and the Israelites, ' Ye are idle, ye are idle ; therefore ye say, let us go and do sacrifice to the Lord.' Men naturally imagine, that time spent in the immediate service of God is wasted : should a professor therefore employ as many hours every week, in reading the Scriptures, in secret and social prayer, in pious discourse, and in attending on public ordinances, as his neighbour devotes to amusement and sensual indulgence ; an outcry would speedily be made, about his idling away his time, and being in the way to beggar his family. As this must be expected, it behoves all believers to avoid every appearance of evil, and by exemplary diligence in their proper employments, a careful redemption of time, a prudent frugality in their expenses, and a good management of all their affairs, to ' put to silence the ignorance of foolish men.' For there are too many favourers of the Gospel, who give plausibility to these slanders, by running from place to place, that they may hear every new preacher ; while the duty of the family, and of their station in the community is miserably neglected. They ' walk disorderly, working not at all, but are busy bodies :' from these we ought to withdraw, and against such professors we should protest ; for they are ' ever learning, but never able to come to the knowledge of the truth.

ered. They told me, that there were archers standing ready in Beelzebub-castle, to shoot them who should knock at the wicket-gate for entrance. They told me also of the wood and dark mountains, of the hill of Difficulty, of the lions; and also of three giants, Bloodyman, Maul, and Slaygood; they said moreover, that there was a foul fiend haunted the valley of Humiliation; and that Christian was by him almost bereft of life. Besides, said they, you must go over the valley of the Shadow of Death, where the hobgoblins are, where the light is darkness, where the way is full of snares, pits, traps, and gins. They told me also of giant Despair, of Doubting-castle, and of the ruin that the pilgrims met with there. Farther, they said I must go over the Enchanted Ground, which was dangerous. And that after all this I should find a river over which I should find no bridge; and that that river did lie betwixt me and the Celestial country.

Gr.-h. And was this all?

Val. No; they also told me, that this way was full of deceivers;* and of persons that lay

* ' Deceivers'—Worldly people, in opposing the Gospel, descant abundantly on the folly and hypocrisy of religious persons; they pick up every vague report that they hear to their disadvantage, and narrowly watch for the halting of such as they are acquainted with; and then they form general conclusions, from a few particular, distorted, and uncertain stories. Thus they endeavour to prove, that there is no reality in religion, that it is impossible to find the way to heaven, and that it is better to be quiet than to bestow pains to no purpose. This frivolous sophistry is frequently employed, after all other arguments have been silenced. But it is

in wait there, to turn good men out of their path.

Gr.-h. But how did they make that out ?

Val. They told me that Mr. Worldly-wise-man did lie there in wait to deceive. They also said, that there was Formality and Hypocrisy continually on the road. They said also, that By-ends, Talkative, or Demas, would go near to gather me up: that the Flatterer would catch me in his net ; or that, with green-headed Ignorance, I would presume to go on to the gate, from whence he was sent back to the hole, that was in the side of the hill, and make to go the by-way to hell.

Gr.-h. I promise you, this was enough to discourage thee. But did they make an end there ?

Val. No, stay. They told me also of many that tried that way of old, and that had gone a great way therein, to see if they could find something of the glory then, that so many had so much talked of from time to time ; and how they came back again, and befooled themselves for setting a foot out of doors in that path, to the satisfaction of the country.

vain to deny the existence of hypocrites and deceivers ; or to excuse the evils to which they object : on the contrary, we should allow these representations, as far as there is any appearance of truth in them, and then shew that this teaches us to beware lest we be deceived, and to try every doctrine by the touchstone of God's word ; that counterfeits prove the value of the thing counterfeited ; that we should learn to distinguish between the precious and the vile ; and, finally, that while danger may attend a religious profession, irreligion ensures destruction.

And they named several that did so, as Obstinate and Pliable, Mistrust and Timorous,
Turnaway and old Atheist, with several more ;
who, they said, had some of them gone far
to see what they could find ; but not one of
them found so much advantage by going, as
amounted to the weight of a feather.

Gr.-h. Said they any thing more to discourage you ?

Val. Yes ; They told me of one Mr. Fearing, who was a pilgrim ; and how he found
his way so solitary, that he never had a comfortable hour therein ; also that Mr. Despondency had like to have been starved therein ;
yea, and also (which I had almost forgot),
Christian himself, about whom there has been
such a noise, after all his ventures for a celestial crown, was certainly drowned in the black
river, and never went a foot farther, however
it was smothered up.

Gr.-h. And did none of these things discourage you ?

Val. No ; they seemed as so many nothings
to me.

Gr.-h. How came that about ?

Val. Why, I still believed what Mr. Tell-
true had said, and that carried me beyond
them all.

Gr.-h. Then this was your victory, even
your faith ?

Val. It was so ; I believed, and therefore
came out, got into the way, fought all that set
themselves against me, and, by believing, am
come to this place.

Who would true valour see
　　Let him come hither ;
One here will constant be,
　　Come wind, come weather
There's no discouragement
Shall make him once relent
His first avow'd intent,
　　To be a pilgrim.
Who so beset him round
　　With dismal stories,
Do but themselves confound
　　His strength the more is,
No lion can him fright ;
He'll with a giant fight
But he will have a right
　　To be a pilgrim.
Hobgoblin nor foul find
　　Can daunt his spirit :
He knows, he at the end
　　Shall life inherit.
Then fancies fly away,
He'll not fear what men say
He'll labour night and day
　　To be a pilgrim.

By this time they were got to the Enchanted Ground, where the air* naturally tended

* ' Air'—The subsequent view of the Enchanted Ground
seems rather to vary from that which has been considered in
the first part. The circumstances of believers who are deeply engaged in business, and constrained to spend much time
among worldly people, is here particularly intended. This
may sometimes be unavoidable ; but it is enchanted ground :
many professors, fascinated by the advantages and connexions
thus presented to them, fall asleep, and wake no more : others are entangled by those thorns and briers, which ' choke
the word, and render it unfruitful.' The more soothing the
scene the greater the danger, and the more urgent need is
there for watchfulness and circumspection : the more vigilant
believers are, the greater uneasiness will such scenes occasion them ; as they will be so long out of their proper ele-
ment : and the weaker and more unestablished men are, the
more apt will they be in such circumstances to yield to discouragement. The society and counsel of faithful ministers

18*

to make one drowsy (Part i. p. 143—316) ; and that place was all grown over with briars and thorns, excepting here and there, where was an enchanted arbour, upon which if a man sits, or in which if a man sleeps, 'tis a question, say some, whether ever he shall rise or wake again in this world. Over this forest therefore they went, both one and another ; and Mr. Great-heart went before, for that he was the guide, and Mr. Valiant-for-truth came behind, being rear-guard ; for fear lest peradventure some fiend, or dragon, or giant, or thief, should fall upon their rear, and so do mischief. They went on here, each man with his sword drawn in his hand, for they knew it was a dangerous place. Also they cheered up one another, as well as they could ; Feeble-mind, Mr. Great-heart commanded, should come up after him, and Mr. Despondency was under the eye of Mr. Valiant.

and Christian friends may help them to get on : but they will often feel that their path is miry and slippery, entangling and perplexing, dark and wearisome to their souls. Yet if this be the case, their sighs, complaints, and prayers, are hopeful symptoms : but when worldly employments and connections which perhaps at first were in a sense unavoidable, induce prosperity ; and men seek comfort from this prosperity, instead of considering it as a snare or burthen, or improving it as a talent ; then the professor falls asleep in the enchanted arbour. It behoves, however, all who love their souls, to shun that hurry of business, and multiplicity of affairs, and projects into which many are betrayed by degrees in order to supply increasing expenses that might be avoided by strict frugality, and more morderate disires : for they lade the soul with thick clay ; are a heavy weight to the most upright ; render a man's way doubtful and joyless ; and ' drown many in destruction and perdition.

Now they had not gone far, but a great mist and darkness fell upon them all ; so that they could scarce, for a great while, one see the other ; wherefore they were forced, for some time, to feel for one another by words, for they walked not by sight. But any one must think that here was but sorry going for the best of them all, but how much the worse was it for the women and children, who both of feet and heart also were but tender ! Yet nevertheless so it was, that through the encouraging words of him that led in the front, and of him that brought them up behind, they made a pretty good shift to wag along.

The way was also here very wearisome, through dirt and slabbiness. Nor was there, on all this ground, so much as one inn or victualling-house, therein to refresh the feebler sort. Here therefore was grunting and puffing, and sighing ; while one tumbleth over a bush, another sticks fast in the dirt ; and the children, some of them, lost their shoes in the mire : while one cries out, I am down ; and another, Ho, where are you ? And a third, The bushes have got such fast hold on me, I think I cannot get away from them.

Then they came to an arbour, warm, and promising much refreshing to the pilgrims : for it was finely wrought above head, beautified with greens, furnished with benches and settles It had in it a soft couch, where the weary might lean. This, you must think, all things considered was tempting; for the pilgrims already began

to be foiled with the badness of the way ; but
there was not one of them that made so much
as a motion to stop there.   Yea, for aught I
could perceive, they continually gave so good
heed to the advice of their guide, and he did
so faithfully tell them of dangers, and of the
nature of dangers, when they were at them,
that usually, when they were nearest to them,
they did most pluck up their spirits, and heart-
en one another to deny the flesh.   The arbour was called, the slothful's friend, on purpose to allure, if it might be, some of the
pilgrims there to take up their rest when
weary.

I saw then in my dream, that they went on
in this their solitary ground, till they came to
a place at which a man is apt to lose* his way.
Now, though when it was light, their guide
could well enough tell how to miss those ways
that led wrong, yet in the dark he was put to
a stand : but he had in his pocket a map of
all ways leading to or from the celestial city ;
wherefore he struck a light (for he never goes
also without his tinder-box), and take a view
of his book or map, which bids him be careful, in that place, to turn to the right-hand.
And had he not here been careful to look in

* 'Lose'—This emblem inculcates the duty of constant
attention to the precepts and counsels of Scripture, as well
as reliance on its promises ; and of an habitual application to the Lord by prayer, to teach us the true meaning of
his word, that we may learn the way of peace and safety,
in the most difficult and doubtful cases ; and the advantage
of consulting such ministers, as are most experienced in
the ways of God, and most conversant with his sacred oracles

his map, they had in all probability been smothered in the mud ; for just a little before them, and that at the end of the cleanest way too, was a pit, none knows how deep, full of nothing but mud, there made on purpose to destroy the pilgrims in.

Then thought I with myself, who, that goeth on pilgrimage, but would have one of these maps about him, that he may look when he is at a stand, which is the way he must take.

They went on, then, in this Enchanted Ground, till they came to where there was another arbour, and it was built by the highway-side. And in that arbour there lay two men,* whose names were Heedless and Toobold. These two went thus far on pilgrimage ; but here, being wearied with their journey, sat down to rest themselves, and so fell

---

* 'Two men'—Such men as take up a profession of the Gospel, in a heedless manner, and proceed with overbearing confidence, the result of pride and ignorance, may long maintain a form of godliness, though it be a weariness to them : but after a time, they will gradually be drawn back into the world, retaining nothing of their religion, except certain distorted doctrinal notions. They find excuses for their conduct from false maxims, and bad examples : they fall asleep in the arms of worldly prosperity : nothing can awaken them to fear, or self-suspicion ; but they will, as it were, talk in their sleep about religion, in so incoherent a manner, as to excite the laughter of children ; while they who understand the case will bewail their deplorable delusion. Such awful examples should excite us to redoubled diligence, in searching the Scriptures, and in prayer ; lest we too should be overcome with a destructive sleep, and perish in this fascinating way. For scenes of worldly prosperity have detected the hypocrisy of many, who have long persevered in an unsuspected profession, and amidst difficulties and trials.

asleep. When the pilgrims saw them, they stood still, and shook their heads ; for they knew that the sleepers were in a pitiful case. Then they consulted what to do, whether to go on, and leave them in their sleep, or step to them and try to awake them. So they concluded to go to them and awake them ; that is, if they could ; but with this caution, namely, to take heed that themselves did not sit down nor embrace the offered benefit of that arbour.

So they went in, and spake to the men, and called each by his name (for the guide, it seems, did know them), but there was no voice nor answer. Then the guide did shake them, and do what he could to disturb them. Then said one of them, I will pay you when I take my money. At which the guide shook his head. I will fight so long as I can hold my sword in my hand, said the other. At that, one of the children laughed.

Then said Christiana, What is the meaning of this ? Then the guide said, They talk in their sleep ; if you do strike them, or beat them or whatever else you do unto them, they will answer you after this fashion ; or, as one of them said in old time, when the waves of the sea did beat upon him, and he slept as one upon the mast of a ship, 'When I do awake, I will seek it yet again' (Prov xxiii. 34, 35). You know, when men talk in their sleep, they say any thing, but their words are not governed either by faith or reason. There is an incoherency in their words now ; ever as there was before, betwixt their going on pilgrimage and their sitting down here. This then is the mischief on't, when heedless ones go on pilgrimage; twenty to one but they are served thus. For this Enchanted Ground is one of the last refuges that the enemy to pilgrims has; wherefore it is, as you see, placed almost at the end of the way, and so it standeth against us with the more advantage. For when, thinks the enemy, will these fools be so desirous to sit down, as when they are weary? And at what time so likely for to be weary, as when they are almost at their journey's end? Therefore it is, I say, that the Enchanted Ground is placed so nigh to the land Beulah, and so near the end of their race. Wherefore let pilgrims look to themselves, lest it happen to them as it has done to these, that, as you see, are fallen asleep, and none can awake them.

Then the pilgrims desired, with trembling, to go forward; only they prayed their guide to strike a light, that they might go the rest of their way by the help of the light of a lantern. So he struck a light, and they went by the help of that through the rest of this way, though the darkness was very great (2 Pet. i. 19).

But the children began to be sorely weary; and they cried out unto him that loveth pilgrims, to make their way more comfortable. So by that they had gone a little further, a wind arose, that drove away the fog; so the air became more clear. Yet they were no off, by much, of the Enchanted Ground, but only now they could see one another better, and also the way wherein they should walk.

Now when they were almost at the end of this ground, they perceived, that a little before them was a solemn noise of one that was much concerned. So they went on, and looked before them : and behind they saw, as they thought, a man upon his knees,* with hands and eyes lifted up, and speaking, as they thought, earnestly to one that was above They drew nigh, but could not tell what he said ; so they went softly till he had done. When he had done, he got up, and began to run towards the celestial city. Then Mr. Great-heart called after him, saying, Soho, friend, let us have your company, if you go, as I suppose you do, to the celestial city. So the man stopped, and they came up to him ; but so soon as Mr. Honest saw him, he said, I know this man. Then said Mr. Valiant-for-truth, Pry'thee, who is it ? 'Tis one, said he, that comes from where abouts I dwelt : his name is Standfast ; he is certainly a right good pilgrim.

So they came up to one another ; and presently Standfast said to old Honest, Ho ! father Honest are you there ? Ay, said he, that I am, as sure as you are there. Right glad am I, said Mr. Standfast, that I have found you on

* ' Knees'—The case of Standfast shews us, that, when believers feel the propensity of their hearts to yield to worldly proposals, it renders them jealous of themselves, excites them to earnest prayer, and thus eventually tend to preserve them from the fatal delusions.

this road.   And as glad am I, said the other,
that I spied you on your knees.   Then Mr.
Standfast blushed, and said; But why, did you
see me ? Yes, that I did, quoth the other,
and with my heart was glad at the sight.
Why, what did you think ? said Standfast.
Think ! said old Honest, what should I think ?
I thought we had an honest man upon the
road, therefore should have his company by-
and-by.   If you thought not amiss, how happy am I : but, if I be not as I should, 'tis I
alone must bear it.   That is true, said the
other ; but your fear doth farther confirm me,
that things are right betwixt the Prince of
pilgrims and your soul : for he saith, ' Blessed
is the man that feareth always.'

Val. Well, but brother, I pray thee tell us,
what was it that was the cause of thy being
upon thy knees even now ? Was it for some
obligations laid by special mercies upon thee,
or how ?

St. Why, we are, as you see, upon the
Enchanted Ground ; and as I was coming
along, I was musing with myself of what a
dangerous nature the road in this place was ,
and how many, that had come even thus far
on pilgrimage, had here been stopt and been
destroyed.   I thought also of the manner of
death, with which this place destroyeth men.
Those that die here, die of no violent distemper ; the death which such do die is not
grievous to them ; for he that goeth away in
a sleep, begins that journey with desire and

pleasure : yea, such acquiesce in the will of that disease.

Then Mr. Honest interrupting of him, said, Did you see the two men asleep in the arbour ?

St. Ay, ay, I saw Heedless and also Too-bold there ; and, for aught I know, that there they will lie until they rot (Prov. x. 7) : but let me go on with my tale. As I was thus musing, as I said, there was one in pleasant attire, but old, who presented herself unto me, and offered me three things ; to wit, her body, her purse, and her bed. Now the truth is, I was both weary and sleepy : I am also as poor as an owlet, and that perhaps the witch knew. Well, I repulsed her once and twice , but she put by my repulses and smiled. Then I began to be angry ; but she mattered that nothing at all. Then she made offers again, and said, If I would be ruled by her, she would make me great and happy ; for, said she, I am the mistress of the world, and men are made happy by me. Then I asked her name, and she told me it was Madam Bubble. This set me farther from her ; but she still followed me with enticements. Then I be-took me, as you see, to my knees, and with hands lifted up, and cries, I prayed to him that had said he would help. So just as you came up, the gentlewoman went her way. Then I continued to give thanks for this great deliverance ; for I verily believe she intended no good, but rather sought to make a stop of me in my journey.

Hon. Without doubt her designs were bad
But stay, now you talk of her, methinks I
either have seen her, or have some story of
her.

St. Perhaps you have done both.

Hon. Madam Bubble! Is she not a tall
comely dame, something of a swarthy complexion?

St. Right, you hit it, she is just such a
one.

Hon. Doth she not speak very smoothly,
and give you a smile at the end of every sentence?

St. You fall right upon it again, for these
are her very actions.

Hon. Doth she not wear a great purse by
her side? and is not her hand often in it fin-
gering her money, as if that was her heart's
delight?

St. 'Tis just so: had she stood by all this
while, you could not more amply have set her
forth before me, and have better described her
features.

Hon. Then he that drew her picture was
a good limner, and he that wrote of her said
true.

Gr.-h. This woman is a witch; and it is
by virtue of her sorceries that this groun   is
enchanted: whoever doth lay their head down
in her lap, had as good lay it down upon that
block over which the axe doth hang; and
whoever lays their eyes upon her beauty, are
counted the enemies of God (James iv. 41;
John ii. 14, 15). This is she that maintain-

eth in their splendour all those that are the enemies of pilgrims. Yea, this is she that hath brought off many a man from a pilgrim's life. She is a great gossipper ; she is always, both she and her daughters, at some pilgrim's heels or another, now commending, and then preferring the excellencies of this life. She is a bold and impudent slut ; she will talk with any man. She always laughed poor pilgrims to scorn ; but highly commend the rich. If there be one cunning to get money in a place, she will speak well of him from house to house ; she loveth banqueting and feasting mainly well ; she is always at one full table or another ; she has given it out in some places that she is a goddess, and therefore some do worship her. She has her time and open places of cheating ; and she will say and avow it, that none can shew a good comparable to hers. She promiseth to dwell with children's children, if they would but love and make much of her. She will cast out of her purse gold like dust, in some places, and to some persons. She loves to be sought after, spoken well of, and to lie in the bosoms of men. She is never weary of commending her commodities, and she loves them most that think best of her. She will promise crowns and kingdoms, if they will but take her advice : yet many hath she brought to the halter, and ten thousand time more to hell.

Oh ! said Standfast, what a mercy it is that I did resist her ! for whither might she have drawn me ?

Gr.-h. Whither ! nay, none but God knows.
But in general, to be sure, she would have
drawn thee into 'many foolish and hurtful
lusts, which drown men in destruction and
perdition' (1 Tim. vi. 9). It was she that set
Absalom against his father, and Jeroboam
against his master. It was she that persuaded Judas to sell his Lord, and that prevailed
with Demas to forsake the godly pilgrim's
life : none can tell of the mischief that she
doth. She makes variance betwixt rulers
and subjects, betwixt parents and children,
betwixt neighbour and neighbour, betwixt a
man and his wife, between a man and himself,
betwixt the flesh and the Spirit. Wherefore,
good master Standfast, be as your name is ;
and 'when you have done all, stand.'

At this discourse there was, among the
pilgrims, a mixture of joy and trembling ; but
at length they brake out, and sang—

> What danger is the pilgrim in !
>   How many are his foes !
> How many ways there are to sin
>   No living mortal knows.
> Some in the ditch spoil'd are, yea can
>   Lie tumbling in the mire :
> Some, though they shun the frying-pan,
>   Do leap into the fire.

After this, I beheld, until they were come
unto the land of Beulah, where the sun shineth night and day (P. i. p. 316). Here because they were weary, they betook themselves awhile to rest : and because this country was common for pilgrims, and because
these orchards and vineyards that were here

19*

belonged to the king of the Celestial country, therefore they were licensed to make bold with any of his things. But a little while* soon refreshed them here ; for the bells did so ring, and the trumpets continually sounding so melodiously, that they could not sleep ; and yet they received as much refreshing, as if they slept their sleep never so soundly. Here also all the noise of them that walked in the streets, was, More pilgrims are come to town. And another would answer, saying, And so many went over the water, and were let in at the golden gates to-day. They would cry again, There is now a legion of shining ones just came to town : by which we know that there are more pilgrims upon the road ; for here they come to wait for them, and comfort them after their sorrow. Then the pilgrims got up and walked to and fro : but how were their eyes now filled with celestial visions ? In this land, they heard nothing, saw nothing, felt nothing, smelt nothing, tasted nothing, that was offensive to their stomach or mind ;

* 'Little while'—The lively exercise of faith and hope, the anticipation of heavenly felicity, and the consolations of the Holy Spirit, soon make the believer forget his conflicts and sorrows, or only remember them to enhance his grateful joy. The ensuing description represents the happy state of those that live in places, favoured with many lively Christians united in heart and judgment ; and where instances of persons dying triumphantly are often reported or witnessed. It has frequently been observed, that aged believers, in such circumstances, have been remarkably delivered from fears and temptations, and animated by hopes and earnests of heaven ; so that while death seemed bitter to nature it became pleasant to the soul, to think of the joy and glory that would immediately follow it.

only, when they tasted of the water of the river over which they were to go, they thought that tasted a little bitterish to the palate, but it proved sweet when it was down.

In this place there was a record kept of the names of them that had been pilgrims of old, and a history of all the famous acts that they had done. It was here also much discoursed, how the river to some has its flowings, and what ebbings it has had while others have gone over. It has been in a manner dry for some, while it has over-flowed its banks for others.

In this place, the children of the town would go into the King's gardens, and gather nosegays for the pilgrims, and bring them to them with affection. Here also grew camphire, and spikenard, saffron, calamus, and cinnamon, with all the trees of frankincense, myrrh, and aloes, with all the chief spices. With these the pilgrims' chambers were perfumed while they staid here ; and with these were their bodies anointed to prepare them to go over the river, when the time appointed was come.

Now while they lay here, and waited for the good hour, there was a noise in the town, that there was a post* come from the Celes-

* ' A post'—These messengers seem to be merely emblems of the different diseases or decays, by which the Lord takes down the earthly tabernacle, when he sees good to receive the souls of his people into his immediate presence. In plain language, it was reported that Christiana was sick and near death, and she herself became sensible of her situation. The arrow sharpened by love implies, that the time, manner, and circumstances of the believer's death are appointed by him, ' who loved us, and gave himself for us. He, as it were,

tial city, with matters of great importance to one Christiana, the wife of Christian, the pilgrim. So inquiry was made for her, and the house was found out where she was : so the post presented her with a letter : the contents were: Hail, good woman ! I bring thee tidings, that the Master calleth for thee, and expecteth that thou shouldest stand in his presence, in clothes of immortality, within these ten days.

When he had read this letter to her, he gave her therewith a sure token that he was a true messenger, and was come to bid her make haste to be gone. The token was, an arrow sharpened with love, let easily into her heart, which, by degrees, wrought so effectually

says to the dying saint, It is I, be not afraid. The address made by Christiana to each of the company, and the circumstances of her passing the river, are well deserving of attention : but require no comment. When such believers as have long walked honourably are enabled to bear a dying testimony to the truth, and to recommend the ways of the Lord with the last remains of their breath, a great effect will often be produced : but the confidence of some professors, in these circumstances, has a very different tendency. Many excellent persons, however, are incapacitated from speaking much in their last hours ; and we ought by no means to judge of men's characters on these grounds : for it is remarkable, that the Scripture is generally silent about the manner in which its worthies terminated their lives ; and only a few exceptions are found to this rule. We are particularly instructed in the nature of their faith, and its effects upon their conduct during life ; and thence we may assuredly infer, that they died in the Lord, and entered into rest. The happy death of an eminent Christian is a loss to relatives and connexions, to the church and the community ; and in this view may be lamented : but it often yields great encouragement to ministers and other spectators of the interesting scene, and excites their adoring praises and thanksgivings.

with her, that at the times appointed she must
be gone.

When Christiana saw that her time was
come, and that she was the first of his company that was to go over, she called for Mr.
Great-heart, her guide, and told him how
matters were. So he told her, He was heartily glad of the news, and could have been
glad had the post come from him. Then she
bid that he should give advice how all things
should be prepared for her journey. So he
told her, saying, thus and thus it must be ; and
we that survive will accompany you to the river side.

Then she called for her children, and gave
them her blessings; and told them, that she had
read with comfort the mark that was set in
their foreheads, and was glad to see them
with her there, and that they had kept their
garments so white. Lastly, she bequeathed
to the poor that little she had, and commanded her sons and daughters to be ready against
the messenger should come for them.

When she had spoken these words to her
guide and to her children, she called for Mr.
Valiant-for-truth, and said unto him, Sir, you
have in all places shewed yourself true-heart-
ed ; be faithful unto death, and my King will
give you a crown of life. I would also entreat you to have an eye to my children ; and
if at any time you see them faint, speak comfortably to them. For my daughters, my
sons' wives, they have been faithful, and a
fulfilling of the promise upon them will be

their end. But she gave Mr. Standfast a ring.

Then she called for old Mr. Honest, and said of him, 'Behold an Israelite indeed, in whom is no guile.' Then said he, I wish you a fair day, when you set out for mount Zion, and shall be glad to see that you go over the river dry-shod. But she answered, Come wet, come dry, I long to be gone ; for, however the weather is in my journey, I shall have time enough, when I come there, to sit down and rest me, and dry me.

Then came in that good man Mr. Ready-to-halt, to see her. So she said to him, Thy travel hitherto has been with difficulty ; but that will make thy rest the sweeter But watch and be ready ; for at an hour when you think not, the messenger may come.

After him came in Mr. Despondency, and his daughter Much-afraid ; to whom she said, You ought with thankfulness for ever to remember your deliverance from the hand of giant Despair, and out of Doubting-castle The effect of that mercy is, that you are brought with safety hither. Be yet watchful, and cast away fear ; be sober, and hope to the end.

Then she said to Mr. Feeble-mind, Thou wast delivered from the mouth of giant Slay-good, that thou mightest live in the light of the living for ever, and see the King with comfort ; only I advise thee to repent thee of thy aptness to fear and doubt of his goodness, before he sends for thee : lest thou shouldest, when he comes, be forced to stand before him, for that fault, with blushing.

Now the day drew on, that Christiana must be gone. So the road was full of people, to see her take her journey. But behold, all the banks beyond the river were full of horses and chariots, which were come down from above to accompany her to the city gate. So she came forth, and entered the river, with a beckon of farewell to those that followed her to the river side. The last words that she was heard to say, were, I come, Lord, to be with thee, and bless thee.

So her children and friends returned to their place, for that those that waited for Christiana had carried her out of their sight. So she went and called, and entered in at the gate, with all the ceremonies of joy that her husband Christian had entered with before her.

At her departure the children wept. But Mr. Great-heart and Mr. Valiant played upon the well-tuned cymbal and harp for joy So all departed to their respective places.

In process of time, there came a post to the town again, and his business was with Mr. Ready-to-halt. So he inquired him out, and said, I am come* to thee in the name of

* ' Am come'—Evident decays of natural powers as effectually convince the observing persons, that death approaches, as if a messenger had been sent to inform him. But men in general cling to life, wilfully overlook such tokens, and try to keep up to the last the vain hope of recovering ; and others, by a kind of cruel compassion, sooth them in the delusion : so that numbers die suddenly of chronical disorders,

him whom thou hast loved and followed,
though upon crutches : and my message is to
tell thee, that he expects thee at his table, to
sup with him in his kingdom, the next day after Easter : wherefore prepare thyself for thy
journey. Then he also gave* him a token
that he was a true messenger, saying, I have
broken the golden bowl, and loosed the silver cord (Eccles. xii. 1—7).

After this, Mr. Ready-to-halt called for his
fellow pilgrims, and told them, saying, I am
sent for, and God shall surely visit you also.
So he desired Mr. Valiant to make his will ;
and because he had nothing to bequeath to
them that should survive him, but his crutches
and his good wishes, therefore thus he said,
These crutches I bequeath to my son that
shall tread in my steps, with a hundred
warm wishes that he may prove better than I
have been.

Then he thanked Mr. Great-heart for his
conduct and kindness, and so addressed himself to his journey. When he came to the
brink of the river, he said, Now I shall have
no more need of these crutches, since yonder

even as if they had been shot through the heart. Perhaps,
however, the author had some reference to those inexplica-
ble presages of death, which some persons evidently experience.

* ' Gave'—The tokens are taken from a well known por-
ion of Scripture (Eccles. xii. 1—7) ; but it would be inconsistent with the plan of his work to enter on a particular explanation of them. The dealings of the Lord are here represented as uniformly gentle to the feeble, trembling, humble
believers, and the circumstances of their deaths comparatively encouraging and easy.

are chariots and horses for me to ride on.
The last words he was heard to say were,
Welcome, life ! So he went his way.

After this Mr. Feeble-mind had tidings
brought him, that the post sounded his horn
at his chamber door. Then he came in, and
told him, saying, I am come to tell thee, that
thy master hath need of thee ; and that in a
very little time thou must behold his face in
brightness. And take this as a token of the
truth of my message : ' Those that look out
at the windows shall be darkened.'

Then Mr. Feeble-mind . called for his
friends, and told them what errand had been
brought unto him, and what token he had received of the truth of the message. Then he
said, Since I have nothing to bequeath to any,
to what purpose should I make a will ? As
for my feeble mind, that I will leave behind,
for that I have no need of it in the place
whither I go ; nor is it worth bestowing upon
the poorest pilgrims ; wherefore, when I am
gone, I desire that you, Mr. Valiant, would
bury it in a dunghill. This done, and the
day being come in which he was to depart,
he entered the river as the rest : his last
words were, Hold out, faith and patience.
So he went over to the other side.

When days had many of them passed away,
Mr. Despondency was sent for ; for a post
was come, and brought this message to him :
Trembling man, these are to summon thee to
be ready with the King by the next Lord's
day, to shout for joy, for thy deliverance

from all thy doubtings. And, said the messenger, that my message is true, take this for a proof: so he gave a grasshopper to be a burthen unto him. Now Mr. Despondency's daughter whose name was Much-afraid, said, when she had heard what was done, that she should go with her father. Then Mr. Despondency said to his friends, Myself and my daughter, you know what we have been, and how troublesomely we have behaved ourselves in every company; my will, and my daughter's is, that our desponds and slavish fears be by no man ever received, from the day of our departure, for ever; for I know that after my death, they will offer themselves to others. For, to be plain with you, they are guests which we entertained when we first began to be pilgrims, and could never shake them off after; and they will walk about and seek entertainment of the pilgrims; but, for our sakes, shut the doors upon them.

When the time was come for them to depart, they went up to the brink of the river, The last words of Mr. Despondency were, Farewell night! Welcome day! His daughter went through the river singing, but none could understand what she said.

Then it came to pass awhile after, that there was a post in the town, that inquired for Mr. Honest. So he came to his house, where he was, and delivered to his hands these lines: Thou art commanded to be ready against this day se'nnight, to present thy-

self before thy Lord, at his Father's house.
And, for a token that my message is true,
' All the daughters of music shall be brought
low.' Then Mr. Honest called for his friends,
and said unto them, I die, but shall make no
will.   As for my honesty, it shall go with me ;
let him that comes after be told of this.

When the day that he was to be gone was
come, he addressed himself to go over the
river.   Now the river at that time overflowed
the banks in some places ; but Mr. Honest,
in his life-time, had spoken to one Good-
conscience to meet him there ; the which he
also did, and lent him his hand and so helped
him over.   The last words of Mr. Honest
were, Grace reigns ! So he left the world.

After this, it was noised about that Mr.
Valiant-for-truth was taken with a summons
by the same post as the other : and had this
for a token that the summons was true, that
his pitcher was broken at the fountain.   When
he understood it, he called for his friends, and
told them of it.   Then, said he, I am going
to my Father's ; and though with great difficulty I got hither, yet now I do not repent me
of all the trouble I have been at to arrive
where I am.   My sword I give to him that
shall succeed me in my pilgrimage, and my
courage and skill to him that can get it.   My
marks and scars I carry with me, to be a witness for me, that I have fought his battle, who
now will be my rewarder.

When the day that he must go hence was
come, many accompanied him to the river side,

into which as he went he said, Death, where
is thy sting ? and as he went down deeper he
said, Grave, where is thy victory ? So he passed over, and all the trumpets sounded for him
on the other side.

Then there came forth a summons for Mr.
Standfast. This Mr. Standfast was he that
the pilgrims found upon his knees in the Enchanted Ground, and the post brought it him
open in his hands. The contents whereof
were, that he must prepare for a change of life,
for his Master was not willing that he should
be so far from him any longer. At this Mr.
Standfast was put into a muse. Nay, said the
messenger, you need not doubt of the truth
of my message ; for here is a token of the
truth thereof ; ' Thy wheel is broken at the
cistern.' Then he called to him Mr. Great-
heart, who was their guide, and said unto him,
Sir, although it was not my hap to be much
in your good company in the days of my pilgrimage, yet, since the time I knew you, you
have been profitable to me. When I came
from home, I left behind me a wife and five
small children ; let me entreat you, at your
return (for I know that you go and return to
your Master's house in hopes that you may
be a conductor to more of the holy pilgrims),
that you send to my family, and let them be
acquainted with all that hath and shall happen
unto me. Tell them, moreover, of my happy
arrival at this place, and of the present and
late blessed condition that I am in. Tell them
also of Christian and Christiana his wife, and

how she and her children came after her husband. Tell them also of what a happy end
she made, and whither she is gone. I have
little or nothing to send to my family, except
it be my prayers and tears for them : of which
it will suffice if you acquaint them, if peradven-
true they may prevail.

When Mr. Standfast had thus set things in
order, and the time being come for him to
haste him away, he also went down to the river. Now there was a great calm at that time
in the river ; wherefore Mr. Standfast, when
he was about half way in, stood awhile and
talked to his companions that had waited upon
him thither : and he said, This river* has
been a terror to many : yea, the thoughts of

* ' River'—This speech has been justly admired, as one
of the most striking passages in the whole work : but it is so
plain, that it only requires an attentive reader. It may, however, be worthy of our observation, that in all the instances
before us the pilgrims are represented as resting their only
dependence, at the closing scene, on the mercy of God,
through tne righteousness and atonement of his Son : and yet
recollecting their conscious integrity, boldness in professing
and contending for the truth, love to the cause, example, and
words of Christ, obedience to his precepts, delight in his ways,
preservation from their own iniquities, and consistent behaviour, as evidences that their faith was living, and their hope
warranted ; and in this way the retrospect conducted to their
encouragement. Moreover they all concur in declaring, that
while they left their infirmities behind them they would take
their graces along with them, and that ' their works would
follow them.' Thus the scriptural mean is exactly maintained,
between those who place their supposed good works as the
foundation of their hope ; and those, who would exclude
even real good works from being so much as looked upon,
as evidential of saving faith, or as in any way giving encouragement to the believer in his dying hour (2 Ti a. iv. 6
—8).

20*

it also have often frighted me : now, methinks, I stand easy ; my foot is fixed upon that on which the feet of the priest that bare the ark of the covenant stood, while Israel went over this Jordan (Josh. iii. 17). The waters, indeed, are to the palate bitter, and to the stomach cold ; yet the thoughts of what I am going to, and of the conduct that waits for me on the other side, doth lie as a glowing coal at my heart. I see myself now at the end of my journey ; my toilsome days are ended. I am going to see that head that was crowned with thorns, and that face that was spit upon for me. I have formerly lived by hearsay and faith ; but now I go where I shall live by sight, and shall be with him in whose company I delight myself. I have loved to hear my Lord spoken of ; and wherever I have seen the print of his shoe in the earth, there I have coveted to set my foot too. His name has been to me as a civet box ; yea, sweeter than all perfumes. His voice to me has been most sweet ; and his countenance, I have more desired than they that have most desired the light of the sun. His words I did use to gather for my food, and for antidotes against my faintings. He has held me, and has kept me from mine iniquities ; yea, my steps have been strengthened in his way.

Now, while he was thus in discourse, his countenance changed ; his ' strong man bowed under him :' and, after he had said, Take me, for I come unto thee, he ceased to be seen of them.

But glorious* it was to see, how the open
region was filled with horses and chariots,
with trumpeters and pipers, with singers and
players on stringed instruments, to welcome

* ' Glorious'—The view given in this place of the peaceful and joyful death of the pilgrims, cannot but affect every
reader in some degree; and many perhaps may be ready to
say, ' Let me die the death of the righteous, and let my last
end be like his.' But, except they make it their principal concern to live the life of the righteous, such a wish will most
probably be frustrated; and every hope grounded on it is evidently presumptuous, as the example of Balaam sufficiently
proves. If any man therefore doubt whether this allegory do
indeed describe the rise and progress of religion in the soul;
the beginning, continuance, and termination of the godly man's
course to heaven; let him diligently search the Scriptures,
and fervently pray to God, from whom alone ' cometh every
good and perfect gift,' to enable him to determine this question. But let such as own themselves to be satisfied that it
does, beware lest they rest on this assent and notion, in the
pleasure of reading an ingenious work on the subject, or in
the ability of developing many of the author's emblems. Let
them beware, lest they be facinated, as it were, into a persuasion, that they actually accompany the pilgrims in the life
of faith, and walking with God, in the same measure as they
keep peace with the author, in discovering and approving
the grand outlines of his plan. And let every one carefully
examine his state, sentiments, experience, motives, tempers,
affections, and conduct, by the various characters, incidents,
and observations, that pass under his review: assured that
this is a matter of the greatest consequence. We ought not
indeed to call any man master, or subscribe absolutely to all
his sentiments, yet the diligent practical student of Scripture
can scarcely doubt, but that the warnings, counsels, and instructions of this singular work, agree in general with that
sacred touchstone; or that characters and actions will at last
be approved or condemned by the Judge of the world, in a
great degree according to the sentence passed on them in this
wise and faithful book. The Lord grant that both the writer and readers of these observations may ' find mercy in
that day,' and be addressed in these gracious words, ' Come,
ye blessed of my Father, inherit the kingdom prepared for
you from the foundation of the world.'

the pilgrims as they went up, and followed one another in at the beautiful gate of the city.

As for Christiana's children, the four boys that Christiana brought, with their wives and children, I did not stay where I was till they were gone over. Also since I came away, I heard one say, they were yet alive, and so would be for the increase of the church in that place where they were, for a time.

Shall it be my lot to go that way again, I may give those that desire it an account of what I here am silent about ; mean time, I bid my reader

FAREWELL.